THE HERO'S LOT

THE STAFF ☉ THE SWORD

THE HERO'S LOT

PATRICK W. CARR

BETHANYHOUSE
a division of Baker Publishing Group
Minneapolis, Minnesota

© 2013 by Patrick W. Carr

Published by Bethany House Publishers
11400 Hampshire Avenue South
Bloomington, Minnesota 55438
www.bethanyhouse.com

Bethany House Publishers is a division of
Baker Publishing Group, Grand Rapids, Michigan

Printed in the United States of America

Library of Congress Cataloging-in-Publication Data
Carr, Patrick W.
    The hero's lot / Patrick W. Carr.
        pages cm. — (The staff and the sword)
    Summary: "Falsely accused of terrible crimes, Errol Stone is placed under com-
pulsion and sentenced to undertake a perilous quest. He must succeed . . . or die
trying"—Provided by publisher.
        ISBN 978-0-7642-1044-0 (pbk.)
        1. Title.
PS3603.A774326H48 2013
813'.6—dc23   2013007569

Cover design by Lookout Design, Inc.

Author represented by The Steve Laube Agency.

12   13   14   15   16   17   18   7   6   5   4   3   2   1

This one goes to the men in my life:

To my father, Joe William Carr,
who awoke in me an appreciation of
and love for a well-told tale.

To Joe Si Carr,
who was and is my brother and friend
through all the craziness of being Air Force brats and after.

And to my sons:
Patrick, Connor, Daniel, and Ethan.
Every father wants his sons to surpass him—you do.

1

ACCUSED

SWEAT, HOT AND SALTY, flowed into Errol's eyes in the sticky heat of the early fall afternoon. He forced a quick blink to shed the distraction, not daring to risk the split second it would take to wipe his brow. A welt as long as his hand burned his left rib cage. Its twin worked to numb his right shoulder. The staff in his hands blurred and buzzed like an angry insect, nearly invisible, but as yet he had managed only a single strike against his opponent.

And he was tiring.

The man opposite him, stronger and fresher, darted like a snake, the blade of his sword disappeared as his arms corded and he struck. Errol parried at the last moment and flowed into a counterattack. The clack of staff against sword filled his ears like the sound of a drummer's rim beats.

For a moment he dared hope that he would penetrate his opponent's defense, but the attack exhausted itself, and he retreated to defend against those cursed whiplike strokes of the swordsman's counter.

Pain blossomed in his side as the sword found its mark. It was no use. Four weeks of food and rest had nearly restored him to complete health after Sarin's attack against the kingdom. But "almost" was insufficient against such an opponent.

He backed away and grounded his staff. "Enough, Liam, I am no match for you today—perhaps not ever again." One of the watchmen, Lieutenant Goran, offered him a wad of cloth. He lifted his shirt. A trickle of blood tracked a crooked rivulet down his side. It could have been worse. Only his foolish pride—and Weir's goading—had impelled him to spar with Liam so soon after his release from the infirmary. All in all, he'd been lucky.

The blond-haired man across from him relaxed from his stance and favored him with the same smile that made every girl, woman, and widow in the kingdom swoon. On Errol the effect failed to dazzle, but it reminded him his fellow villager walked a bit closer to perfection than other men.

Liam inclined his head. "You're nearly as fast as you were before the attack."

Captain Reynald nodded his agreement from his vantage point just to the side. "The lad speaks the simple truth. Had you sparred with any other man—" he paused to glance at Weir—"you would have won, easily. As it is, there are only two men I can think of that could best either of you. Merodach and—"

"Naaman Ru," Errol finished.

The captain grunted. "Yes."

Eagerness flared in Liam's eyes. "How good is he, Errol?"

"I don't know. I never saw him in an actual fight, and we never sparred. I'm just as happy about that, though. His best student, Gram Skorik, pushed me to my limit. Rokha, his daughter, told me Ru bested Skorik without breaking a sweat."

Liam's eyes shone. "Wouldn't it be glorious to go against him, the best swordsman in the world?"

A catarrhal laugh erupted from Errol's throat before he could stop it. "Glorious? No, I don't think so. The last time I saw Ru, he had naked steel in his hand and was furious with me."

Errol panicked as he said this last and cursed himself for a fool. His admission might lead to questions about his escape from the caravan master he could not answer. Before Reynald or Liam could inquire after the means of his deliverance from the legendary swordsman, Adora, flanked by Weir and a dozen ladies of the court who gazed in longing toward Liam, joined the trio.

"Are you well?" the princess asked him.

His breath caught at the sight of her . . . as always. The green of her eyes unmade him, so he busied himself with his staff, twisting the knobblocks back onto each end. "A couple of welts. They're a small price to pay for letting Weir goad me into a match with Liam."

At the mention of his name, Lord Weir elbowed Errol on his way to congratulate Liam on his victory. "It's too bad you called a halt, peasant. A couple of blows to the head might have taught you respect for your betters."

Errol made a show of looking around Weir and over his head. "If I see any I'll let you know."

Weir yanked his hand toward the pommel of his sword, as if to draw.

Errol darted to his right. He needed space. His eyes caught Weir's, and his hands slid to the ready position on his staff. Reynald's voice came from behind him.

"Please do, Lord Weir. The minute you bare steel in this yard you free him from restraint. Don't forget, he's an earl now."

Weir slammed his sword back into its scabbard. "He'll always be a filthy peasant." He spat and brushed past.

Errol watched him leave, didn't relax his grip on the staff until Weir and his friends disappeared from the yard. "Why does he hate me so much?" he asked Adora.

"You have something he wants," she said.

Before he could ask for an explanation, the crowd split and a wave of bows announced the arrival of a newcomer of importance. He pulled his gaze from Princess Adora with reluctance to see Enoch Sten, Illustra's primus approaching. The set of his shoulders and the compressed line of his mouth hinted at displeasure. The pair of watchmen who trailed behind him kept their hands on their swords, ready to draw in an instant. Sarin's treacherous legacy had left more than bloodstains in the hallways.

Errol bowed in greeting. "Primus."

Enoch Sten stopped within arm's reach and fanned his florid face with one hand. "I'm not made for haste, my boy. Haste is for younger men who can still afford notions of self-importance. Ah well. When the Judica commands haste, even the head of the conclave must hurry." His shoulders bunched under his tunic with mirth, and he greeted Adora, the king's niece, with a nod. "My dear, your radiance outshines the sun." The primus simpered over the object of Errol's affections for a moment before turning serious. His smile drained away. "Errol, you are commanded before the Judica."

"Me?" His heart skipped like a calf. The proceedings of the benefices' council stymied him. The church's highest-ranking clergy were assembled to determine the process for choosing King Rodran's successor. According to Martin they seemed more intent on arguing arcane points of church law than in choosing the next king.

Enoch Sten, thin and gangly, like a scarecrow with tufts of gray hair that defied grooming, licked his lips. "They're talking about you."

Adora's hand wormed its way into Errol's, where it fluttered like a trapped bird. She paled. Her reaction frightened him more than Sten's comment.

"What do I have to do with choosing the next king?"

An amused chuckle put a slight bend in Sten's posture as it drifted up from his midsection. "Ah, Errol, your innocence becomes your youth, but it is a trait you can ill afford just now." The primus turned toward Adora as he took Errol by the elbow. "Your Highness, will you excuse us?"

As they traced the winding route through native-granite hallways toward the hall of the Judica, Sten's voice adopted a cadenced pattern, as if instructing a young group of postulates to the conclave. "This isn't flattery, Errol, though I can see that you might be flattered by the attention. You really don't want churchmen talking about you."

"Why would they be interested in me? What are they saying?"

Sten cleared his throat with a grimace. "Short questions with long answers, my boy."

"But why me? Isn't selecting Rodran's successor more important?"

"Who knows the minds of men—especially the benefices. Sometimes it is easier to argue over the lesser concerns. But they will get to it eventually. Archbenefice Canon has the situation in hand."

Primus Sten shook his head as if dispelling a fog. "Illustra might well fall apart without a strong, ready leader, and the kingdom of Merakh would welcome such chaos. We must have a king. Even a bad king—and we've had our share of those—is better than none."

The process seemed a trifle ridiculous to Errol, like taking the long way around the Sprata instead of taking the Cripples when the stones were safe and dry. "Why doesn't the archbenefice just tell the rest of the benefices what to do? Isn't he the head of the church?"

The primus smiled and stroked the wayward grizzle on his chin. "He cannot. Think of the archbenefice as first among equals."

They left the halls of the watch and emerged onto the green that separated the kingdom's three powers—monarchy, conclave, and church. Up ahead the soaring cathedral and attached buildings loomed over the landscape proclaiming the preeminent power of the ecclesia. Errol shivered as they passed into the shadow of the spire.

The primus guided him toward the main entrance of a massive building beside the cathedral. The dressed blocks of stone rose above him as he approached, and he suddenly felt small and insignificant next to the giant gray slabs. An arched entrance, wide enough for ten broad-shouldered guards to march through abreast, awaited them. Just inside, four pair of church guards dressed in red with purple armbands stood with sharpened pikes.

As Errol and the primus ventured to pass through, a functionary stepped from the shadows and raised his hand palm out, signaling them to stop.

"Your pardon, Primus." The man bowed, a marginal bend from the waist, less than what Errol would have expected the head of the conclave would receive.

If Enoch Sten noticed the slight, he gave no sign. "Is there a problem? This is Earl Stone; we are commanded here by the archbenefice."

The functionary nodded agreement, his dark eyes heavy-lidded. "The earl will have to surrender his staff. None but the watch and church guards may enter the Judica armed."

Errol turned to present the black armband that proclaimed him an honorary captain of the watch. "Will this do?"

The functionary shook his head. "It will not. I am under orders to ensure you do not enter the Judica under arms."

The hackles on Errol's neck rose as alarm traced an icy finger down the nape of his neck. Why would they insist on making him defenseless? "Then I will not enter."

Four of the guards closed in behind him, their pikes leveled at his back. "You are commanded before the Judica," the man said. "You will attend."

The primus clutched Errol's arm just above the elbow. "There is no choice in this. Give them your staff."

The churchman stepped forward and took the polished ash from him. His fingers ached at their sudden emptiness. Helpless, defenseless, he rounded on the head of his order. "Did you know they were going to take my staff?"

At Sten's nod, he went on. "Why didn't you warn me?"

"Because you might not have come, and whatever else we of the conclave may be, we are servants of the church."

"Not we," Errol said.

"Quiet, boy," the primus snapped. "Any word you speak against the church can be used against you in the Judica."

Errol fumed. When he hesitated the guards moved closer, the points of their pikes now only inches from his back. With a snarl, he gave a curt nod of acquiescence to the functionary. The guards retreated a pace but kept their weapons leveled. Why was he being escorted like a prisoner?

He walked the long corridor toward the Judica's meeting hall. Questions tumbled through his mind like lots in the drum. Why had the primus been sent to retrieve him? Where was Martin? Every time Errol dealt with the church in the past, Martin had been there to guide him—giving him the words to say, helping him to keep his tongue in check.

They rounded a sharp turn, and the doors to the domed hall of the Judica rose before him. The functionary stepped forward to speak with a detachment of guards at the entrance. The pike-men maintained their vigilance as if they expected Errol to bolt at any moment. Then the functionary gave a curt wave of his hand to motion him over.

Errol nodded and moved to step forward. The primus grabbed his arm, hauled him backward. "A word of warning, Errol. This isn't the informality of the conclave or the camaraderie of the throne room. In many ways these churchmen run the kingdom. Most of them are good men, but some of them are sharks. With the king dying, they smell blood in the water. Speak only when you're spoken to, be respectful, and don't lose your temper."

Trapped. He was trapped as surely as if Antil had locked him in the stocks. What did they want with him?

The doors opened, and a voice from within announced his presence before the archbenefice and the Judica.

"So summoned, the accused, Errol Stone, has presented himself before the Judica."

A chorus of voices, hundreds strong, replied, "Judica me, Deas."

Accused?

What had he done?

2

A NECESSARY SACRIFICE

THE GUARDS BEHIND HIM shouldered their pikes after a trio of church soldiers with bared swords came forward to escort Errol between the raised seats of the amphitheater to present him to the head of the church. A sea of implacable faces regarded him—some young, most old, all without a hint of acknowledgment or recognition.

The meeting place of the Judica was an enormous half-circle composed of raised seats focused on the dais where sat Bertrand Canon, archbenefice of Erinon and mediator of the Judica. In front of each of the seven sections of the half circle a blue-robed reader waited, the implements of his craft and a stack of blanks ready for carving on a simple table next to him.

Errol searched for Martin, found him up and to the left. Yet when they locked gazes, the benefice showed no recognition, no gesture of support. The planes of his broad bluff face were closed to human emotion. Errol's stomach hollowed as his gaze drifted across the mass of scarlet and purple and came to rest again on his supposed friend.

By the three, what was the charge?

His breath came in short gasps as he surveyed the blue-robed readers and saw no sign of Luis. He knew each and every one of the men chosen to cast lots if the need arose, but he could not count any of them as friend. Watchmen, officers all, guarded the doors and the archbenefice, but Cruk was not among them.

Someone—one of the church guards—prodded him into motion, steering him toward the raised dais. The archbenefice acknowledged him with a grave nod, the barest inclination of his head. His captors guided him to a simple wooden chair on the floor to the right and below the archbenefice, where he endured the scrutiny of the Judica.

"Who would speak?" the archbenefice intoned in a cadenced singsong.

A withered benefice with thin, bloodless lips rose. "I would speak."

"Approach, Benefice Kell. Speak no word before the Judica that is untrue. Make no statement that is incomplete. You are adjured by Deas."

Benefice Kell gave a perfunctory nod. "Judica me, Deas," he said. Whispers of hair framed his head like the remnants of a halo as he approached the dais. When he gestured his accusation at Errol, the sleeve of his robe slid up to reveal a desiccated arm. His flesh hung slack on his body and parched face, yet his eyes burned in his skull. They burned.

"From his own mouth," the benefice said, "Errol Stone has admitted traffic with herbwomen, those foul beings who consort with evil spirits."

Mutters ran through the Judica. Some sounded reproving while others verged on exasperated. Confusion rocked him. Hadn't this been discussed and resolved already?

"I would speak." A younger benefice popped up from his seat.

The archbenefice held up a hand, forestalling the new speaker. "Patience, Benefice Kerran." He regarded Benefice Kell with a sigh. "Have you any other accusation to bring?"

Kell's face mottled with indignation. Red blotches marred his waxy complexion and he lifted a finger that quivered with rage to point at Errol. "Any other? What else could be required? That fiend among us has defied the law of this body and must be punished."

The archbenefice looked like a man trying not to roll his eyes. "Benefice Kell, the Judica will weigh your charge, so please restrain your zeal and answer the question. Do you have any other charges to bring against Errol Stone?"

Benefice Kell looked on the verge of launching another tirade but instead shook his head and reseated himself with a growl.

Bertrand Canon addressed the body. "Who would speak?" he inquired again.

A benefice with red hair and white soft-looking hands rose with a delicate clearing of his throat. "Hmmm, yes, well, I would speak." He ducked his head as if the sudden attention of the Judica embarrassed him, and he gave a coy smile to the benefices seated to his right.

"Approach, Benefice Dane. Speak no word before the Judica that is untrue. Make no statement that is incomplete. You are adjured by Deas."

The benefice minced toward the stand. "Oh, yes, yes, of course. Judica me, Deas." The benefice stood in the accuser's box without speaking until the archbenefice sighed and prompted him.

"Your charge, Benefice Dane?"

"Hmmm? Oh my. Well, it's not a charge so much as a concern."

The archbenefice rubbed his temples. "The Judica is met, my dear benefice, to hear charges of a clerical nature against one of the nobility. So far, Earl Stone is accused of trafficking with herbwomen."

"And evil spirits," Benefice Kell yelled from his seat.

"Yes, yes, and evil spirits," the archbenefice said in a resigned tone. "Now, Benefice Dane, do you have a charge to bring?"

The benefice looked on the verge of returning to his seat, but at the last minute some inner resolve seemed to embolden him. He straightened and his voice strengthened. "I accuse Errol Stone of conspiring with Benefice Martin Arwitten and Secondus Luis

Montari to cast lots for the next king without authorization from
the Judica."

Stunned silence covered the assembled. Men too dismayed to
gasp stared at Errol as if he'd committed regicide while they slept.
Errol tried to catch the eye of the primus, but Enoch Sten, pale
and motionless, refused to look his way. Benefice Dane threw
back his shoulders and preened at the effect of his words.

Then the hall erupted. Men old enough to be Errol's father
or grandfather started out of their seats to voice their shock and
disapproval. Whether the target of their ire was him or Benefice Dane, Errol couldn't tell—the cacophony of voices defied
order. Many of those assembled turned to face Martin, their
looks horrified, supportive, or dumbstruck. The archbenefice
rose from his seat, yanked the metal-shod staff of office from
its holder, and struck the floor, calling for order, but the din
drowned his efforts. He signaled the guards, who drew swords
and crossed blades.

The sound of steel did what the staff could not. By twos
and threes, the benefices quieted, and the archbenefice's voice
rose above the din. "Sit down! Is this college nothing more
than a collection of excitable boys that we should react so?
My benefices, where is your self-control? Where is your sense
of decorum?"

The head of the church gestured to the guards. "Seal the chamber." The archbenefice's order silenced throngs of benefices who
moments before had threatened to riot within the dome. The
muffled boom of the giant doors being barred echoed from the
stone walls like a knell of Errol's doom. His fingers made seeking
motions, twitching at the ends of his hands as they sought the
comfort of a staff they no longer held. Dane's charge brought
spots of darkness to his vision. Errol was innocent, but somehow
the benefice had learned of Martin and Luis's cast.

How?

Splotches of emotion colored the archbenefice's face as he
raised a finger to address Errol's accuser. "Benefice Dane, conspiring to usurp the authority of the Judica is a serious charge.

Understand that you will be asked to provide corroboration to this charge. Perhaps your recent elevation to the orders of benefice has given you an undue enthusiasm for these proceedings?"

The archbenefice regarded Benefice Dane, and silence settled like a blanket over the hall as the Judica waited for its newest member to respond.

"Hmm? Oh my. Perhaps I've erred, Archbenefice. Does the Judica not have the right to examine any noble, including the king?"

It seemed some hint of danger or intent warned the archbenefice. Errol watched the man's eyes narrow as his hands dropped to cradle his staff of office. He nodded assent before answering. "As much is written in our law. However—"

"And does not each member," Benefice Dane interrupted, "have the Deas-given right to pose a question, any question, to the accused?"

Bertrand Canon took a moment to resume his seat before answering. With fastidious care he arranged the fold of his robe and replaced his staff of office in its holder with a soft clank. Whispers filled the hall with expectancy in the silence of the archbenefice's consideration.

"My compliments, Benefice Dane. Seldom do new benefices come to us with such . . . confidence in their ability to navigate the intricacies of church law. Yes, you do have the right to question the accused."

Benefice Dane leaned forward, his eyes sparkling and his manner sharp. "Thank you, Archbenefice Canon. I would like to begin by—"

"However," the archbenefice interrupted, "I am sure you are aware that we must take the charges in order. Benefice Kell's charge of consorting with spirits must be heard first. And we have yet to hear from other esteemed members of the Judica who may wish to speak."

A glimmer of hatred flashed in the look Dane directed at the archbenefice, but a moment later he fumbled with his stole of office, looking distracted and subservient once more. "Hmm?

Of course, of course. Your pardon, Archbenefice." He retreated up the stairs to resume his seat.

The archbenefice surveyed the hall before again offering the now-familiar intonation. "Who would speak?" Every line of his posture seemed to warn the remainder of the benefices against speaking. A moment passed that Errol measured in the still-panicked beat of his heart before the archbenefice spoke again. "The Judica has spoken. The charges have been set before this body. Let none seek to swerve the arm of Deas from its quest for the truth."

Three raps of the archbenefice's staff upon the floor interrupted Benefice Kell's approach toward the questioner's box. Disappointment wreathed his features, and he chewed his lips in obvious frustration. The assembly rose as one. "The Judica will resume at the third hour after dawn tomorrow. The accused, Earl Errol Stone, is remanded to the watch until such time as the charges are disproven or penance prescribed."

The archbenefice scribbled a note before beckoning a pair of guards from the back of the chamber and passing the scrap of parchment to them. Two members of the watch, men whose names and handclasps were known to Errol, came forward to lead him away. Vladic, tall and dark-haired, made a gesture for him to follow without lifting his gaze above Errol's chest. Itara, short and bluff faced, fell in behind.

The crowd of benefices and their assistants thinned as the watchmen made their way toward the exit that would take them away from the church's compound and back toward the squat rectangular building that served as the quarters for the watch.

Behind Errol, Lieutenant Itara snorted. "Right waste of time this is. Takin' an honorary captain of the watch into custody on the say-so of some pampered little church toadie."

Vladic's and Itara's unrelieved black clothing comforted Errol. For too many years the red and purple of the church meant the stocks or another beating at Antil's hands, punishment for trying to drink away the memory of the death of his adoptive father, Warrel. Though his situation remained unchanged from that of an accused prisoner, his removal from the benefices and their signature colors served to calm him. Now, if only he could devise some way to get his staff back, he would feel almost normal.

He slowed. "Lieutenant, would it be possible for us to retrieve my staff? The church guards stripped it from me on the way to the Judica. It's nothing special, but I've had it a long time now and I'd hate to lose it."

Vladic's eyes clouded at the request, but Itara merely shrugged and changed direction at the next corridor. "Can't see as that should be a problem, milord. This is all foolishness, anyways, far as I can see. I can't let you hold it, of course. The fellows in the Judica would have a frothing fit, they would."

Errol clenched his jaw and nodded. It had been a slim hope that Itara would let him have his staff—and slimmer still that it would have done him any good—but now any chance of escape was denied him.

Moments later, removed from the Judica and back in the familiar environs of the watch, Errol followed the lieutenant, who walked two paces in front of him with his staff tucked under one arm. He sighed. The church needed a scapegoat, and they would vent their collective wrath on whomever they wanted.

They wanted him, it seemed.

He tensed as they rounded a corner, recognition bringing him up short. "Itara, where are you taking me?"

"Eh? Oh, that. Right strange, that is. The archbenefice wanted me to deliver you to Cap'n Reynald's quarters. Told us to hold you inside."

Vladic rapped at the door and moved aside when the captain, the head of the watch, answered.

Reynald took in the presence of the three men, noted Errol's position between the other two. His face hardened until it took on the aspect of weathered rock. With a sharp nod, he gestured them in.

Errol refused to take the bait. "Why am I here, Captain?"

Captain Reynald shrugged as if the question were trivial. "The archbenefice ordered you brought here. Too many eyes might witness you being escorted to his quarters."

The answer only raised more questions, questions he doubted the captain would answer. "What do we do now?"

"We wait."

3

DIVIDE AND . . .

SWEAT COVERED MARTIN as if he were some wastrel seeking absolution. Perhaps in a sense he was. When dispatching Martin and Luis to find Illustra's heir more than five years ago, the archbenefice's imperative had been simple: Find the king; let no one find out.

Yet someone had found out, and though the accusation had come primarily against Errol, Dane had hit close enough to the mark to endanger not only Martin and Luis but the archbenefice and the primus as well.

Luis, newly elevated to secondus of the conclave, stood at his side. The reader's manner betrayed no hint of nerves. Then again, Luis had less to lose. Martin reflected on that for a moment and then amended the thought. No, if the wrong people discovered their purpose, they would all die, killed by the very people they sought to protect.

He wiped his hands on his cassock and lifted a blunt fist to announce himself on the thick oak planks of Enoch Sten's door. The entrance to the primus's private quarters bore mute testimony to the longevity of the office. Untold fists and knuckles had worn the finish where he pounded his presence to a deep honey color that contrasted with the age-darkened hue of the rest of the wood.

The door opened to reveal the primus's secretary, a short waddle-throated man. Martin forced his mouth open in imitation of a smile. "Good evening, Willet. Is the primus in?"

Like any secretary, Willet guarded his employer's prestige. "A moment," he said with a half bow. "I will see if he is up to receiving guests."

A moment later, Sten appeared at the door, shooing the guardian of his image out as he beckoned Martin and Luis into his apartments. "I will see you tomorrow, Willet."

Martin inclined his head, respectful as Sten closed and bolted the door. "Will the archbenefice be joining us, Primus?"

Sten shook his head. "No. Bertrand considers the risk too great—as do I. You will both have to leave the island, of course." He sighed. "We can't risk Dane calling you to testify. I'm sorry, Martin. It means you'll no longer be entitled to the red of the Judica."

Martin waved a hand to indicate it was unimportant, but a stab of loss struck him even so. "It's not unexpected, Primus. You'll watch after them, won't you?"

Sten nodded. "Liam and Errol are too valuable to lose. Bertrand will think of something. And Errol is innocent, is he not? He didn't help with the cast, did he?"

Luis shook his head. "No, but it hardly matters. The boy is clever—he figured out what Martin and I were doing weeks ago. If Dane examines him, the truth will come out."

Sten blew air through the white wisps of his mustache. "Worse and worse. Will you cast for your destination?"

Luis gave a shy smile, the skin around his brown eyes crinkling. "I already have. It didn't take any great wit to see we would be forced to leave. There was no time to cast in stone, of course, but for this, wood suffices. We're going back to Callowford. Errol and Liam's village came up seventeen times out of twenty."

Enoch Sten grunted. "I can't say I'm surprised. It makes sense."

He paced the room. His old-man's feet shuffled across the carpet in slippers. "We need to determine what makes Errol so blasted important. Have you cast for the person who holds the answer?"

Luis gave a brief shake. "Not yet. I'm taking blanks with me. We'll have weeks on the road. I'll fashion the lots as we go."

The primus stalked the carpet like a caged animal, his frustration evident. Martin could hardly blame him. Years of planning and work had failed to provide the answer the kingdom desperately needed. The best readers in the conclave had failed. "Are you sure you didn't misread the cast, Luis?"

Luis's dark brown eyes clouded, and he rubbed the naked dome of his head with one hand before answering. "Those lots were as perfect as I could make them, Primus. I've never seen the like on a cast before—first Liam, then Errol, over and over again, as if the drum and the lots were spelled."

"And your question?" the primus asked. "You cast for the soteregia—our savior and king? The question frames the answer."

Luis nodded. "For five years I thought of little else."

The primus uttered an uncharacteristic oath under his breath. Martin wanted to join in.

"I'm sorry, Primus," Luis said. "In some fashion that escapes me, I've failed."

"Don't be ridiculous," Sten said with a snort. "You're the conclave's most skillful reader now that we've lost Sarin." He spat the renegade's name like an epithet.

"Other than yourself," Luis amended.

"I'm old, Luis. I can't hold the question and its possible answers the way I used to. My concentration slips."

Martin leaned forward in his chair to catch their attention. Blame and confession would not answer their questions. "I should have realized Errol's importance. Every attack on the way to Erinon came against the boy."

Sten shrugged his shoulders under the blue robe of his office. "What kind of king would Errol make?"

Martin snorted. "The boy? He's not going to be king, Primus." The idea was ridiculous. "Luis cast in wood first—Liam is our soteregia. But there is something about Errol we do not know, and I fear the enemy knows what that is."

Luis demurred. "I think your preconceptions have blinded you, my friend. According to the lots, Errol may very well be our next king. He may not be Liam, but he has courage, and Erinon's past is littered with sovereigns who lacked even Errol's nominal statecraft."

Martin grunted to concede the point, then waved his hand to brush it aside. "The boy would be a disaster, Luis, and you know it. He has a deep-seated mistrust of the church."

"Can you blame him, Martin?" Luis asked.

A weight of regret settled onto his shoulders. Too many times he'd been too slow to act. "No, but speculation gets us nowhere."

The primus nodded his agreement. "Quite. If the Judica determines that we have already cast for the king, they will make an example of us that will make readers and priests shiver for a hundred years."

Sten turned his attention to Luis. "The boy is an omne. I shudder to think what will happen if he comes across your lots and finds he may be the next king. He'd run. I know I would."

"He can't," Luis said. His eyes pinched and his voice dipped. "After the cast, I destroyed the lots. They are only so much dust now."

An empathetic pang like an empty longing opened in Martin's chest at Luis's declaration. For five years, his dear friend had worked the stones to perfection, threescore lots as identical as craft and Deas's gift could make them—his greatest work. Countless days and nights had been spent sculpting, shaping, and polishing the stones to ensure the cast would be unassailable.

And the cast had failed.

He rested his hand for a moment on Luis's shoulder.

"When will you leave?" Sten asked.

Martin sighed. Going back to Callowford would be a step back in more ways than one. Church law prohibited any benefice from leaving the Judica until its stated purpose concluded. When his fellow benefices discovered his absence from the city, they would likely demote him to priest. His shoulders twitched with a mental shrug. "Before dawn. Cruk will come with us."

Reynald stalked the edges of the carpet, each footstep landing half on, half off the covering. "Well, he did it—curse the old fool." He sounded as if he were chewing rocks. "Kell actually brought his charge."

"Beggin' your pardon, Captain," Itara said. "But I don't think Kell's the problem."

"No, he's not," a voice at the doorway said.

Errol turned to see the archbenefice filling the entrance to Captain Reynald's chambers. Behind him stood the primus.

"Thank you, Lieutenant," the archbenefice said to Itara. "You have performed your duty. You've earned yourself a nice drink after today's boring post of duty. I won't keep you from it. I think you can leave Earl Stone his staff as well."

Itara and Vladic bobbed their heads and retreated through the open doorway. Primus Sten closed the door after them and shot the bolt home. Errol restrained himself from bowing to the archbenefice or the primus. His anger wouldn't allow it.

"The boy's a quick study," the archbenefice said to the primus. "He's become as proud and arrogant as any other noble."

Reynald growled behind him. "Show the archbenefice some respect, boy."

"I'd be more inclined to bow and scrape if I weren't a prisoner," Errol shot back. "Now I'm accused of something I haven't done, and a roomful of churchmen are just waiting for the chance to throw me into prison. That's if Kell and Dane don't have their way and have me executed instead."

The archbenefice chuckled. "Well, at least you're perceptive, boy. Under the circumstances, I think we can forego the genuflections. It gets tiresome after a while, anyway. Do you have a place where we can sit and talk, Captain? I think we owe Errol an explanation of the day's events. And then, of course, we'll have to devise a means for keeping Benefice Dane at bay."

Errol followed the most powerful men of the church, the conclave, and the watch to a small dining room deep in Captain Reynald's apartments. The furnishings reflected their owner in their straight-lined elegance and simplicity. A walnut table burnished to a satin glow dominated the room, cabinets of a red wood Errol couldn't identify flanked the table and chairs, and monochromatic paintings adorned the walls. Errol compared the room to Abbot Morin's decadent sumptuousness in the abbey at Windridge and found the captain's quarters to his liking. Everything spoke of a well-made functionality he appreciated.

"Have a seat, Earl," the archbenefice said. It took Errol a moment to realize Bertrand Canon had spoken to him. He seated himself and laid his staff across his lap, but under the table his hands clenched the ash wood as if he could wring comfort or security from it.

The archbenefice took a chair at the head of the table flanked by Primus Sten on his right and Captain Reynald on his left. They arranged themselves as if their seating held some significance, but Errol couldn't discern the import.

"I need answers regarding Benefice Dane's charges, Earl Stone," the archbenefice said. "Truthful answers, or so help you, that jackal of a benefice, Duke Weir's sycophant, will have you in front of the headsman, and I will be powerless to prevent it."

Errol nodded but didn't speak. These three men wanted something from him, and that realization alone made him wary. Martin, Luis, and Cruk had made it plain that, though they liked him, in the end they considered him nothing more than a necessary sacrifice. He doubted their superiors would see things differently.

"Let's deal with Benefice Kell's charge first," Bertrand Canon said. "Perhaps we can use it to blunt Benefice Dane's line of inquiry. Have you consorted with *herbwomen*?" The archbenefice's mouth twisted around the word as if he'd bitten into something bitter.

Errol's face heated. "Yes. As I have explained before, I hunted herbs for them." He locked eyes with the archbenefice. "They used them to help sick people in my village."

"Don't play games with me, boy," the archbenefice shot back. "I'm not interested in their deeds or your justifications. Were you touched by their spirit?"

Errol's back stiffened, and he glared at the men around the table. "Yes. And if I had to do it over again, I would welcome the embrace."

The archbenefice jerked, but before he could speak, the primus raised one hand to interject. "Perhaps we should hear the boy out, Bertrand."

The head of the church settled himself back into his chair and signaled Errol to speak with a curt nod.

"Somebody poisoned us—Pater Martin, Luis, and me—with moritweed. I went to Adele, but she couldn't figure out what poison had been used. I remember lying on her floor. I was dying. Then the herbwoman went out back and called out in a language that sounded like the sighing of trees. Then there was something there with me. It spoke to Adele in a voice of wind, told her how to cure me. She said it was Aurae."

The archbenefice's face pinched in disapproval. "Ridiculous. Aurae is unknowable. Of the three, only Deas and Eleison can be discerned. It must have been some other spirit, possibly even a malus. It would have been better had that thing never touched you."

Errol laced his voice with as much scorn as he could manage. "I'll try to remember that the next time I'm poisoned. Then I can die all nice and clean and pure."

The archbenefice jerked as if stung. His voice cracked across the space between them like a whip. "Boy, I'm trying to help you. Don't you know I have the power to send you to the inquisitor?"

Errol's staff clattered to the floor as he rose from his chair. Reynald mirrored him and drew his sword.

Errol jerked loose the laces of his shirt and slipped it over his head. Months of working with a weighted staff had added muscle to his frame, but he would always be leaner than most men. "We have our own inquisitor back in my village," Errol said. "I don't think he ever asked me why I was drunk. I'm pretty sure he didn't care. He was too eager to get to the punishment." Errol turned his back, let them see the network of old wounds that laced and relaced his skin with puckers and scars until almost no normal skin showed. "Our inquisitor's name is Antil—Pater Antil."

He jerked his shirt back into place. "I'm sure the church is very proud of him, Archbenefice. He's a very zealous priest. When he would get done beating me, I'd walk or crawl to Radere, a cursed herbwoman, and she'd tend to my wounds."

Errol dressed and seated himself, took in the ashen faces in front of him. With deliberate care, he retrieved his staff and placed it in the crook of one elbow.

Archbenefice Bertrand Canon stood and gave a slight bow of acknowledgment, bending from the waist, his movements oddly formal. "The church owes you recompense, Earl Stone. You have more than just cause to doubt her intentions, but I promise I will do whatever I can to keep you from harm."

He turned to Captain Reynald. "Good captain, please summon a pair of the watch to escort Earl Stone to his quarters. I'm sure the events of the day have left him fatigued."

4

WHAT PASSES FOR PENANCE

ROUGH HANDS SHOOK ERROL until he sat up from the austere comfort of his bed to squint against the light of lamps that blinded him. He tried to see past the glare, but his eyes had yet to adjust. He sensed rather than saw a group of four men about him.

"Come, lad." A man, the primus he thought, urged him. "There's much to be done before you're brought before the Judica."

Errol turned toward the window. It reflected only the lamplight of the men in the room with him. So it was sometime before dawn. He clenched his teeth against the retort that would surely start another argument. The figures of the primus, the archbenefice, and Captain Reynald resolved into clarity. Another watchman, unknown to him, stood behind the other men—his guard, no doubt.

"Come, Errol," the leader of the conclave urged again. "You must dress. And then you must work your craft."

The archbenefice handed him a blue doublet and hose, the clothes Oliver Turing had given him when he'd been presented to the king. They were his best. "You should always look good if

30

you're going to be condemned, boy. It's important to have style, and it will sow a seed of doubt in the minds of your judges."

A bolt of anger flashed through Errol, heated his skin. "So, it's already been decided, has it?"

"Of course it has, boy," the archbenefice said. His tone still held its flippant humor. "Otherwise we'd have to leave things to chance, and I don't think you'd like that."

His confusion must have shown on his face, because the primus cut in. "He doesn't understand, Bertrand. He thinks you've deprived him of a fair trial."

The head of the church snorted his derision. "Fair? Somebody's been feeding the boy fables. Probably the king's niece. Humph. Nice girl. Too many romantic notions, though."

The archbenefice tapped him on the chest with one finger. "If we don't allow you to be convicted on Benefice Kell's charges, Benefice Dane will press his accusation in front of the Judica, and no power in the church can keep him from pulling the truth from you."

Errol shrugged into his clothes. "But I'm innocent. I didn't cast lots for the next king. It was Martin and Luis."

The archbenefice rolled his eyes. "I know that, boy. Who do you think told them to do it?" He turned to Primus Enoch Sten. "For an omne, the boy's remarkably dense. Haven't you taught him anything?"

The head of the conclave chuckled. "The boy's been busy, if you'll recall."

Archbenefice Bertrand Canon straightened, rubbed his chin. "Ah yes, saving the kingdom and all that. Well, he's about to get a harsh lesson in church politics."

He turned to the watchman at the door. "Resume your post, Lieutenant. I assure you we are quite safe."

After the lieutenant closed and bolted the door, Canon turned back to Errol, all signs of his bantering tone gone. "Listen closely, boy. I tried to call a grand Judica six years ago." He laughed at Errol's surprise. "Ha. I see that means something to you. The primus and I decided we couldn't afford to wait for the king to die; we needed an heir. But the motion was rejected by the lesser Judica. Too many of the benefices said it was risky to select a new king while the old one still lived, that it begged for civil war."

Now Errol understood. "So you had Luis cast for the location of the next king and they came to Callowford."

The archbenefice nodded. "Very good. Yes, Primus and I violated the will of the Judica with Martin's and Luis's help. If they find out, we'll be excommunicated and possibly executed. They must not find out."

Errol's face flushed. "So you want to use me to keep yourselves safe?"

The archbenefice snorted in disgust and turned to Sten. "What is the matter with this boy, Primus?" He shook his head like an exasperated teacher. "Of course I want you to keep me safe, boy. If the Judica banishes me, I can't find the snakes in my own house."

His voice dipped, and his gaze bored into Errol. "Our kingdom's enemies in the church and the conclave are counting on blinding us by getting you out of the way. An omne is the only way to verify a reader's cast. With you gone, we don't know for sure whom to trust."

That didn't make any sense. Their enemy was gone. They'd cast for Sarin. The former secondus had escaped Erinon and passed beyond retribution into Merakh.

The archbenefice gripped his shoulder, gave him a little shake. "Do you think Valon worked alone, boy?"

Errol's stomach floated as if he'd jumped the cliff overlooking the Cripples and was waiting for the fall to end. "What's going to happen?"

The archbenefice nodded. "Better. We're going to let Benefice Kell rant and rave about your involvement with evil spirits—I have enough influence to get you convicted on the charge—and then we're going to impose penance that will keep you sequestered here in Erinon, where we can use your abilities to help us kill the snakes in the Judica."

"But what about Benefice Dane?"

The archbenefice chuckled. "That's the only fun part about

this. I can use church law to defer action on his charge until your penance is complete."

The realization of what the archbenefice intended swept through him. Errol experienced the sensation of waking from a dream to find the bad men and dire situations were mere phantoms. "Nothing's going to be any different, is it."

"Hopefully not, Errol," the primus said.

"Hopefully," the archbenefice echoed. "But the Judica is unpredictable. I guide; I don't control. That uncertainty brings us to our task, Errol."

Primus Sten stepped forward with a pair of hardwood blanks and his carving knife. "We need you to use your talent to verify a cast, Errol."

This made no sense to him. They didn't need him. "Why?"

The archbenefice's eyes darted to the primus and the captain. "Because we dare not trust each other until you do, boy. The Judica and the conclave are made up of men who have known each other for decades, and I'd call most of them friend." A muscle in his jaw jumped. "But we know there are traitors within the Judica and the conclave. I won't risk putting a viper to my chest just because I might hurt someone's feelings. We're going to begin by testing Dane and Kell. The primus will cast to see if they're an enemy or ally of Illustra, and you will verify. I wish we had time for more, but after the Judica has decided your fate, you'll cast for the rest of the benefices. We're going to sweep the house clean, boy."

The edge of Enoch Sten's knife had just touched the golden brown grain of the wood when a thought occurred to Errol. "It won't work."

The knife stopped.

"Why not?" the archbenefice demanded. "He casts, you verify."

Errol's hands anticipated his apology. They fluttered in the air before he spoke. "Because that's all I can do. I can read the primus's lot, but I can't read his question. For this to work, we need to question all—even the primus. What if he asks whether Dane is an enemy or an ally of Merakh?"

Color drained from the archbenefice's face until it resembled the white of his robe.

Enoch Sten chuckled. "What was that you were saying about the boy being dense, Archbenefice?"

The archbenefice's face tensed. "I've no choice but to trust you or the boy to cast, Enoch," the archbenefice said. He looked like a man who'd been given a choice of losing an arm or a leg.

"Perhaps not," the primus said. "Have us cast the same question, but in silence. We can write down the answer. If they agree, then you have the information you need. If they don't agree, then you will know at least one of us is a traitor to the kingdom." He chuckled. "Given that the boy's survived this long by merest chance, it's not likely to be him."

Canon shook his head. "And what if you're both traitors? Your answers would still agree."

"Trust the boy, Bertrand. He has no reason to love the church or the conclave, but I think he's perceptive enough to know who his real enemies are."

The archbenefice nodded but looked unconvinced. "Then I want the two of you to cast for Dane first."

"I don't have a knife or blanks," Errol said.

"You may use mine, once I'm done." Enoch Sten nodded, his fingers resting on the handle of his knife the way a musician would his instrument. Errol watched him turn the hardwood blanks into lots with deft strokes of his knife. The scent of walnut rose from his hands until it permeated the room. The primus's economy of motion amazed Errol. The blanks rounded with amazing speed, even though his hands appeared to turn each lot in deliberate increments, never slowing or stopping.

"I've always loved walnut," the primus said. "Hard, but if your knife is sharp, it shapes like butter." Before twenty minutes had passed, the sound of wood clacking against wood came from the bag Captain Reynald held.

Canon directed Errol to the other side of the room. "You can work over there, lad, if you're willing."

For a moment he was tempted to say no. Why should he help

these men who seemed intent on putting him into danger over and again until he was inevitably killed? Inwardly he raged. He didn't want to be an omne; he held no desire to be a person of importance.

What *did* he want? To dance with the staff, to knock lightning from the sky.

And Adora.

But to win the princess, he had to be a person of importance.

Oh, they had him. The archbenefice, the primus, Martin, Luis—they all had him more than they knew. They'd never need to lay a compulsion on him again. As long as the faintest whisper of hope remained of winning Adora's heart, he would do anything they asked.

Curse it.

"I'm willing."

The archbenefice nodded as if he had followed the winding track of Errol's thoughts. The primus pressed his lips together, and his eyes narrowed the way people looked when they're trying not to cry.

He didn't have time or use for their pity. If casting lots for them kept him in the city, then he would carve until his hands bled. "So, I cast for Dane—whether he is friend or foe of Illustra—and then for Kell?"

The Archbenefice nodded and Errol set to work.

Two hours later, sunlight streamed through the window, giving the men in the room a yellowish cast that accentuated the lines of sleeplessness and age they shared. Errol stared at the lots he had cast for Benefice Kell. Strange, he thought, how men who were supposed to be allies could do so much harm.

"So, Kell is an ally." His breath gusted from his lungs in what would have been laughter if he'd smiled.

Archbenefice Canon harrumphed. "More or less. As much as I'm loath to admit it, Benefice Kell's charge against you has afforded us the opportunity to delay Dane's charge indefinitely."

The primus smirked, and his eyes twinkled. "Divine providence."

"Perhaps," the archbenefice said. "Benefice Dane is not a surprise, really, but most certainly a disappointment."

"What will you do?" Errol asked.

The archbenefice exchanged glances with the primus and Captain Reynald. "Whatever is best for the kingdom, my boy." He rose from his chair with the creaks and groans of an old man. "For now we need to leave. I don't want to be seen departing your quarters, if I can help it. The Judica convenes in an hour. You should eat." He stopped at the door. "As accused, you'll be assigned an interpreter of sorts."

Errol let his surprise show on his face. "Interpreter?"

Canon retraced his steps, closed the distance between them until he stood over Errol where he sat. "A priest assigned to translate the traditions of the Judica so that laymen can understand them. Primus Sten and I have agreed on the man for the job. We are certain you can trust him."

The archbenefice patted his shoulder in a gesture Errol had seen fathers give their sons when they were proud or tried to be comforting. The touch felt alien to him—not unwelcome, but strange.

Benefice Kell, white-haired and furious, stood in the accuser's box to present his case. Errol tried reminding himself he was an ally of the kingdom. It didn't help much to hear himself described as a deadly incarnation of evil.

"This evil youth has deceived you all," the benefice said. Flecks of spittle flew from his passionate denunciation. "Under the guise of rescuing the kingdom, he has consorted with spirits. Made bold by his acceptance at court and in the conclave, he has actually admitted to contact with these so-called herbwomen and their sinister familiars."

"By the three, listen to him go on," Benefice Credo said. The tall clergyman from the province of Dannick, the man assigned by the archbenefice to interpret events for him, muttered a continuous commentary on his right. The benefice sat so close, Errol could have touched his far shoulder without completely extending his arm. He liked Credo. In looks he resembled Luis, with lighter skin, but his sense of humor could have come straight from Cruk's mouth. After Conger he was the most unpriestlike churchman he'd ever met.

Few of the benefices displayed an interest in Kell's diatribe. Most sat with their chin resting in one hand, their eyes heavy-lidded. A few involuntary nods of sleepiness decorated the crowd. The archbenefice, towering over the blustering benefice from his position on the raised dais, suppressed another sigh—perhaps his sixth or seventh. Errol had lost count.

"Another five minutes of this and the archbenefice will have to wake everyone up with his staff," Credo said.

Benefice Dane looked neither sleepy nor bored. He was intent, like a river rat watching the shallows, waiting for his turn to strike. He twitched at odd moments, and adjusted the deep crimson of his robe in sharp jerks that spoke of impatience. The red-haired benefice punctuated those movements with hungry looks at Errol and glares for Benefice Kell and the archbenefice.

Credo dropped his voice to a whisper. "Dane doesn't look happy, not happy at all."

"Why's that?"

"He thinks he has you, and not only you but Martin and Luis as well."

After another ten minutes Benefice Kell finished reciting the charges and his evidence. The archbenefice lifted himself from the comfort of his seat with a deep sigh and rapped his staff on the floor. "Who would speak to the charges?"

Benefice Dane sprang from his chair. "I would speak."

"Well, there's a surprise," Credo said. His voice must have carried to the first row. Several of the benefices there snickered.

The archbenefice nodded as if he'd expected no less. "Speak no word before the Judica that is untrue. Make no statement that is incomplete. You are adjured by Deas."

"Judica me, Deas," the benefice answered. "This is all very entertaining, Archbenefice, but quite beside the point. The status of the herbwomen and their claim to know unknowable Aurae has been debated for centuries without conclusion, a fact that will almost certainly be unaltered by today's deliberations."

Dane's lip curled. "With all due respect to Benefice Kell, the matter I placed before the Judica is of far more importance. I respectfully request that we suspend the charges of consorting with spirits so that we may consider the far more serious charge of usurpation of authority."

Credo patted him on the leg. "Here we go, lad. Pay attention. This could be as unpredictable as a lot blank bouncing across the floor."

Kell spat. "You insolent young pup. You speak of respect, then attempt to brush my charges aside as if they were of no consequence." He pointed a shaking finger at Errol. "He consorted with spirits!"

Credo snorted. "Any fool knows the herbwomen are harmless."

Dane smirked. "Please calm yourself, Benefice Kell. I did say with all *due* respect. Please don't blame me if the amount given seems unsatisfactory."

The archbenefice's staff interrupted Kell's apoplectic reply. "Benefice Dane, as I've said before, you're well versed in church law. However, I find your attentiveness to church tradition less than exemplary. It is the custom of this body to deliberate with solemn dignity. Baiting your fellow benefice and servant of the church is hardly in keeping with the expectations of your office."

Errol saw Credo nod his approval out of the corner of his eye.

Dane's smirk never wavered, but he bowed toward the archbenefice. "I crave your pardon and that of Benefice Kell. I was momentarily overwhelmed by the gravity of our situation."

The archbenefice's voice remained cold. "Your apology is accepted. In accordance with church tradition, the Judica will hear and pass judgment on the charges as they've been presented."

"Archbenefice, I have presented a motion, surely you'll want the Judica to vote on it," Dane said.

A sea of red-robed benefices nodded.

"Clever, clever man," Credo said under his breath.

"Why?" Errol asked.

The benefice put his mouth close to Errol's ear, shielding his face from the Judica with one hand. "He seeks to go against tradition by appealing to the benefices directly. I don't think it will work, but it will cost the archbenefice later."

"Cost him how?" Errol asked.

"I don't know, lad, but the Judica is jealous of its power. Church tradition or not, they'll feel slighted if the archbenefice denies them the chance to vote on Dane's motion."

Archbenefice Canon rapped the floor twice with his staff. "It has been the church's tradition to rule in succession. The motion is denied."

A knot of tension in the back of Errol's neck loosened at the ruling. This was insane; he actually felt relieved to be facing charges of conspiring with spirits.

A sea of faces, stiff and disapproving, now faced Errol—as if he'd overruled them himself. Dane's eyes glittered, and he smiled like a wolf as he bowed to the archbenefice and resumed his seat.

"The charge of consorting with spirits is presented," the archbenefice said. "Who would speak?"

A thin, blond-haired benefice rose from his seat. He barely looked old enough to be a priest, much less a benefice. "I would speak."

"Benefice McKeran," Credo said. "Good man. He hasn't aged in the last twenty years."

He exchanged the ritual charge with the archbenefice and addressed the Judica. "It has not been established that the herb-women do, in fact, consort with spirits or that the spirits are evil. The proscription is against contact with evil spirits, made before Magis's war as a safeguard against contact with a malus. What if they do, in fact, know Aurae?"

Robes rustled as a benefice at the far end of the room burst from his seat with his arm waving for the archbenefice's attention. "I would speak." Without waiting for the charge, he presented his counterargument. "Though I hold Benefice McKeran in highest esteem, I must point out that . . ."

The debate turned interminable, but the archbenefice seemed perfectly content to let it continue. And continue it did.

They broke for lunch, and the deliberation extended into the afternoon. After several hours, during which time nearly every member of the Judica voiced his opinion at least once, the hall stood silent.

"Who would speak?" the archbenefice asked. No one moved. Bertrand Canon fingered his staff but made no motion to close the debate. A sea of red regarded him. "Who would speak?"

Three raps, like the toll of a funeral bell filled the hall, bounced back from the far walls and died, creating a silence more absolute and profound than before.

"Benefices, you are to vote. There can be no dissembling. Earl Stone is guilty or innocent. You are adjured by Deas."

Errol leaned toward Benefice Credo. "Now what?"

"The benefices will vote by stone—white for innocent, black for guilty. Simple majority."

Two church guards hefted a large heavily lacquered box onto the dais. The box held no ornamentation, only a hole in the top a little smaller than the palm of Errol's hand. By rows the benefices came forward to drop their vote in the box, each palming their stone of choice so that it remained hidden.

Sweat ran beneath Errol's tunic. If they found him innocent, Dane would have the right to question him on the charge of usurping authority, and readers would check his every word. He darted a glance to the archbenefice, but Canon remained as impassive as rock.

The last of the benefices voted, and Benefice Kell and Benefice McKeran came forward. The archbenefice removed the top and began dividing the votes, counting the black votes placed in front of Kell and the white votes in front of McKeran.

Errol's face flushed. From his seat he couldn't tell which pile was bigger, and the archbenefice's count was too soft to reach his ears.

"Benefice Kell, Benefice McKeran, do you agree?" Canon asked. A curt nod came from both men.

The staff rapped three times on the floor, the sound muted by the proximity of the two benefices. "Earl Stone is guilty."

Errol might have imagined it, but the archbenefice's voice seemed to hold a smug, satisfied tone to it.

The archbenefice rapped once to quiet the murmurs of the hall. "Errol Stone, are you prepared to accept the penalty of your crime?"

Benefice Credo leaned toward him. "Stand up, face the archbenefice, and say 'I am.'"

Before he could rise, a large benefice with iron-gray hair who'd spoken in Errol's defense rose. "I would speak, Archbenefice."

"I am about to pronounce sentence, Benefice Horvath, in accordance with church tradition."

Horvath nodded. "Yet, it is the right of the Judica to determine sentence, according to a strict interpretation of the law."

On Errol's right, Benefice Credo stiffened. "What is that old fox up to?"

For the space of a dozen heartbeats, the archbenefice remained silent. "That is so," he said at last, his tone cold. "Are you requesting a formal vote, Benefice Horvath?"

The benefice shook his head. "Not if it may be avoided. I seek to ensure that the will of the Judica, this college of benefices, is observed." A near-unanimous nod of heads greeted this.

Bertrand Canon nodded. "I see."

Benefice Credo muttered something under his breath that sounded like a curse. "Well, the fat's in the fire now, lad. The Judica's got their back up and there's nothing the archbenefice can do about it. They've got the law on their side on this one."

Horvath made a placating gesture toward the dais. "What I propose is that we order Earl Stone to serve his penance and the kingdom at the same time. The former secondus and our enemy, Sarin Valon, escaped to Merakh. Earl Stone's valor is unquestioned by most in this body. Moreover, he is an omne, equipped by Deas as no other reader in the conclave—not even Valon."

The archbenefice leaned forward, his faced pinched. For an

instant he looked like a trapped animal before he reasserted his composure. "What do you propose, Benefice Horvath?"

"Place a compulsion upon Earl Stone to track down Sarin Valon wherever he may be in Merakh—there to capture or kill him."

Gorge rose in Errol's throat. There would be no need to vote. A sea of nods condemned him.

5

COMPANIONS OF NECESSITY

T HE ARCHBENEFICE'S MOOD could only be described as sulfurous. Yet even as Bertrand Canon paced the rug in Enoch Sten's quarters vowing reprisals and doom on his enemies in the Judica, he maintained a veneer of austere dignity. Enoch Sten and Captain Reynald sat off to the side—the primus the picture of patience, the watchman a study in restrained violence.

Errol understood. The primus would lose his omne, the captain his staff instructor. With all his heart, he wished it weren't so.

"A compulsion," the archbenefice snarled. He spit the words as if they were a curse. "Just like that, they voted to put a compulsion on you, boy—as if we hadn't spent the last three hundred years trying to weed that abominable practice out of the church."

"But even that tells us something," Sten said.

"Ha! What it tells us is that our enemies in the Judica are more numerous and stronger than we suspected." He grimaced. "I could do without such news."

Errol posed the question that lurked in his heart close to the spot where his mistrust of the church and its clergy lay. "I don't

43

understand. Why do you let people like that in the church in the first place?"

Bertrand Canon stopped midstride. Anger slid from his face like a sheet of ice slipping from a cliff wall. He gazed at Errol, his blue eyes intense and unwavering until Errol looked away. "I keep forgetting he wasn't raised here," he said to the primus.

"I'm just as happy about that," Primus Sten said. "We've already filled our quota of schemers."

The archbenefice grunted. "No doubt. The truth, Errol, is that the church exercises considerable temporal power in addition to its spiritual authority. Power attracts men of all types. Some see it as a way to accomplish good." He sighed. "Others see it as a way to exercise authority over others or to become wealthy."

"But why?" Emotions he couldn't begin to identify threatened to overwhelm him. "Why let them in? They hurt . . . people."

"I'm sorry, Errol. The church is vast, too vast to keep them all out. And people change. Some lose themselves along the way, but some find themselves too. A priest is just a man who's taken a vow, Errol, just a man."

Errol pinched the bridge of his nose. It didn't matter. The Judica had voted, and Benefice Weir, Lord Weir's uncle, had gleefully and savagely laid the compulsion on him. As nearly as Errol could figure, he'd be dead in a few weeks. "How long will it take the compulsion to force me from Erinon?"

The archbenefice grimaced. "I think you can answer that better than we. Despite what people outside the church believe, to this point the Judica has only used compulsion to ensure those with the talent for reading come to the isle." He shrugged. "Even that has become rare. The threat of compulsion is usually enough. You've had it used on you twice in less than a year. How long did it take?"

He thought back. Luis had laid the coercion on him in Callowford. "We left for Erinon immediately. But when I was stopped along the way"—such as in Windridge, where he'd jumped into the river to escape, only to be washed downstream, and was nursed back to health from pneumonia by Rale and his family—"it took quite some time for the compulsion to overwhelm me again." He exhaled. "At least a month."

"That gives us some time," the archbenefice said.

"Time for what?"

The archbenefice's heavy brows rose in surprise. "To pull together the men to go with you. You didn't think we were just going to put you on a horse and send you off to get killed, did you?"

Errol stammered. "I didn't know, but who'd be willing to go with me?"

"I'll go with you, boy, and gladly," Reynald said.

The archbenefice stilled. "No."

"But—"

"No."

Reynald nodded, but his lips compressed into a thin line of disapproval.

The archbenefice barked a laugh. "As for the rest . . . Willing? I don't care whether or not they want to go. Those we can't order, we'll buy." He paced the carpet. "I need recommendations, gentlemen. I have no intention of losing an asset to the enemy. Who do you think we should send, Primus?"

"That's easy enough—Martin, Luis, and Cruk."

Distaste twisted Archbenefice Canon's features at the mention of the three. "Yes, if they hadn't already left on their own penance." His face closed. "They're not here. I need people we can put our hands on."

A desire built in Errol's chest, grew until it demanded utterance. "I want Rale."

The archbenefice turned to him, gave him a look of patient forbearance. "Who?"

Errol's tongue spilled words that tumbled over each other. He wanted Rale more than he could hope to express. "He's the farmer who taught me how to use the staff. Cruk told me his real name is Elar Indomiel."

"No!" The archbenefice reddened. "I forbid it."

Errol edged back from the archbenefice's sudden anger. He looked to the primus and Captain Reynald for explanation, but the pair sat in their seats with the look of men willing to wait out a storm. The archbenefice employed an extensive vocabulary to describe Rale and his ancestry. Quite a few words were unfamiliar to Errol.

What had Rale done to warrant such a tirade?

After the archbenefice's tempest passed, Primus Sten fingered his blue robe of office and offered a diffident proposal. "It's unlikely that Elar would willingly consent to a trip into Merakh." He picked a piece of lint from the front. "Anyone would consider it a long-overdue penance."

"He is quite good with a staff," Reynald said, "and the second-best tactician I know."

"No," the archbenefice said. "I will not lay eyes on that man again."

Enoch Sten kept the same constrained tone to his voice as before. "You wouldn't have to actually see him, Bertrand. Let a low-level assistant deliver the order. You'd deprive Elar of a chance to respond."

"Ha." The planes of the archbenefice's face softened. "Elar always did insist on being the last to speak." He rounded on the primus. "I know what you're doing, Enoch. Do you honestly think appealing to my vanity will induce me to work with him?"

Enoch Sten chuckled. "I'd hoped so. He's needed, Bertrand. He can't help but be needed, and the boy trusts him. Begging your pardon, Archbenefice, but you're inconsistent. First you say you're unwilling to lose an asset, and then you refuse one of the best tactical minds in the kingdom." He gestured toward Errol. "Look at his face. Have you seen this look on him for anyone other than the princess?"

Warmth rose in Errol's cheeks. Were his thoughts so easy to read? The archbenefice looked at him, and a cascade of emotions played across his wrinkled face. "You're right, of course, Enoch. If he can be found, he will be brought."

Captain Reynald gave a polite cough as he held one hand palm up. "If I may venture an observation, how do you suggest the boy and his company penetrate the Merakhi interior?"

The archbenefice nodded as if he'd expected the question.

"Merchants. As long as they travel the permitted routes, they'll be able to seek Valon's place of concealment without contest."

"And if Valon is not close to the routes?"

The archbenefice leaned back. "Then things will become more difficult."

Reynald shook his head. "Blithely said, Archbenefice, but if they're caught, we'll lose Errol and the entire company."

Bertrand Canon flushed. "What would you have me do, Reynald? The Judica has voted! I have no authority to overturn their decision." His voice rose until it cracked like a whip. "If you can provide a solution to this, then out with it."

Reynald took the archbenefice's lashing in stride; his manner remained calm, thoughtful. "I mean no accusation or disrespect, Archbenefice. I merely meant to point out that we need someone with knowledge of those parts of Merakh that are forbidden to kingdom men."

"There aren't any," the archbenefice snapped.

"I know a man," Errol said.

The three men turned toward him as if they'd forgotten his presence. The archbenefice gave a small shake of his head, but Captain Reynald wore a grin as if a voice only he could hear had just said something amusing. "Who would that be?"

"His name is Naaman Ru," Errol said. "I worked as a guard in his caravan."

Primus Sten's face lit as if he now shared the captain's joke, but the archbenefice shook his head. "Granted, he has the knowledge we're after, but he can't be trusted, Errol. You of all people should know that."

Errol shrugged. The solution seemed simple to him. "Put a compulsion on him."

"The boy learns fast," the primus muttered.

"He doesn't know what he's saying," Canon said. "Compulsion is . . ."

"Wrong?" Errol asked with a sarcastic tone.

Canon huffed. "Yes, boy, it's wrong. I know it's been done to you . . ."

"Twice," Errol said.

He nodded. "Agreed, but my heart misgives me in this. We can compel Ru to guide you, but you will make an enemy of him for as long as he lives. Do you want that?"

Errol shrugged to show how little he cared. "He's already my enemy. I want to live, and for that I need a guide. Is there anyone who has the knowledge Ru has?"

Silence ruled for a moment as Errol, Primus Enoch Sten, and Captain Reynald all watched the archbenefice struggle with the decision. At last, he threw up his hands in surrender. "I can't gainsay you in this, Errol, but my heart tells me there will be a reckoning for this decision. I have tried to discontinue compulsion for two reasons."

"You said it was wrong," Errol said.

"Yes, and I believe it is. I believe Deas created the church to serve, not to enforce obedience." Canon licked his lips. "But compulsion for a benefice is similar to lots for a reader—the results are dependent on the wisdom of its practitioner. Just as in casting the question frames the answer, so in compulsion the requirement frames the response." He sighed. "We will want to give careful thought to the wording of Naaman Ru's compulsion."

"Now, I want you to take a priest with you," Canon said.

Something deep in Errol's gut rebelled at the suggestion. Unbidden, an image of Antil rose in his mind. He shook his head.

"You'll need a priest, Errol," the archbenefice asserted.

"Why?" He hadn't meant for his voice to pop that way.

"Our feud with the Merakhi and the Morgols goes back centuries, boy. Rodran's childlessness is only the spark that lights the tinder. You'll need someone who knows the history. That knowledge is confined to the priesthood."

Errol laughed out loud. The archbenefice's face grew stiff and cold, as if affronted. Errol raised a hand to explain. "There was a man in Ru's caravan . . . I don't think you'd like him very much, but the only time I saw him without a book on church history was when we were fighting. After we'd been attacked, he was back in his book before the blood dried."

"Who is this man?" Primus asked.

"His name is Conger," Errol said.

"Never heard of him," the archbenefice said. "How do you know he has the knowledge you need?"

"He's a defrocked priest."

The archbenefice wore a momentary look of horror. Then he laughed. "The boy seems determined to gather the worst sort of refuse for his mission to Merakh. For someone who has every reason to despise the concept of penance, Errol, you seem quite willing to impose it on others."

It was meant in jest, but the words cut. The archbenefice was comparing him to the Judica. "I just want to live. Rale and Conger are men I can trust, and Naaman Ru knows the way." He shrugged away the comparison. "How long will it take to get everyone together? I think they'll be tough to find."

The archbenefice and the primus smiled. "My dear boy," the archbenefice said, "you are about to find out just how long the arm of the church can be."

"I heard," Adora said. Undercurrents Errol couldn't interpret stirred in her voice. They sat in the shade of the sparring yard. The clack of practice swords came from Errol's right, where Liam educated two minor nobles. Periodic grunts of pain indicated those times Liam's weapon struck home. Errol didn't bother to watch if either of the nobles landed a blow on his friend. The notion was ridiculous.

A long-familiar twinge of jealousy pricked him at the thought of Liam, but today his fellow villager had Errol's gratitude. Liam's presence and the adoration it engendered among the men and women of the court, assured Adora and him of an uninterrupted conversation.

"How soon will you leave?" An unaccustomed tightness at the corner of her eyes warned him, like a portent of danger.

"As soon as the men I asked for are brought," Errol said.

When he offered nothing more, Adora slipped a hand up her

sleeve and brought forth her fan. She snapped it open and began fanning herself with brusque, imperious strokes. She shifted in her seat so that she no longer faced Errol, but rather the yard and Liam. With a nod she indicated him, or so Errol thought.

"Lord Weir's father, the duke, has petitioned the king for me on Weir's behalf." Adora said this with so little inflection Errol couldn't begin to guess her thoughts on the matter.

"Oh," he said.

The fan snapped shut with a soft crack of sound. Adora's eyes widened, and their green darkened to slate. "Oh? Some man comes to my uncle to ask for my hand for his son and all you have to say is 'Oh'?"

For the first time, he grew angry with her, fed up with her expectations of him, tired of her seeing him as more than he really was. "What else is there to say? The church is sending me to Merakh! After Valon! He's a reader. No, I'm sorry, he's more than a reader—he's a possessed reader who's linked to a circle of readers. He's going to see me coming!" The words spilled from him now, as if a dam had burst in his heart. "Don't you under-stand? They're sending me off to die!"

Tears welled in her eyes. Errol had seen such interactions between husbands and wives in his village. This was the part where the woman ran away crying and the man chased after her, apologizing for telling the truth, telling her and himself with soft-spoken lies how mistaken he'd been. Adora blinked, and a tear dropped from each eye to darken the light blue of her dress. Then, with motions slow and deliberate, she rose from her chair and came to him.

A crack sounded in his ear. A split second later heat blos-somed in his left cheek. The princess stood before him, shaking the tingle of the slap from her fingers. "You are an omne and the best fighter I've ever seen." She bit her lower lip.

"Second best," he corrected.

"Hush." Her voice dropped, moved from steel to velvet. "And I have seen you show mercy to supposedly greater men who've used and insulted you." She breathed deeply. "Do you want me?"

He did his best to ignore the stares that registered in his peripheral vision. "What?"

She huffed, her exasperation obvious. "Do you want me?" she repeated.

He took a deep breath, forced himself to speak past the weight that sat like a draft horse on his chest. "More than life."

"Then find a way to live."

With a swirl of skirts she passed through the onlookers and left without a backward glance.

Smiles came to him at her departure. Men, young and old, nodded their approval, as if he'd won a bout.

Except for Lord Weir.

He stood at the edge of the crowd with the look of a man bent on murder.

6

WHAT LIES AT WINDRIDGE

MARTIN HELD HIS BREATH as a group of horsemen, their faces hooded, their dark cloaks flailing and
snapping behind, thundered by their hiding place. As the sound
of pursuit faded, Luis dropped from his horse, pulled a pair of
pine blocks and a knife from his saddlebag, and began carving.
The secondus muttered imprecations under his breath in time
to the strokes of his craft, some of them directed at Sarin, some
at the men and ferrals who served Illustra's enemies, but most
directed at Martin.

"Told him we shouldn't chance Windridge," the reader said
under his breath. Stab. "Even cast lots for it." Stab. "Safer to go
around to the south."

Just ahead, from the position he'd assumed guarding the entrance to the copse of trees that concealed them, Cruk grunted
with amusement. The watchman spoke little, but five years in
Callowford had given Martin insight into the taciturn captain's
vocabulary. Cruk was laughing at them.

Martin decided to address Luis's concern. "You only cast for
the safest route, old friend, not the route we should take. There

are questions—questions that may have their answers in the abbot's cathedral."

"Would it have made any difference if I had cast for the route we should take? Would you have skirted Windridge then?" Luis's voice held exasperation. The three of them had spent too much time together. Keeping secrets or even private thoughts had become difficult.

"No," he answered.

Cruk grunted again.

Luis' voice softened. "You couldn't have done anything about it, Martin. You didn't have the authority."

His ears heated. "I did, Luis. You and I both know it. Had I gone to Morin's superior, I could have used my position as benefice to win the herbwoman's release."

"Aye," Cruk said. His gravel voice rasped across Martin's hearing like a saw blade cutting wood. "And at what cost? You can't save everyone during a battle, Pater. If you try, you'll lose the battle and the men. Any soldier knows that."

"Is this a battle, then?" Martin asked.

"Ha. You know it is—it is, in fact, a war."

The captain's correction rankled all the more for being true. He could have saved the herbwoman from Morin's foul use. He'd chosen not to. His failure obligated him to her. And she might be able to answer questions. He rubbed his backside. A whiff of horse and his own sweat wafted up to him. There could be no doubt about the matter. His years of being able to ride all day and still function had long passed. Luis's lighter build and Cruk's tougher constitution allowed them to endure the four-footed torture better than he. Men of his maturity and bulk were more suited to carriages than horses.

"I've replayed every minute of our journey, Luis." He shifted in his saddle. "Cruk, do you remember what happened in Abbot Morin's prison?"

The watch captain snorted; the lumpy contours of his face pulled his reddish beard to one side. "It's not the kind of incident I'm likely to forget. I've seen plenty of strange things during twenty years in the watch, but I've never seen a woman try and batter through the bars of her prison that way."

"Nor I," Martin said. "If I had known beforehand a malus awaited us, I could have tried the rite of purification."

"Not exactly your area of expertise," Luis said. The reader replaced his knife and pulled a piece of rubbing cloth to finish the lots.

He couldn't deny it. Like most of the priests who attained the red of benefice, theology was his primary focus. "No matter. I'm more interested in that creature's target. I'd assumed it to be Liam at the time."

"As did I," Cruk said, "but Errol stood right beside him."

"You don't think you'll be able to find the malus's host and question her, do you, Martin?" Luis asked.

"No, of course not. According to Errol, the woman is almost certainly dead. Shot by Merodach as he jumped from the bridge."

"So, we come back to the herbwoman," Luis said.

Martin nodded.

"I think they're ready," the secondus announced. Two indistinguishable pine spheres rested in his hands. He retrieved a rough canvas sack, deposited the lots inside, and bounced the bag a couple of times.

Soft clacking sounds drifted to Martin, the gift of Deas. "What question did you cast?"

A slight smile tugged the reader's face into an expression of resigned surrender. "Whether or not there is anything valuable to be learned in Windridge." He presented the bag to Martin for the draw.

Yes came up eight times out of ten.

"Not much of a surprise," Cruk said. "When you know nothing, almost anything you learn is bound to be helpful."

"True enough," Martin said. Luis had wasted a pair of lots and his craft on a question that didn't need to be cast. The secondus gave a small lift of his shoulders. No, the draw wasn't wasted. This was Luis's way of standing with him, of giving Martin his support. "Thank you, my friend. Now, can you check for the safest time for us to resume our journey?"

With a nod, Luis pulled a dozen blanks from his pack and began the process of delivering them to Windridge.

The clouds, threatening throughout the morning, surrendered their rain as the three of them approached the city gates. Fat drops struck Martin's head with soft pops and hisses before he pulled up the hood of his cloak.

Windridge had changed. The guards at the city gates no longer waved carts into the city with casual, bored gestures. A line of wagons and carriages stretched from the left side of the main entrance to the city, while a shorter line consisting of those on horseback or on foot snaked in from the right. Martin and Luis loosened their swords. Cruk's free hand rested on the pommel of his saddle, inches from his throwing knife. The guardhouse bristled with a full complement of guards.

Martin surveyed the line. As each cart approached the gate, the merchants and their guards lowered their hoods and offered their goods for inspection.

Cruk stiffened as they rode past a caravan displaying a flag of vertical red and blue stripes. "Martin." They edged their horses closer together. "That merchant train back there . . . One of the guards is Merakhi."

Martin schooled his features and leaned forward as if to check his horse's tack. "Are you sure?"

"I'm not likely to be mistaken."

Dread blossomed in his stomach at the watchman's certainty. Then Luis put words to his apprehension. "They're scouting us. We need to get away from that caravan, Martin. If they have a reader with them, we'll be hard to miss."

As they approached, the guard took note of their hoods and leveled a crossbow at Cruk. "No one approaches the gate hooded."

They threw back their hoods. Martin shook the rain from his hair. He gave Cruk a nod.

"Name your business in Windridge," the guard said.

Cruk's hand rested on the pommel of his dagger. "Rest and food as we pass through."

The guard nodded and waved them through, but Cruk kept his horse still. "Things have changed since we last visited your city, Sergeant. Why is there extra security at the gate?"

The guard's eyes darted, flashed a warning before he waved them through without answering. "Be about your business." He signaled the next rider to approach.

Smells of food, mud, and men washed over them. The rain muted the cries of the marketplace, where people moved from stall to stall, their heads uncovered and water dripping from their noses. Those closest to the gates looked at each set of newcomers in fear.

Cruk headed to a large covered stall whose owner hawked swords in a dispirited voice. Martin dismounted and edged close to Cruk, followed by Luis. "I think it best to find rooms and information before we approach the new abbot."

"I understand your caution, Martin," Luis said, "but if we don't keep moving, they'll have us."

"How about an inn close to the market?" Cruk asked. "If it's busy enough, it should keep pursuit at bay, even if they find us."

The suggestion made sense. Martin nodded his approval to Cruk. "Find the busiest inn available. Something close so we can get out of this cursed rain. Get a room so Luis can cast for the best approach to the cathedral. Then see if you can find one of the off-duty guards and get him to talk."

Cruk barked a laugh. "A couple of tankards of ale and it'll be hard to get him to stop. Every guard alive wants a sympathetic ear." He cast a look up at the rain. "I wouldn't mind one myself." The captain remounted and disappeared into the sodden press of the crowd.

Martin watched the throng, trying to remember how many years it had been since he'd drawn a sword in earnest. "Was it wrong to come here, Luis? You could have advised against it."

"I did."

The dry tone of the secondus's voice belied the seriousness of their situation.

"I know you too well, old friend," Martin said. "You're mulish when pushed to do something you don't want to do. I tried to advise you against taking Errol to Erinon. Little good it did me."

The reader nodded. "Deep down I agreed with you. We needed to come here. Lots are stupid things, Martin. They can only tell you what you ask them. We asked them if coming here was safe. Humph. Any fool would realize coming here wasn't safe. The question should have been, should we come here?"

Martin saw his point. Insights such as this made Luis Montari a rarity among the conclave: a man who looked beyond his next cast. "But then we wouldn't have known whether it was safe."

"Exactly," Luis said. "I don't speak for Deas, but I think it only right that you try to free the herbwoman if she is still held."

The crowd shifted and flowed in front of them, and Cruk soon emerged in front of their stand. He dismounted and joined them under the awning, his eyes slits against the rain and his mouth tight. "I saw a Morgol." He paused. "I think." His hand clenched and reclenched around the pommel of his sword.

"You must be mistaken," Luis said. "They never come off the steppes."

Cruk corrected the reader. "Almost never."

"How do you know it was a Morgol?" Martin asked.

The captain's massive shoulder shifted under his cloak in a shrug. "Morgols have a yellowish tinge to their skin. And they're shorter. I saw an arm come out of a cloak. This is bad, Pater." Cruk waved at the crowd at large. "Most of these people couldn't tell a Merakhi from a Basqu or a Morgol from a Bellian."

Martin pulled the misty air into his lungs. "Our enemies know King Rodran's time is short. Do you have an inn for us?" At Cruk's nod, Martin pushed himself away from the shelter of the seller's stall and into the rain. "Come. Haste is needed."

Cruk led them through the soaked crowd to a square on the far side of the market. Martin nodded his approval at the captain's choice. The inn's large common room thronged with customers who showed no sign of leaving anytime soon, yet there were still rooms available.

"The question, Martin?" Luis asked.

Gratitude spread warmth from his chest outward. "As it seems best to you, Secondus." He gave a small bow, and Luis retreated up the stairs. Cruk gave his pouch an exploratory heft and wandered from the table in search of one of the city guards, leaving Martin in the corner with his thoughts.

Questions chased each other through his mind like unruly acolytes playing tag before vespers. What made Errol so important? What had turned Sarin Valon, the brightest mind in the history of the conclave, to serve the enemy? Abbot Morin was dead, executed by the king without surrendering any of the information that might have remained in his broken mind, but what enemies remained in the watch, the conclave, or the church?

And what of Liam?

All instinct and reason told him that Liam would be the next king. So why did their enemies show so little interest in him? Martin cursed himself for a fool, so blinded by his quest to find and protect Liam that he'd ignored events taking place right in front of him.

He took a pull from his tankard—dreadful stuff—and waited.

Luis joined him an hour later, his brows furrowed and his eyes wary. Across the room, Cruk still sat, exchanging stories and tankards of ale with a medium-sized man with thinning light brown hair and a scar that ran through one eyebrow.

"Well?" Martin asked.

Luis shrugged. "Dawn."

"That doesn't explain the crease in your forehead," Martin said.

The secondus gave a small shake of his head. "The lots . . ."

"What about them?"

The reader threw up his hands. "I don't know. They felt strange."

A seed of doubt took root somewhere in Martin's middle. They shouldn't have come to Windridge. "Strange . . . how?"

Luis forced a mirthless laugh. "It felt as if I were reading someone else's question."

Martin tried to wave away Luis's concern. "I'm sure your art is still as strong as ever. If the lots say dawn, then dawn it will be."

Across the room, Cruk plunked a coin down on the bar in front of two frothy tankards, grabbed one, and weaved his way through the patrons to rejoin them in the corner. He grabbed a seat and proceeded to take a long pull from the tankard that left it as full as before.

"Ferrals," he said.

Luis slumped back, his face lost in shadow. "That would explain the order at the gate. They can walk upright, but there's no disguising their faces."

"It gets worse," Cruk growled. "They attacked the abbey. A band broke into the sanctuary. Tore the throats out of a pair of acolytes before the night watch knew anything was amiss. One of the brothers heard the cry of the acolytes and locked himself and the ferrals into the sanctuary and threw the key through a window. When reinforcements arrived they found the ferrals still inside. The monk was torn to pieces."

"A brave man," Luis said.

Martin bowed his head and recited the panikhida, the prayer for the dead. "We commend into thy mercy all thy servants which are departed hence from us with the sign of faith and now do rest in the sleep of peace: grant unto them, we beseech thee, thy mercy and everlasting peace, Deas, Eleison, and unknowable Aurae."

After a brief moment of silence, Cruk continued. "The ferrals were killed and their bodies burned. The abbot is trying to keep the matter quiet to keep from hurting trade in the city." Cruk's smile looked almost amused. "Fastest way I know of to spread information is to tell people to keep it quiet."

"What were the ferrals trying to do?" Luis asked.

Cruk grimaced. "Ferrals don't do, they kill."

Martin rubbed a sudden ache in his temples. "Gerold is the new abbot. Would he have just left her in prison?"

"Left who?" Cruk asked.

That brought Martin up short. Then he gave a rueful laugh. "I don't even remember her name. The herbwoman Morin imprisoned."

"Odene," Luis said. "Her name is Odene."

Luis would be the one to remember that. Not for the first time, Martin wished he was gifted with a reader's memory.

The smoky air of the common room burned his lungs. He let it out in a sigh. One more night before they might get some answers. "We should retire to our quarters before the crowd thins enough to make us conspicuous."

Cruk's hand caught his arm as he started to rise, forced him back to his seat. "Too late for that. Look there."

At the entrance to the inn, four men in dark cloaks scanned the crowd. The torchlight, bright and cheery, reflected from the sallow-tinged skin of the one in back.

7

FLIGHT

MARTIN LIFTED HIS TANKARD and took a pull that wet his lips and nothing more. He cast a look toward the door again when he lowered his mug. Palpable relief washed over him as the men by the door turned to survey the crowd at the opposite end of the common room. A knot somewhere in his gut started to loosen. He had no doubt Cruk would exact a costly price if they were attacked, but his own best days with a sword were far behind him, and Luis had never been a fighter. And fights were risky, unpredictable.

He leaned toward Cruk, moving so as to attract as little notice as possible. "I think they missed us."

The captain nodded, pulled his dagger to slice a wedge from the block of cheese in front of them. The blade passed through the dark yellow block with ridiculous ease. He grunted, not sounding convinced. "Maybe. If I were hunting someone, I'd do everything in my power to keep them from knowing they'd been spotted."

The knot in Martin's midsection re-formed.

Luis ran one hand over the rough wooden texture of their

table. "Perhaps we should slip into the kitchen and out through the door by the stables."

Cruk gave the best shake of his head. "No. If we do that, they'll know we've spotted them. Let's continue up to our room as if we had no suspicions. Then we can slip out through the window onto the roof and down into the stable yard."

"The roof? I'm not exactly built for rooftop adventures, my friend." He gave his paunch a pat. "The trusses may pay a penance for my gluttony."

Luis laughed under his breath, but Cruk remained stoic.

"I'll go first," the captain said. "Step where I step." His brows drew together as if he resented the direction of his thoughts. "I'll go up to the room first. That should cement the idea that we don't know we've been spotted. The two of you follow me after a moment." He rose and upended his tankard, spilling beer in a cascade down the front of his tunic.

Martin let his head nod as if he were sleepy. "How did they find us, Luis? Sarin is a thousand miles away. Even if he can cast for us, there's no way he could put men on us at such a distance."

Luis brushed his fingers across a dark stain in the wood—blood or oil, impossible to tell which. "You know as well as I do. Sarin isn't the only reader they have. The conclave can only guess at what the circle he's formed can do—a group of readers bonded to his will and thoughts by a malus . . . I shudder to think of the possibilities."

Martin exhaled in an attempt to defuse the flash of anger washing over him like the sudden heat from an oven. "By the three, it's the conclave's job to know."

"And how could we, old friend? To plumb the depths of Sarin's ability we would have to replicate what he's done. Our enemies are beyond restraint."

Martin accepted the rebuke. "You are right, of course." He lifted himself from his chair. "The roof awaits." He permitted his feet a stumble to give the appearance of fatigue and made for the stairs that led to their room. Luis's footsteps made shuffling noises behind him.

Cruk closed the room's door behind them and knelt to hammer a wedge-shaped piece of wood between the floor and the door with the butt of his dagger. With deft movements he rose and hammered two more wedges in between the door and the jamb. "Hopefully, by the time they get through those into our room, we'll be long gone."

Martin followed him to the narrow window whose dirty glass reflected the lamplight, keeping the night beyond shrouded. Cruk forced the latch and swung the frame open. The sound of distant laughter spilled in on the warm breeze. The watchman turned and squeezed through the narrow opening, then beckoned Martin to follow.

He turned sideways as Cruk had done and stepped through. His foot found purchase on the slanted wooden shingles of the roof, but the window frame scraped against his side, then his middle.

Then he got stuck.

"This would be funny if our lives didn't depend on getting away from here," Cruk said. His mouth twitched to the right in an amused grimace.

Luis smiled. "Most people won't trust a thin priest. It makes them wonder what vice he has instead of gluttony. Still. I think you've skipped too many fasts."

Martin exhaled and sucked in his stomach in a vain attempt to get through the window. The rough wood scraped another couple of inches across his belly before the need for air curtailed his effort.

Cruk grabbed his arm. "Push, Luis."

Together the two of them forced him through the window accompanied by the creak of wood and the rasp of tearing cloth. Cruk caught him as he fell toward the roof. The watchman's grip crushed his forearm. "You weren't this fat in Callowford, Pater. I think Erinon is bad for your health."

Martin assessed the damage to his middle. "My health is fine, thank you. I just need to stop eating so much."

Luis stepped through the window as he would have a door

and alighted on the roof next to him with a grace Martin found annoying.

The reader's face betrayed no further hint of amusement. "I think that's what the captain just said."

Cruk rolled his footsteps toward the stable. "This way."

The sound of soft knocking drifted to Martin's ears through the open window. A moment later a sharp crack of splintering wood split the air.

Cruk hissed a curse. "Run!"

Martin forced himself across the slanted roof, tried to ignore the sound of cracking trusses that sounded with each step. Snatches of prayers pulled from half a dozen different liturgies merged into a plea for help. "Deas, please strengthen this roof." He slowed when Cruk turned the corner and disappeared. Another staccato sound of cracking wood sounded from their room.

"Hurry, Martin," Luis said. "We're an easy target on this roof for a bow or a well-thrown knife."

He nodded in the gloom. "Me, especially."

Around the corner, Cruk stood at the edge of the roof overlooking the grounds in front of the stable. He shifted to his right and jumped. Martin stopped, dismayed by the expectation implicit in Cruk's actions. If he jumped from this height, he'd break his ankles.

Luis nudged him from behind. "Martin, we're going to have company out here very soon."

Sweat plastered his tunic to his skin. With a shake of his head and a rebuke for his lack of faith, he forced himself forward. When he got to the edge of the roof, he laughed with relief. Beneath him a pile of hay beckoned. Across the enclosed yard, he could just see Cruk moving into the stable. With a quick intake he stepped off. A cloud of chaff rose on impact, and the grassy smell filled his nose. The landing hit him harder than he expected. His teeth clacked together and a spasm of complaint shot across the muscles of his back, but everything seemed intact. Luis landed next to him and bounced up.

Sounds of pursuit came to them from behind.

Martin scrambled out of the hay and lumbered toward the stables. He found Cruk just inside the darkened entrance, the reins to three horses twined through his fingers. "They're not as good as ours, but they're decent. More important, they're saddled."

Martin nodded his approval. "Maybe the difference in horse-flesh will pay the innkeeper for the broken shingles."

"It'll leak the next time it rains," Luis said.

Cruk's amused grimace froze halfway, interrupted by the buzz of an arrow. With a yell he dove into Martin and Luis, knocking them deeper into the stable. Martin fell with Cruk on top, his ribs groaning under the weight. He motioned the captain to slide off, but the watchman's hiss of pain stopped him. He rolled, his face knotted in agony.

The point of a broadhead arrow, wet with crimson, protruded from Cruk's shoulder. Blood grew in an ever-increasing stain around the wound.

Cruk staggered and led them to the back of the stable that opened onto the streets of Windridge. "Orders, Pater?" His voice sounded thin and pinched.

"Orders? By the book, man! Take us to a healer before you drop dead."

Cruk shook his head, gave a low growl of negation. "We can't do that."

Martin balled his fists until they ached with his impotence. "Why not?"

Luis stepped up to his shoulder. "They'll find us if we stop long enough to get Cruk medical attention."

Cruk's voice wheezed past a spasm of pain. "Listen to him, Pater. I can still ride. I've been wounded before. I know what to do."

Martin's blood dropped from his face to settle somewhere in his gut. "When we get to a safe stopping point, Luis and I will pull the arrow for you."

"No," Cruk said. "You'll disturb the wound if you do—and we don't have the time. We have to leave it. I promise to try not to bleed to death." He barked a weak laugh. "Last rites would take too much time."

Martin's middle constricted with fear despite Cruk's banter. A ride through the city would kill him as surely as a headsman's axe.

Cruk bit his lips as he threw the bar to the broad doors at the back of the stable and led them out to the street. He mounted, his face pale and pinched. "Stay close. Once we get away from the inn, walk your mounts unless you see pursuit."

Luis coughed. "If we follow a course chosen at random, they can't cast for our path. Don't plan our route."

Cruk gave the barest nod, then yanked the reins to the left.

Earthy smells of horse came to Martin as he mounted and nudged his mare into motion. Hooves clopped against cobblestones, and the outlines of the buildings around them, already muddied in the gloaming of the day, blurred until the lines of the city became indistinguishable from each other. Cruk led them on a meandering path that defied logic or prediction.

Martin held his breath whenever they rounded a corner, waiting for Cruk's strength to fail him. Each time he swayed in the saddle, then righted. They continued on. Behind them the streets were silent as death. An agony of minutes and miles later, Cruk held up a hand in the weak torchlight and motioned them to slow.

Martin pulled the reins and turned to Cruk. Blood clotted the arrow's fletching and a rich, dark stain covered most of Cruk's tunic. For all that, his face looked worse. Pain and blood loss leached the color from him until his skin held no hue of its own; it merely reflected the sickly yellow of the streetlamps.

When Cruk pulled to a stop, he looked like a ghoul. "I think we have some time to spare. I need you to bind the wound."

Martin nodded. Inside he quailed at the layers of thick, sticky blood on his friend's tunic. "Tell us what to do."

"Fold up four pieces of cloth into tight bundles. Place them around the arrow—both front and back. Then take long strips and wrap my shoulder as tightly as you can. The pressure will help slow the bleeding." Cruk grinned, his lips bloodless. "You might want to pray, Pater. I'm likely to say some things I'll need to be forgiven for."

Hot tears blurred Martin's vision. He rebuked them. This was no time for maudlin sentimentality. Determined to adopt Cruk's stoicism, he pulled his dagger and began ripping his cloak into strips. Luis stepped in with his carpenter's knife. The sound of tearing cloth filled his ears like the growling hiss of a predator.

Luis rolled four strips into tight wads, his reader's hands deft, practiced. With slow, careful motions he moved to Cruk's side and pressed the wads in place. When Martin made the first pass to secure them, Cruk's gasp sounded like the quench of white-hot metal, and he swayed.

Martin paused to touch his forehead to Cruk's, steadying him. "Deas, Father of us all, we plead for the life and well-being of this your servant, and do petition for your succor in our time of need."

Cruk didn't speak but smiled and gave an almost imperceptible nod. He winced but didn't cry out when Martin made the next wrap.

He'd just finished and was tucking the ends of the cloth under when hooves sounded in the distance, coming their way.

Cruk shook his head. "Battles never go according to plan. I don't think I can lead. Hopefully this excuse for a horse will have enough sense to follow."

"Luis, take the front." Martin's command came out harsher than intended, but if his friend noticed, he made no sign.

Luis set an easy canter, halting at intervals to listen. Each time he moved away from the suggestion of other riders on their left. Martin brought up the rear, turning back often to check for the sound of pursuit. The other hooves faded but never quite disappeared. A hard knot of desperation formed in Martin's throat as realization hit him: they were being herded.

He rode past Cruk, who rode slumped over his saddle, the reins loose in his pale hands. "Luis."

The reader jerked his head up and down, his manner brusque, tense. "I know. Unless we run the horses, they'll have us."

A sob formed somewhere inside the knot that filled Martin's

throat, tried to claw its way out. He swallowed thickly. "He can't." But if not, they would all die. His mouth refused to open, to give utterance to the command that would kill his friend. A clatter of hooves sounded, and a brush of air moved past him.

Cruk.

The big horse galloped past them. Cruk whipped the flanks, his head down, unable to see or determine his direction. Luis followed, spewing epithets at the stubborn watchman. Martin scrubbed his tears away and kicked his horse into motion. His hand lifted to clutch the emblem of his office that hung beneath his tunic. How long could Cruk stay in the saddle?

Luis passed the watchman, grabbed the reins to Cruk's horse on the way, and galloped away from the two groups that threatened to trap them. Martin groaned inside. The reader was taking them to the poor quarter. If their enemies didn't kill them, the cutthroats who preyed on Windridge's destitute would.

The streets narrowed and darkened. Furtive motions at the edge of his vision caught Martin's attention as they raced through the slums. Up ahead a flurry of activity diverted Luis, forced them into a shrouded alleyway. Cruk swayed in his saddle.

Then he slid.

"Luis! He's down."

The reader's horse gave a neigh of complaint as Luis sawed the reins. Martin dismounted, felt at Cruk's neck for a pulse, and cried with relief when he found it, but a fresh stain of blood oozed from the watchman's wound. Somehow the arrow was still intact, and the damage from the fall appeared minimal. "We'll have to get him back up on his horse."

Luis shook his head. "He can't ride, Martin."

"He can if we go at a walk and I ride alongside to help steady him."

"We can't afford to walk, Martin," Luis said. "If our enemies don't catch us, footpads will swarm us."

As if he'd summoned them, a pair of dark shadows filled the end of the alley behind them, the wan light glinting from long daggers.

"Well now. Are we havin' a bit o' trouble?" the figure in front asked. His clothes hung in tatters, and he limped toward them, his knife low and steady.

"Not our enemies, at least," Luis muttered.

Martin pulled his emblem and held it out. "I'm a priest. Our friend needs help. I can reward you if you get us safely away from here."

"Oh, you're a priest now, are ye?" the one in front said. "Well, you best be sayin' your prayers, then."

The man in back laughed. "Sayin' yer prayers."

Martin turned to point back toward Luis and Cruk, using the motion to draw his knife and hide it behind his forearm. "You would defile yourselves by attacking a priest?"

The leader barked his derision. "Don't rightly know you're a priest, now, do I? Nob, how many priests you ever seen in the poor quarter?"

The second laughed. "Oh, there's priests here all the time, there be." His voice grew harsh. "But never in the night. I'm startin' to think they don't trust us as live in the poor quarter."

The two men quickened their advance. Martin blocked half the alley with his horse. If he had to fight, he didn't want to take them at the same time. Bile burned the back of his throat. He wiped his mouth with a shaky hand.

The leader jumped, his knife cutting from underneath toward Martin's belly. He caught the thrust with his dagger's quillon. The thief gasped in surprise, tried to disengage, but Martin grabbed his wrist, squeezed until the man's knife clattered to the ground. When the man tried to kick himself free, Martin slammed an elbow into his face. Bones crunched, and the man fell back with a scream, pressing his hands to the ruin of his nose. The man behind turned and ran, followed a moment later by his leader.

A tug on his sleeve caught his attention. "Come," Luis said, "we must get him on his horse. We've been here too long."

Martin sheathed his dagger and helped lever Cruk onto his mount. He tried to take encouragement from the low moans that came from Cruk's lips. His friend still lived. Luis mounted, urged his horse forward at a walk while Martin came alongside. The darkness closed in, forcing him to follow by sound. Rats skittered out of their way with soft squeaks.

Up ahead their alley opened to a street where light from some unknown source relieved the gloom. Martin's blood rushed through his veins as if he still fought. Despite his priestly vows, he rejoiced at defeating their attackers, and he struggled to hear over the exultant beating of his heart.

Ten paces from the opening, Luis reined in. It took Martin a moment to notice the reader had stopped, and he almost walked Cruk's mount into him. Past his friend's silhouette, he saw the reason for their halt.

A figure, cloaked and hooded and bent forward at the waist, blocked their way.

8

THE SOLIS

MARTIN WATCHED as the figure lifted its head as if scenting, then lifted an arm and beckoned them forward. The sounds of pursuit from behind grew closer. In another minute they would have company. Trusting the stranger seemed their only hope.

They were nearly within arm's reach of the figure before it moved to their left down another alley. When they got to the juncture, their guide stood at the other end beckoning them on, urging haste with choppy waves of its arm. "Our benefactor moves quickly," Martin said.

Luis nodded. "But to what purpose?"

"I imagine we'll find out in time. If his intent is to lure us to capture"—Martin gestured toward the pursuit behind them— "there is no need." Yet tension filled him as he clenched his dagger.

"Agreed." Luis nudged his horse into motion, and they zigzagged through alleys that smelled of dank rainwater and filth. Always their guide stayed far enough ahead to keep himself hidden. The sound of pursuit dropped away, and no more thieves appeared to trouble them. The entire city could have been deserted for all Martin could tell. He heard the echo of their horses' hooves, the faint jingle of tack, and the breathing of men and animals—nothing else.

Up ahead, their guide moved to the right, disappearing once again.

And half a dozen paces ahead, Luis stopped and pointed at a door, short, narrow, and almost indistinguishable from the rest of the dirty stone and timber of the building. A soft glow of light illuminated a handsbreadth of space between the wood of the door and the frame. A voice beckoned them in.

"The light will betray you to any who venture into the alley. Besides, your friend needs help." The hooded figure opened the door and stepped past them. "Take him in. I'll hide the horses."

Luis and Martin dismounted, and together they lifted Cruk from his horse. The captain's groan of pain fell like a benediction on Martin's ears. He lived. They struggled to get him through the narrow door. Cruk's groans softened and then stopped as they bumped and stumbled down a short flight of stairs to the room beyond.

Martin's heart quailed at Cruk's pallor. A massive pool of blood had congealed on his clothes. With as much care as they could manage, they laid him on a low table—on his side to avoid pressure on the arrow. Martin begged a prayer as he knelt to Cruk's chest, unmindful of the blood, and listened for his heart.

"He lives," their guide said as he reappeared at the entrance. He stopped to bar the door and stooped to stuff a roll of burlap against the crack underneath. "Light the other lamp and let me see what we have." He pushed back his hood, allowing Martin his first look at their rescuer.

"Ra . . ." He stopped. The man before him bore such a strong resemblance to the herbwoman of Callowford that he nearly called him by her name. "Your pardon." He gave a slight bow. "You remind me of someone." On further inspection, the man was even younger than he, with thick brown hair that matched the hue of his eyes.

The man smiled. "Aurae leaves a mark. If you look closer, doubtless you will find me different than others you have met." He moved to Cruk's side and began cutting away his blood-soaked clothes. "Do either of you possess any knowledge of herb-lore?" At their wide-eyed stares, he shrugged. "No? Pity."

He stabbed a finger at Luis between cuts with his knife. "You. Bring me the seven jars on the left of that shelf over there." As if an afterthought, he added "Oh, my name is Karele," and continued with his commentary.

"Clever to leave the arrow in," Karele said. "It saved his life, if he lives. Whose idea was that?"

"His," Martin said. "He has some experience with battle wounds."

Karele's face grew solemn as his finger traced old scars on Cruk's torso. "Doubtless. Pity, that." He probed the flesh around the wound. "No sign of poison, thank Deas. He wouldn't survive that on top of the blood loss."

Martin started at Karele's words. "You believe in Deas, then?"

Karele snorted without turning his attention from his patient. "Who else would I believe in?"

Martin sensed he was on the verge of something important, some fact or discovery that made his skin tingle. "I thought you believed in Aurae alone."

The healer made a dismissive sound deep in his throat. "There is Aurae, sent from Deas and Eleison. Now be quiet unless you want an extra horse for your travels." He continued to probe Cruk's skin.

Cruk's breathing barely lifted his chest. Karele moved to the side of the room and opened a cabinet door. Inside, several saws hung on the door. He ran his hand along the blades before selecting the smallest. Then he moved to the shelf to uncork a bottle and pour a watery amber liquid down the blade.

Martin sniffed the air. "Is that mead?"

Karele shook his head. "Close, but this is stronger and thinner. I'm going to cut the arrow so we can more easily pull it. You two must hold him very still, and once we pull it, we're going to pack the wound with urticweed to stop the bleeding. It's in that second jar. We'll have to apply pressure to the wound for as long as it takes the bleeding to stop. Then we'll have to find a way to get water into him." He looked at Martin and Luis by turns. "Do you understand?"

They nodded.

"Good." Karele took the saw and, with gentle strokes that resembled Luis at his craft, cut the arrowhead free from Cruk's chest. Karele cupped a generous helping of white powder in each hand, nodded toward Luis. "Pull the arrow from his shoulder. Don't turn it or twist it. Bring it out exactly as it went in, or your friend will bleed to death. And whatever you do, don't jerk it out."

Luis pulled the shaft, winced at the sucking sound the wound made as it came free. Karele put a hand on each wound and pressed, working the powder into Cruk's injury. Blood mixed with the flour-like substance to make a gruesome paste on his hands, but he continued the gentle circular motions until his hands were empty.

He lifted two thick pads of white linen and placed one on Cruk's chest and one on his back, covering the wounds. "Now, gentle pressure, please." He surrendered the front to Martin and Luis.

As much as his heart urged him to help, Martin motioned Luis to take the pad. "You do it, friend. Your hands are better suited to such tasks than mine."

They waited. Karele neither spoke nor invited conversation, but after nearly a quarter of an hour, he checked his hands and nodded to Martin. "Use that strip of linen and wrap his wound. Don't disturb the pads or we'll have to do this all over. Go over the shoulder and then under, until you run out of cloth."

When he'd finished, their guide nodded and moved to retrieve a waterskin. To it he added a variety of powders. Pungent aromas as of burning spices filled the room—the scent of bitter cloves mixed with cinnamon. Karele shook the skin and lifted it to Cruk's mouth and crooned. "Drink, my friend."

To Martin's surprise, Cruk's mouth widened and he took a

few weak swallows. The healer lowered the skin and then raised it again. Again Cruk drank, but not as much this time. On the third attempt, the captain didn't move.

A spasm shot through Martin's chest. "Is he all right?"

Karele huffed and shook his head. "Of course he's not all right. He almost bled to death. But he should live and heal with time."

"How long will that be?" Luis asked.

Karele shrugged. "As long as it takes. Your friend is a strong man. With plenty of food and drink, he should be able to ride at a walk in two weeks. If he doesn't bleed anymore, he'll be back to normal in two or three months." He moved to a small fireplace in the corner, filled a pot with water, and swung it over the tinder and wood that lay ready for use. Karele lit a taper from one of the lamps and started the fire. "I assume you want tea?"

At a nod from Martin and Luis, he retrieved three worn but serviceable cups from a nook and set them on a small table. "I always think better when I hold a cup of tea," Karele said. "It keeps my hands from running away with my thoughts." He turned to look at Martin, his dark eyes luminous in the growing fire. "After you've rested, we can talk about why you're here."

A prickling sensation danced across Martin's skin like a sudden gust of cold air. "I thought we were here for Cruk."

Karele gave him a heavy-lidded smile a grownup would give a child. Then he moved to a small bed on the far side of the room, where he rolled himself into a blanket. "Your friend's injury is unfortunate, but that's not why Aurae sent me to you."

Martin and Luis finished their tea with furtive whispers and settled for the night into piles of what appeared to be rags but only found fitful sleep. Cruk stirred three times during the night. Perhaps some instinct or response in his warrior's constitution fought for survival even while he slept. Each time Karele rose from a seemingly deep sleep, mixed a draught of water laced with the powders that smelled of burnt spices, and drugged the captain back to motionless sleep with soft crooning noises.

Dawn came, visible only by the sunlight that limned the cracks around the door. Martin rose from his makeshift pallet, scratched at some uninvited guest beneath his clothing, and knelt by his friend's side to say lauds. When he rose, he saw Cruk's healer standing to one side, a half smile creasing his swarthy complexion.

"Do you find some cause for amusement?" Martin asked. Worry and fatigue so deep it made the muscles in his legs ache sharpened his tongue.

"You pray more than most priests I've met," Karele said. "Though to be honest, I haven't met that many. Like most of us, I avoid priests. They keep mistaking us for kindling."

Martin gave a sour grunt that rumbled through his throat. "Barbaric practice, and stupid."

Karele appraised him with a lift of his eyebrows. Martin knew that look, but he wasn't used to being on the receiving end of it. His mind filled with questions—the reason for Karele's aid uppermost—but he held his tongue. He'd used silence in the past as a way to pressure others to speak. Yet the healer seemed to see no need to break the silence; he busied himself with Cruk's care, carefully checking the wound underneath the blood-soaked pads they'd used the previous evening.

For his part, Cruk's color seemed more normal, though rings like deep bruises surrounded his eyes. His slightly pink lips held the hope of eventual health.

"He seems better this morning." Martin grimaced inwardly. He hadn't meant to speak. Doing so felt like a concession to his host, as if he'd put himself in Karele's debt. He chided himself for his attitude. The diminutive man had put himself at risk to save them from pursuit and had undoubtedly saved Cruk's life. They *were* in his debt.

A nudge at Martin's elbow broke his train of thought, brought his awareness back to their squalid surroundings and Luis.

"It's morning," Luis said. The reader stressed the last word as if it carried significance.

Martin nodded.

"We're still here," Luis said.

Then it dawned on him, and his blood dropped to his stomach so fast he probably resembled Cruk. "Heaven help us. They should have found us by now. How much time do we have?"

"As much as you need, actually," Karele said. "Although, I'll need any coin you might have. I've only enough food to last a day or two." He said this without turning around, and it took Martin a moment to realize the healer was serious.

Luis had already pulled a set of blanks and his carving knife from his bag in preparation to cast. Karele eyed the cubes with a smirk and a slight shake of his head.

"Luis, I don't think that will be necessary," Martin said.

Doubt creased the reader's brows, and he cut his eyes back and forth between Martin and Karele. "Martin, they have readers. There's no other explanation for the way they tracked us last night."

He nodded. Luis's logic defied refutation, but it didn't go far enough. "So they should have been on us minutes after we stopped, Luis."

The reader paused. "Fortune is with us, it seems."

This elicited a snort from Karele. He finished his ministrations and then, like a teacher calling students forth for a lesson, beckoned to Martin and Luis to join him at a small table. When they'd seated themselves, with one forefinger Karele tapped the blanks Luis still held. "This is why Aurae sent me to you, part of it anyway."

"The spirit of Deas is interested in the cast?" Martin asked.

Karele smiled and gave a small shake of his head. "No, Aurae is interested in your instruction. The lots are the beginning point."

Luis stiffened. "I don't think there's much an herbman can teach me about lots."

"Ha, a name given to us by peasants and people who didn't know any better," Karele said. "We are the solis."

Martin struggled with the word, tried to pull the meaning from his lessons as a postulate and later as an acolyte in the church. "Protector?"

Karele nodded. "Close. Actually, it means being alone and having no protector. For those who obey Aurae it describes us and our call. We have no companion or protector save Deas, and we minister to those whose circumstances have placed them in the same position." He favored Martin with a half smile at this. "The solis are chosen from every people to help the least of our world. Most of us become healers, thus the label *herbman* or *herbwoman*."

"But you look so much like the others I have seen," Luis said.

"Aurae leaves its mark upon us, but we come from every province—Basquon, Soeden, Bellia, Einland, all of them." He spread his arms and gestured at himself. "Don't be fooled by my appearance or that of the herbwomen you've met. Some of us are quite large."

Martin's impatience impelled him forward in his chair. "Why didn't Aurae instruct us before now? We lived in Callowford near two of your kind for five years."

Karele raised one hand palm up. "I don't know. We do not command Aurae. If anything, it's the other way around, though that's not exactly accurate either."

Martin's gut refused his order to relax. Despite his attempts to save the herbwoman from Abbot Morin, he couldn't shake the feeling he now dabbled in heresy. Imagined heat from a heretic's flames made him sweat.

Karele's face took on a look of blank distraction, as if he were listening to a conversation across the room. "Aurae tells me war is coming."

Martin snorted. "We've known that since we found Rodran couldn't father an heir."

"No. You've suspected. When Aurae speaks, you know."

Martin shrugged.

Karele edged forward. "You will need the solis. The conclave will not be sufficient for this task."

Luis made a noise of protest in his throat.

The healer sighed. "Your pardon. I mean no offence. I have not dealt with kingdom men for many years." He pointed at the softwood cubes on the table in front of the reader. "Cast for a question to which you already know the answer."

Luis turned to Martin, his eyes inviting.

Martin smiled. "There's no sense getting exotic with the question. Ask if I am a priest or something similar."

Luis gave a curt nod and picked up his knife, yet he sat with the stiff posture of one offended. The short, quick strokes of his knife spoke of his insulted pride.

"While the reader prepares his cast, I will instruct," Karele said to Martin. "You know of Magis's war?"

"Of course."

"And the loss of the book?"

Martin's heart must have stopped. There was no other way to explain the weight on his chest or his inability to draw breath. He stared at the small man before him. "You cannot know about that."

Karele smiled. "Yet I do. The book was lost to the kingdom. Magis's mistake."

Luis's knife stopped. "What is he talking about, Martin?"

Martin shook his head. Only the benefices knew of the first king's tragic, colossal error. "I am forbidden to speak of it. I will not break that vow."

Karele laughed softly as he faced Luis. "Had it not been shrouded in secrecy, things might have been easier to fix. Oh well, if the benefice is forbidden to speak of it, I am not.

"Magis took the book, the holy history of the church, the communicated stories of Deas and Eleison, with him to fight the evil that came at Illustra from across the straight. He thought it would protect him. At the last he learned that his survival was not what Deas intended, and he bought the barrier.

"But the book was lost. The men who guarded him, the forerunners of the watch, couldn't find it. Ever since Magis died, the church has had to rely on the passed-down memory of its priests to relate the words of Deas." Karele shrugged. "They've done well, but an oral tradition is bound to lose things over the course of hundreds of years."

Martin's empty stomach twisted. "They did the best they could. As soon as they realized the book was lost, the benefices wrote every piece of the sacred writ they could recall. They compared notes, used each other's quotations to check for accuracy."

"Yes." Karele's nod might have been sympathetic. "Reader, if you will continue your craft?"

Luis resumed carving the first lot.

"Magis's loss birthed the conclave," Karele said. "The church collected the readers throughout Illustra to help the new kingdom survive. Now something new is coming." His gaze bored into Martin's eyes. "Deas has chosen you, Martin, to take the knowledge of Aurae to the church."

"No." He would not. "I have protected the herbwomen, have risked my position within the church to keep them from harm, but I will not consort with any spirit save Deas."

Karele's answering smile unnerved him. "No one is asking you to."

Martin straightened in his chair. "I will ignore your implied blasphemy and simply restate my position. I will not agree to contact with your spirit—no matter what name you give it."

The healer shrugged. "We shall see." He pointed to the pair of rounded wooden lots that lay among a pile of slivers and sawdust in front of Luis. "Are you prepared to cast, reader?"

Luis nodded.

"And the question?" Karele asked.

"As Martin said, something simple—whether or not he is a priest."

Their strange host nodded. "Very well. Proceed while I tend to your friend."

Luis put the lots into a makeshift bag and drew. "Yes. Yes. Yes. No. Yes. Yes. Yes. Yes. No. Yes." He dropped the lot back into the bag and shrugged at Karele, perhaps with satisfaction. "My craft is intact."

The healer nodded as he inspected Cruk's bandage. The watchman slept, his chest rising and falling with comforting regularity.

"Again, please," Karele said. His eyes twinkled as if at some private joke.

Luis drew. A small crease of a frown etched the area between his brows. He replaced the lot, shook the bag and drew again. And again, continuing. He never spoke a word, but the look he directed at Martin might have been the look of a child whose father has died.

"They say *No*, Martin." Luis's plaintive voice cracked. "They all say *No*. Not most of them. All."

Martin didn't want to speak, didn't wish to acknowledge the thought that lay hidden at the bottom of his heart where he'd locked it away. Shame would never let him reveal it: They should have run—they should have let Cruk die.

9

A Breaking

RALE GAVE ERROL A NOD and a smile of pleasure. This was as much as a bear hug from other men. He eyed Errol's staff critically. His gaze paused at the worn spots where Errol's hands found the balance, swept to the ends of the staff where the wood had become frayed from the knobblocks. Rale stepped forward and tapped Errol on the head and shoulders with one hand. "You've eaten well."

Errol laughed. How long had it been since he'd done that? "I didn't have much choice." And with a great sense of release, he related all that had taken place on the way to Erinon.

Rale's face lit with pleasure under twinkling eyes. "That last part I hadn't heard."

That caught Errol off guard. "What?"

The farmer laughed. "Didn't you know, boy? They entered you in the record. Your exploits are common knowledge. On the way here, I heard a bard declaim your exploits. You're seven feet tall and muscled enough to make your friend Liam look underfed, by the way."

A somber cast crossed Rale's face, like a wisp of cloud dimming the sun. "Myrrha wanted to come. I think you've grown in her memory like some mythic figure out of the tales. Anomar forbade it."

The realization of what he'd done washed Errol's joy away. On his orders, soldiers had brought Rale to the isle, tearing him away from his family. "I'm sorry, Rale. Cruk and Martin and Luis are all gone. I didn't know who else to trust."

The man everyone else knew as Elar Indomiel gave a brief chuckle and shrugged Errol's concerns away. "Don't apologize, boy. I've had to order men into battle. Now someone is ordering me." He shrugged his cloak to the ground and slid his hands along his oak staff until they each came to rest a foot away from the midpoint. He smiled. "Let's see if the minstrel's tales are true."

Errol stepped back, stashed the knobblocks into his pocket, and lost himself in the movements that Rale had taught him months before. They sparred lightly at first, moving in the point and counterpoint of the staff, like partners in a dance after a long estrangement, but in mere moments the pace quickened. Rale no longer flowed like a lazy stream. Now he rushed, his attacks coming quick, the buzzing of his staff loud in Errol's ears.

Yet he turned each of Rale's attacks aside. His memory played tricks on him. Rale was faster than this. Then Errol realized Rale hadn't changed—*he* had. An opening presented itself, but Errol ignored it.

Rale growled a curse. "Boy, if you don't stop holding back, you're going to annoy me. Try this."

The farmer launched an all-out attack that would have overwhelmed Errol months ago. Now he slipped to the side, let Rale's momentum carry him past, and struck. He pulled the blows, reduced them to no more than a hard slap, then dropped low to the ground to sweep Rale's legs with a kick.

The farmer ended on his back, defenseless. And laughing. "Where did you learn that?"

Errol extended a hand and helped the man to his feet. "There was a guard in Ru's caravan. I think she's part Morgol. The first few times we sparred with the staff I never knew what she would hit me with next."

"By the three, boy, what do you need me for? You could have left me on the farm. I had my doubts, but that swatch of black cloth on your arm isn't just a decoration. You really could be a captain."

Errol shook his head. "No one's told me your story, but the primus says you're one of the best tacticians in the kingdom." He lifted his shoulders. "I have no idea how to wage a battle, how to lead."

The man who'd been more of a father to him than anyone else regarded him with his dark blue eyes, appraising him with the same frank gaze he'd give a horse. "You've learned more than I thought."

Errol ducked his head to hide the blush and smile.

"Stop!" The yell erupted from the far end of the yard where a figure in purple-and-black merchant clothes stomped across the grounds. He held a bared sword in one hand. With almost casual parries he slipped past the watchmen who tried to bar his way. He paused to scan the grounds.

Then he headed straight for Errol.

Naaman Ru.

"He moves well," Rale said, as calmly as if the man bearing down on him didn't have violence written in every line of his face. "Who is he?"

Errol's palms grew moist, lending the wood in his hands a slippery, untrustworthy feel. "Naaman Ru. The caravan master."

Rale nodded. "Boy, you're wearing a captain's band. I think you should exercise some of that authority and make sure he doesn't get to you. I'd love to see him fight, but I'd hate for you to be the opponent."

Errol chewed his lower lip in thought. "I don't think he wants to kill me. If he attacks, I can always call the guard then."

"Aye," Rale nodded, "assuming you have time. A man like Ru doesn't require much of it."

Errol stepped back, signaled the guards to make way for the

caravan master, and waited. Ru's eyes burned, and he swiped his blade back and forth, cutting the air as he came. The blade moved absurdly fast in his hands.

The watchmen gathered into a broad circle as Ru approached. If he attacked, Errol would have to parry a half dozen times before sheer numbers rescued him. Could he survive that long?

Ru's steps quickened, and his blade steadied, coming up to the ready position. The late-afternoon sun gleamed along that length of steel. Errol bent his legs and held his staff. At ten paces Ru charged, his sword high for a slashing attack.

Then he stopped—not as if he'd hit a wall, but as though the air had thickened around him until forward motion was no longer possible. The cords on his neck stood while he strained to reach Errol, and he leaned forward as if struggling against a headwind.

Errol straightened, grounded his staff. "You're not the only one who's been placed under compulsion, Naaman Ru."

Ru fought for a moment more, then dropped to one knee, spent, but his eyes burned and his voice carried savage promises of reprisal. "They'll kill her, boy. You know that."

Rokha. "I didn't ask for your daughter—just you. Rokha will be safe here in Erinon. She won't be going with us, Ru."

A contralto's throaty laughter greeted his declaration. The guards parted, and Rokha, fierce and gleeful, swaggered forward and placed herself between him and her father. "Hello, Errol."

Nobles and watchmen eyed the caravan master's daughter in appreciation. Dressed in a man's shirt and breeches, Rokha's movements were decidedly not manlike. The timbre of her speech turned Errol's name into an aural indulgence.

His ears heated from the caress of her voice. With an effort, he forced his thoughts back to the track they'd left at her appearance. "You're not going with us, Rokha."

Her light brown eyes flashed a challenge, but she kept her smile. "You're not the head guard of the caravan here, Errol, and I'm not the sixth. I don't take orders from you."

His face flushed. What made women so stubborn? "The church has compelled me to find Sarin Valon and kill him. I've been given the authority to choose those companions who will give me the best chance of succeeding and surviving." He edged closer to Rokha and dropped his voice. "That puts me in charge. You're not going."

Her smile turned frosty, and the glint in her eyes became hard, like flint. "I wish you luck in leaving me behind."

Errol kept himself from shouting, just. "I don't need luck. Take a look around you, Rokha. You're at Erinon. At a word, I'll simply have one of the priests compel you to stay here until we return—if we return."

Rokha's smile returned. "That might be difficult, seeing as they've already compelled me along with my father to guide you into Merakh."

Errol's retort fell from his throat into his stomach, where it lay like a stone. "You're lying."

Ru growled a curse. "No, boy, she's not. Your churchmen wouldn't listen to me. They reasoned two guides could succeed where one might fail."

"That's ridiculous," Errol said. "She doesn't know anything about Merakh."

Ru's right hand twitched as it held his sword, the blade jumping, hungry for blood. "Don't you think I know that? I watched as they laid the compulsion on her." His tone softened, taking on the bargaining note Errol knew well from his days as one of Ru's caravan guards. "But you can change that. If you're really in charge, you could have them remove the compulsion."

"No," Rokha said. "If you must go back to Merakh, so must I."

"Why?" A plaintive note crept into Ru's voice.

"Because you're my father." She eyed Errol. "And he owes me for my humiliation when he challenged me for the sixth."

Laughter interrupted Errol's reply. Rale stood to one side, obviously enjoying Errol's consternation. "You should have stayed in your village, boy."

He shook his head. "I think I should have stayed in the ale barrel. Life was a lot less dangerous when I was a drunk."

Naaman Ru eyed Rale the way a dog might eye a potential rival. "Who's this?"

"This is Elar Indomiel," Errol said. "He'll be going with us."

"I've heard of you," Ru said, his tone dismissive.

Indomiel's eyes hardened. "I go by Rale now." He held out a hand. "The boy seems to have amassed some notable acquaintances."

Ru ignored the proffered hand. "Including yourself. They've put me under a compulsion, so why send a tactician?"

Rale lowered his hand and shrugged. "I'm just a farmer now."

Naaman Ru matched him, his voice cold. "And I'm just a merchant, am I not?"

Rale turned to Errol, his jaw muscles working. "When do we leave, Earl Stone?"

Errol noted with satisfaction Rokha's and Ru's reaction to his title. He turned to Ru. "As soon as we have everybody together. My compulsion is three weeks old now. It's starting to make my feet itch. Where's Conger?"

Ru laughed—a sarcastic bark, not the laugh of a man genuinely amused. "The church's coercion doesn't force me to answer your questions. Find him yourself."

Rokha sighed. "If you hadn't used Errol for profit, Father, we wouldn't be here." She pointed to the chairs in the shade of the overhanging balcony. "He's over there, trying to go unnoticed."

Conger had pulled his shoulders up so high, his head was almost invisible. Errol gestured to the two guards on either side of the defrocked priest. They hauled him to his feet and escorted him into Errol's presence, where he stood staring at his feet and darting glances at those assembled around their group.

"So now you wave your hand and the watch does your bidding?" Ru asked, his voice caustic. "How high you've risen. Do you think that will save us when we get to Merakh?"

Their hands on his back, the guards pushed Conger closer to Errol. As his old friend straightened, Errol could see he still wore the tattered remains of his priestly garments—a threadbare collar, and a stained chasuble. "By our G— I mean, that is, to say . . . I'm glad to see you again . . . uh, Earl Stone." Sweat beaded on Conger's forehead, and he darted quick, furtive glances at the crowd.

"I'm still Errol, Conger. The title's still new, and most of the nobles here refuse to use it anyway."

Conger frowned as he paused to scratch an armpit and belch. "Beggin' your pardon, Errol, but why am I here?"

Guilt, sharp and cold, laid an icy line across his throat. "The archbenefice insisted I take a priest. My friend, Martin, is gone. You're the only other priest I know . . . and trust."

Conger shook his head. "Can't see how it applies—I've been dismissed." He gave a slight lift of the shoulders. "But if the church says go to Merakh, who am I to argue?"

His attitude toward a penance that could likely result in his death caught Errol off guard. "You'd go just because the church told you to? So many of the men I've met in the church are out for their own interests."

Conger's face and tone became solemn. "Errol, the church is made of men, and wherever you have men, you have problems, but the church has been the bulwark against the evil that's over-taken Merakh and the steppes. Without its influence . . ." He shrugged.

"Without the church, we might actually live our lives in peace," Ru finished for him.

Errol looked at the small band gathered around him. There was nothing more to be gained by talking. "We'll leave tomorrow disguised as merchants."

Ru sneered. "I suppose you'll be the merchant and make me your guard."

"You'll do whatever Earl Stone tells you to do," Rale said. He shifted his weight, slid his hands closer to the center of his staff.

"You would try me?" Ru asked.

Errol stepped between them. "You're the merchant. I will be your second."

The caravan master's eyes narrowed. "And who will be my first?"

Errol nodded toward Rale. "Him."

88

The smell of horses permeated the thin mist early the next morning. Despite himself, Errol's heart quickened with excitement. A small train of empty wagons, appropriated by the arch-benefice, lined the roadway just outside the main walls of the imperial compound. Ru shook his head in disgust. "Doesn't anyone on this island know anything about being a merchant? We'll be found out before we've gone a league."

"What's wrong?" Errol asked.

"Look at the wagons."

The caravan train wasn't as big as Ru's, but the wagons looked pretty much the same, as far as Errol could tell. "So?"

Naaman rubbed his temples. "Didn't you learn anything while you were with me? They're empty, boy. Are your church friends trying to get us killed?"

That was a question Errol didn't want to answer. Rale shifted closer on his horse. "The king's isle is the ultimate destination for goods, Ru. They don't produce anything here. We're just taking the wagons to the port. We'll find a cargo then."

Ru's face showed what he thought of this arrangement, but for the moment he seemed satisfied.

A tap at Errol's shoulder startled him and he spun. Liam stood before him, hand outstretched and smiling. Errol clasped hands, kept his own from being crushed, just.

"I wish I could go with you," Liam said. "But the archbenefice and Captain Reynald forbade it when I asked."

Errol nodded. As well they should. Liam would be Rodran's successor. Erinon could hardly risk sending its future king on a mission designed to kill a minor nuisance. "They'll need you here, I think," Errol said.

"Still, I'd prefer to meet the enemy of our kingdom head on, as you are doing, rather than stay here endlessly teaching nobles the art of the sword when they have no intention of using it."

Errol didn't know what to say, so he merely nodded.

"Deas keep you and grant you favor, Errol," Liam said. He spoke the customary parting with sincerity, laying it on Errol's hearing like a blessing.

"Thank you. I'll need it."

The sun rose, cleared the trees to burn off the thin mist, and still they waited.

"What's the holdup, boy?" Ru asked. "The sooner I'm away from this place, the better."

"Think, Father, what would make a man delay his departure?" Rokha asked. She stood to one side, smiling.

After a few more minutes that dragged like hours, she came. Accompanied by one of her ladies, she stopped a dozen paces away and waited. He crossed the intervening space with no conscious awareness of having moved.

"You're leaving," she said. The princess sounded almost angry.

As if he had any choice in the matter. "I am compelled, Your Highness."

Adora nodded. "Will you . . . come back?"

Her voice caught on the last two words. Errol knew the question that lay behind her hesitation. Would he live? "I will try, my lady." Ever so softly, he let his voice caress the last two words.

Her companion bristled at this. "Your tone is overly familiar, Earl Stone."

Adora coughed. "My uncle has been persuaded to have me accompanied. This is the Lady Sevra, the daughter of Duke Weir."

"And sister to Lord Weir," the woman said.

Errol saw him then—Lord Weir, standing twenty paces back, staring at Errol, smiling, his eyes gleaming with triumph. Errol's face burned, and he gripped his staff until his knuckles cracked. "Your uncle would really marry you off to him? That strutting toad?"

"Lord Weir's blood is the noblest in the kingdom," Sevra spat. "Daughters of privilege are not permitted to marry beneath themselves."

Errol let his voice carry. "I don't see how you could marry any lower than him."

Weir's hand went to his pommel, but he didn't draw, didn't give Errol the excuse he wanted.

Adora's companion laughed in Errol's face, her breath hot,

sour with wine despite the early hour. "You taunt him in vain. My brother will not sully his reputation with the blood of an uncouth peasant."

Errol stepped forward, thrusting his face down until his nose nearly touched Sevra's. "Your brother would fight the meanest beggar as long as he was sure of winning. He's a coward and a bully."

She paled, retreated a step. "My lady, I think we should withdraw." Without waiting for Adora's consent, she showed her back to Errol, moving to join her brother.

Adora dropped her gaze to the grass at her feet before she peered up at him through her lashes. "I have to go. My uncle says my reputation is to be guarded." Her posture appeared meek, but glints of anger and plans flared in her eyes.

Errol watched her leave. After she disappeared into the guardhouse to the palace grounds, he mounted Midnight and turned the horse toward the sea.

At that moment he didn't care whether he lived or not.

10

THE BERON STRAIT

THEY LEFT THE WAGONS BEHIND with a trader at the docks and prepared to board a three-masted ship to cross the Beron Strait. They would sail with their horses and then obtain a commensurate number of wagons in Port City, where their trip south would begin in earnest. The smell of fish and the detritus of the shore filled Errol's nose as they coaxed the animals aboard. The rocking motion of the ship brought back vivid memories of his last miserable crossing, and the back of his throat tightened in expectation.

A voice broke the sound of the sea. "Horses? I hate horses. They mess up my ship. Why don't you just get new ones in Port City?"

Errol fought a premonition of nausea and made his way forward, leaving Naaman and Rale to deal with their Bellian captain, a thin, bearded man named Salo. At sea the breeze would blow from behind him and carry the scent of his seasickness away.

For a few happy moments after the lines were cast, Errol allowed himself to hope he might weather the crossing in fair order. Then they sailed through a gap between two of the breakwaters that defended the island, and he lost hope. His stomach rolled as if the moors of his internal organs had been removed. The ship pitched, yawed, and seemingly moved in two directions at once. He grabbed the rail and puked violently into the sea. It would take three hours to make the crossing. It might as well be three days. He slumped to the deck, flung an arm over the manrope, and tried to aim between the balusters of the rail.

Rokha came to him sometime later, put a hand to his forehead, and laughed. "I should challenge you now."

What was it that people found funny about seasickness? "I concede. You can have the second, and I'll give you the first if you'll kill the captain."

She patted him on the head. "Here, take this. It will help a bit. Not as much as if you'd taken it before we sailed, but it will keep you from the worst of the stomach pains and sweats. I don't leave port until I've had some."

He pried his eyes open. She held a cup of a brownish-red powder, offering it to him. "What is it?"

"Zingiber root. Why didn't you ask the captain for some before we sailed?"

This pulled his gaze up to hers. She looked pale, but otherwise seemed hale enough. "I've never heard of it before. The herbwomen in my village don't use anything like it. Of course, Callowford is far from the sea, so there would be no use for such." He grabbed the cup with an unsteady hand and took a mouthful of the powder. It turned to paste on his tongue as he struggled to choke it down. "Why would the captain carry this? He doesn't need any—he's a sailor."

Rokha laughed again, but it carried a sympathetic sound to it. "All captains carry it. Sick passengers are bad for business, Errol. A ship's captain is just a merchant with a boat."

He stared. All captains had it. *Jonas Grim.* "I know a sailor I'd like to kill." He closed his eyes, willed the zingiber root to take effect as she laughed. "What makes you think I'm joking?"

She sat on the deck beside him and looped an arm through the rail. "You're not a vengeful man, Errol."

The powder might have started working, or possibly the sound of Rokha's voice kept him distracted. "How do you know?"

She chuckled. "I don't lie to myself, Errol. My father used you. He kept you locked up for weeks, forced you to cast lots so he could profit, and threatened to kill you. Then you escaped and won the favor of the king."

This last pained him. "For a while, anyway."

"The point is," she went on, "you could have used your influence to find my father and have him—and me—imprisoned for what he did. But you did not."

"I was too busy for revenge."

"My point exactly." She stayed by his side in silence.

He gulped another mouthful of powder, amazed that the first had managed to stay down.

"Do you love her?"

His stomach tightened at the question. Errol tried to convince it to relax. "It doesn't matter."

She stiffened. "I didn't think you were the type to surrender."

Errol shrugged. Was he giving up? He didn't know. So many of his choices had been taken away. "I'm not surrendering, but there's not much I can do about Adora now. She's back in Erinon with Weir, and I'm on my way to Merakh." His eyes burned behind his lids. "It's like a challenge in the guard—sometimes you lose whether you surrender or not."

They rode the swells, the smell of salt heavy in the air, wet from the spray.

"What about Skorik?" he asked.

"He's like my father."

"How so?"

Rokha laughed. "He hates you too."

Errol snorted.

"Skorik wanted to own me, not win me," she said finally.

Rokha had always reminded him of a hawk, so proud, so fierce. She—

A distant thumping of feet brought his eyes open. Men lined the ship on the starboard side, pointing, intent. Shouts of alarm carried forward on the wind from the poop deck. The ship heeled hard to port, rolling Errol and Rokha across the boards until they hit the bulwark in a tumble of arms and legs.

Errol pulled himself up, followed the points of the sailors closest by. Salo's ship bounced up and down on the chop, obscuring his vision. Then he saw it—a lean ship with three masts bearing down on them out of the south.

"Foolish, foolish." He cursed himself over and over.

Rokha shook him, had been shaking him. Her words registered at last above the sound of the sea. "What's happening?"

He spun to meet her, yelled over the tumult. "We planned too far ahead. Valon is attacking."

Five hundred paces distant, men with crossbows lined the deck of the other ship—it appeared to be a cog. Errol did a quick count. They were outnumbered at least three to one. On the aft deck Salo screamed orders to add sail. Errol watched with sick fascination as the cog turned to port, trying to come in behind them. He wobbled his way back to the captain.

The ship lurched, moving away from the enemy and away from Port City as well. What was Salo doing? He stumbled into Rale, screamed to get his attention. "We have to get to Port City."

Rale gave a brusque shake of his head. "No, lad. We turn or we die. Salo knows what he's about."

Errol stared across the distance. The other ship seemed larger already. "But they're gaining."

"Aye. The question is, can we make the mainland before they get close enough to pincushion us with those crossbows? If they pick off enough of the crew, they'll be able to overtake us and board." His face hardened. "That would be bad."

An empty feeling in the pit of his stomach washed over him. By the three, he was tired of fighting. "How close do they have to be?"

Rale shrugged. "Crossbows are fairly long but not accurate. If they close to two hundred paces, they'll fill the sky with bolts. Thank Deas for the rough sea." He grabbed Errol by the arm, guided him to the ladder that led up to the aft deck. "Let's find out what our captain intends."

Salo called orders as he watched the enemy ship pull inexorably closer. A glance told Errol that he and Rale were not welcome on the deck, but Salo didn't order them away.

"How long before they're in firing range, Captain?" Rale asked.

A scowl creased Salo's face, turning the weathered cracks of his skin into crevices. "An hour—maybe a little more."

"Is that long enough to make land?" Stress pulled Errol's voice higher, merged it with the wind screeching through the rigging.

"No."

Rale nodded. "What do you need, Captain?"

Salo rolled his eyes. Errol heard him say something about landwalkers with a lot of swear words in front of it. "I need a way to keep those cursed bowmen from shooting my lads out of the rigging, and if someone does get shot, I'm going to need a replacement."

"You don't have extra crew?" Errol asked.

"It's a three-hour crossing, boy. Why would I waste profit on men I don't need?" He turned back to Rale. "As long as I'm asking for the impossible, I'd like to know the intentions of that other ship out there."

Other ship? Errol followed Salo's gaze. At first he couldn't make out anything except the gray-green swells. Then the silhouette of a low-decked ship appeared in the distance, dark figures at the rail. The zingiber root roiled in his stomach.

"Your thoughts, Captain?" Rale asked.

"If they mean us ill, we're done for. That longship is faster than these high-decked cogs, and it'll be on us inside an hour. On the other hand, if they mean to aid us, it'll cost them sore to buy our passage. Those crossbows will wreak havoc from the cog's higher decks."

"Could we signal them?"

"Aye, but are you willing to bet our lives on the answer?"

Rale nodded. "Come, Errol. We have work to do."

He followed Rale down the ladder. Every man not a part of the crew lined the starboard rail, staring at the gaps closing between the three ships. Rale moved to the first watchman. "Do you have a longbow?" The watchman shook his head. "Have you ever served aboard ship?" Another shake.

Rale moved on, moving from watchman to watchman, always asking the same two questions. Afterward, two men with long-bows stood beside him. Another man, who possessed a sure gait despite the rolling of the ship, walked aft to put himself at Salo's disposal. Two bows. One additional seaman.

Rale pointed. "We're about to discover the intentions of that second ship."

Rokha stole up beside Errol, her hand on her sword, her teeth bared. The faster vessel, the longship, pulled within two hundred paces of the cog as it in turn continued to pursue Salo's ship. The cog's high decks fore and aft were filled with crossbowmen. Yet the longship appeared empty. Where had they gone?

With a suddenness that made Errol start, a dozen black-garbed men sprang into view pulling longbows. Watchmen. The longship crested a swell, and the bowmen launched. A volley of arrows sailed toward the forecastle of the other ship, peaked, and then plum-meted. Cries and shouts sounded, and two-score crossbows loosed.

The men on the longship ducked behind the low bulwark, and bolts that would have pierced chain mail instead plunged harm-lessly into the side of the ship. Now the men rose and fired volley after volley at the cog. Screams of the wounded and dying came to Errol over the waves, and over them the sound of command.

Another set of bolts came from the cog, but merely a third of what had come before. Errol's heart soared. The men in the longship ducked again. Hidden and unseeing, they didn't see the cog immediately release another volley. Black shafts streaked toward the deck.

Errol's throat closed around his warning. *Stay down. Stay down.*

The watchmen rose as the second volley arrived. Three men went down. The rest loosed their arrows in the face of wither-ing fire.

"Their commander's good." Rale nodded toward the cog. "He doesn't make the same mistake twice." He turned to the two watchmen with longbows. "Can you make that distance?"

The first, tall and blond-haired, nodded. "It's about three hundred paces. I can make the distance, but it'll be a lucky shot if I can land it on the ship, much less hit anything. I've only got a dozen shafts. The percentage will improve if we can move a bit closer."

A hail of arrows flew back and forth between the other ships. The longbows fired faster, but there were more crossbows, many more.

Rale strode over to Salo, who clearly was not inclined to move any closer to the cog, but in the end he bellowed the order as Rale returned. "The captain will provide a few paces, the rest is up to you. Distract them as much as you can."

The two men stood side by side. As one they fired, nocked, pulled, and fired again. Errol marveled at their smooth efficiency. He watched in fascination as pairs of arrows flew across the distance. He'd never dreamed a bow could shoot so far.

The first volley splashed into the water to port. And the second.

The third hit the main deck between the fore and aft castles. The fourth found the water again, but the deed had been done. A roil of confusion rippled through the crossbowmen, and the cog's crew turned its attention from the longboat to Salo's ship. After dodging a rain of arrows from the longboat, the crossbowmen turned and fired a volley in the direction of Salo's ship. Errol watched it come.

Rale's voice cracked through the noise of men, wind, and water. "Everyone down!"

Watchmen and crewmen threw themselves behind the bulwark. Errol pressed himself against the rough wood of the deck and waited. A bolt lodged itself in the main mast. Another flew overhead. Errol peeked over the rail. It appeared the rest had fallen short.

No more missiles came. Beside him Rale cursed. "He knows what he's about." He pointed. "We're nothing more than a distraction, and he's returned all his fire to the longship. Now it's a matter of luck."

Errol watched, horrified. It was like no battle he'd ever seen or heard of. Time stretched as the two ships fought in silence, the air filled with bolts and arrows. Absent were the sounds of steel and staff. He heard no screams. Most of the noise from the combatants was carried away by the wind.

The rate of fire from each ship had slowed. Only five bowmen loosed arrows from the longship, and twenty crossbows still fired from the cog. It seemed the watchmen were losing. "Who'll win?" Even as he asked, his stomach sank with a swell.

"Tough to say, lad. A good man with a longbow can fire three times as fast as a man with crossbow, but the numbers are against our friends out there." Rale turned to the two watchmen with bows. "Garrigus, Molney, how many arrows do you have left?"

Garrigus, the lieutenant Errol had challenged on his arrival to Erinon, answered. "Six each."

"How close do we have to be for a high-percentage shot?"

Garrigus ran a hand through his hair. "Do you want us to kill someone specific?"

Rale shook his head. "No. Just take out a few more of those crossbows."

The two bowmen conferred. "A hundred and fifty paces."

Salo had returned to outracing the cog. Their distance was close to two hundred fifty.

Rale studied the battle over the aft rail and again went in search of Salo, his eyes filled with dire choices. Errol followed. His shoulders twitched in expectation of a bolt. He glanced at the sky, searching for the black streaks.

Salo handled the wheel, casting quick glances at their pursuers and making minute adjustments to their course, striving for speed and distance.

"Can we get away, Captain?" Rale asked.

Salo shook his head. "They'll have us as soon as they finish off the longship. Their captain doesn't distract easily."

Rale nodded once. "Furl the fore sails, Captain."

Salo glared, his bushy dark brows nearly hiding his eyes. "Is there some reason you want to die soon rather than late?"

"We need to close the gap again. They're focused on the last dregs of the longship and, with Deas's help, won't see us furl the forward sails. I'm hoping by the time they notice they're within range of our bows, we'll be able to kill enough of them to buy us another day."

"That's a lot of hoping, landwalker," Salo said. "No, I won't do it. Once we lose that distance, we won't get it back."

Rale drew his dagger and pressed the point against Salo's neck. "Captain, that wasn't a suggestion. Furl those sails or die now."

Salo's eyes bulged. His hands stilled on the wheel, and he strained to see the dagger at his throat. "Filthy landwalkers. I hope they kill you first. At least I'll have one last laugh before I die."

The knife didn't move. If anything, Rale pushed it a little harder against Salo's neck. A bead of blood appeared. "For your sake, I hope we don't hit an unexpected wave, Captain."

Salo managed to yell down the length of the boat without moving. "Fulke, take in the forward sails."

Fulke relayed the order, and a trio of sailors scrambled in the rigging to wrap the canvas. Deprived of one-third of their speed, they slowed and the other two boats leapt at them. Rale sheathed his knife, strode to the edge of the deck, and nodded for the bowmen to be at the ready.

As he turned his attention to the other ships, Rale blinked, bowed his head. "Brave man." Errol turned to see what had caught his attention. The distance between the longboat and the enemy ship had lessened so that now only fifty paces separated them.

"What's he doing?"

"The only thing he can if he's to break their pursuit. Any man can handle a crossbow, but men on the longbow are raised to it. They're much more accurate. The captain of the longship knows that. If he can keep the rest of his bowmen alive long enough, they'll slaughter the men on the other ship."

Errol swallowed, tasted the salt on the air. "But how long can they last at that distance?"

"Not long." Rale hailed his two bowmen. "Gentlemen, fire as soon as you're assured of hitting your target."

The watchmen on the longship nocked and fired without pause, filling the space between the two ships with a steady rain of arrows. Errol's heart exulted to see their attack. The cog's bolts flew wide and disappeared into the sea and then stopped altogether. The longbows continued to shoot, raining death on the elevated decks of the other ship.

Then at some signal, the twang of a score of crossbows firing at once came across the water. Bolts sprouted from the flesh of the bowmen like quills. The longbows stilled.

Except one.

Protected by the mast, a single archer continued to draw and fire.

"We need those bows, gentlemen," Rale shouted. "Their attention will be on us soon."

Garrigus and Molney each nocked, pulled the bowstring to their cheek, and waited, bodies swaying with the movement of the ship. Molney loosed first. The arrow shot from the bow, flew low over the deck of the other ship until it sprouted in a man's throat.

Rale nodded. "Nice shot."

"Luck, or nearly so. Bound to hit something shooting down the length of another ship like that."

Garrigus loosed. The shaft sped across the distance, punched into a crossbowman's shoulder, and didn't stop until the broadhead erupted through the other one. Furious shouts came from the cog, and all the crossbows on the foredeck turned to aim at the new threat. The lone longbow still fired, but more weakly now, and a handful of bolts from the aft deck kept its owner pinned down.

Molney loosed another shaft, then slumped to the deck. A short bolt stuck out from his chest. He plucked feebly at it with one hand. Then his eyes glazed and the hand fell away.

A muscle twitched in Garrigus's cheek, but he fired as if nothing had happened. "I'll need someone to bring me his arrows."

Errol ducked into a crouch, stepped over Molney's body, and grabbed the four remaining arrows. He put them within Garrigus's reach, then ducked back behind the aft mast. The watchman nocked, paused, and let fly. On the longship, the sole remaining bowman still fired, but the shots came infrequently now, and they barely cleared the distance to the other vessel.

A scream overhead pulled Errol's gaze upward. One of Salo's sailors clutched a bolt stuck in his abdomen, lost his balance, and plummeted to the deck headfirst. Errol turned away, squeezing his eyes shut against the crunching sound.

Garrigus hissed. Errol opened his eyes to see the watchman's bow on the deck, his left hand pressed to his right bicep, blood leaking through his fingers.

"Can you fire?" Rale asked.

The watchman shook his head. "But I can work a sword with my left if someone can bandage this."

Errol cupped his hands around his mouth. "Rokha!" Ru's daughter broke off her study of the battle, came running.

"Can you bandage his arm?" Errol asked.

Her dark hair, cut short, waved in the wind. "I have supplies below." She pushed Garrigus to a sitting position against the ship's protective wall and ran for the hold.

Errol stared at the bow. There were four arrows left. Rale stood on the aft deck speaking with the captain. The longship drifted now, a derelict. No more arrows came from it.

He'd never used a longbow before, had rarely shot the shorter versions hunters used around the Sprata. But how different could it be? Errol nocked an arrow and pulled. He clenched his teeth, straining. How did men do it? He grunted with effort and finally managed to get the bowstring a handsbreadth from his cheek, where it stopped, refusing to go any farther. He loosed. The ship was so close, he could hardly miss it.

He didn't. The arrow stuck fast in the side, useless. A bolt whizzed by, close enough for him to hear its passage. Errol drew and fired again, aiming a little higher this time. A short scream came across the water. Salo shouted an order to unfurl the forward sails, but it would be too late. The other ship was only twenty paces away. In another moment grappling hooks would fly across the space to haul them within boarding distance, and then they'd fight.

Errol aimed for the men holding crossbows—got lucky enough to hit one, completely missed another. All the arrows were gone.

11

BOARDED

CROSSBOW FIRE kept them pinned to the deck. Errol hugged the bulwark while grappling hooks pulled the two ships closer. The hulls thumped together with a hollow booming sound. Behind the foremast, Rale held up a hand, signaling Errol and the rest to wait. When the first man from the enemy ship landed on the deck, he yanked his arm down.

Errol dove away from the ship's rail, his staff tight in his hands. Stray crossbow bolts still whined through the air. He rolled to his feet, the wood buzzing in the air. Merakhi, dark-skinned and dour, swarmed over the rail wielding heavy, curved swords.

The boat's rocking confused his footwork, and he almost stumbled into the point of a sword. He parried a thrust, stabbed the end of his staff into his attacker's throat.

"'Ware!" Garrigus yelled behind him. Errol dropped to the deck, felt a rush of displaced air, and thrust at the source. A grunt, followed a heartbeat later by a scream, started his heart beating again.

A hand hauled him back to his feet. Garrigus. Blood spatters covered the blond watchman. A pace away a Merakhi warrior screamed, tried to hold the stump of an arm.

"Back to back," Garrigus ordered.

Errol turned, met the charge with a swing of his staff as the deck canted and pulled his feet from underneath him. Behind him, Garrigus swore. With a flurry of sword strokes he dispatched his man and bought Errol enough time to get to his feet.

"Short strokes," the watchman yelled. "Keep your balance."

Time stretched into an endless series of thrusts and parries. Errol's world contracted to the face and sword of the man in front of him. Blood slicked the deck. Screams tore across his hearing, and he tried in vain to identify owners—friend or foe?

The swordsman in front of him feinted. Errol sidestepped to his right to counter, put his foot in a pool of blood and went down. His opponent pressed in. Errol tripped him with his staff, but the man fell on it. As Errol fought to pull it from underneath the man's weight, the swordsman rolled toward him, blade flashing.

With a flurry of sword strokes, Garrigus dispatched his opponent with a cut through the chest. With an overhand cut, the watchman struck Errol's attacker across the throat. Fresh blood wet the deck. Errol regained his feet and his staff. Thick streams of red ran from Garrigus's side. Errol's rescue had come at a price.

Before he could voice his concern, they were set upon again. Twice more Errol lost his footing on the deck. Each time he fell, Garrigus bought him the time he needed to rise and keep fighting.

Then the fighting stopped.

Bodies lay everywhere. Blood and salt water flowed across the deck. Errol turned to thank Garrigus, but his smile wavered and collapsed at the sight of the watchman. Garrigus stood, his hand pressed against his side, trying to staunch the blood that leaked through his fingers. His smile stretched his bloodless lips. "Are you well?" His voice barely rose above the sounds of the ocean.

Errol nodded.

Garrigus slow-blinked twice, then crumpled to the deck. His chest stilled.

Errol dropped to Garrigus's side, tore open the watchman's jerkin, and pressed his hands against two of the wounds on Garrigus's chest. Talons of despair tore at Errol's heart. "No, please. Not again."

Men kept dying. For him. He fingered the black armband Reynald had given him. Maybe he could use his authority to order the watchmen not to die for him. An instant later he cursed himself for a fool. They wouldn't listen. Captain Reynald had gotten to them already.

A cold knot formed in his chest. Valon would pay. Oh yes, Errol would make him pay.

Footsteps drew close. "You carry death lightly, boy, or you drown."

Errol leaned forward to brush his hand across the valiant lieutenant's eyes, laid the man's head gently on the hard timber of the deck, and stood.

His gaze locked with Rale's. "I'll kill Valon."

The farmer nodded, his eyes somber over the strong nose. "You know that won't stop what's coming."

It wouldn't. He knew it wouldn't. Killing Valon couldn't make Rodran young again or conjure an heir the kingdom didn't have. "Maybe it'll keep them from killing the people around me."

Rale's smile held grief in it. "I hope so, lad. I hope so. Come, I'll need your help." He pulled a dagger from his belt and jumped the rail to the enemy ship. With as much apparent feeling as a butcher, he moved from body to body and thrust his blade through the heart. The sound made Errol sick to his stomach.

"Do you have to do that?"

His teacher shook his head. "Probably not, but I've lost more than one man to an enemy that played dead only to spring up and fire an arrow at our backs." He waved an arm at the scat-

Patrick W. Carr

tered bodies. "Salvage as many of the arrows as you can. We'll probably need them."

"Is it always like this?" Errol asked. He'd meant to say *battle*, but Rale seemed to understand his question even so.

"No, usually it's worse." Memories shadowed Rale's eyes as he spoke. "I've seen battlefields that stretched for hundreds of paces, the dead so thick you could walk from end to end without your feet ever touching the ground. The dead aren't the worst of it." He stabbed, rose, and moved to the next body. "It's the dying—men or boys with gut wounds trying to hold themselves together, crying for water, crying for their wife or mother."

Errol tried to shake the spell of Rale's words. He didn't want to hear them, but he didn't want to be alone, so he followed behind, waited until Rale struck, and then pulled the arrows he could. Many of the shafts had broken on impact, some had fouled the head, and others were stuck so deeply they couldn't be retrieved. But by the time they were halfway through he held a thick armful of shafts that could be cleaned and used again.

In the space between breaths he saw Rale bend next to a Merakhi with a single arrow in his back. The Merakhi rolled and thrust. By luck or skill, Rale caught the sword's edge on his guard, but the man kicked out and swept Rale's feet from beneath him. His teacher rolled, tried to get space, but the Merakhi was faster.

Errol leapt across the space and took the Merakhi through the eye with one of the arrows. With a moan, the man's bones turned to water, and he dropped to the deck.

Rale straightened and gave Errol a grateful nod. "My thanks. Age seems to have dulled my sense of caution as well as my reflexes."

Errol followed him more closely after that, one arm wrapped around the arrows, the other ready to strike. After a half hour, supplied with crossbows, bolts, and arrows, they crossed back to their own ship. Salo's crew set fire to the enemy vessel, Rale

107

and the surviving watchmen cut the grappling lines, and they left the burning vessel behind.

On the aft deck their captain employed the rough side of his tongue on Rokha as she stitched up a jagged cut on his arm. Ru's daughter just smiled and yanked the thread holding his flesh together.

"You evil woman! You did that on purpose. Don't pull so hard."

Rokha flashed him a saucy smile. "I thought sailors were tough. You cry more than a soft-handed courtier, Salo."

Her words seemed to have the desired effect; Salo stifled his complaints in spite of Rokha's obvious pleasure at employing more force on the stitches than necessary. When she knotted off the last one, she approached Errol, swaying with the movement of the ship like a dancer.

Rokha moved in so close her breath brushed Errol's ear like a caress. "I thought I'd give Captain Salo a little of his own back for your seasickness." She moved on to the next injury, her hands clutching her pack.

"Captain," Rale said, "we need to circle back and see if there are any survivors on that longship," Rale said.

Salo spat. "You want us to stay out here in the strait? Who knows what other ships may be out there hunting us? No. By all the gods of the sea, no."

Errol brought his staff up, waved the bloody end of it in front of Salo's face. The man's eyes followed it as if it were a venomous snake. "Captain, if any other vessels were within striking distance of us, they would have attacked along with that first ship. Valon doesn't strike by half measures. He didn't expect us to be aided."

The captain's eyes bulged at the mention of the secondus, as if Errol had invoked a malus.

"Without the men on the longship, we'd be dead. Yes?" Errol asked.

The captain didn't answer. He continued to watch the end of Errol's staff as if it might strike him at any moment.

"Nod your head, Captain."

Salo bobbed his head once.

Errol allowed a measure of his helplessness and frustration into his hands. The staff twitched a fraction. "I think we should go back and see if there are any survivors."

The matter proved to be more complicated than Errol realized. Sails had to be reconfigured to turn about and tack against the wind in a zigzag course to bring them to the drifting form of the longship. From his vantage point on the aft deck of Salo's ship, Errol witnessed the carnage the cog had wreaked on the watchmen who'd appeared to save them. No one moved. Crossbow bolts by the score had turned the vessel into a floating prickle hog of wooden skin and iron quills.

Salo thrust his arm at the derelict. "Are you satisfied?"

Rale stood next to Errol, his gaze focused on the longship as he scrutinized one body after another. "Pull her in, Captain. I want to board her."

A torrent of muttered imprecations poured from Salo at this command, but he gave the order, and within minutes the longship bobbed alongside. Errol's feet rocked underneath him as the two hulls bumped together. The carnage looked even worse up close. Those men had fought death to the last. He followed Rale across the rail, dropping to the lower deck of the longship.

Dead watchmen lay everywhere. Errol found himself examining each pale, lifeless face, but none of these men were known to him. As far as he could tell not one of these men dressed in black had ever graced the courtyard in Erinon. Rale collected crossbow bolts as he went. Then he jerked in surprise and rushed to a man lying next to the main mast.

"Errol, get Rokha."

He rushed back to the other ship, pulled Rokha away from stitching a deep but not life-threatening cut on a sailor, and ran back to Rale. They found him next to a tall watchman, a captain's sword emblem stitched to the breast of his cloak. Sweat matted blond hair so light it was almost white. The man lay unconscious, or nearly so. Strong hands clenched his thigh so that the tendons corded.

Rokha ripped a strip of cloth from a dead man's cloak, wound it tight around the watchman's leg just above his hands. She snatched a length of a broken crossbow bolt and inserted it through a knot in the cloth.

The captain's eyes flew open at the first turn. "No, not the tourniquet," he gasped. "I need my leg."

Errol caught sight of familiar icy blue eyes.

Rokha brushed aside the captain's objection. "I want to make sure you live, Captain."

The watchman jerked his head toward Errol. "And I want to make sure he lives. You've stitched arteries before?"

Ru's daughter nodded. "But not on a rolling ship, and never without something to knock the patient out."

"Do it," the watchman ordered.

Rokha stared down at him, her face unreadable. "If you flinch, you'll die."

"Then I'll have to make sure I don't flinch. Hurry. I don't know how long I can stay conscious."

Ru's daughter loosened the tourniquet just long enough to place a pad of cloth underneath it against the artery. "Lie back, Captain. Errol, elevate that leg and keep it steady. Rale, keep just enough pressure on the tourniquet to keep him from bleeding. Too much and you'll crush the artery, too little and he'll bleed to death."

Rale took the tourniquet from Rokha. "Release your grip, Captain. Let the lady do her work."

A rope of blood squirted across Rokha's tunic. "Tighten it."

The bleeding slowed. Rale turned the bolt by increments as Rokha wiped the blood away.

"That's it. Stop."

Errol could see the ends of the watchman's severed artery. With deft movements, Rokha threaded a small needle and began sewing the captain's leg together. The watchman clenched his teeth and stared at the sky. Sweat poured from him, but he never moved.

At last Rokha tied the last knot and put away her needle. As Errol watched she dug through her pouch, unstopped a bottle that held a gray powder, and sprinkled a generous amount on the captain's wound. The watchman hissed, his lips drawn tight against his teeth, and then appeared to lose consciousness.

Rokha drew a deep breath and nodded to Rale. "Release the pressure slowly, very slowly."

Errol's gaze locked onto the watchman's artery, willing Rokha's stitches to hold. Blood welled in the wound.

"It's not holding," he said.

Rokha watched for a moment longer. "Yes it is. The blood is from smaller veins—serious, but not life-threatening." She wrapped the wound with long strips of cloth in a figure eight and tied them off.

"Now what?" she asked.

Rale sighed. "We'll drop him off at Port City. There are healers there who can take care of him."

"No," Errol said. Every gaze turned to him where he still held the watchman's leg. "He'll want to come with us. And we won't be going to Port City. I made a mistake planning our route too far ahead. The only way to avoid Valon's net is to make our decisions quickly, randomly. That way, by the time he knows where we're headed, it will be too late for him to catch us." As the words left his mouth, his eye twitched. His plan was sound, but he was missing something.

"Makes sense," Rale said.

"He won't be able to travel for at least a week, Errol," Rokha said. "That artery needs time to heal."

Errol shrugged. "Then we'll get him some urticweed to help with the bleeding so he can recover more quickly."

Rale regarded him with serious brown eyes. "How do you know he wants to come with us?"

Errol met his gaze. How much could he say? He glanced down at the captain of the guard. "He said he wanted to make sure I lived. When he wakes we'll ask him what he meant. In the meantime we'll need a stretcher." He turned away before they could ask him any more questions.

111

The ship heeled over to bypass Port City and sailed for the next major port north, a hundred-league journey to Steadham, the capital of the Einland province. Merodach woke halfway there, his eyes sharp, darting. Errol held vigil by his side. Everyone else had been kept away, ostensibly by Rale's orders, but in reality by Errol's request.

The watchman nodded. "You're alive."

Errol's fingertips floated across the smooth grain of his staff. "You seem to be of two minds about that, Captain. First you try to kill me, and then you seem bent on keeping others from doing that very thing."

Merodach didn't smile, but something in his countenance lightened for a moment before he grew somber again. "My men?"

Errol shook his head. "You were the only survivor, Captain. I'm sorry."

A sigh. "They wanted you very badly, Errol, to chance so many men in the strait."

"Why would the number of men make any difference?"

Merodach stared at the ceiling of Salo's cabin, commandeered as the watchman's makeshift infirmary. "That ship is a declaration of war. I have no doubt the Merakhi had hoped to keep us asleep for a while longer, preying on our desire for peace."

Errol waited for more. Merodach lay with his eyes closed. Only the twitch of his sword hand gave evidence of wakefulness.

"What is your part in this, Captain? You seem determined to go to extreme lengths to keep me alive." Errol's pulse quickened. Each time he'd encountered Merodach, the captain of the watch had appeared without warning—to fight or save him and then disappear without explanation. Now the captain's wounds held him captive. An unexpected opportunity to interrogate Merodach presented itself.

Merodach opened his eyes, stared at the ceiling.

If only Errol could find the key to unlock the man's tongue. Desperate acts meant desperate motivations. Attacking a three-masted cog loaded with crossbows was definitely desperate.

Errol leaned in, drawing closer to his erstwhile assassin. "We're headed north, Captain. Our plans for Port City were made too far ahead of time. Valon, or one of his circle, knew of them."

The captain acknowledged this but didn't speak.

"I'll send Rokha to you now that you're awake." Impatience rankled Errol like an itch he couldn't scratch. "We'll make provisions for your care once we reach port." He rose, turned his back to the watchman. Merodach's voice caught him at the entrance.

"You cannot afford to leave me behind, Errol. I will be able to ride as soon as it is necessary. Valon gambled much on this attack and lost. It will take him time to marshal enough men for another strike—but when he does, you'll need me with you."

12

THE CATHEDRAL

MARTIN STARED AT HIS FEET while he worked his way toward the cathedral. A light drizzle, unexpectedly chill in the early autumn air, aided them. The people of Windridge who had cause or desire to be on the streets went with their heads down. Martin and Luis wouldn't attract attention.

He hoped.

In the week since the solis rescued them, Cruk had strengthened, but his ability to travel was still some days off. Martin chewed on this thought with resentment. Time spent with the solis, implacable as a Frataland glacier and sometimes as distant, had left Martin shaken. Every argument of theology and training he'd used to refute the herbman's statements had been ruthlessly turned aside.

Karele's rejoinders put Martin on the defensive. They all came down to a simple position: If Deas was supreme in power, then how could a simple herbman frustrate a consecrated benefice and the secondus of the conclave?

Luis walked next to him in silence that defined their interactions in Windridge. An urge, like a desire to shed a physical burden, filled him, and he turned to the secondus to speak, to voice his desperate doubts. He swallowed his words, forced them down deep to his belly, where they churned. *Tell the church the spirit of Deas talks to men directly? Me?*

They'd never believe it. The only real question was how they would kill Martin after he uttered such blasphemy. He stumbled at the thought and righted himself. He'd done his part. The priests in his diocese were forbidden to persecute the solis. Since Deas wanted someone to tell the Judica that Aurae spoke to the herbwomen directly, let someone else do it.

If, he corrected with self-excoriation. *If* Deas wanted someone to tell the Judica!

"Not a sign," Luis said.

Startled, Martin pulled his gaze from the grimy cobblestones to search for the object of Luis's comment. "What?"

The secondus almost sounded mournful. "There's no sign of pursuit, Martin. Not a trace. We've been out on the street for at least an hour, walking in a straight line toward the cathedral. The worst reader in Erinon could have tracked us by now."

"Thank the three they cannot find us," Martin said. Yet even to his own ears he didn't sound very thankful.

"It will mean the end of the conclave," Luis said.

Martin nodded. Yes, and who knew what else?

They turned a corner, and the cathedral rose before them. A weight like a cloak of lead settled onto his shoulders. They'd come to Windridge looking for answers; now he wasn't sure he wanted them.

They crossed the broad plaza to the cathedral. The local guards, dressed in faded red uniforms of the church, stood watch over the approach, ignoring the complaints of those they ordered to raise their heads in the gray drizzle. Martin lifted his head, shivered a bit as the damp found his neck, and approached the lieutenant.

"We would like to see Abbot Gerold."

The guard took in their nondescript clothing and shook his head. "So would most of the supplicants who come to the cathedral. The abbot can't see you all. I'll let one of the brothers know you're here."

Martin stepped close enough to the lieutenant to shield himself from casual passersby. Then he reached into his tunic and pulled out the heavy symbol of his office, cupping it in his hands so only the guard could see it. "Do you know what this is?"

The guard's eyes widened. He nodded, took a step back.

Martin stepped forward to keep the guard from bowing. "And do you know what it means?"

"Y-Yes, Your Excellency." The guard stood, his body twitching as if he couldn't decide whether or not to genuflect.

Martin sighed. "Keep your voice down." The lieutenant was probably a good man, but he wasn't very bright. Martin waited, but the man in front of him showed no sign of recalling his request. "The abbot?"

Relief washed over the guard's face at being presented with an opportunity to leave. "Yes, Your Excellency." He turned and disappeared into the cathedral at a trot.

The guard returned a minute later with one of the brothers in tow. He practically flung him at Martin. "This is Brother Gilis."

A short man with a bulbous nose and an unruly crop of thick black hair stood in front of Martin, trying to free his arm from the lieutenant's grasp. The church solider stared at Martin, seemingly unaware that he still held the brother's arm.

No, not a bright man. "Thank you, Lieutenant. I think you can let him go now."

Gilis nodded his thanks. "I'll take care of our guests, Otto," he said to the guard. Otto nodded but showed no signs of moving. The brother looked heavenward, muttered something that sounded like a prayer for patience under his breath. "You can go now, Otto."

The lieutenant nodded several times, pumping his head up and down and smiling before he left.

Gilis lifted his hands. "A nice lad, the third son of a local lord." He stepped to one side, raised an arm in an invitation to follow him into the cathedral. "If you'll follow me, I'll take you to the abbot."

They passed from underneath the overcast skies into the deeper gloom of the cathedral. Candles burned in the narthex, where pilgrims offered prayers. The shadows of their bent forms danced on the walls in parody. Gilis led them to the right— through the sanctuary, past the sacristy, and down a hallway. He stopped before a pair of double doors Martin recognized as the previous abbot's personal dining room. With a knock, Brother Gilis escorted them into Abbot Gerold's presence, bowed, and withdrew.

Martin paused to appreciate the change in decor. Abbot Gerold was cut from different cloth than Morin, thank Deas. Morin's opulent furnishings had been replaced with a simple trestle table and chairs. Except for the signs of the abbot's office and a pair of detailed drawings of the cathedral, the walls were bare.

Martin nodded to Gerold. "My compliments to your decorator, Abbot. The furnishings are much improved since I visited last."

Gerold, tall with a hawklike nose and that bird's piercing hazel eyes, waved his arms to show his dismay. "You saw that? When I arrived, I thought I'd walked into a brothel. As bad as this room was, Morin's private chambers were a nightmare. I had Brother Dominic sell the furnishings. He bargains well, but I'm afraid the sheer quantity of Morin's frippery overwhelmed the market for such things."

The abbot's casual manner melted away, and his eyes became even more piercing. "I'm given to understand that you are a benefice. You'll forgive me if I seem doubtful, but we live in troubled times, and those who wear the red have been called to the Judica, in Erinon."

Martin brought forth his symbol of office. "I am Benefice Martin Arwitten. This is Secondus Montari. A matter of urgency—those troubled times you spoke of—called us unexpectedly away from the proceedings on the isle."

Gerold nodded his apology. "Please forgive my hesitation. How may I serve you?"

Martin pulled a deep shuddering breath into his lungs. "Abbot

Morin kept a prisoner here, an old herbwoman guilty of nothing more than helping peasants in the countryside. I would like to have her released into my care."

The abbot's face fell.

"She's dead!" Martin waved the bitter truth at Karele. In his peripheral vision, he saw Cruk stir and push himself up to a sitting position on arms that trembled with the effort.

"Yes," Karele said. "I know."

For some reason that simple acknowledgment stoked Martin's anger. He closed the distance between himself and the healer. "Do you know how she died?"

Their host shrugged. "She was killed in her cell, probably the night you escaped from Windridge."

Why had he hit Morin? Martin tried to speak, but his words shattered in his throat. Tears burned his eyes as he gathered the broken shards of his speech and threw it at Karele. "I could have saved her!" He hid his face. "She was torn to pieces."

Martin spun away from their stares, gathered himself. People died. He pulled a cloth from his pocket and scrubbed his face. "You could have saved us a trip to the cathedral. We never should have returned to this place."

He could almost hear Karele shrug his feeble accusation away. "I don't think you would have believed me, and your trip to Windridge accomplished something necessary."

Martin didn't respond. Their trip to Windridge had been a disaster; they should have trusted the lots and gone south. The herbwoman—the solis—was dead, and Cruk had almost died as well—all for a fat benefice's pride.

"What did we accomplish coming to this place?" Luis asked.

Karele's smile held more in it than Martin could discern. "You now know that the solis, with Aurae's guidance, can nullify a reader's craft."

Martin held up a hand, as if he could keep the consequences of this new knowledge away. For hundreds of years the church's decisions had been guided and confirmed by lot, by the skill and dedication of the conclave. What would they do now?

"Martin," Luis called to him. "We will need all the allies we can get. They will be needed." He gave a helpless laugh. "They can't help but be needed." The secondus stood next to Cruk, his brown eyes filled with resignation. "Since Magnus's time, the conclave has belonged to the church, Martin, not to men. If casting lots becomes worthless, I will find another way to serve."

Martin gave himself a shake. Enough talk. Despite the revelations they'd uncovered at Windridge, their mission remained the same. They needed to discover the truth behind Liam's and Errol's importance. He turned to Cruk. "How soon can you travel?"

"I can travel now," the captain answered. Spots of fatigue on his sunken cheeks told a different story.

"Of course he can," Karele said, "if you want him to die. I can't protect you outside the walls of Windridge."

"Can you go with us?" Luis asked.

Martin stared at his friend in shock, vowed he would never again underestimate him.

Karele's gaze passed through Luis where he stood, and he cocked his head as if listening. When his eyes focused on Martin again, the solis's eyes were resigned. "I am commanded. Aurae says I am to submit to you."

"When can Cruk travel?" Martin asked.

"Two days." The healer shook his head. "But he'll be useless in a fight."

The fact that their captain didn't protest Karele's assessment told Martin it was true.

Two days after leaving Windridge, hooves thundered on the hard-packed road behind them. Panic sucked the air from Martin's lungs as they wheeled their horses and drew swords. Their pursuers slowed to a trot.

"No bows on them," Cruk said. Fatigue leeched most of the customary growl from his voice.

The riders came on. Luis pointed. "That one's wearing a nuntius's armband, and unless I miss my guess, that's Willem on his right." He indicated a tall man who flopped in his saddle like a scarecrow, arms out from his body, reins held in a death grip.

Relief and fear met midway in Martin's chest. They wouldn't have to fight, but what had happened at Erinon? Was he being commanded back to the Judica? That would mean the archbenefice and primus had been forced to acknowledge his absence. Fear nailed his tongue to the roof of his mouth. The riders approached to five paces, then stopped.

"Greetings, Willem," Luis said. "You're a long way from the conclave."

Willem let loose a string of curses that made Cruk nod in appreciation. The word *horse* was sprinkled liberally through the tirade.

Martin's trepidation didn't allow for patience. "Enough. How long have you been searching for us?"

Willem gave a bow and almost slid sideways from the saddle. "Your pardon, Excellency. I thought I'd found you back in Windridge, but . . ." He gave his head a little shake. "No matter. I've been ordered to guide this nuntius to you." The reader jerked his head back toward the watchman in the rear. "Jan has been tasked with our safety. He's done a lousy job of protecting me from this horse."

Martin nodded once and turned to the nuntius. "You may deliver your message."

"Nay," the man said. "I do not know you. The message cannot be delivered until your identity has been confirmed by the reader."

Willem rolled his eyes. He raised his arm to point at Martin. "I hereby vow that this pillar of the church, this paragon of virtue, this epitome of theological prowess is indeed Benefice Martin Arwitten."

Luis snorted, but the nuntius showed no signs of possessing a sense of humor. "Until the benefice's identity is verified by lot, I cannot speak."

Martin interjected even as Willem drew breath to argue. "The message is sensitive, good reader. Unless we follow the protocol laid on the nuntius, it cannot be delivered." He turned to Karele, who sat his horse with his eyes half-lidded as if he would fall asleep any moment. "Can he cast?" Martin asked under his breath.

At Karele's disinterested nod, Martin gave the reader his assent.

Willem growled. "I'll have to carve on horseback. If I dismount from this foul beast, I won't be able to stand. I don't think I'll ever walk normally again." After a few minutes, he held two identical spheres. His large hands dwarfed the lots. "How many times do I have to draw?"

"I am commanded to have you draw twenty times."

"That seems a bit extreme," Luis said.

Twenty draws later, Willem presented his results to the church messenger. "He is Benefice Arwitten seventeen times out of twenty."

The nuntius nodded, satisfied.

Martin intoned the ancient command that would release the message to him. "Nuntius, you may speak."

The messenger demurred. "I cannot. It must be delivered in private."

With a sigh, Martin twitched the reins and led the messenger away from the rest of the party. When he judged the distance great enough to prevent eavesdropping, he stopped. "Do you have a written copy of the message?"

The nuntius shook his head. "I was commanded to deliver it verbally only, Excellency."

Gooseflesh rose on Martin's skin. So, the message required even more precautions than standard church protocol afforded. He spoke the ritual command again. "Nuntius, you may speak."

All thought and self-awareness dropped from the messenger's face until he resembled a mask of himself, speaking as though a wax sculpture had been given the gift of speech. "'Greetings to our brother in the church, Martin Arwitten, from the Arch-benefice in Erinon, Bertrand Canon. I regret that I must send you ill tidings. As planned, Errol Stone has been found guilty of conspiring with spirits in order to save him and us from ruin, but the penance I planned for him was thwarted by a coalition of benefices within the Judica. Errol has been compelled to journey to Merakh, where he must find Sarin Valon and kill him.'"

Spots danced in Martin's vision. He locked his knees to keep from falling. Compelled to Merakh? They'd killed the boy. Those snakes in the Judica had killed Errol.

The messenger continued. "'We have enemies in the Judica and the conclave, Martin. Without the omne to confirm each cast for confidence, we cannot be sure of whom to trust. My friend, I should not order you to do this, but the need of the kingdom requires I do so. Make haste to discover the boy's importance, and if you can, find a way to join him and help him survive. I trust you and remain your brother in the faith, Bertrand Canon.'"

Awareness came back into the nuntius's face. Martin started breathing again and tried to school his features into some semblance of calm. He ached everywhere, as if he'd been beaten with a stick, and made a conscious effort to relax.

"Will there be a return message, Your Excellency?" the nuntius asked.

"Yes." He waited for the messenger to compose himself. What should he say? Dear Deas, what could he say?

"To our brother Archbenefice Bertrand Canon from your humble servant Martin Arwitten. I have received your message and will do all I can to comply." He thought for a moment.

"Even unto death."

13

THE CARAVAN

THICK HAWSERS SECURED Salo's ship to the pier at Steadham, the shipping capital of the Einland province that lay a hundred leagues north of Erinon. Men in half-sleeved shirts and trousers worked the docks, calling to each other in a guttural dialect so rough Errol could only make out every other word. Their speech carried the cadence of the sea, floating and crashing through their words.

Rale oversaw the transport of the horses. The animals trembled and their ears twitched forward and back as the survivors of Errol's party coaxed them across the broad gangplank to the pier. Of the twenty watchmen who'd sailed with Errol from the isle, only five survived.

Errol looked at the remnants of his party and berated himself again. He was a reader. The responsibility for avoiding Valon's attacks belonged to him. No one else could do it.

Rale approached as Rokha gave directions regarding Merodach's transport to two of the surviving watchmen. She stopped as they passed by. "I want to take him to a healer."

This caught Errol by surprise. Rokha was as good as any of

the healers back in Erinon at patching a wound, and better than most. She had more experience with battle injuries. "Why?"

"I want to make sure that wound doesn't foul." She shrugged, but her face held a pinched cast to it Errol had never seen on her before, and she darted looks to Merodach's litter. "And I need to restock my kit."

She followed on the heels of the men carrying the litter. Errol's attention moved from the docks inward. Something he couldn't identify bothered him, a worry that chewed at his mind, generating unease, as if he'd missed an enemy poised with a sword at his back.

"Rale, where did that cog come from?"

The farmer massaged his jaw muscles for a moment before answering. "We killed anyone who could tell us, but to catch us in the strait it either had to launch from Port City or was waiting at anchor."

Errol nodded. He'd thought as much himself. "But it couldn't have been anchored in the strait. Not without a reader on board."

"How do you know there wasn't?"

He allowed himself a smile. "There were no lots, no wood shavings, and no sawdust on the ship."

Rale considered his logic, eyes narrowed. When he spoke, his voice carried tones of respect. "Very good. What do you think it means?"

Errol pulled a deep breath into his lungs, then let it out in a long sigh. "I think it means we can't count on the longship captain's estimate. Valon is in Merakh, but he's tied to a circle—a linking of readers." He paused, wondering if he needed to explain, but Rale nodded, so he continued. "He must have left one of his circle behind to catch us. I can't think of any other way that ship could have found us so quickly. There must have been a reader in Port City."

He turned, looked across the docks toward the city that sprawled on the low bluff above them. He pointed to Merodach's retreating litter. "Merodach said Valon won't be able to muster another attack for some time." The thought of being hunted by the former secondus brought a skittering of rat's feet down his neck. He scratched, turned to Rale. "It took us three days to sail a hundred leagues. How long would it take a man to ride that distance?"

His mentor rubbed his jaw. "They'll have to follow the curve of the coast. Unless they're willing to kill horses, it'll take them five or six days." He pulled at his jaw muscles. "What if Valon left more than one of his circle behind?"

Errol searched for a memory, cudgeling his brain into cooperation. Lots had filled the warehouse where Luis had discovered the depths of Sarin's depravity. How many different men had cast lots there? He closed his eyes, pictured each lot as it came to rest in his hands. His hands moved with the memory of choosing a pine sphere, reading it, and putting it away. By the three, there were so many. How could they fight that?

Moments passed. Rale didn't speak, but Errol could feel his gaze. "He has at least twenty readers in his circle, possibly more—and they're all connected by a malus."

Rale's brown eyes hardened to chips of flint. "Explain."

He sighed. Rale wasn't going to like this. "Sarin Valon was the secondus of the conclave. Luis said he went insane trying to create a versis—a single lot that can cast any question. We found a mill where he'd been hiding after he faked his death. It was filled with lots that Sarin didn't cast, but it appeared they were tied to the same question. The only way to do that was to use a malus to form a circle."

Rale's eyes narrowed. "Explain the capabilities of this circle."

Errol lifted his hands in surrender. "I'm not sure, but Luis thought the malus would allow them to communicate mind to mind. That way they could all carve a different answer to a question. Their ability to cast would be twenty times faster than a single reader."

Rale sighed and staggered to lean against the railing of the ship, like a farmer dropping a sack of grain. "We're in trouble, boy."

Errol nodded. "I know."

Rale shook his head. "No, boy, you don't." He held up a

hand, palm out. "I don't mean to offend you, lad. You're bright. You've got as much courage as a whole squad of watchmen, and you handle a staff like something out of legend, but you haven't fought in a war." He cocked his head to one side. "Do you know what wins battles, Errol?"

He shrugged. "Good soldiers?"

Rale shook his head.

"Superior tactics?"

Rale shook his head again. "Those are all pieces of the whole, lad. Every captain fights with the best soldiers he can train and the best tactics his generals can devise. There are captains that spend their entire lives studying the art of war." Rale held up a finger. "But most battles are won and lost on one thing—communication. Whoever can deploy and redeploy his men most effectively wins."

Errol flopped next to Rale, feeling as if a boulder had landed on his shoulders. The Merakhi didn't need to kill Rodran. They had the kingdom beat already. With Valon and a score of linked readers, they could react to any change in the battle instantly.

"We're going to have to kill the entire circle, aren't we?" Errol asked.

"That's a good idea, but I don't think we can."

"Why not?"

Rale's shoulders bunched under his tunic. "Let's suppose you're Valon. You've got your circle spread throughout the kingdom. Suddenly, you lose one or two. What do you do?"

Errol leaned forward, put his hands on his knees, thought. "I'd pull all the rest to Merakh, where no one could get to them."

"That's right."

Flame burned across his skin at the thought. "You're saying we can't win."

His mentor nodded. "Not as things stand."

"How do we change them?"

Rale laughed without humor. "I think that's what you've been tasked with."

Errol let that sink in. "But even if we kill Valon, won't one of the other readers in the circle take his place?"

"I don't know, Errol. I'm just a soldier."

"It's hopeless, isn't it?"

A trace of a growl entered Rale's voice. "The only battles that are hopeless are the ones that have already been fought. We now know that finding and killing Valon is going to prove more difficult than we first thought, but we haven't lost yet."

Startled laughter burst from Errol's mouth. "More difficult? It's going to be impossible. How do you kill someone who can see you coming?"

Neither of them had an answer.

Moments passed in which Errol wallowed in hopelessness. He pushed himself off the deck. "We need to know what's waiting for us." He went down into the hold in search of his reader's kit. He'd never officially joined the conclave, but the primus had employed him to confirm casts already. Before they left the isle, Errol had helped himself to a knife and a generous amount of pine blanks.

Back on deck he motioned to Rale, seated himself in a quiet corner of the ship, and considered which question to ask. Master Quinn had often told him the question frames the answer. A reader had to beware of his assumptions. Readers spent years in the conclave learning to question everything.

What did he know?

They'd been attacked in the strait through the guidance of a reader. No. He knew they'd been attacked; he only assumed a reader lay behind it. With precise strokes, he shaped a pair of pine blanks into lots to determine whether a reader orchestrated the attack. He held the two lots side by side for inspection. Except for the imprint of his thoughts upon the grain, which only he could see, they appeared identical. Errol dropped them into his bag and shook it. Hollow clacks muffled by the burlap came to him. He drew.

Yes. He grunted. No surprise there. Ten more times he drew. Eight of them matched the first answer. He nodded to himself, confident his assumption had been confirmed.

"There was a reader behind the attack in the strait," he said.

Rale's smile pulled to one side. "I thought we knew that."

"No, we assumed that. Master Quillon says assumptions are dangerous to a reader. That's why they train for years to get rid of them."

Errol paused to think through the possible chain of events, determined not to skip any steps in his logic. He and Rale had assumed the reader would pursue them to Steadham. It seemed logical, but assumptions always seemed logical. Errol sighed. That is until you crossed the strait and dozens of good men died. A dozen different questions came to him, each as plausible as the one before. Which one should he choose?

He looked to Rale. "What is the most important thing we need to know?"

His friend looked across the railing to the steep slate roofs of Steadham that rose above the harbor before he looked back at Errol. "You know Valon. What is the worst possibility you can think of?"

Errol shook his head in denial. "I don't know him. I've never even seen him, and he's nearly killed me twice."

"Yet you keep surviving. You must be doing something right."

His throat constricted against sudden grief. "It's not me. It's the people around me—the watch mostly. They keep sacrificing themselves. I don't think Valon counted on so many people being willing to die to keep me alive."

Rale nodded, his eyes somber. "We're here in the harbor, Errol. What's the worst possible outcome?"

Errol felt a bitter laugh tear through the tightness in his throat. "Valon could have put readers in all the major cities close to Erinon." He threw up a hand in surrender. "We could be attacked our first night in port." As he spoke the words, a dagger of ice slid down his back. At a slow nod from Rale, he picked up a pine blank and began to whittle.

Twenty minutes later he drew the lot for Yes again. The sun dipped to touch the sea to the west, painting the sky with fire. Errol wasn't comforted. He turned to Rale, but to his surprise his mentor wore a savage grin.

"What am I missing?"

Rale's laugh was almost a cackle. "Oh, you're not going to miss anything. I think it's time we give back some of what we took in the strait. I'm going to send runners to call everyone back to the ship. In the meantime I want you to cast and see if we're going to be attacked tonight. I pray to Deas we will be." He clapped Errol on the shoulder and left, his stride light.

Errol crouched in Salo's cabin as waves and moonlight bathed the ship. The gentle lapping and the distant voices of rowdy tavern customers were the only sounds he heard. For two hours he had done nothing but cast, determining the number of men that would come against them, seeing if the reader would be there, uncovering their intent.

Two score men would come against them in an hour, led by one of Valon's circle. Errol shook his head in amazement at the enemy's colossal underestimation. Surely Valon or his reader in Steadham would test to see if they were expected. They must.

But Errol had cast that question as well. They did not. At least, the lots told them they hadn't.

"What if the cast is wrong?"

The lantern light lit Rale's face in planes as absolute and uncompromising as stone. Even his smile appeared to have been carved. "I never met Valon, but I know his kind. His towering ego will hardly credit the possibility that he's been outfoxed. They believe they will take us unaware now, just as they have time and again."

Errol cast a glance out the porthole. That small opening facing the bay would be their only means of escape should the counterattack on Valon's men fumble or stall. They would plunge into the icy waters of the harbor and then have to swim to safety. They were the only men left on the ship. Rale's presence was unnecessary, even dangerous, but he'd refused to leave Errol to be the bait alone.

Errol cradled a pair of blanks in the moonlight, considered

the timing of his final cast. It would take him fifteen minutes to shape the lots into spheres he could trust, perhaps three to draw a dozen times. He didn't know what question to ask.

Would they attack the ship as planned?

Was Sarin's reader still with them?

Did they suspect a counterattack?

He cradled the wood, felt the rough end grain slide under his fingertips like rubbing cloth, smelled the bits of pine resin, immersed himself in the questions as if the blanks could resolve his dilemma. But no question came.

A hand came to rest on his shoulder. "Lots can only answer your question, Errol. They can't guide your query."

"What should I ask?"

A change in the air told him Rale had shaken his head. "I can't tell you, Errol. What do the church and the conclave teach?"

Errol twitched his shoulders, felt the pull of old scars across the skin on his back. "The conclave says the question frames the answer." He paused, unwilling to say any more, but Rale's stillness in the darkness prodded. "The church says the question should come from Deas."

"Then why don't you ask him for it?"

Errol's hands tightened until the corners of the blanks dug into his flesh. "I don't think he'd answer."

"Why not?" Rale's question—soft, so soft it hardly disturbed the air in Salo's cabin—landed on his shoulders like a yoke.

Errol stifled a shrug in the darkness, tried instead to make his voice light. "Deas hears other men." That hadn't been what he meant to say, but it came close enough.

"Someday I will tell you how I came to be a farmer, Errol. Few men have more reason to dislike the church than I do, but I've seen what we're fighting. If the Morgols or the Merakhi conquer us, you'll wish for the worst day under the church you've ever had."

His grip eased on the wood. "That's it? The best we can say for the church is that there are some things so much worse?"

"The church has power, Errol. Power attracts men of all types."

Errol sniffed. "I've heard that before."

"That doesn't make it any less true."

"I still don't know what question to ask." Something tightened in Errol's chest, refused to unclench.

Rale's sigh sounded resigned in the dim light. "Trust your talent, then. It comes from Deas, after all."

"So does Sarin's."

His mentor nodded. "No doubt, every man's talent does. What choices do you intend to make with yours?"

"You sound like a priest." Errol threw the accusation across the space that divided them.

"No," Rale said. "I'm just a soldier. If you don't like the church, Errol, why do you continue striving to save it?"

That was easy enough to answer. "They keep compelling me. I don't have any choice."

"You could have left Erinon after you presented yourself to the conclave. Months went by before they laid another compulsion on you. Why did you stay?"

Errol's eyes burned. He turned away from Rale to check the candle. It was almost time to cast.

"Ah," Rale said with a smile. "So you've found a way to fill the hole left by the ale barrel."

He didn't turn. "I'm a fool. The king has given her to a strutting peacock, the son of a duke."

Leaden silence filled the cabin, stifling any further conversation. He checked the candle. It was time, but what question? Out in the darkness, watchmen and dozens of church guards waited.

It came to him like a whisper in his sleep. He tried to shake it, cursed himself for his heart's ambition, but the query lodged in his head, refused to move. Even if he tried to cast differently now, the lots would be ruined by his scattered thoughts. His eyes brimmed as if each stroke of the knife cut him instead of the wood, but he surrendered himself utterly to the question. Tears splashed the deck as he made the first draw.

Yes.

In disbelief he placed the lot back in the bag. Disappointment and resignation stabbed through him when the next lot came up *No*. But the next ten times came out *Yes*. He couldn't help himself. Tears stung his eyes, gathered at the corners to track down his cheeks. He sniffled like a broken child.

Rale's voice, soft and low, came to him across the cabin. "That must be some question, lad."

He lifted his tear-streaked face, wiped his nose on his sleeve. "She loves me."

Arms enfolded him and squeezed until he thought his ribs would break. "Ah, Errol. I saw how she looked at you. Why did you doubt?"

Errol buried himself into Rale's embrace.

Footfalls hit the deck above them. It had begun.

Cries split the air followed by the hollow thumps of bodies falling. Frantic scrabbles and scratches on the planks above him told where a dying man thrashed. Arrows thunked into the topside of the ship. Sounds of swordplay came through the porthole.

Errol gripped his staff, checking the bladed knobblocks at each end. His palms sweated with the effort of staying within the captain's quarters. "Shouldn't we go fight?"

Rale smiled. "You're an honorary captain in the watch, Errol, but you don't know much about command yet. The commander doesn't put himself in the vanguard. His responsibility is to lead, not to fight."

"I'm not a captain."

"Not yet," Rale said in agreement. "But you're the focal point of the enemy's attacks. If it's you they want dead, then it's you we need to keep alive."

Errol's mind conjured a tapestry of blood and carnage as the rain of arrows, the thump of bodies, and the clanging of steel went on. When it ended he was surprised to see only a quarter hour had passed on the candle. In less time than it took to make a cast, Valon's attack in Steadham had been nullified.

Rokha's voice followed three knocks on the cabin door. Errol rushed to it, flung it open. "Well?"

Ru's daughter wore a fierce smile and exertion colored her cheeks. "It's done."

"How many men did we lose?" Rale asked.

"A handful of church guards." She scowled. "They didn't believe me when I said Valon's forces would turn from their retreat."

"Do we have the reader?"

Rokha lifted and dropped her shoulders. "It's hard to tell in the dark, but everyone who's not dead is under guard on the aft deck."

Rale questioned Errol as he led the way. "Will you be able to pick him out?"

Errol shook his head. "Probably not. I think Sarin's circle left the conclave before I arrived." He pointed at Rokha. "But I think she might be able to find him."

Ru's daughter smiled, but the glance she gave Errol and Rale was wary. "How would I do that?"

"You can spot compulsion," Errol said. "I think the malus's influence works something like that."

"Possession isn't the same thing as compulsion. I don't know if that will work," Rokha said. "But I'll try."

The prisoners, bloodied and weaponless, lined the aft deck. Their variety shocked Errol. He'd expected a homogenous row of swarthy, dark-haired, black-eyed men. Instead, a collection of Bellians, Soedes, and Fratalanders shifted their feet under the intense stares of the watch.

Errol stared. "By the three, how many traitors are there in the kingdom?"

Rale made a sound that might have been a laugh but for the look of death he wore. "Money buys men anywhere."

Rokha moved down the line, searching the face of each man as she went. She stopped, turned, and retraced a step. In front of her a tall Fratalander with dark brown hair and blue eyes stood trembling.

She pointed. "Something's not right with this one."

Errol marveled at Rokha's understatement. The Fratalander sweated and twitched as muscle spasms rocked his body. His eyes rolled, and spittle bubbled from one corner of his mouth.

When he saw Errol he stilled and smiled. "Greetings, omne. I'm pleased to find you will be a more worthy adversary than I first thought."

Steel flashed in the moonlight. The Fratalander's head flew off the deck to splash in the water of the bay. Blood fountained in the darkness. Naaman Ru stood, sword in hand, looking no more bothered than if he'd just slaughtered a chicken.

Errol choked as the body folded in on itself and slumped to the deck. "What did you do that for?"

Ru gestured with his sword to Rale. "He ordered it."

Errol's mentor nodded. "That was Valon. He was using the Fratalander's eyes. I wanted the reader killed before he could see what we all look like." Rale sighed, his chest filling, then falling. "We won't be able to catch him off guard again." He turned to Ru. "Master Ru, please give each of the prisoners the choice between the sword and the noose. I want to be out of Steadham by noon."

Errol looked at Rale as if his teacher had become someone unrecognizable. "You're just going to kill them?"

Rale's face clouded. "Yes. These men tried to kill you, Errol, and would have killed us all. They've betrayed their kingdom. There's no going back for any of them. Look at them. Any one of these men would sell his soul again for the chance to strike you down. Would you put them in a jail to rot for the rest of their lives, take the chance that they might escape and betray their countrymen to the Merakhi again?"

Errol followed Rale off the ship, trying to ignore the sounds behind him.

14

WROUGHT

THREE DAYS OUT from Steadham, in the midst of the Einland province, Errol watched Merodach haul himself into the saddle of a horse with the labored breathing of a woman giving birth. By the time the captain righted himself, his face was nearly as white as his hair. Rokha stood to one side, her eyes filled with the grudging admiration one gives to an underestimated opponent.

"Well done, Captain," she said. "Let's see if you can stay up there."

Merodach gave a mocking bow to his physician and raised a hand to point at the wagons of furs that Ru had procured to set up their disguise for the trip south. "I think I should be able to match any pace our caravan will set."

Errol had never seen Merodach smile before, and the captain didn't now, but he held a sense of amusement about him whenever Rokha challenged him that hinted at jests and teasing. Rokha stood to one side, her eyes considering. With a start she jerked as if waking, gave Errol a frown, and moved away.

A voice hailed him from ahead, and he turned to see Rale and

Naaman Ru bearing down on him as they did every morning. Rale brought forth a map of the province, the parchment littered with the names of every village that boasted even a single inn.

Ru stood to one side, chafing as he always did under Rale's authority, but even more so now that they had taken on the guise of a caravan. "What aimless wandering do you mean to plot out for us today, boy?"

Errol smiled, allowing himself to enjoy this moment when his former captor was forced to take his direction. "I don't mean to plot it out, Ru. I keep telling you that. As we hit each crossroads, we'll decide where to go next." He gave a pointed glance to the furs. "By delaying our decisions until the last possible moment, we deprive Valon of the weapon of being able to cast our position. We're keeping your cargo safe."

Ru's shoulders twitched as if casting off an unwelcome hand. "It's not my cargo." He gestured toward the watchmen posing as caravan guards. "And these aren't my guards."

Errol shrugged. "What's wrong with them?"

"What's wrong?" Ru asked as if the answer should have been obvious. "Any idiot can tell they're not merchant guards. Look at them. If you or Rale go anywhere near them, they snap to attention as if they are forming ranks. It's taken me three days to get them to stop doing it anytime I come around. And their clothes—look at their clothes. Not a button missing, not a stitch out of place. It's disgusting."

Rale laughed. "Come now, Ru. I'm sure that any number of caravan masters run an orderly operation."

"But not mine," Ru said. "Do you want this disguise to work?" he asked Errol. At his nod, he went on. "Then get these men to act a little more like Conger there—else the first real trading town we come to, our disguise will be ruined."

Errol glanced at Conger. The former priest was busy shaking a boot, his clothes so rumpled he looked like a pile of dirty laundry with arms and legs. When he felt their gazes on him, he gave a good-natured wave and belched.

Rale nodded. "Point taken, Master Ru. I'll speak to the guards and see if I can get them to take the edge off their usual discipline." He turned to Errol with the map extended before him. "Now, where to today, lad?"

"Where are we?" Errol asked.

Rale pointed, his index finger resting on symbols denoting two large villages, almost towns—Unich and Trier. Of the two, Unich lay closer to the great caravan route that ran through Longhollow, and then on to the province of Talia, and finally to the Forbidden Strait, which separated Illustra from Merakh.

"Trier sounds nice. Let's go through there."

Rale nodded as if the decision held little consequence. Errol hoped so, but he didn't intend on mapping out a route that would leave the caravan open to attack either. They were under way in minutes. Errol mounted Midnight, the horse Rale had given him months ago. Ru drove the caravan master's wagon, its side splashed with the purple-and-black diamond that identified him to other traders.

Errol gave him a smile. "I can't recall ever seeing a caravan that broke camp so quickly, Master Ru. Impressive, isn't it?"

Ru grunted without looking in Errol's direction.

"Yes," Errol continued, "quite impressive." He turned in his saddle to gesture at the precisely spaced wagons, each one with a guard at exactly the same point, as if each were a copy of the other. "And look how attentive they are to their duties. Yes, sir, you won't find any men like Loman Eck in this caravan."

Ru twisted in his seat to stab an icy glare at Errol. "Ha! Loman Eck would reduce half these men to buzzard food."

Errol's smile grew. "You mean *if* he was sober enough to be able to tell dirt from sky, right? You had just busted him to fifteenth for being drunk on duty when I joined the caravan, yes?"

The caravan master shifted in his seat and set his gaze forward. A touch on Errol's arm kept him from making his next verbal jab at Ru's expense. Rokha, her light brown eyes serious, rode next to him.

"Rale wants to see you at the back of the caravan."

A band tightened around Errol's chest. "Trouble?"

Rokha shook her head. The motion sent waves through her thick, black hair, which caught the sunlight. Over her shoulder, Merodach studied her, his face inscrutable. "I don't think so," she said. "But it's hard to tell with that one. He doesn't respond to trouble the way most men do."

Errol grimaced. "Probably because he's seen so much of it."

He pulled on the reins and clucked to Midnight. Rale rode at the rear of the caravan as if nothing untoward had happened. Errol eased his mount in beside him with a lift of his eyebrows.

"We're being followed," Rale said without turning around.

Errol cast a glance behind but the hilltop they'd just crested remained empty. "I don't see anything. Is it Valon?"

"I don't think so. These people ride like they're simply trying to overtake us. There are only three of them, so they're no threat in and of themselves." He pointed back over his shoulder. "They should crest the hill any moment now. When they do, tell me what you see. My eyes aren't as sharp as yours."

Rale's voice carried a strange undercurrent that Errol couldn't identify, but his mentor's face carried no hint at what might be amiss. Errol watched the hill, and when the riders crested it, he squinted in an effort to make out details. There were three men, one of them on the small side, sparsely provisioned for a quick journey.

"Perhaps they wish to ride with us for safe passage to the next village," Errol said.

Rale gave a slow nod. "Perhaps."

The small rider in the middle pointed in their direction, and the three eased into a canter. As they drew closer, Errol noticed the horses and their tack. "I think they're from Erinon. Might they be church messengers?"

Rale nodded, but there was something in the way he cocked his head to one side that put Errol on his guard. "The one in the middle bears the armband of a nuntius, and you are correct—the horses are from Erinon. They look good enough to come from the king's stables."

As the riders narrowed the distance a horrible suspicion

dawned on Errol. He knew what color the middle rider's eyes were, knew what must be tucked under the tight-fitting cap. A swirl of wind lifted the cloak of the rider on the left to reveal a splash of bright blue cloth. So that's how she found them.

"It can't be."

"I usually find that when I say those words, not only can it be, it probably is," Rale said. The smile in his voice was unmistakable now.

Errol turned on him. "I don't see what's so funny. If she can find us with a reader, so can Valon."

Rale waved away Errol's objection. "Valon has always been able to find us, Errol. What we're trying to prevent is his ability to organize an attack. Wiping out his forces in Steadham probably set him back a bit."

His voice dipped, and his dark eyes became intent. "Be careful of what you say before we know what game the princess plays."

Adora was close enough now that Errol could just begin to make out her delicate features. She closed the distance, reined in, and smiled at him, her green eyes flashing in the early light.

He was undone.

The watchman to Adora's right cleared his throat, ducked his head, and swept his arm to indicate the princess. "Nuntius of the first order, Dorrie Barwin, seeks Captain Elar of the watch."

"I trust the message is urgent, *nuntius*," Rale said with a bow from his vantage point on horseback. His tone emphasized Adora's feigned title as if urging everyone present to use it. "Else I would not expect the church to overtake us so soon after our departure." The amusement in his voice carried hints of steel within it.

The princess nodded in acknowledgment. "It is indeed, Captain Elar, but is of a sensitive nature and must be given to you and the omne, Earl Stone, privately."

Rale smirked, but his eyes remained serious. "Then, let us go apart so that you may disclose this urgency, nuntius."

Errol's mind descended into panicked burbles of semi-lucid thought. *Messenger?* Inconceivable. The king would never send Adora. *Private?* What could that mean? Through it all a horrified refrain of *no-no-no* echoed and reechoed through his mind. He wanted to run away but could think of no way to subvert the church's compulsion or the princess's claim on his heart. Instead he closed his mouth and followed Adora and Rale to the side of the road.

Rale bowed again. "Nuntius, I await your convenience."

"You are clever, Captain," Adora laughed.

Errol stared at the two of them, his head working back and forth as he searched for some acknowledgment of their danger. He darted a glance at the rest of the company. So far no one seemed to notice that things had just gone horribly, horribly wrong. "Are you insane," he hissed. They stared at him as if seeking some clarification of whom he addressed. He wasn't sure himself.

Adora smiled at his discomfort. "Earl Stone, I bear messages from the king for you and Captain Elar. Will you hear them?" She held herself erect as she recited the ritual greeting from a nuntius and spoke in tones that carried to the rear of the caravan.

"You do not," Errol shot. "The king would never send you to find us. By the three, are you trying to get me hanged?" He pulled at his hair in frustration. "No, they won't hang me." He made prancing motions with his hands imitating hooves for Adora and Rale to see. "They'll have me drawn and quartered, and then Lord Weir will have the horses stomp on the bits."

Rale put a hand on his arm. "Errol. Hear the prin . . . the messenger out. Perhaps there is more here than we suspect."

"More?" Errol clenched his jaws together, but his mouth ran ahead of him, and he bit off his words. "I don't want there to be more. By all that's holy, what is the penalty for kidnapping the king's n—?"

Adora stepped close, filled his vision. "They've given me to Lord Weir."

He gaped.

"That's right," she said, pointing back at her companions. "I spent the last week driving those two"—she nodded toward the reader and the watchman—"before me, searching for you." She gave a little smile. "Would you like to know where I was supposed to be yesterday?" The lift of her brows mocked his ignorance. "I was scheduled to be in the cathedral at Erinon entering into a formal betrothal."

Adora moved closer, until her eyes filled his vision. "Whether you want me or not, I will not marry that coward, that peacock." She stepped back. "You are in no worse danger now than you were before."

Rale bowed. "You are welcome to our company, Princess. Tell me, how did you convince those two to help you?"

Adora laughed. "Reader Whitcomb is so infatuated with me, he would have ridden directly to Merakh had I commanded it. Watchman Jens plays a more skilled game. He knows my departure from the palace is unsanctioned but refuses to acknowledge, even privately, that our trip is anything but a mission of the church."

Rale's face closed into cautiousness. "What persuaded Jens to help you, Princess? It seems to me he plays a dangerous game."

She smiled. "When he returns, he can feign shock and indignation at being so foully used by the king's niece. No one will believe him, of course, but what can they do? If your mission is successful, you and I will owe him a favor—a considerable advantage for an ambitious member of the watch."

Errol's pulse pounded through his temples. "I'll tell you what they can do. They can make me responsible for this insanity."

"But you're not responsible," Adora said.

His eyes bulged. "When has that mattered? They make me responsible for things that have nothing to do with me all the time. It's like I'm still a whipping boy—only now instead of a rod they're using politics." Feeling his panic starting to run away with him again, he took a deep breath.

"Do you want me to go back and marry Weir?" Adora asked.

Errol stared, unable to breathe or blink. He knew his mouth was hanging open. His teeth clicked when he closed it. "Why, of all the cheap, manipulative, underhanded—"

"Answer the question," Adora said. The look of confidence written in the hint of a smile and the unwrinkled skin between her brows told him she knew his answer already.

His heart, heavy as a stone, sank through his chest to end somewhere near his feet. "Of course not." He shook his head. "But they'll never let us be together now. Your uncle and Duke Weir will roast me as a kidnapper and a rogue for putting your life in danger. I can't say I'd blame them much. You should be someplace safe." He sighed. "Away from me and where I'm going."

"I outrank you."

"What?"

She laughed. "Earl Stone, I rarely stand on my title, but you are mine to command, became my uncle's and mine when you received your title and swore your oath." She shook her head. "No. The blame will be mine. I will make sure of it."

He felt relieved and hated himself for feeling it. "Is there any message?"

Adora's face grew serious, almost somber as she dismounted. "Only whatever meaning you derive from my presence, Earl Stone." She drew a dagger and made to cut a lock of hair that had escaped her cap.

Rale gasped and darted forward. His hand closed over the princess's, forcing it down. "Do not!" He hissed. "Not where you can be seen." His face flushed, and he checked over Errol's shoulder toward the rest of the company.

"Who knows why you left Erinon, Princess?" he growled.

Adora drew herself up. "I don't like your tone, Captain."

Rale's sudden change mystified Errol.

"Your likes and dislikes are no concern of mine, Princess. If you're going to draw attention to yourself, I will insist you leave. As Deas is my witness, if you even think of doing anything else to proclaim your royal blood, I'll drop you off with the nearest priest with instructions to take you back to Erinon—in chains, if necessary."

A swirl of thoughts made Errol dizzy. *Proclaim . . . ?* What had she done?

"You wouldn't," Adora said, but her eyes betrayed her doubt.

"I don't allow threats to my men, Princess. Not from you, not from the archbenefice, not from anyone. Others have made that mistake, to their regret. Does anyone besides those two know you were searching for us?"

Adora crossed her arms and presented her profile to the captain, refusing to answer.

"Errol," Rale said, "please have Master Ru pick two of the guards to accompany the princess back to Erinon."

She spun, met his gaze. "No. No one knows. I left a note for my ladies that I needed time to think and that I was headed for my uncle's estates outside of Baden.

Rale nodded. "Good. That's well north of here, but we still need to get rid of your companions." Sternness etched fissures in his smooth baritone. "I don't want dead weight on this trip."

She nodded. "I'll dismiss them immediately. I am certain they will keep their silence."

"You're going to let her stay?" Errol asked.

The look the captain gave Adora carried the threat of expulsion in it. "Yes. I don't want to diminish our company. And if I simply order her back to Erinon in the company of her companions, she'll just follow us."

"But we're going to Merakh."

His former master grew somber. "Boy, if we don't break Valon's circle, it won't matter where the princess is—we'll all be dead."

15

RETRACEMENT

MARTIN LOOKED across the rolling hills of Lugaria and winced. For most of his life, his ample stomach had been one of his most reliable advisors. If all was well, it merely growled when he ignored it for too long. When danger threatened, it tightened in anticipation of physical conflict. Yet now it lurched and roiled in his midsection like a boiling pot.

The source of his stomach's complaint mystified him. They'd eaten their midday meal only an hour ago. Martin could only conclude that his midsection had become aware of some subconscious train of thought that troubled him. But what?

Karele sat his horse, a small placid mare, as if he neither knew nor cared where they were going. The sight of the solis sent Martin's stomach into a series of tumbling maneuvers. He belched. The healer's presence unnerved him. Perhaps his stomach protested the death of his pride. The little man they'd picked up in Windridge, the man who'd saved them, might very well be his theological superior.

That Karele wielded power superior to Luis could no longer be contested. The survival of their mission in Windridge would have been proof enough, but the solis's ability to block or allow the casting of lots seemingly at will turned all of Martin's clerical experience and knowledge on its head. Knowledge—yes, that was the key and the curse all wrapped up in the same package. Every time Martin attempted to refute Karele's eldritch power, he learned—and regretted learning—something new.

He laughed out loud at himself, waved away the questioning looks from the rest of the party, and continued to chuckle at his foolishness. Oh yes, he'd disguised it to himself as prudence, but what he'd really wanted was to figure out a way to be rid of the solis. But three nights ago, camped in the middle of the grasslands of northern Avenia, he'd completely outsmarted himself.

Martin had waited until the solis snored in his blanket, tiptoed across the ground, and forced Luis to cast to test the healer's allegiance. Luis had carved the lots as if he'd known what the cast would be before he made it. Perhaps he had, but he went through the motions anyway. Three dozen times they pulled one of the spheres from Luis's burlap sack. Thirty-three times the lots said the solis served Deas.

As he now rode, Martin chortled. "I'm a coward." His horse cocked one ear at the sound and continued his plodding.

Luis smiled. "Really?"

"Hardly that," Karele said. The small man straightened in his saddle. "I doubt Deas would have chosen you to bring the knowledge of Aurae to the Judica if you lacked courage."

The words failed to comfort Martin or his stomach. The sound of a single horse ridden at an easy canter offered a welcome distraction. Cruk, looking almost normal, reined in.

He directed his concern to Luis. "Are you sure this is the main road between Lugaria and Sorland?"

The secondus nodded. As a reader, Luis knew the provinces of the kingdom in exhaustive detail. His training demanded it.

Cruk shook his head as if he were trying to rid himself of a suspicion that refused to leave. "It feels wrong."

Martin surveyed the way ahead. The hard-packed earthen road, interrupted by cobblestones or bricks in the villages, seemed peaceful enough. A farmer hauling turnips to the next village, Goran, preceded them by a couple hundred paces. Other than that, they had the road to themselves. After all that had happened in Windridge, Martin was just as happy for the solitude.

"Do you sense anything amiss, Luis?" Martin asked.

The secondus shook his head.

Martin turned to Karele. The solis sat his horse as before, calm, unperturbed. Martin forced the words past the stubborn knot in his throat. "And you, master healer, do you sense anything wrong?"

Karele smiled as if he sensed Martin's internal struggle. "No. Aurae isn't telling me anything, but if I may make a suggestion . . . ?"

Cruk nodded.

"We could overtake the farmer ahead of us and ask him if he knows if aught is amiss."

Martin hid his surprise. "So you credit our captain's unease without confirmation."

Karele's smile held a note of triumph whose justification eluded Martin. "I'm sure we'll find the captain's suspicions are justified. This is his area of expertise, after all."

They kicked their horses into a canter, but as they neared the farmer he cracked the reins to force his team into a gallop. Turnips flew from the cart at each bounce. Martin caught a brief look of white-faced terror on the driver. Cruk urged his mount to a gallop and caught the farmer after a quarter mile. Even Karele's placid mount would have had no trouble catching farm horses.

Martin drew even with the farmer opposite Cruk. Tears rolled down the man's face while he urged his horses on, reins clutched with one hand and trying to unsheathe an ancient-looking sword with the other.

"Goodman!" Martin yelled. "Goodman farmer, stop." He held up the symbol of his office. The sun glinted off the polished emblem, and the reflection hit the farmer in the eyes. He started, dropped the sword, and sawed the reins. The horses skipped to a stop.

Tears rolled down his cheeks and his chin quivered. "Thank Deas, Pater. I was sure you were raiders come to take my turnips."

Cruk's eyes narrowed. "Why would you think that?"

The farmer avoided looking at Cruk, chose instead to address his answer to Martin. "Because of the raids."

Cruk's jaw came forward and he inhaled, but Martin held up a hand.

"What sort of raids?"

The farmer's eyes widened. "Have you not heard, Pater?"

Martin kept his tone gentle. "We're just lately come to Goran, goodman."

"Well, they burned Tomlin's farm to the ground not three leagues from here—all the rutabagas went up in flames. And I heard tell that they hit the villages and farms to the east as they came through, stealing the produce they wanted and torching the rest."

Cruk cursed, his patience at an obvious end. "Who came through?" Martin could hear the captain grinding his teeth.

"Why, the Morgols, Pater."

"Have you seen them?" Cruk grated.

The farmer jerked. "I don't need to see them to know what the mayor in the village says or to know what smoke in the sky at midday means." He pointed down the road. "I'm bound for Goran with my first load of turnips of the season. If I didn't need the money, I wouldn't be going. I raise the best turnips in the region." He held a purple-and-white sample up for Martin's inspection, beaming with pride. "Are you bound for Goran, Pater?"

Martin nodded. "We'd be happy to accompany you, goodman. Please lead on." He signaled Cruk, and the captain fell back to join him, Luis, and Karele at the rear of the wagon.

Cruk snorted. "I'll warrant the farmer doesn't know much beyond growing turnips. Any idiot who's seen a Morgol could tell we weren't from the steppes, even at two hundred paces."

Luis nodded. "True, but something has him spooked, and the traffic on the road is less than it should be."

A new worry dropped into Martin's gut to fester there with the rest. "I dislike what he said about the villages to the east. Morgol raiders here? Now? Might they have overtaken Callowford?"

They crested a hill. Below, a cluster of thatched roofs and chimneys drifting welcome tendrils of woodsmoke told Martin they'd arrived at Goran. A low fence reinforced with a new palisade of sharpened poles surrounded the village. The road in and out was manned by a middle-aged man who brandished a sword like a club and a younger man in a bedraggled uniform of some local nobleman. Martin stifled a flash of disappointment at the absence of a church. A priest would give a more coherent report.

"Perhaps the villagers will provide us a more cogent report than our farmer," Luis said.

Cruk harrumphed. "It would be difficult to give less."

The men on the road swung open the fortified gate at a wave from the farmer, but the looks they gave Martin and the rest were hard. Cruk reined in, leaned forward in his saddle toward the guards. "Could you direct us to your mayor?"

The first man, burly with a blacksmith's shoulders, gripped his sword and eyed Cruk with open distrust. "What's your business in Goran, stranger?"

"Our business is our own, neighbor, and—"

Martin put a hand on Cruk's arm. "We're heading east, goodman. We're hoping your mayor will be able to advise us on the best route."

The second guard hawked and spat. "There ain't no best route, leastways none that head east. Morgols are coming over the mountains. Blast me if they ain't."

The blacksmith nodded. "That's it."

The knot in Martin's gut twisted tighter. Witnesses were piling up, and even accounting for the natural unreliability of people who spoke from fear, the agreement among tales spoke of something very wrong in the province. "Our business cannot be delayed, I'm sorry to say. Which way did you say the mayor was?"

The blacksmith jerked his thumb toward a small timbered inn with a slate roof halfway down the street. "Bolger's in the inn."

Martin nodded thanks, which the two men didn't bother to

return, and followed Cruk through the mud of the village's main thoroughfare. The smell of turnips mingled with the sour odors of sweat and fear of the villagers he passed. Furtive looks came to them from old men and youths, widowers and lasses, and even children. This last stuck to him like a sodden tunic. Children in villages all over Illustra greeted visitors with frank curiosity. What had happened to make these little ones so cautious of strangers?

Bolger sat at a large round table in the inn, an empty tankard in front of him, his tunic stretched over girth that made Martin feel slim by comparison. A handful of men with short bows stood behind him, attentive. Martin's first impression was dispelled by the presence of maps spread across the expanse of the table and the sharp eyes that searched him and his friends as they entered the dim interior.

"Are you Mayor Bolger?"

The man snorted. "Only when there's trouble. When there's not you'll likely have to ask after me by less complimentary names." Bolger's eyes scanned them again, rested on Karele as if the man were a riddle and then moved on. "You have the look of authority. You'll not be in the market for turnips, I'm guessing." He pointed with his chin at Cruk. "He wears his weapons like they're a part of him."

Martin nodded. "You're a perceptive man, Mayor Bolger. We'd prefer not to announce our presence too loudly in the region."

The man's eyes, little more than slits in his fleshy face, narrowed until they almost disappeared. "If you bring trouble on us, I'll do my best to make sure you regret it. Now, unless you can prove to me you're not highwaymen on the run, I'll have to ask you to leave."

A whisper of movement behind Bolger caught Martin's attention. The mayor's men, dour and efficient, had each nocked arrows. A small movement, too small to be prevented, would bring those bows up to target each of them.

Martin held up his hands, palms forward. "I'm going to reach into my cloak very slowly, Master Bolger. I'd appreciate it if your men didn't take my movement as a threat."

Bolger held up a hand. The arrows didn't rise to their target, but they didn't lower, and the bowstrings still held their tension. Martin pulled his symbol of office from his pocket and placed it on the table.

Bolger didn't seem impressed. "How do I know you didn't take this off someone?"

Martin allowed his irritation to show. "The soldier behind me is a captain of the watch. I can perform any rite of the church you care to name"—he shot a suggestive glance at Bolger's men—"including last rites."

The mayor's cheeks bunched up like summer clouds before a rain with laughter. The men behind him didn't laugh. Instead they eyed Cruk the way dogs looked at a wolf.

"What can I do for you, Excellency?" Bolger asked.

Martin pulled a chair and seated himself. Karele didn't wait for an invitation. Luis followed suit. Cruk remained where he was, standing like a plinth of granite, his hand on his sword.

"We need information on the villages to the east."

On a thinner man, Bolger's scowl would have brought his eyebrows together. As it was, it only succeeded in bunching the flesh of his forehead into concentrated lumps of ire.

"It's not good." The mayor's expression transformed him into a clothed bear. "So far we've only seen scouts and small raiding parties. But here . . . " He pointed to the closest map in front of him, his pudgy finger covering the Sprata Mountains that lay east and north of Callowford. "The routes to Sligo and Muin are gone."

"Gone?" Cruk asked. "What do you mean gone? Be clear, man."

Bolger's face grew stiff. "There's no traffic in or out of those villages."

"Why not?" Martin asked.

"Haven't you been listening, Pater? The Morgols have them."

"Nonsense," Cruk said. "There's no way to get enough men to stage a raid over the mountains, much less hold a pair of villages. They'd lose eight out of ten just trying. Then they'd have to fight their way past the garrison at Balinsloe first."

Bolger didn't bother to refute Cruk's assertions—just gazed at him with the unassailable certainty of a man confident in his own knowledge. "Eight out of ten, you say? It makes you wonder what's so important here in the land of sheep and turnips that they'd sacrifice so many men." His sarcastic growl answered Cruk's. "Balinsloe is gone, watchman."

"How would you know that?" Cruk demanded.

"You rode past one of the few survivors of the garrison on your way to see me. Soldier Bier was scouting when the Morgols came pouring down out of the icy mountains like the vengeance of Deas."

A knife of cold certainty pierced Martin's stomach. He knew. Luis could cast for it, but it wasn't necessary. The kingdom's enemies outpaced them. How many hundreds or thousands of Morgols had died in the mountains to get a raiding party into the Sprata region?

He pointed at the map. "How far have they come?"

The mayor's mouth pulled to one side in a gesture equivalent to a shrug. "I don't know for certain, but the best reports we have indicate that there are two contingents heading west toward this area."

Martin watched with dread as Bolger's finger landed on an area marked with two names: Berea and Callowford. Karele stirred at his side. Dread chased acceptance across the healer's face. Martin put a hand against the splintered boards of the table to steady himself. What was happening in Callowford? A voice in Martin's head told him he was already too late.

"Pincer movement." Cruk's brief assessment fell like the stroke of an executioner's axe.

Martin squeezed his eyes shut, as if he could deny the truth. His military experience amounted to listening to the occasional tale from one of the watch or the confession of some postulant who'd come to the priesthood from the guard. Even with his limited experience, however, he knew the fate of the villages they traveled toward.

Karele stepped forward, and Martin noted again just how

small the solis was. "Do you have any idea when those bands will reach Berea and Callowford, Mayor Bolger?"

The mayor considered the question while he squirmed. The joints of his chair squeaked in protest. "We don't know how fast they can travel. According to Soldier Bier, only one Morgol in ten had a horse. How fast can men bred to the saddle march?" One fat finger shifted significantly on the map. "They have to cover twenty leagues, all of it mountainous."

"Have the villagers been warned?" Luis asked.

Bolger's neck waddled with his answer. "Not by us. But I'm sure someone from the garrison has gotten word to them by now."

"Really?" Cruk's voice cut across the mayor's assertion like a crashing of boulders. "Assumptions like that kill people, Bolger."

The mayor's eyes challenged Cruk's before he nodded. "True enough, but I can't spare a man to run messages. You tell them."

Karele turned to Martin, a sudden air of authority lending him stature. "We must beat the Morgols to Callowford." His eyes burned as he clutched Martin's sleeve. "We must."

Cruk stepped forward. "I want to talk to Bier first. We need to know what happened at Balinsloe."

Karele brushed aside his demand as if Cruk's concern were inconsequential. "We know what happened, Captain. The Morgols attacked with enough numbers to overrun the garrison, and brave men of Illustra died. Their bodies are lying in Balinsloe Pass, frozen in the snow. What else do you want to know?"

Cruk glared, but Karele's ruthless assessment silenced his dissension.

16

BY MOONLIGHT

THEY ROTATED HORSES to pull every league possible from the beasts each day. Luis and Karele, thin and light, offered Martin's mount a breather as they rode up and down the slopes for Berea. The hardwoods sprinkled through the hills showed brilliant colors any weaver would envy, and the scent of pine and cedar in the cool moist air was like a friend's greeting after a long absence. But Martin's initial joy of reacquainting himself with the Sprata region turned to worry that left the muscles of his face weary with fatigue from constant frowning. After each change he found himself urging his new horse to a canter. Karele matched his pace, his lower lip tucked between his teeth, a mannerism of which the solis seemed unaware.

Each time Martin and the healer kicked their mounts to a gallop, Cruk would call to them in his voice like breaking rocks, telling them to keep it to a trot or risk losing the horses altogether. After the fourth time in the same day, Martin ground his teeth.

"Walk the mounts," Cruk said.

Martin tried not to take the command as a personal insult.

"Why? We're still ten leagues out, and they don't seem that tired yet."

Cruk didn't bother to nod or shrug, he merely pointed at the empty road ahead as if that explained everything.

For the last six hours Martin's mind had conjured scenes of their return to Callowford, each more disastrous than the one before. Caught within a product of his imagination where everyone and anyone who could help them had been killed, he snapped his reply. "Explain your command, Captain."

Cruk's eyes widened, then narrowed at the tone and the use of his rank. He pursed his lips and bowed, deep and extravagant for being on horseback. "There's nothing on the road, *Pater*. We haven't seen a farmer or merchant since before noon. In the last day, not one caravan loaded with Callowford stone has passed us going west." He pointed ahead to the peak of the long hill they climbed. "We have to get off this road. Let's circle around that hill."

"Impossible," Martin's frustration at his ignorance boiled over. "We have to get to Callowford." He turned to Karele, searching for an ally against Cruk's suggestion.

The solis shook his head. "If the captain is here to guide us in matters concerning combat, then, in the absence of any other knowledge, we should defer to his experience."

"Well said," Luis murmured.

Cruk nodded as if that settled the matter. "We need to make a decision."

Martin forced his voice to a neutral tone. "Which is?"

"Do we make for Berea or Callowford?"

The intent of the captain's question was plain. Berea was closer, but Callowford was more likely to hold the answers they sought. Unbidden, a score of faces rose before him, all residents of Berea whose names and grips were known to him. How could he just ride past them, leaving them unwarned?

"Berea," Karele said before Martin could answer. When they looked in his direction, his posture gave no hint of apology or compromise, but Martin sensed an odd reluctance within him. "Adele is there. I must speak with her."

"Did Aurae tell you this?"

The solis shook his head.

Martin nodded. "My heart says Berea as well. At the very least we need to warn them of the Morgols—if it isn't already too late."

Cruk's response was a twitch of the reins that took his mount off the road into the woods that lay south. Martin followed, his imagination resuming its assault.

The trees thickened, and they picked their way through the underbrush at a walk. Cruk eschewed any path that showed signs of recent use. Time and again, the captain had them wait until he scouted the area ahead. When they stopped for the night, they were still five leagues short of Berea.

They tethered the horses, and the four of them sat in a rough circle around the spot where a fire would have given them warmth had they dared risk such a beacon. A gibbous moon cast shadows, giving them the look of phantoms. Luis stirred, his hands twitching in the moonlight as if they itched to cast.

Martin allowed himself a smile. In moments Luis would retrieve wood and steel from his pockets or saddlebags and find some pressing question that required the use of his craft. When he rose a moment later, Karele put out a hand to stop him.

"It would be unwise to cast just now."

The moon glinted briefly off Luis's eyes, turning his pupils green for a split second as he turned. "Why? I think we should check to see if the Morgols are in Berea before us." He paused. "Adele may have left already."

Karele nodded. "True, but if the Morgols have brought theurgists over the mountains, we will all be in danger."

The healer's tone suggested more than just familiarity to Martin. "What do you know of the Morgols and their religion, Karele?"

Karele shrugged. "The people of the Jhengjin have a reverence for horses. Much of their religion comes to them from so long ago that the origins have been lost, but their legends tell of a tree that both saves and condemns the world." Moonlight reflected from the healer's gaze.

"That sounds a bit like our own history," Luis murmured.

Karele nodded. "Yes, before the book was lost to us. The Morgols do not have a rich tradition of writing like Illustra or Merakh. Their tradition is oral, and many of the truths that Aurae placed into their tradition have been corrupted."

Karele stirred, but it appeared as if the shadows moved the man. "They are ruled by a jheng, a type of clan chief, and by their theurgists, those who are born with the same talent that gives Illustra its readers and Merakh its ghostwalkers." As he turned to face Luis, the moonlight lit half his face, but the other half lay in complete shadow.

"If they have a theurgist with them, the exercise of your talent will call to him, Secondus, like a lodestone to iron."

"What of Aurae?" Martin's voice sounded clipped, brusque in the confines of their circle. He didn't care.

"As I told you before, Aurae has not spoken to me since I was told to come with you."

"That's pretty inconvenient," Cruk said.

Karele nodded, but now the moonlight glinted off his amused smile. His hand lifted to take in their small camp. "I have often thought so myself, but Deas does not answer to me."

Karele's imperturbability grated. The only time Martin had seen him show concern of any type was when they discovered the Morgols had crossed the mountains and that Adele and Radere might be in danger. Martin had liked him better then. The solis seemed more human when he looked worried. This unflappable peace the healer exuded unnerved him.

Cruk rose. "I'm going to scout. There must be a reason for the lack of traffic on the roads." His shape melted into the forest. Martin's gaze followed him for as long as the moonlight allowed, but the watchman moved through the underbrush with the ease of a deer. When Martin blinked, his friend was gone.

Curiosity warred with his discomfort. As usual, curiosity won. "You speak as if you'd journeyed to the steppes, Karele. Your words have the ring of firsthand experience."

The solis nodded. "You're perceptive, Pater. I was taken captive by the Morgols in the Steppes War twenty years ago."

Luis's gasp of shock was slightly louder than Martin's. He wouldn't have heard it otherwise. "The horsemen don't take captives."

Karele shrugged, and his teeth flashed again in the silver gleam of the moon. "True. As a general rule they do not."

The solis paused, whether in memory or unwillingness to remember, Martin couldn't tell.

"What was it like?" Luis asked.

"It was the life of any slave," Karele said. His voice dipped so that Martin had to lean forward to catch every word. "I served Ablajin. His rank would have been equivalent to a lieutenant, I think. He made me a menial servant, and I waited upon him with all the diligence I could muster." Karele shrugged. "He was a very practical man. Ablajin did not believe in wasting slaves or supplies. Competence he rewarded with life, incompetence with death." His chuckle nestled behind Martin's ears. "I tried very hard to be competent."

"Why do they fight us?" Martin asked. He wished very much that the kingdom would not have to fight a two-front war. Even the most incompetent soldier knew the likely outcome of such an eventuality.

"The Morgol society is at once simple and complex," Karele said. "Like the Merakhi, they hold the family and the clan as the means to govern. Their language has a beauty and economy of speech that makes even the dullest conversation sound like poetry."

The solis let forth a stream of syllables that fell on Martin's ears like a clarion call to battle, and his heart raced in spite of his incomprehension. "I just said the weather looks to be turning colder." He sighed, his breath catching the moonlight in the cool air like the hint of mist. "Yet unlike the men of the southern continent, they do not maintain cities as such, and interclan fights over water and pasture are common."

"Perhaps their numbers are not as great as we've heard," Luis said. The pitch of his words rose toward the end, the effort of a man trying to sound hopeful.

"They are greater and yet not so great," Karele answered. "The steppes stretch for a thousand leagues to the east, and the Morgols rule all of it through their cunning and horsemanship. Yet, the far eastern Morgols have no interest in the kingdom."

He turned toward Martin. "But to answer your question, the Morgols of the western steppes see the kingdoms as nothing more than an opportunity ripe for plunder. They have no interest in our religious war with the Merakhi, but once we've committed to the southern flank, I expect they will come pouring through the gaps in the mountains in a tide that will make the Steppes War of twenty years ago look like a border skirmish."

"How do you know all this?" Martin asked, his tone holding a hint of demand.

"I told you, Pater. I was a slave among them." Karele's voice and the tilt of his head in the gloom held hints of amusement as if at some unspoken jest.

Luis leaned forward, caught the healer's attention. "How long were you a slave, Karele?"

"Over nineteen years."

"But . . . that's impossible."

Karele's voice came to him gently mocking. "Don't you say that with Deas all things are possible, Pater?"

He spluttered, trying to find words—no, trying to find thoughts that wouldn't come. "How did you get away?"

"Nine years ago, Ablajin made me master of his horses. You must understand; the horselords worship their mounts. For him to make me master of his horses was like a man of the kingdom adopting a servant as his heir. A Morgol barbarian raised me from the status of slave to son."

Karele grew silent, then continued. "There is much in the Morgols that is worthy of redemption, Pater."

"Why didn't you return to the kingdom then?" Luis asked. "Why did you stay?"

"The briefest answer is that Aurae didn't tell me to—" a brief catch, almost a sob, interrupted Karele's words, but he quickly continued—"but the truth is that I had come to see Ablajin not just as my master, nor as my adoptive father, but my father, in truth. My own father is unknown to me, and I discovered a hunger for Ablajin's approval that surprised even me." His exhale sounded like a soft moan of loss and regret. "The word of Aurae came to me . . . a year ago, telling me to return to the kingdom. I made my way at last to Windridge."

"How did you escape?" Karele's words held him spellbound, as if the solis had learned the theurgy of the Morgols and was using it to hold Martin captive.

"I didn't," Karele answered. "I went to Ablajin and told him everything. I think I was secretly hoping that he would lose his temper and enslave me, but I underestimated Deas's call. My father embraced me as a son and gave me the best of his horses." The healer's voice cracked, splinters of pain filled Martin's ears. "Do you know what that means to a horselord? No, of course not. It took me nearly two decades to learn.

"I was amazed at how easily I slipped through the clans to the north of us and over the gap into Frataland. When I showed up at the first outpost, the guard nearly passed out from fright when he saw me. I spoke to him in unaccented kingdom speech, and he laughed with such relief I understood what the weight of war would mean."

They fell silent. Martin dozed as the shadows from the moon shifted and stretched as that silver orb tracked through the sky toward her appointment with the horizon.

A hand on his shoulder startled him. He hadn't been aware that he slept. In the east a swath of slate gray against the black of the nighttime sky told him dawn approached.

"We have trouble," Cruk said.

The others came awake. "How so?" Luis asked.

"Berea and Callowford are surrounded."

A twig crunched under Martin's foot. He winced and froze. Thirty paces away a Morgol guard, part of a large patrol, jerked his head, but a deer close to Martin broke cover, and the guard continued his patrol. Twelve men, most with dark, wispy beards and almond-shaped eyes, argued in the same language Karele had used last night. Despite his lack of understanding, Martin thought their voices carried the tension of doubt.

One of the Morgols, a young man with slashes of blood or paint running down each jawline, made peremptory gestures, ordering the rest. But his motions held the rushed jerkiness of a man in authority who did not wish to be questioned because he didn't know what to do. Another Morgol, a thickset man with broad shoulders, addressed the commander and received a blistering tirade in response. The men of the patrol split to resume their cordon of Berea.

Cruk settled into the undergrowth next to Martin. "There's no way to get through during the daylight, with or without the horses. We'll have to wait for dark."

Martin's stomach tightened. Waiting put them at the mercy of events and the capriciousness of whoever led the Morgols. "What if they find us? What if they march on Berea today or tonight?"

"I think we're safe," Cruk said. "For a while, anyway. We're outside the perimeter they've set." He shook his head, his dirty blond hair lifted with the motion. "Curse me, but I have no idea what's keeping them from squeezing Berea and Callowford like overripe grapes."

"They don't know what to do," Karele said.

"What's holding them back?" Martin asked.

"The one with the red slashes is a theurgist. That means this is a holy mission to them. They won't make a move unless he tells them to."

"So why aren't they moving?" Cruk asked. "Not that I'm objecting, mind you."

Karele smiled. "Aurae is blocking the theurgist's access to his familiar. They've come this far, but they don't know what to do next."

Martin nodded. "That would explain his temper. I've noticed insecure men don't handle uncertainty well."

Karele nodded.

Cruk's soft laugh punctuated the healer's nod. "All right, we'll wait until dark, but I don't see any way to take the horses with us."

"I can keep them quiet," Karele said.

At a look from Cruk, the healer shrugged. "It's a long story, and already told, but I know horses."

Cruk nodded but looked doubtful. "I just hope we get there before the soldiers decide to ignore that popinjay and take the assault into their own hands."

"It won't happen," Karele said. "A theurgist's word is absolute. More's the pity. If it were not, war with the Morgols might be avoided."

They withdrew and spent the day sleeping in shifts. Karele and Cruk fell asleep as soon as they settled into their cloaks, but though Luis insisted he take the first watch shift, Martin struggled to quiet his mind enough to rest. He opened his eyes to find the secondus staring at him from his lookout spot by a large beech log.

"You can't sleep?" Luis asked.

Martin shook his head. "My head is filled with thoughts that chase each other 'round and 'round."

"It's odd, isn't it?"

Martin could tell from Luis's tone that he wasn't addressing Martin's statement. "What is?"

"That the person who saves us in Windridge is one of the few people in the kingdom with firsthand knowledge of the Morgols."

Martin sighed. That had been one of the thoughts that denied him rest. "Too coincidental."

Luis chuckled. "Is it so hard to see the hand of Deas in his appearance, my friend?"

Martin shook his head. "No, it's too hard to miss. It has all the subtlety of a hammer to the skull." He sighed again. "Which gives me no opportunity to refute that we are guided by Deas's hand. He has always dealt with my stubbornness that way." He pressed his palms to his forehead. "The church will look like an anthill that's been kicked."

"Perhaps not," Luis said.

"I consider myself an open-minded man, Luis, and Karele's revelations scare me right down to my toes. Churchmen don't give up their cherished beliefs easily."

The secondus shrugged. "No one does."

They fell silent after that. But though the others took turns at the watch, Martin could not shake his restlessness and did not sleep.

After an eternity, the sky in the east began to purple. Karele returned from his watch by the road and began rummaging through his bags. The healer brought forth an array of bottles, testing the contents of each. When he appeared to find the one he wanted, he rose and sought Cruk.

"We'll need to muffle the horse's hooves, Captain."

The watchman shook his head. "They won't like it. They'll shy on us."

Karele shook his head in denial. "No. I'll take care of it. Just make sure that their hooves don't clatter against any stones. The Morgols have few horses with them. If they hear ours, they'll know we're here."

Cruk's search for material to wrap the horse's hooves yielded little. Finally, with a curse he shed his cloak and began ripping it into wide strips with his dagger. "I've had this cloak for seven years." His face took on a look of pain, as if bidding a fond acquaintance farewell.

"We'll get you a new one," Martin offered.

"It won't be the same," Cruk grunted. "I knew the circumstance behind every bloodstain on this one." He huffed, turned to Karele. "Do you think you could get your spirit guide to give us a little cloud cover? The moon will be almost full tonight."

Karele laughed. "Your prayers are as effective as mine or the priest's, Captain. If you want clouds, ask for clouds."

Cruk's face pinched into a sour expression of disappointment. "What if Deas says no?"

The healer shrugged as he poured a thick amber liquid from the bottle onto his hands. A scent of camphor, lemongrass, walnut, lavender, and other less definable odors pierced the air. "Then you won't get any clouds."

Luis laughed.

Martin pointed to the sheen on Karele's hands. "What is that?"

"It's an ointment the Morgols use to soothe their horses."

Cruk grunted. "Liniment? Salve is going to save us?"

Karele drew himself up. "It's not salve. I was master of horses for nine years. Every master makes his own oil. This is mine. Watch."

He moved to Cruk's horse.

"You don't want to do that," Cruk said. "He's trained not to trust any hand but mine."

"I'll accept the consequences of my actions, Captain." Karele approached, hands forward, making soft noises in the Morgol language. The smell of the healer's oil hung in the air and the singsong of his voice lulled Martin into a sudden lassitude. His head bobbed forward, and he jerked upright in an effort to stay awake.

Cruk's horse bared his teeth when the healer drew near, but Karele continued his slow advance, hands forward. The stallion shook his head, mane flying, but the teeth were no longer bared. Then Karele caught the horse's nose with one hand and the bridle with the other. He led the horse forward and back, then side to side, crooning all the while. After a few minutes the stallion quieted, standing still.

"Impressive." Luis nodded in acknowledgment of the healer's skill.

Cruk looked awed and annoyed at the same time. Karele moved to the next horse. When the last trace of light died from the western sky, they set out for the Morgol perimeter. Karele moved to lead.

"How are you going to lead us, healer?" Cruk asked. "You've never been here before."

Karele's voice floated out of the darkness. "You'll direct me, but unless anyone else here knows how to speak the Morgol tongue, I'm the only one who can talk us past the guards if we're seen."

Cruk snorted. "Do you think that will save us?"

"Save us?" Karele echoed. "No, I'm hoping I'll be able to buy you enough time to get clear." When no one spoke, the solis went on. "When we get to the road I'll take each of the horses across."

Martin's insides jumbled into a disordered pile. The more he tried to calm himself, the worse the tangle became. His diaphragm worked to pull the cool autumn air into his lungs. What neither Karele nor Cruk had said stared him in the face, threatening and unavoidable. He possessed no woodcraft.

Cruk, large though he might be, had practiced the ways of the watch for years, learning how to move through the forest without a sound. Karele, small and nimble, might have been a rabbit for all the traces he left. Even Luis moved by the glow of the newly risen moon with assurance.

He, however, was a fat priest whose stealth was limited to theological discussions and political maneuvering. With his reluctance beating in his chest, he tugged on Karele's tunic. "I need to go last."

The solis opened his mouth to object, caught Martin's glance, and pressed his lips together with a nod.

It took them an hour to reach the spot where they had seen the patrol that morning. Cruk had been forced to clear a path, necessitating unnumbered pauses to move obstacles that might give them away. Even so, it seemed Martin's every step brought the telltale crack of a twig. Nervous sweat soaked his tunic. Curse his clumsy hide, he was going to get them all killed.

They hid in a gully at a turn in the road between Berea and Callowford and waited. Martin watched in sick fascination as the moon climbed higher in the cloudless sky and prayed the guard in charge of this section of road would come and go quickly. Once the moon cleared the trees, the light would provide more than enough illumination to discern the bulk of a comfortably fed priest.

He'd just mustered the courage to suggest they retreat and wait for another night and more cloud cover when the soft crunch of footsteps on the road stopped his breathing. A short figure, lightly clothed despite the chill, approached from a large open track in the woods, walking with the lazy, disinterested steps of the bored. He stopped in the middle of the road to gaze in the distance each way and with an audible sigh moved on.

Karele pulled his hands from beneath his cloak, the sudden odor of liniment strong in the air, and led Cruk's horse down the road. Cruk followed, his sword glinting like a promise of death in the silver light of the moon. Neither the horse nor the men who moved with it made a sound. Martin watched them until distance or darkness—he couldn't tell which—swallowed them.

Martin waited next to Luis, determined not to speak. The minutes passed in a tortured agony of uncertainty when Karele did not return. How long would it be before another guard passed by?

The moon crested the trees. To Martin the sudden flood of reflected light looked like a condemnation. Still Karele didn't return. A ghost of movement to his right caught his attention, and he hunkered lower to the ground like a turtle withdrawing into its shell. A guard moved with purposeful strides, as if assured in the knowledge that there was nothing to see on his patrol, now or ever. He swung a sabre as he moved, slicing through stray plants that presented themselves. The edge of his sword glinted and disappeared by turns, and the tops of the plants he cut fell straight down, testimony to the keen edge he kept on the blade. Martin rubbed his neck.

Ten minutes after the guard passed, a figure emerged from the far shadows of the road and approached their hiding spot. Karele.

"What took you so long?" Martin whispered.

"Their path parallels the road for a way," Karele said. "It was necessary to get beyond it before returning. Cruk and his horse are safe. Come, reader. You and your horse will accompany me now." He moved his hands to stroke the horse's nose with his oil.

A sudden terror gripped Martin, and he grabbed Luis's hand. "Take care, my friend."

The reader nodded and moved to take his place next to Karele, who surveyed the roadway with studious intensity. On impulse, Martin stepped up to Luis's horse, took its head in his hands, and blessed it. *Be silent.*

The three—healer, reader, and horse—moved off into the semi-darkness to leave Martin in the gully once more. Ten paces behind him his horse, probably lonely, whickered softly. He moved back to the mare and rubbed her nose the way he'd seen Karele do it. Bemused, he stroked the horse, the smell of liniment wafting up to him from his hands.

He drifted, lulled by the smell and the rhythm of his hands stroking his mare. When Karele touched his elbow, he started, and his horse shied.

"Quiet, Pater," the healer said. "We must move quickly. Something has agitated the patrol. They no longer move predictably."

They retraced their steps to the gully by the edge of the road and stopped. There, a single guard stood, turning in slow circles, his head lifted and his sword clenched tight in his hand. Without the blade he would have made an almost comical figure. A minute passed, but the guard refused to move on, continued to turn.

Karele's breath, hot and urgent, fell on his ear. "Cover your hands if you want to see dawn, priest. He smells the oil." The healer covered Martin's horse's nose with his cloak.

Martin shoved his hands under his tunic even as his brain yammered, *It's not enough! It's on my clothes!*

The guard turned a few more circles, interrupted at intervals as if he'd lost the scent, and then moved on.

Karele pulled at him, urging him up from the gully. "Go, I'll be right behind you."

His feet shuffled against the dirt and rock of the road. He couldn't breathe. Cramps in his side kept him from drawing air, and spots of darkness danced on the moonlit landscape. He pulled his hands from under his tunic and sniffed. Calmed, he moved down the road, across the path of the patrol and into safety. Behind him, Karele followed with the horse, the sound of Morgol assurances flowing from his lips.

Forty paces behind them, a guttural voice cried a challenge.

17

THE MASTER OF HORSES

MARTIN PRAYED THE MORGOL wouldn't hear his heart beating like a hammer against an anvil in his chest. The sentry's voice cried out another challenge.

"Goreth ulalor ujin!"

Karele's voice came, whispered and urgent. "Don't move. Don't speak." The solis pivoted where he stood to face the Morgol sentry. *"Alath nejisin ulaat. Korenanath ul ujinsa ta."*

The guard's voice came to them from out of the darkness, closer now. A surge, like the rushing of the tide, roared through Martin's ears. His horse stood between him and the sentry, offering him cover, but flashes of moonlight glinted off the Morgol's curved saber, illuminating a wicked hook at the end.

Karele took a step toward the guard, his hands at his sides, and responded, his voice framing an unfamiliar mix of words that sounded as if he were trying to swallow his own tongue.

"Verya?"

The question in the Morgol's voice was unmistakable, and he brandished his weapon. Martin gripped his horse's mane and prayed he would be able to launch himself onto the horse's back before the guard came too close.

Karele barked a laugh laced with derision back at the sentry. *"Nejisin neighisa ulan, sopt."*

Martin reiterated desperate prayers as he tried to peer through the darkness where death waited. Spots swam in his vision against the backdrop of night. He'd forgotten to breathe. With the best effort he could muster, he pulled a quiet, shuddering breath into his lungs. When the hammering of his heart subsided, he picked up sounds of the sentry moving off. Karele's grip on his arm blocked a sob of relief that threatened to tear its way past his lips.

After another minute the solis's hand dropped. "Deas is merciful," he said. "Come, a Morgol guard is as unquestioning as a kingdom soldier, but a chance conversation with another sentry will reveal our deception and bring them down on us."

After his vision cleared, Martin drew alongside his guide. "You were brilliant," he offered. "Had you not been by my side, I wouldn't have been able to tell the difference between the two of you."

Karele's laughter came to him, soft, breathy, and amused. "It would seem that Deas saw fit to use my extended captivity on the steppes. Who knows? Perhaps this encounter tonight is the very reason he allowed me to be held prisoner for so long."

This last comment struck Martin as an overly harsh view of Deas, but Karele's logic and his own relief precluded argument. "What did you say to him?"

"He smelled horse and horse liniment. He knew someone was out there with a horse. I simply pointed out to him what he should assume—that only a Morgol with a Morgol horse would be using that salve."

"He believed you?"

Laughter drifted through the cool air. "Yes, after I called him *horse-brained.* The guard doubtless thought it only slightly unusual to find another Morgol so out of place in the cordon around Berea. Soldiers on duty just want someone to tell them what to do. They'd prefer not to bear the burden of having to think for themselves." They walked in silence, which Martin filled with thanks to Deas.

"The Morgols are unmatched in their ferocity on horseback," Karele said. "But their hierarchy is looser than that of Illustra's forces."

Martin grunted in agreement. "I have heard as much from Cruk. He said their lack of structure was the only thing that saved the kingdom twenty years ago."

The soft whicker of a horse a few minutes later heralded their reunion with the rest of their party. Luis's face appeared, ghosting above his dark cloak like a disembodied head, silver in the light and pinched. "Are you all right, Martin? We nearly started back for you."

"I'm fine. I got a bit careless with Karele's liniment, and it nearly betrayed us. A sentry sniffed us out. Karele managed to bluff us through."

Cruk grunted. "Only one? And you didn't get him close enough to slip a knife between his ribs?"

The healer's voice answered the captain in hard, brittle tones, his words clipped. "I prefer not to do that. Images of Deas are not meant to be destroyed."

"Huh," Cruk said. "You left an enemy alive that you could have eliminated. That's one more we'll have to kill when Rodran dies. Or do you not remember the damage they did twenty years ago?"

The moonlight carved Karele's face into a set of intersecting planes, hard, unyielding. "I think I'm in a position to remember as well as any man. I've seen the Morgols. I've lived as one. They are like the Merakhi, held captive by their theurgists as the Merakhi are controlled by their hoteps and akhen. Most of them are our combatants, not our enemies. They are images of Deas."

"Small difference," Cruk retorted, "when they're trying to rip your guts out with those hooked swords."

Martin rubbed a hand across his belly, remembering the glint of steel in the moonlight.

"So you say," Karele said. "But tell me which is better—to kill an enemy or to redeem him?"

Cruk growled but didn't respond. Martin looked away, unwilling to see the accusation in Karele's face. What would Martin have done? Kill? It was easier and safer. His heart and mind split, his priestly vows warring with his responsibility to the kingdom. Their lives hung on the thread of Rodran's unstable heart. Could they afford mercy?

"If it will make you feel better, Captain," Karele said, "the guard was taken in. And alive he will cause less commotion than if he were gathering blowflies in the dirt. His absence would be noted at first light."

The grinding of Cruk's teeth sounded in the darkness. "Glibly spoken, healer, but whose side are you on?"

"I am on Deas's side, Captain—not yours, and not the Morgol's either." He swung himself up into his saddle. "And that will never change. Now, since this is your territory, not mine, I think it's time you lead us out of here."

Cruk mounted and snapped the reins as if his horse had somehow offended him. "This way."

The tracked road ran from Callowford to Berea. By the time they neared the bridge across the Sprata, the sky had lightened from black to a dark gray, casting the world in uniform hues of drab that sent chills of foreboding down Martin's neck. This is what defeat would look like. The light gone and the world forever doomed to live under the unrelenting darkness of the Morgol and Merakhi spiritists. With a shake of his head, he castigated himself for such thoughts. No. They would not lose. They must not.

Cruk held up a hand for a halt. "If it is acceptable, I'd prefer not to alert the entire town to our presence. I doubt the Morgols have bought any eyes and ears in Berea, but I don't want to take a chance on someone selling us to save his own skin."

Martin nodded. The ashen gray of predawn light seeped into his mind. Even his thoughts felt muted. "Agreed. Do as you think best, Captain."

Cruk nodded and led them onto the bridge, walking his horse. The captain's head swiveled from side to side, and he peered ahead into the darkness.

"What?" Martin prompted.

"I know the men in Berea, Pater," he said. "They're not watchmen, but a few of them fought in the Morgol war. They're not stupid enough to leave the bridge into the city unguarded or unwatched. Someone should have challenged us by now."

Martin's mouth dried. When he licked his lips, his tongue felt like cloth. "Did the Morgols wipe out the village?"

Cruk shook his head. "It wouldn't make sense. Why hold the cordon off Berea if there was no one alive inside it? No, it's something else."

As they neared the far end of the bridge, a whiff of corruption and bowel wafted to Martin on the breeze. Then he heard it—the buzzing of flies.

The captain held up a hand. Martin was only too happy to comply.

Cruk pointed. "There."

A body, no, two bodies lay face up in the dirt just beyond the bridge. As Cruk went to investigate, Martin covered his mouth and nose with a corner of his cloak. Cruk returned a moment later, his voice flat and hard as stone. His eyes sought Karele. "They've been gutted. One of them looks to be a week dead or so, the other a couple of days. For some reason, the Morgols seem intent on keeping the Bereans inside their homes."

Martin coughed. A gust filled his nose with the sickly sweet smell of rot. "Deas help us, they wouldn't even let them bury their dead."

"Evidently not. It looks like the second man tried to drag the first one back toward the village." Cruk impaled Karele with his gaze, or tried to. "What was that you were telling us about the Morgols, healer?"

Karele shook his head without answering.

They skirted the village and found the path to Adele's cabin as the sky moved from charcoal to the hue of doves. The muted light surrendered colors like a miser parting with his gold. Even so, they looked wrong, as if the cordon had somehow robbed the greens, reds, and yellows of their autumn vitality. Martin fixed his eyes on the road ahead, trying to dismiss the blemished colors as a vain imagination. He could do nothing about them.

They rounded a corner and stopped. Adele's cabin squatted among the trees some twenty paces away. The herbwoman stood like a statue on the stoop, her arms crossed in the manner of one whose company is expected and late.

Karele dismounted and tied his horse to the closest sapling, leading the way on foot. Adele remained in her pose, stern as winter.

When Karele came within arm's reach of the old woman, he went to both knees before her, head bowed. "As Aurae bids, so I have come, mother."

Adele's face showed its emotions by various shifts of her wrinkles. Now they tightened into disapproval, though Martin could discern no cause for it either in Karele's manner or their own.

"And did Aurae tell you to tarry on the steppes, my son?"

Karele jerked as if whipped. "I came back, mother, at Aurae's command."

Adele's face hardened further. "Do not dissemble with me, son. You are many turns of the moon late in obeying the call to return."

The healer hung his head. "Yes, mother."

"And did your master mean so much to you, son?"

"He was like a father to me."

Adele harrumphed. "An earthly father, you mean."

Karele nodded.

Martin stepped forward. The man's tardy answer to Aurae's call explained his odd reluctance, but he had made the journey, if a little late. If the solis worshipped the same Deas as the church, then it was time to prove it. "Stop, Adele. There is grace also, even for those who are slow to answer."

The herbwoman's eyes glinted in the dawn like chips of agate. "Does your church not impose penance on those who are too slow to obey?"

Martin nodded but refused to yield the point. "Yes, as part of forgiveness."

"Well then, priest, since you stand for this reluctant son, this recalcitrant solis, are you willing to share in his amends? I will not speak of penance." Adele's eyes, carved from stone, still challenged him.

"If need be," Martin answered. "I will not commit to folly in my ignorance. Speak plainly, and I will as well."

Karele's voice croaked from beneath his bowed head. "No, mother, please."

His plea might as well have been given to rock; Adele's face remained graven. "The kingdom rests on a knife's edge, my son, an edge made keener and narrower by your tardy obedience, and you entreat me to forbear from speaking of it."

Karele nodded.

Something so personal passed between Adele and the figure crouched at her feet that Martin felt as if he eavesdropped on lovers. He wanted nothing so much as to turn away and leave them, but Karele's pain called to him. It was too familiar, too much like Errol's, for him to ignore. Blinded by his obsession with keeping Liam safe, he'd done nothing for Errol. His need to expunge his guilt would not let him turn away from Karele now.

"I will share his amends."

Cruk and Luis stared. He didn't care. If Deas wanted the kingdom saved, then He would find a way to save it.

Softness seeped into Adele's face in the lessening of the lines that marked her disdain, and the look she turned on Martin made him straighten his shoulders in preparation to accept the burden of his words. What had he done?

"As you wish, priest, but if you would share the doom of Karele's geas, we must find Radere. I do not presume to solely speak for Aurae."

What had he done?

The herbwoman stumped from her porch, past the still-kneeling Karele, past Martin, Cruk, and Luis. She stopped and called back over her shoulder. "Well, bring your horses, noble sirs. I am old. I have no intention of walking to my sister's when one of you can give me a ride."

"I can give you a ride," Cruk said. The captain eyed Karele with something like satisfaction across the planes of his hard face.

"Ha!" Adele laughed. "Your horse has enough of a burden." She stabbed a finger at Luis. "He will carry me."

The reader reacted as if she'd speared him in the side. Then he nodded, his head dipping in surrender.

Martin's head swam. Unexpected events spun his carefully laid plans out of control each time he tried to dictate the next move. Luis's reaction betrayed hidden familiarity with the herb-woman and hinted at a relationship previously unknown to him. The revelations washed the foundation of his confidence from beneath his feet.

As they backtracked the way they'd come, Martin tried to ride close to his friend, hoping to eavesdrop on whatever snippets of conversation he shared with Adele. The herbwoman saw through him with shameful ease.

"Ride ahead, priest. I would speak with the reader, the secondus of the conclave, alone." She filled the titles with sarcastic condescension, as if she intended to repudiate their value. Martin looked to his friend, but Luis bowed his head in assent to Adele's wish and would not meet his gaze.

He edged his horse forward to ride beside Cruk. The captain of the watch scanned the forest that hemmed in the road as if resenting man's intrusion. His eyes darted back and forth, occasionally coming to rest on a tree or shadow that required greater attention.

"Waste of time," Cruk said. "There could be an entire phalanx of Morgols in these woods and I wouldn't be able to see them."

Martin followed Cruk's gaze, but his attention slid past the shadows and trees to scrutinize the foliage itself. The plants seemed normal at first glance, but if he looked long enough the colors appeared . . . off, as if the sun withheld a portion of its light. The greens of the laurel and rhododendron that dominated this close to the river held a yellowish tinge that contrasted with the deep, rich green he expected so late in the year.

Rodran's doing—curse him. He had no right to die now.

Martin caught the train of thought, shunted it aside. The king still lived—however tentative his grip on life had become. Martin reached back with one meaty hand to try and squeeze the tension out of his neck. Rodran wasn't to blame for his sterility. That consequence had been set into motion by his father, and Rodrick IV lay moldering in the royal mausoleum, entombed beyond all retribution for his folly and pride.

He tore his gaze from the plants and turned his attention to his companions. Luis and Adele still rode beyond earshot at the rear of the group. The herbwoman noted his attention, and the lines of her face tightened. Cruk continued to submit to his soldier's training, his head turning in methodical increments. Karele rode on the other side of Cruk, as far from the group as possible, head bowed, eyes hidden. The healer's pain was palpable.

The road to Callowford narrowed, forced Karele to bring his horse closer to Cruk and Martin until only a span separated their mounts. Karele's curled posture, as if he were trying to hide within himself, accentuated his small stature. His loose brown curls merged with his horse's mane of the same color, giving the appearance the mount and rider had become one.

The solis's mare stumbled, startling Karele into awareness. He looked around, his eyes slowly coming into focus to something beyond his thoughts. He addressed Cruk. "You're wasting your time."

Cruk's disdain for the solis etched itself in the jaw muscles that bunched in his face. "How's that, healer?"

If Karele noted the watchman's contempt, he didn't bother to acknowledge it. "The Morgol theurgists will not order the soldiers to attack until their divinations are answered." He jerked his head back toward Luis and Adele. "Mother would not have ordered us to Callowford had not Aurae indicated Deas's protection." A ghost of a smile flitted across his face. "The theurgists are doubtless unsure of how to proceed. Their art is blocked. I have seen the Morgol holy men at work. They are unaccustomed to failure. Mother is administering unfamiliar chastisement."

Karele's reverence for the herbwomen struck Martin, and he forced himself to revisit his assumptions regarding them. "Why do you call her *mother?*"

The solis hunched his shoulder as if against unseen blows. "Unlike the church, those who are solis are loosely organized. Yet every organization requires authority." His mouth twisted. "And submission to that authority. Adele and Radere were chosen by Aurae over twenty years ago to lead the solis."

The timing caught Martin's attention. He didn't believe in coincidence. With a wrench, as if his thoughts had become externalized by some arcane means, he knew the question that needed answering above all others: Why had the Morgols invaded twenty years ago? What goad had driven the nomads over the mountains to attack?

With a sigh, he put that question aside with the rest. His inability to see more than a small portion of the reasons behind the kingdom's threat discouraged him. Errol, Liam, the solis, and the Morgol invasion taunted his ignorance as if he were the most naive acolyte of the church.

Two hours later, with the sun a handspan above the treetops, they approached Callowford. Radere's cabin lay in their path. Adele's sister waited on the stoop, her eyes hooded in shadow, but Martin imagined he could see expectation there. Luis's horse, with Adele aboard, almost like a child in the front part of his saddle, came past Martin and the rest. Luis dismounted first and then, his moves deferential, reached up and lifted Adele down to the hard-packed earth.

"Well met, sister," Adele said.

Radere nodded toward Karele. The healer, out of intent or accident, had positioned his horse behind Cruk's. "I see you've brought him. Does he know of the amends he must make?"

Adele shrugged her thin shoulders. "He knows he must make them, but I have not shared the specifics."

Radere nodded as if she expected no less. "Thank you, sister." She cast an eye at the rest of the party before coming to rest on Luis. "Have you come here to accept your call, reader?"

For the briefest of moments, Martin's closest friend looked pained. Luis shot him a glance that mixed equal parts embarrassment and contrition.

"I have come at the behest of my friend, Martin," Luis answered.

Martin hoped for elaboration, but none came.

Adele joined Radere at the front of the cabin, and the pair of herbwomen beckoned them in. "Come inside, all of you," Radere said. "Adele and I have completed our task, and I'm ready to go home. I'm sure you'll want to pester two old ladies with your questions."

Shafts of sunlight highlighted the austerity of Radere's cabin. Stoneware containers of herbs and powders lined rough planks along the walls. There were only two chairs within. Adele and Radere perched themselves upon them like nobles passing judgment. Martin caught himself at the thought, but it was probably true. He shouldn't have agreed to share Karele's amends. With a shake of his head, he berated himself. How many times would his emotions make his decisions for him?

"Speak, priest," Radere commanded, her voice and manner formal. "The keeping is in our hands. Tell us of the boys. How do they fare?"

What? Martin struggled to control the look of surprise he knew must be written across his features. Weren't they supposed to answer his questions? "Liam is well."

The herbwomen settled into their chairs as if a threat or burden had been removed. "And what of Errol?"

Martin swallowed. "The Judica has sent the boy to Merakh."

The herbwomen jolted forward in their chairs, eyes wide and blazing, and in unison demanded, "How did this happen?"

A smothered moan came from Karele, and the healer dropped to his knees. Adele snapped her fingers at him. "Ignore him, priest. Speak."

Martin ripped his gaze from Karele with an effort. "Certain benefices brought accusations against him." He coughed. "Accusations the church could not afford to answer. To keep Errol from the executioner, it was decided to impose penance for consorting with spirits."

Martin licked his lips. How could two shriveled old women make him feel like a boy caught stealing? "Errol was commanded to find Sarin Valon and kill him."

Adele waved a veined hand in dismissal. "Ridiculous. Valon is tied to a circle. No reader will be able to catch him unawares. Tell me, priest—are they all fools in this Judica?"

"Peace, sister," Radere said. "The enemy worms in wherever he can." She skewered Martin with her rheumy old eyes. "But I would have the truth of this matter. Errol was sacrificed to avoid what charge?"

A touch on Martin's arm kept him from answering. "This is my burden, friend." Luis stepped forward to answer, but his gaze never left the dirt floor of Radere's hut. "Errol was convicted on the lesser charge of consorting with spirits to avoid a more damaging charge. Benefice Dane accused Errol of helping Martin and me cast lots for the next king. Usurpation of the Judica's authority would have meant death for him . . . and us as well."

Radere hung her head, shook it slowly. "Did I not tell you years ago your art was unnecessary? Aurae would have told you who was to be king if Deas wanted you to know. But you were unwilling to believe Aurae was knowable."

The room spun in Martin's vision. They had told Luis?

"Yes, mother," Luis whispered.

Adele spat. "Worse and worse. Sister, we are surrounded by idiots. The reader endangers the boy by casting what is forbidden, and the master of horses arrives late."

Martin's curiosity wedged his mouth open. "Late for what?"

The women turned their gazes upon Karele. Martin shivered. Those gazes held understanding, even pity, but over those, ruling, blazed a look of unyielding, remorseless necessity. The herbwomen, wrinkled and stooped, might as well have been cast from iron.

"Tell them," Adele said.

Karele lifted his head, his eyes sunken and haunted. "I was to accompany you to Erinon. Errol's safety should have been in my charge, but I tarried on the steppes. If I had been with you, the malus would not have known him or Liam for what they are."

Martin dropped to the floor. What had they done? What had they all done?

18

STRUCK

"GET UP, PRIEST," Adele said. "You have knowledge we need, and there are amends to be paid."

"Why don't you ask Aurae?" Martin said. His voice cracked. Errol was lost. How many times could a man be betrayed by circumstance before he surrendered his capacity to believe?

"I share your pain," Radere said. "But we cannot aid the boy if you will not share your council."

"What do you wish to know?"

Adele's birdlike little head peered at him. "Everything that happened to the lad since he left our protection."

Martin slumped. "That will take some time."

Adele's face sharpened. "Best you get to it, then."

Radere laid a hand on her sister's arm but didn't speak.

Martin raised his chin from his chest and began. He laid the tale before the herbwomen, pausing to collect his thoughts when they interrupted him to prod or jostle him for details or impressions. The herbwomen's appetite for knowledge seemed insatiable. They would make him explain in different words or have Luis or Cruk relate the same tale from their point of view.

Toward the end, icicles of fear stabbed him as realization threaded its way through his despondency. None of their questions concerned Liam.

The herbwomen were so sure in their knowledge of Liam that they needed nothing further, but hours of questioning were not enough to satisfy them about Errol. Martin could feel the blood dropping from his head, as if someone had opened the veins in his legs.

"You don't know," he accused. "Errol is as much a mystery to you as he is to us."

Adele snorted. "About time, priest. If the boy was known to us, we wouldn't have you in here."

Martin shook his head in dismay. "I thought Aurae told you everything you needed to know."

Radere nodded, her lips curved in the bow of a smile. "Understandable, but Aurae tells us what *he* wants us to know, not what *we* want to know. If Aurae does not speak, then we must obtain information much as you would."

"Yes. Yes. Yes," Adele said, waving one hand. "The boy poses a problem."

"How do you mean?" Martin asked.

"Go easy, sister," Radere said.

Adele drew breath and shook her head. "No, sister. Not this time." She leaned forward, thrusting her head toward Martin on the thin stalk of her neck. "You want to know what Aurae has told us? Very well. The fate of the kingdom rests on two men, Errol and Liam, and one of them will be king. Liam is unassailable. From the first, Radere and I were sent by Aurae to Callowford to watch over him and instruct him."

Martin's mind exploded. "Instruct? You . . . you taught him?"

Adele's eyes sparkled. "From birth, priest."

"They never attacked him," Luis said. "The malus, the ferrals, Abbot Morin. It was always Errol they went after."

Martin couldn't breathe. The air in the cabin turned to jelly, thick and unyielding. "He's one of you. Liam's a solis."

"Yes," Adele nodded. "The protection of Aurae is on him."

"But what about Errol?" Martin asked, but guilty relief flooded his mind. Even if Errol died, Erinon would still have Liam, would still have a king.

Adele settled back in her chair. "We didn't know Errol was important until you were poisoned. You all should have died. The boy should have gasped out his last breath on my floor, but Aurae came—not simply his voice, but the wind of Aurae himself—and told me how to save him."

She stabbed a finger at Martin. "That boy may be the savior of the kingdom."

"What does that mean?" Martin asked.

"We don't know," Radere said. "Aurae has not . . . fully explained."

"We do know this, priest," Adele snapped. "Without both of them, the kingdom is doomed. If that boy is lost in Merakh, the kingdom is lost."

"Sister." Radere's voice cut Adele off, sharp, warning.

"We've demanded everything they know," Adele said. "Should we do any less for them?"

Radere closed her eyes and nodded. "As you say, but go gently."

Martin's neck prickled at Radere's words, but when Adele's face softened into something of pity, he wanted to bolt from the cabin and ride back to Erinon as fast as his horse could carry him. *No, Deas, please no;* he begged, not knowing what he pleaded for or against.

"War is coming," Adele said, "and both Errol and Liam must be here to meet the enemy. You know of Magis?" She waved her hand. "Yes, of course you do. It is the same for Errol and Liam. One of them must die."

"Oh, Deas," Martin breathed. "Why?"

"Because salvation is bought by blood, priest. You know this."

"Which one?" Cruk asked.

So like him, Martin thought. Focus on what had to be done. Accept and move on. Why couldn't he be more like the watchman?

"We don't know."

"How can you not know?" Martin cried.

Radere exhaled into the silence, her breath loud in the cramped space of her cabin. "It is not for the solis to question. We are called to obey, not to command."

Spasms shook him, and his arms and legs twitched where he sat on Radere's floor. "But why?"

"You know this," Adele said. "Even as Magis gave himself to buy the barrier with his blood, so will Liam or Errol step forward and renew it."

No. It wasn't fair. "But why them?"

"You know this as well, priest," Adele said. Her voice and face had softened until she no longer resembled iron, just a kindly grandmother. "Is it not Deas's way to sacrifice the innocent to save the guilty?"

"None are truly innocent, save Deas's son, Eleison," Radere added, "but this is the means Deas has provided to pay for Rodrick's pride."

Adele straightened in her chair, and that quickly the grandmother was gone, replaced by the wrinkled lump of iron that was the herbwoman. "Reader and watchman, take the priest and wait for Karele in the village. There are counsels we must share." She caught Martin's eye. "When we are done, Karele will let you know what amends are required."

There was nothing for Martin to do but obey. In silence, he left the cabin with Cruk and Luis.

He untied his horse and led the animal along the path toward the center of Callowford. He didn't bother to mount. Walking fatigued him, but his portion of guilt for Errol's misuse and abandonment wouldn't allow the comfort of horseback.

"The Morgols might as well have attacked," Cruk said from behind him.

Out of courtesy or shared guilt the watchman walked his mount as well. No one else used the road. The crunch of gravel beneath their horses' hooves sounded in a complex and lonely rhythm. Luis walked behind Cruk. There were too many questions for him to answer. The thought of the secondus reminded him of another one: Who was Luis Montari?

Martin thought he knew the reader as well as he knew himself. They'd spent five years in a single-room cabin searching for the next king. Deas have mercy. They shouldn't have cast for it. They'd handed a weapon to their enemy that had been twisted to strike at Errol. How would the boy ever find the strength to forgive them?

The rasp of gravel and hooves became too much. He had to say it. "It's like Rodrick, is it not?"

Cruk grunted a questioning sound, but Luis quickened his pace until the reader walked next to him.

"How so?" he asked.

Martin shrugged. Perhaps it didn't matter. "Rodran's father refused to follow the will of the Judica and marry Lorelle. Then he sired poor sterile Rodran and the line of kings broke. We defied the will of the Judica because in our pride we thought we knew better, and now we've broken Errol." Illustra was doomed. Rodran was fading, and with his death the barrier would fall and the kingdom would die. Truly, they were dead already. All that remained was for the corpse to stop twitching.

To Martin's surprise, it was Cruk who chose to take issue with him. "The boy is stronger than you think, Pater. If he was able to pull himself out of the ale barrel, he can find a way to live."

"He has to do more than live," Luis said. His voice whispered his argument, barely louder than the sibilance of the wind through the trees. "Errol must forgive us."

"We held too much from him," Martin said. "He earned our trust, and we denied it to him."

He straightened, held both hands up as a sudden impulse took him. "I, Benefice Martin Arwitten, in the presence of Deas and witnesses, declare that if I live to meet Errol Stone again I vow to tell him everything. No secret will remain in my heart or mind." A wave of cold spread from his hands through his chest and settled in his heart as his vow, his compulsion, took hold.

"What have you done, Martin?" Luis asked with astonishment on his face.

"Strong words, Pater," Cruk said. "What if he is the one destined to die?"

"A dying man deserves to know the truth," Martin said. His words throbbed and pulsed in his chest. He would make amends to Errol. He would!

"And if he's to be king?" Luis asked.

"Even more so. A king needs knowledge to rule," Martin said.

Cruk sighed. "As you will, Pater, but I hope you don't live to regret your vow."

Luis didn't speak.

They rounded the last bend in the road, revealing the village, the thatched roofed and whitewashed cottages lining the road that led to Cilla's inn and the church. All would have appeared well except the street was nearly deserted. Villagers who ventured from locked doors darted with furtive steps from building to building, their gaits and glances little more than a series of nervous jerks.

"The look of people on the brink of war," Cruk said.

They led their horses down a deserted street while villagers whose names and handclasps were known to them huddled behind doors and windows. When they neared the inn across from the church, and the rectory where Antil lived, a fatigue settled into Martin, as if the curse that had leached the colors from the flora had drained the energy from him as well. Removed now from the energizing influence of the herbwomen, an emotional lassitude swept over him. All seemed pointless. Even in a war the kingdom won, thousands upon thousands would die—some by the mercy of the sword, but far more by plague and famine.

His feet came to a stop. The inn lay directly ahead at the end of the street. He wanted nothing more than to renew his acquaintance with Cilla while he hefted a tankard of thick brown ale. He laughed at the irony. Perhaps Errol had been right all along. Why not just drown his sorrows?

With a sigh he turned left toward Antil's living quarters. Other men might be able to escape into ale, but a benefice could not. "I need to speak with Pater Antil. I'll join you in the inn presently."

"I'll go with you, if you're willing," Luis said. His eyes questioned Martin, as if unsure of his response.

For a moment, Martin almost said no. Luis had kept his relationship with the herbwomen secret from him. From him! Had they not lived knee to knee for five years? Didn't Luis trust him?

Martin thrust his hurt away, kept it from coming out through his eyes, face, or posture. "I'd be honored, old friend. I don't relish the meeting. Antil never liked Errol. Callowford's priest seems to have a singular dislike for drunkards."

Luis nodded, but Martin noted something within his silence that struck him—an odd reticence to speak. Martin didn't pursue it. Any additional revelations and he wouldn't recognize his friend at all.

As they approached the church, he saw the stocks out back, partially hidden by weeds. The evidence of their disuse made him angry. Had Errol been the only sinner for whom Antil exercised punishment? He knocked on the door to the small rectory attached to the church. The barest twitch of a curtain was the only evidence of life within.

Martin knocked again. Antil finally opened the door, his eyes darting to the sides and down the street before he knelt. "Yes, Pater?" He bowed his head.

"Pater Antil, I hope you'll forgive this intrusion," Martin said, his voice slipping into the practiced cadence and phrases he used when dealing with fellow clergy. "I need information that you may be able to provide."

Antil nodded, his face guarded. "Of course." He rose and stepped aside to invite them in.

Martin took a step into Antil's quarters and stopped. The room was nearly bare. A rude wooden table, its surface frayed and splintered, occupied a space against the wall. A chair that appeared to have been designed to maximize its users' discomfort sat to one side. Other than a few cupboards without paint or polish, that was it. The room was as stark and unwelcoming as human intent could make it. Martin's curiosity robbed him of his manners. He stepped to the side door that led to Antil's sleeping quarters.

Even there the same philosophy ruled. Callowford's shepherd slept upon a bed composed of a frame and a broad wooden board. No mattress lay there to relieve the nightly punishment imposed on the user, only a thin sheet. There was no pillow.

Martin turned to find Antil's face guarded and closed. "You live a simple life, Pater."

Antil refused to be drawn in. "How may I serve you?"

Luis stepped to one side, removing himself from the conversation.

"The church finds itself in dire need of information," Martin said. He needed as much leverage here as he could summon. He showed Antil the symbol of his office as benefice. Antil's preoccupation with mortification signaled a deep desire to be punished, but Martin had no time to indulge some village priest's guilt.

"Forgive me, Excellency. I was unaware of your station. I'm not sure how I could help. Callowford is a small village on the edge of the kingdom, hardly important."

Martin bored in. "It seems to be important enough for the Morgols to lay siege to it."

Antil spread his hands. "An unfortunate consequence of being too close to a gap in the mountains."

"No, Pater, only Berea and Callowford have been surrounded," Martin said. "There is something here that brings the Morgols."

"I don't know what it would be," Antil said. "Will that be all, Excellency?"

Martin ignored the invitation to leave. "Oh, we know what it is—or rather, who. I have been dispatched to see if I can find the genesis of their importance."

Antil forced the hint of a smile past his bloodless lips. "If you mean Liam, I would welcome the chance to speak of him."

Martin elected to let Antil speak of Liam at length, allowing him time to pursue other matters. When Antil finally showed signs of exhausting his praise for the young man, Martin prodded him.

"What can you tell us of Liam's birth?"

Antil grabbed at the question like a drowning man reaching for an offered tree branch. "Strange, Excellency. The boy's birth would hardly have been notable had not the mother died bearing him." His face pinched into a look of distaste. "The herbwoman couldn't save her, but one of the mother's friends came running for me that I might say the coda for her before she died."

"What was his mother's name?" Martin asked.

Antil shrugged. "Fallon, I think. It's been a long time." He stopped.

Martin's frustration edged his voice. "Well, what else can you tell us, man?"

Antil sighed. "She was a tavern girl. Prince Jaclin's army billeted in Callowford for a time." His face stretched in a sad smile. "Eight months after the army left to continue their campaign . . . Fallon delivered a baby boy.

"After she died, I put the boy with the Redens family." He smiled. "How is Liam? Well, I hope. I have never seen a child as blessed by Deas."

Martin nodded. "Liam is well and still blessed. He is good enough with a sword to be an officer of the watch and has been made a captain already. He has covered himself with honor."

Antil nodded as if he expected no less but said nothing. Martin waited for the priest to ask after Errol, but Antil's curiosity seemed to be at an end. The priest's thoughtless dismissal brought a flush to Martin's cheeks.

"And what of Errol's birth?" Martin prompted. "Ironic that the two births were so similar in time and circumstance, wouldn't you say?"

Antil's face chilled until it might have been carved from ice. "Doubtless that is where their similarity ends. I placed him with a perfectly decent family and the boy ends up a drunk." His voice heated. "No doubt he's out there somewhere trying to drink the kingdom dry. City priests are too soft on those such as Errol." He panted with suppressed rage, his cheeks flushed and eyes glittering. "A few hours back in the stocks would remind the boy of the price of drunkenness."

Antil's hands had curled into talons, ripping the air with indignations. Martin stepped back. For a moment he wondered if the priest was possessed and under the control of a malus.

"I've seen the boy's back, Antil," Martin said. "It seems that you were very . . . zealous for the boy's punishment."

"No more than the little sot deserved," Antil snarled.

"Even though he watched the only father he knew bleed to death under a block of stone?" Martin asked. "Hardly a gentle way to treat an orphan."

Antil snorted. "Orphan? What would you know? The boy was steeped in sin from birth. Perhaps the noble priests and benefices close to Erinon have grown soft on wastrels and sinners, but here in the outer provinces we still know the value of penance. Only the harshest punishments can drive the sin from a man."

Without permission, Martin crossed the small room to seat himself at the lone chair. It was as uncomfortable as it looked. A support out of line with the rest poked him in the center of his spine, and when he leaned forward to escape it, the front edge pressed against the back of his legs.

Antil crossed his arms, his brows pulled low over his eyes to show his disfavor—the picture of a man waiting for unwanted guests to leave.

Martin closed his eyes and, in the depths of his heart, prayed to Deas for wisdom. Antil's behavior seemingly defied logic, but everything had an explanation, even what appeared to be illogical. The chair, the bed, the table were all clues.

Martin shook his head. Strange that Errol seemed to provoke such strong emotional reactions in people. Love or hate—there didn't seem to be any middle ground where the boy was concerned. But why was there so much hate in Antil? Every village owned a drunk; most had more than one.

He opened his eyes. In that moment Antil turned away, and the priest's ruined nose disappeared and only the line of his cheek and jaw were visible. A tug of familiarity pulled at Martin, teasing him. Antil must have felt his gaze—he turned back toward Martin and jerked away again. *There!* The priest's cheekbones and the hint of dimples in his face reminded him of . . .

A jolt shot up his arm. Something cracked in his knuckles. Crimson filled his vision. Martin struck again. Antil or Luis might have cried out. He couldn't hear. Oceans of rage roared in his ears. He changed hands, beating Antil with the other fist.

A moment or a lifetime later, Luis placed himself between Martin and Antil. The priest of Callowford lay bleeding and crying on the floor. Blood flowed from a cut on Luis's lip. Martin looked at his fist, cracked and bloody.

"Enough, Martin!" Luis yelled. "Remember who you are."

He screamed back. "I know who I am." He flung a hand at the huddled form of Antil. "And I know who *he* is." He thrust Luis aside and hauled Antil to his feet. "Your son! No one else filled the stocks—just your son."

"Filth," Antil muttered past the ruin of his mouth.

"By Deas!" Martin roared. "That boy holds the kingdom in his hands! He has saved the kingdom twice over already, and Deas has made him an omne. *Earl* Stone is the most courageous man I've ever known. What right do you have to call anyone filth? You are as contemptible a wretch as I have ever seen. I . . . I . . ."

There were no words, no violence short of death that would satiate his need for justice. Martin threw back his head to yell at the sky and the deity beyond it. "How could you? He was just a boy!"

Antil said nothing but crawled from the floor to sit in his torture of a chair, elbows on his rude wooden table, face in his hands.

Martin moved to whisper in his ear. "Tell me, *priest*. Tell me it all."

Afterward he ran from Antil's presence, didn't bother to close the door as he left. If the villagers happened to see the ruin Martin had made of their priest's face, let them.

Luis caught up to him before he got halfway to Cilla's. Martin kept his gaze forward. "You knew. You knew and you didn't tell me."

"I suspected. Remember, my friend, I spent countless hours getting to know every villager in Callowford." His gesture took in the surroundings. "I saw past the dirt and drunkenness and noticed Errol's likeness to Antil, but I never cast the question. Even without it, the answer lay before me."

"You didn't even tell me you suspected." Martin threw it at his friend like an accusation.

"We had to stay hidden. Errol seemed to be of no consequence to our task, and we were very focused." Luis took a step forward. "I thought you might kill him if you knew."

Martin spun toward the rectory, disgust roiling in his gut. "I still might."

Luis shook his head. "Would you sever Antil from grace?"

"The man doesn't deserve grace."

The secondus nodded. "That may be. Would you shield him from judgment?"

Martin stopped, dust rose from his feet. "What do you mean?"

"You vowed to keep no secrets from Errol," Luis said. "How much vengeance can an earl exact on a poor parish priest?"

A weight descended on his chest. *No. Oh no, no, no.* He would have to tell Errol. His vow held the power of compulsion. Only death would prevent its fulfillment. For a brief moment, Martin thumbed the knife at his belt. Then he dropped his hands to his side, forced himself to start moving again. He mounted the steps to the porch and entered the shadowed interior of Cilla's inn.

Karele found him there hours later. Martin noted the solis's glance for the array of empty tankards, but Karele held his tongue. "I've been ordered to find Errol and accompany him into Merakh. Those are my amends."

Martin nodded, unsurprised. Of course. And he would accompany Karele because he'd sworn to share his amends. There would be no evading his vow to tell Errol everything. He sighed, tasting ashes. Perhaps he would die on the way.

19

ALONG THE SPRATA

ND HOW DO YOU INTEND to get us past the guards, healer?" Cruk asked.

Martin thought Karele's sigh held a burden of more than just strained patience. The solis's pallid face showed new lines in the morning light. Only the unbroken habit of living seemed to keep Karele moving forward.

"Adele and Radere will take care of them." The healer shrugged. "After that, the Morgols will return to the steppes or stay and fight." His inflection never changed, as if neither option held any interest for him.

"How will the herbwomen take care of them?" Cruk demanded.

Karele's lungs inflated, and he pushed out the air, his cheeks puffing. "Deas is going to suspend His protection."

Cruk stiffened, preparing to demand an explanation. Martin held up a hand, asking the captain's forbearance.

"I can see you're troubled," Martin said to Karele. "Only a fool could miss it, but I think our situation requires that you speak plainly."

Karele's brown eyes were lifeless glass. "Adele and Radere are giving up their position as head of the solis. Aurae will no longer hide and protect them from the theurgists who guide the Morgols. After the villagers in Callowford and Berea have been warned, and once his protection is withdrawn, they'll be able to use their arts to find Adele and Radere and kill them."

"You mean they're just going to let themselves be killed?" Luis asked. "Why?"

"Their death will buy our freedom. The Morgols will attack, and the way south will be open." Karele scanned the forest along the road. "It's unfamiliar country for me, but they've told me where to go." He clamped his jaws against anything else he might say.

Cruk's voice hardened. "How will we know when to hide? I don't fancy blundering into a Morgol patrol."

Karele shrugged as if the question and the answer were unimportant. "We'll know. Aurae will tell me."

A thought came to Martin. "Who will head the solis now?"

Karele slumped in his saddle, and his shoulders shifted beneath invisible burdens under his tunic. "I will, though I am the least and younger than any in the circle of nine. Adele and Radere passed their authority on to me. It seems Deas has placed some importance on your friend Errol."

They rode in silence, Cruk ranging ahead on the road back to Berea. The sun shone a handsbreadth above the trees when Karele reined in his horse. "It's begun."

A moment later Cruk rounded the bend, coming toward them at a gallop. Dust billowed up from the road like seafoam on a wave. "We've got company," he said. The tone of his voice left little doubt as to its nature. "They look like they're in a hurry. We need to get off this road."

Cruk made for a break in the trees and picked a path into the shadows of the wood. The still air carried sound. Every jingle of tack became a clarion call. When Cruk nodded his satisfaction and stopped, Karele dismounted and moved from horse to horse, rubbing the aromatic salve on the nose of each mount.

"Hold the bridles. The Morgols' affinity for horses will lead them to seek us out if they hear our mounts. The oil will make them a little slow for the rest of the day," he said, "but they won't give us away."

"Point taken." Cruk grunted, his face twisting as if displeased to find himself in agreement with the solis.

A few minutes later feet pounded along the dust of the road, making for Callowford. The sound faded and disappeared. Martin turned his horse, but Cruk waved him back. When the noise of birds in the direction of the road resumed, the captain led them out.

"How long will it take them to get to Callowford?" Karele asked.

Cruk pulled at his jaw muscles. "For horsemen, they don't make bad infantry. Probably not more than an hour if they keep that pace."

They remounted and rode. The sun was a semicircle of fire above the treetops when Karele pitched forward in his saddle.

Martin grabbed the solis and held him steady. "Healer, are you all right?" The solis reeled in his grip, his face the color of maggots. Martin held his tunic in one hand and lifted Karele's head to see his eyes. His skin felt clammy to the touch, and his eyes stared through Martin.

"Radere and Adele are dead," Karele said. His mouth appeared to work without his conscious command. "Deas, help me, please," he mumbled. "I am head of the solis now."

Martin dismounted. Karele slipped from his saddle, his eyes fluttering. Martin caught him, then caught Cruk's eye. "We need to make camp. Karele can't sit his horse like this."

Karele's eyes rolled up in his head, and the small man's legs went completely limp. Martin staggered under the weight until Luis came to help. "Thank you. I think I'm better at handling spiritual burdens than physical ones. He's heavy for a small man."

They found a grassy spot off the road and staked the horses. Martin wanted a fire—the evenings had begun to chill—but Cruk overruled him. Karele lay on the ground where Martin had wrapped him in his cloak—apparently unconscious, but his mouth gaped with an expression of loss and dread.

Martin knelt on the soft grass, his knees creaking, and recited the panikhida for Adele and Radere. He shook his head in wonder. Those two shriveled women had protected Liam for a score of years. There was a story there that needed safeguarding. Martin resolved to have it from the healer. He sighed, reciting the familiar liturgy, commending their souls and spirits to Deas. If he had any say in it, their story would be entered into the kingdom's record.

Luis adjusted Karele in his cloak, trying to make the healer comfortable in the midst of his stupor. The solis didn't respond. Then Martin, Luis, and Cruk ate cold rations of cheese and hard bread around the spot where the fire would have been.

Cruk spoke first. "How are we going to find the boy?"

Martin sighed. "I don't know. All I do know is that he has been compelled to go into Merakh to find Valon."

"It's impossible, then," the captain said.

"Perhaps not," Luis said, his voice soft. "There are any number of ports Errol could depart from, but the Merakhi won't allow kingdom men to disembark anywhere but Oranis."

"The boy is weeks ahead of us," Cruk argued. "If he's already in the interior, it would be suicide to seek him out."

Luis nodded his agreement. "They are touchy about kingdom men."

"You've got quite a gift for understatement, Secondus," Cruk said. "When the Merakhi get touchy, they like to take those curved swords of theirs and chop away at the source of their unease until they feel better."

Martin stirred, searching for a more comfortable spot of earth for his backside. Cruk and Luis were right, of course. Both men were knowledgeable and experienced, but their objections were beside the point. Martin had bound himself with vows and oaths. If Karele meant to seek Errol out to make his amends, Martin would go as well. "I think the solis will be able to lead us to him."

Luis's head tilted to one side. "And what makes you think so, my friend?"

Martin licked his lips, nervous. "I think Aurae will guide him."

His stomach tightened as Cruk and Luis stared at him. With that simple admission he'd committed himself to a path that would strip from him the comfort of his familiar clerical traditions. He'd never shied from confrontation, but this would be of a magnitude greater than any change in doctrine he'd proposed. Compared to this, his petition to the archbenefice to let the general populace read the liturgy would be as a lake to the ocean.

They'd haul him before the Judica.

Cruk's voice broke his reverie. "We still need to choose a route to the boy." He grunted. "He's even more inconvenient now that he's sober."

Martin smiled at the captain's note of pride. "Do you have a map? Let us see what options we have before us."

Cruk retreated to his pack and returned with yellowed parchment that crackled as he unfolded it. A dark spot in the lower left might have been blood. The captain clicked his tongue as he considered. To Martin the symbols on the map might as well have been incantations in another language.

Cruk settled back on his heels. "We'll have to backtrack to Windridge and make our way to Longhollow. From there we've only got two choices—we can take a boat downriver to Longhollow or we can cross over and ride overland to Basquon."

"Which one is quicker?" Martin asked.

"Boat," Cruk said. "It's slower, actually, but a good river captain can sail even at night. You can't match that pace on horseback."

Karele sat up, conscious but haggard. Cruk's mouth tightened as the solis brushed past Martin to study the map.

"Going back through the province of Avenia will take too long," Karele said. The tone of his voice precluded argument, and Cruk's face tightened further. "We'll have to go this way." The healer's finger began to trace a route south along the Sprata River, where it hugged the mountains before it split.

The route would be dangerous, but it made sense. They could follow the Sprata until it flowed east. Then they could hug the western side of the mountains until they hit the coast and at one of the villages try to catch a ship that would carry them along the edge of Illustra to Basquon.

But Karele didn't trace the expected route. Instead the healer's finger followed the river east through the Shattered Hills into the shadow lands. No. That couldn't be right, but the solis tapped the map with his index finger indicating his mind was made up.

Luis looked as if he'd been punched in the stomach, and Cruk's hand twitched near the pommel of his sword. Martin pulled a shuddering breath into his lungs. Karele had spent the last twenty years of his life on the steppes. He wouldn't know—couldn't know—about the shadow lands.

"We can't go that way, my friend," Martin said. "If we are to help Errol, we must have aid to do it. Our path must lie another way."

Karele shook his head. His finger tapped the map again. "No, if we are to help Errol, we must make haste. No other route will get us there in time."

"And how do you know this?" Cruk barked.

"Aurae," Karele said.

Cruk shook his head. "I didn't hear anything. Is this an audible voice?"

The solis grew still. "No, Captain, Aurae speaks in silence to those who listen."

Cruk glared. "Then you go to some quiet place and tell Aurae to speak to me, because I am not taking us into the shadow lands to die. The place is troubled by the dead as well as those that live there."

Karele's lips turned ever so slightly up at the corners. "Surely you exaggerate, Captain."

Cruk bolted to his feet. "Surely I do not! The place is a killing ground for young toughs and brainless men who think with their swords. We are not going that way."

The healer looked up. Cruk towered over him, threatening, but Karele remained seated, his finger still on the map, as if his physical connection to the symbol of their intended destination could compel them to take that route.

"We will go to the shadow lands, Captain," he said. "And we will survive. If we do not take this route, Errol will sail into the Forbidden Strait without us, without me to protect him. And he and all with him will be killed by Merakhi sailing on galleys commanded by ghostwalkers."

Martin shuddered. The healer's flat-voiced pronouncement knelled Errol's death as if it had already happened.

"You're a fool," Cruk snapped. "The survival of this mission is in my charge. I choose the route, and I say we're going to Windridge. If you want to choose how we go from there, you may do so." He pointed a thick finger at Martin. "The watch will not let its charge die."

Karele rose, his motions unhurried. "I thought Errol was your charge."

"He's not here; Benefice Arwitten and Secondus Montari are." He pointed to Karele's mount. "Tomorrow morning you will get on that horse and go where I tell you."

Karele's face at last showed signs of anger. "Even if it means Aurae says Errol will die?"

Cruk hawked and spat. "I've never seen evidence you can talk to Deas's spirit, and I'm not going to take the word of an addled healer."

"I saved your life, Captain."

Cruk shook his head. "Not if you take us into the shadow lands—you only prolonged it. I prefer to live a little longer, thank you."

"There is another way," Luis said.

Cruk and Karele turned to the reader.

Luis's hands held a pair of pine blanks and a knife.

The captain's eyes narrowed, and a look of resignation softened the harsh lines of his face. With a slow nod, Cruk accepted the reader's suggestion. Martin could almost feel Cruk's sense of powerlessness. Karele held the power to control the cast of the lots. It was an argument Cruk could no longer win. If the lots indicated they should journey into the perils of the shadow lands, Cruk would gain nothing by accusing Karele of tampering with the outcome. To do so would be tantamount to an admission that a greater power worked through the solis.

Martin left Luis to his craft, the issue settled. Tomorrow they would ride south. Some days from now they would turn east through the Shattered Hills into those blasted lands. So be it. As he settled into his blanket with his saddle for a pillow, Luis's voice came soft and low from a few paces away.

"Deas is in the lot. Let the cast be true. Do we go through the shadow lands?" A moment and a rustling sound later his voice came again. "Yes."

Eleven draws later the issue had been decided.

20

THE DOMAIN OF A WOMAN

A SENSE OF WRONG settled on Errol's mind as they passed the remaining villages of southern Gascony. By the time the caravan zigzagged its way up the Apalian Mountains to approach the hilly farmland of northern Talia, the feeling nagged like a whiff of corruption and weighed on him like an unwanted prophecy. Yet he couldn't identify the source of his discomfort. Nothing appeared to be amiss. The weather had turned fair. Farms teemed with crops, and their caravan even had aerial entertainment of a sort to offer distraction from the tedium of the ride: A large red-banded hawk flew overhead, sweeping the sky each day, looking for prey.

"Errol." Adora's call from the front of the caravan caressed him like the brush of her fingers against his skin. With a last check behind, he left the rear of the caravan, urged Midnight into a canter past Rokha, who rode the middle guard, and slowed as he reached the princess.

"Yes, Your Highness?"

Adora fixed him with green eyes the color of the sea under sunshine and smiled. She reached across and rested one hand on his where they held the reins. A tendon in his wrist jumped involuntarily. "Would you be willing to ride with me for a while, Errol?" She waved a hand at the other members of the party. "I don't know your friends very well, and I find myself wishing for conversation."

Errol nodded. The thought of refusing Adora anything never entered, and would never enter, his head. "Of course, Princess."

"Can't you call me Adora?"

Errol bowed his head, then stole a glance at the tail of the caravan. "If you wish—for a while, anyway."

She favored him with a smile. "I wish. Tell me, why do we keep to such a strange route? It's as if we don't know where we're going from one day to the next."

Laughter cleared away his sense of unease. "We don't." At Adora's look of confusion, he rushed to explain. "Valon commands a circle. He can track us from moment to moment, but so long as our decisions are random, he can only determine where we are, not where we're going to be. That's how he found us in the strait." His laughter died at the memory of Garrigus slumped on the deck, his blood filling the cracks in the boards.

"But surely he's guessed our destination by now—and the provinces we will pass through to reach it."

Errol nodded. "No doubt, but Basquon and Talia cover a large area. Valon could spread his agents and wait for us, but he would be unable to come at us in force. And if he concentrates his men, the likelihood of catching us becomes small."

They spoke for an hour or more, until Errol's conscience forced him back to his position at the rear of the train. Adora, unwilling to suffer the dust the wagons and horses raised, stayed at the front. Rokha drifted back to join him, her lips twisted as if she smelled something foul. "When did you become her pet, boy?"

"What?"

Rokha shook her head as she looked at the ground. "Errol, you have so much to learn about women."

"What do you mean?"

"If a woman becomes too sure of you, she won't want you."

Now he understood. "She's scared. Adora needs to be sure of someone, and I want her to know I'm hers. Wouldn't any woman want her husband to be constant?"

Rokha rolled her eyes. "You're not her husband, boy. Not even close. If you don't plant a seed of doubt in her highness's mind, she'll take you for granted. She wants a man, Errol, not a lapdog."

He could hear the truth of Rokha's advice in her words. With a bitter laugh, he turned and caught Rokha's gaze. "I believe you, but whenever she looks at me . . . I lose myself."

Ru's daughter sighed with her eyes closed, then spat. "Boy, you need to learn to handle a woman as well as you handle that staff of yours or the princess is going to stop looking at you as a man and start looking at you as a plaything." She dug her heels into her mount's flanks and galloped back toward her spot at the middle of the caravan.

The road wound upward through a gap in the mountains ahead. Peaks towered over either side, their tops shrouded in mist and snow. When Errol looked back, he was surprised to see how high they had climbed.

The watchman next to him chuckled. "First time through the twins, my lord?"

Errol nodded.

The guard, a Gascon named Darcy, threw back his arms and sang a song of hills and mountains and snow. When he stopped, he turned a face flushed with excitement toward Errol, his smile crinkling his eyes with wrinkles yet making him appear youthful at the same time. "I was raised not five leagues from here. It is beautiful, no?"

Errol nodded.

"Ah, you have good taste, my lord. At summer's twilight maidens who still your heart with their beauty pour from their fathers' estates to harvest the finest grapes in the kingdom. With their own feet they crush them until the air hangs heavy with the scent of the vineyards. The wine master performs his magic, and then the entire world savors the wines of the Arryth, from the vineyards of Gascony, Talia, and Basquon."

Errol laughed. Darcy, taking his amusement as an invitation, waxed eloquent about the region that had birthed him. According to the lithe, dark-haired watchman, in his home region the stars shone brighter, the women were at once more virtuous and sensuous, and the food was incomparably better than anyplace else in the kingdom of Illustra.

Darcy pointed. "Ah, my young lord, you are in for a treat. Up ahead is the pass between the twins. From that point we will descend into heaven along the border between Talia and Basquon, but there at the crest you will see both provinces spread before you like a banquet, the hills and farms laid out like a blanket to welcome you home to your rest." He paused to kiss the fingers of his hand. "There is no sight like it on earth. You'll—"

The hiss of an arrow interrupted Darcy's eloquence. With a startled curse, he pulled his horse in front of Errol's, a crossbow filling his hands. Up ahead, a rain of arrows fell on the caravan. Men and women dove for cover, seeking protection behind the wagons.

Errol searched for the source of the attack. The sunlight bathed the twins in bright yellow, but down by the gap, huge boulders created deep shadows. Errol tapped Darcy on the shoulder. "Aim your crossbow into those shadows."

Darcy shouldered the weapon and fired. A split second later a cry of pain hung in the cool air. The rest of the caravan seized on Errol's insight and filled the shadows by the road with arrows and crossbow bolts. A chorus of screams echoed and splintered among the rocks. Then a score of riders charged from the shadows toward the caravan.

Darcy grunted, struggled to reload his crossbow from atop his horse. With a curse, he flung the weapon away and drew his sword.

Errol swept past him, his mind filled with one thought— Adora. He unslung his staff, knobblocks on each end, as he galloped to the front of the line. An arrow flew wide of him. He heard her scream first. Then he saw her. A large man in boiled leather charged him, sword upraised. Errol blocked an awkward stroke and cracked the man across the temple. His eyes rolled, and he toppled from his horse. Behind him another man charged, his reins in one hand and a punja stick in the other. Errol slipped the blow and thrust the end of his staff at the man's neck. The weapon and reins slipped from the man's grip as he clutched his throat, trying to pull air past his crushed windpipe.

Adora's cry behind him stilled his heart. He wheeled Midnight to see a man pulling the princess from her horse. Errol charged, his staff whirling above his head.

A hooked knife appeared at Adora's throat. "Stay back or I'll open her up!"

Errol skidded Midnight to a halt. "Free her and I'll let you live."

The man laughed, spittle bubbling on his lips. "Oh, I'll live. I'll be rich." He pressed the point of his dagger against Adora's throat. "Now, drop your weapon."

Errol hesitated, but Adora's eyes, wide and unblinking, compelled him. His staff clattered against the stones of the road.

"Come here," the man ordered.

With the sounds of fighting around him, Errol nudged his horse forward. The man signaled his companion. "Kill him."

The man gave a gap-toothed smile and raised his notched sword. Errol could only watch.

A blur of motion resolved itself into Rokha. With a curse, she launched a sword cut at the arm of the man who held the dagger to Adora's throat. "Roll, boy!"

Errol jumped from his saddle as the sword descended. He landed badly, felt something tear in his chest, and sucked air in pain. Spots danced in his vision as the man spurred his horse, trying to run Errol down. With a gasp, he lurched from the horse's path. In the corner of his eye he saw Rokha backing from the man who had held Adora captive—but he could not see the princess.

A great underhanded sweep of the horseman's sword almost had him. He flattened against the ground, tried in vain to get to his staff, but the man maneuvered his horse over the weapon each time Errol tried to reach it.

Rokha continued backing toward him. With a flurry of strokes she opened up a small space, turned, and stabbed the mount of the man trying to run Errol down. With a scream, the man's horse reared. The rider kicked free of the stirrups, twisted in the air, and landed on his hands and knees.

Errol snatched his staff and rose to his feet. Fire burned across the ribs on his right side. He parried a sword stroke, tried to strike at the man's legs and missed. He couldn't extend the arm on his wounded side. His opponent's eyes flattened, and he circled to Errol's right.

Sword strokes rained on Errol. Each parry sent burning coals of pain across his ribs. He couldn't last. Shallow breathing created black spots that danced across his vision. With a scream of pain and frustration, he countered, striking with the end of his staff as if it were a pike.

The bandit parried the first strike, missed the second. The knobblock crunched into his face. Errol followed with a thrust at his throat. The bandit dropped. Errol spun, looking for opponents. Rokha slipped a stroke from her man and lunged. Her sword found a weak spot in the bandit's mail. With a screech of metal on metal, her blade slid into the man's chest. Rokha twisted her wrist, and the man shuddered and collapsed, pulling her sword down. She put a foot on his ribs and yanked the blade free.

The fighting was over. Fierce and glowing, Rokha turned to Errol, threw her free arm around him, and pressed her lips against his in a savage kiss. When they parted, her mouth brushed his ear with lips and laughter. "You owe me on several counts, Errol. You can thank me later."

Adora's gaze rested on him. He rushed to her. "Are you all right?"

Without answering, she sidestepped him and walked away, her face smooth. Errol could see no emotion written there, but her eyes had darkened to the color of storm clouds. As she passed Rokha, the caravan master's daughter caught her by the arm.

"Unhand me," Adora said. "Do you know who I am?"

Rokha laughed and tightened her grip until the flesh of Adora's arm bunched around her fingers. The princess winced but bit her lip in silence.

"I know exactly who you are," Rokha said. "You're a spoiled little princess who almost got a man killed because she doesn't know how to defend herself. Look at him." She gave Adora a shake. "Look!"

Adora turned. Her gaze froze Errol where he stood.

Rokha growled her words in disgust. "He threw down his weapon for you—for you! If I hadn't been here they'd have split him from head to belt because you were too helpless to offer any defense." She spat.

"Are you finished with my arm?" the princess asked, head high.

Rokha dropped it, tilted her head back, and laughed. "It's nice to see you've got some backbone, Princess."

Adora walked past her.

"Princess," Rokha called, "that's not the first time Errol has felt my lips against his."

Adora's back stiffened at the jibe, but she neither stopped nor slowed.

A cloud that no pastoral beauty of the Arryth or banter from Darcy could alleviate descended on Errol. Even the fact that the caravan had emerged from the fight with only a few injuries failed to cheer him. His attempts to apologize to the princess for Rokha's behavior were rebuffed before they'd begun. Each time he approached her, she would find some purpose or interest that needed her attention and guide her mare away from Errol without a word. After the fourth time, he gave up.

Disconsolate, yet unwilling to ask Rokha's advice—the woman had gotten him into enough trouble already!—he sought Rale. Perhaps the captain could instruct him in the ways of women as well as the staff. Errol nudged Midnight forward until he rode almost knee to knee with the erstwhile farmer.

Rale stared ahead, his eyes scanning the landscape as if searching for new enemies as he chewed on his lower lip. "Strange."

Errol fumed. He needed Rale's advice, not random observa-tions on some trivial oddity, yet a nagging voice told him to put aside his childish behavior. If the captain noticed something amiss and felt compelled to comment on it, Errol should know of it. He sighed. "What?"

"The attack," Rale said. "They seemed intent on killing you."

A burst of caustic laughter erupted from Errol's lungs. "What's so strange about that? It never stops."

Rale gave him a look that brought a blush to the roots of his hair. "Errol, a leader has to be able to set his emotions, his prejudices, and his assumptions aside. When you're in charge, you must notice everything."

Errol accepted the rebuke with a nod. Doubtless Rale knew of his troubles with the princess. How could he not? Rale made a habit of noticing everything. By now he would have seen Adora rebuff his attempts at reconciliation, but his mentor's correction seemed misplaced. "I'm not the one in charge. You're a captain of the watch again and one of the best tacticians in the kingdom. Everyone says so."

"And I'm one arrow or sword thrust from being dead, boy. Who will watch out for you then—one of the watch?" He nod-ded. "Surely, they would do their best to protect you, but none of them are qualified to lead you into Merakh. Perhaps Captain Merodach—but can you trust someone who tried to kill you?"

At a look from Errol, Rale snorted. "No. A man who's changed his mind might just change it back. And then there's Naaman Ru. He's gifted with a sword and has the knowledge to take you into the dunes after Valon, and I don't doubt that he's a reason-able tactician. There's much in common between a general and a caravan master, especially one who's seen as much action as Ru. But tell me, boy, would you be willing put yourself in his hands if I died?"

The thought chilled Errol. Ru's allegiance went as far as the compulsion the church had laid upon him and no further. And Errol did not trust the church's compulsion to keep him safe. He gave a shake of his head.

Rale gave a mirthless chuckle. "I thought not. If I die, you'll have to take charge."

"Me?" His stomach seemed to be forever dropping. "I don't know anything about tactics or leading men." Yet inside he knew that wasn't the whole truth. It went deeper than that. "I don't want to be in charge."

Rale's dark eyebrows converged over his broad nose. Errol sensed he was dangerously close to making the man angry. "Errol, the people who long for power are ill-suited to handle it. I'd prefer to be plowing a field behind this horse rather than sitting on it, but here I am. Our wishes and wants are beside the point."

He leaned in toward Errol. "Do you want to live?"

Errol nodded.

"Good. Now tell me what was different about this attack."

With a long breath, Errol settled a little deeper into his saddle, closed his eyes, and tried to remember everything.

At the first arrow, Merodach had rained fire on the enemy, as if he were a squad of archers. Conger, the ex-priest, had shouted prayers and curses to warn the rest of the caravan. Then the charge had come, and Errol had moved forward to protect Adora. Despite his effort, she'd been taken.

His eyes snapped open. Not killed, taken. "They didn't kill the princess."

Rale nodded. "Good, boy. Very good. Go on."

On? What else was there? He'd been forced to give up his weapon. If not for Rokha, he'd be dead. He could still see the face of the man he'd killed, eyes wide, pale with shock. Pale.

"They weren't from Merakh," Errol said. "But that doesn't mean anything. They used kingdom men in the attack at Steadham. Still, it's strange, no Merakhi and no ferrals." His mind backtracked. "And why would they want Adora alive? They've got no use for her alive. She's worth more to the Merakhi dead to ensure the royal line dies completely. It's almost as if this attack didn't come from the Merakhi at all."

Rale nodded. "I came to the same conclusion."

"But who besides Valon would want to keep us from Merakh?"

His mentor shrugged. "That's a good question, Errol. Unfortunately, there's no way to know. All we can assume is that whoever struck at us wants you dead and the princess alive. To me, that speaks of someone in the Judica."

Icy waves rippled down his back at the suggestion. "The Judica? I know a lot of them hate me, but why attack? Why not let Valon do the job for them?"

Rale hunched his shoulders. "Perhaps they think you might succeed. Maybe they desire to keep the princess from accompanying you. Adora left a trail easy enough to follow." He turned a somber gaze to Errol. "You must learn to command."

He swallowed. "What should I do first?"

Rale nodded. "Every commander must get to know the people he leads. Men won't die for a stranger, boy. Go check on everyone. See how they fare."

Errol nudged Midnight forward. If he needed to know those he commanded, he would begin with Rokha. It would be easier to start with the familiarity of Ru's daughter, and he owed her his life. He had yet to thank her for her assistance.

He advanced to the middle of the caravan to approach Ru's daughter as she rode on the opposite side of the fur wagons. He prepared to drop back and circle around the wagon when the voice of the princess drifted to him.

"Lady Ru, I would speak with you," Adora said. Stress laced her voice, clipped the cadence of her words.

Rokha's laugh, deep and amused, answered the princess. "I'm not officially titled, Princess. Most of my friends call me Rokha."

"And what do your enemies call you?" Adora's voice challenged.

"I try not to let them live long enough to call me anything."

"That is why I wanted to speak to you," Adora said.

"How so, Princess?"

"I want you to teach me how to fight." Adora's words tumbled over each other. Errol leaned toward the conversation. He'd never heard the princess sound so unbalanced, so unsure.

"Why?" Rokha's voice was flat.

"Because I don't want Errol to die," Adora said.

Rokha laughed. Errol blushed.

"Do you know what you're asking, Princess?" Ru's daughter mocked. "You're volunteering for bone-deep weariness, unforgiving correction, and acknowledgment that I am your superior. On top of all of that, you're asking for blisters—and what's not blistered will be bruised. I won't take it easy on you just because you have a title." Rokha's voice dripped with sarcasm. "Is that boy worth so much to you? I'm sure Erinon offers plenty of other lapdogs at your beck and call. Why go to so much trouble just to keep this one alive?"

"Errol is no one's dog!" Adora's voice throbbed with repudiation. "He's genuine and kind and merciful. I want to learn the sword. If you won't teach me, I'll find someone who will."

Rokha's laughter drifted over the wagon. "I'll teach you, Princess, but remember what I said."

"I'll remember," Adora shot back. "But don't underestimate me just because of my title. You may find yourself wearing bruises of your own."

Rokha laughed until the princess rode ahead, her shoulders tense.

Errol dropped back to circle around the wagon to confront Rokha. This had gone far enough. She wouldn't hesitate to beat the princess black and blue, and she'd enjoy it.

21

BEATING

THE CLACK OF SWORDS drifted through camp, jarring in their lack of rhythm, accompanied by bursts of laughter from Naaman Ru's daughter. She laughed alone. Doubtless the rest of the guards found the spectacle of the princess learning the sword amusing, but none of the watchmen present would dare allow their mirth to show. To a newcomer it would appear the men who lived their lives in the unrelieved black of the king's guard had been carved from stone.

Errol knew better. For four days he'd lived Rale's advice to become familiar with every guard in the caravan in case circumstance forced him to lead. Gial Orth, the flame-haired warrior from Erinon, stood erect as ever. Yet the twinkle in his eyes and the set of his mouth, pressed into a thin line that hid his lips, spoke of a towering mirth that threatened to explode any minute. Next to him, burly Lelan Nassep's normally pale visage, now ruddy as a sunset, betrayed the watchman's glee to those who held even a passing acquaintance with him.

Only Merodach rebuffed Errol's efforts at familiarity. The

rangy captain hoarded his words as if they were precious jewels. Errol still knew nothing of him or his motives.

The only exceptions to the silent stoicism the princess's lessons fostered were Naaman Ru and Rale. The caravan master savored combat the way a glutton luxuriated in food. The fact that Rokha served up a nightly beating to the only princess in the kingdom only added relish to his repast. Ru hated nobles.

As for Rale, his enjoyment was more academic. He shouted encouragement to both participants, though Rokha hardly needed it. On those rare occasions when Adora managed to do something right, the captain's praise and smile would bring an answering grin to her lips, a grin that Rokha took pains to erase with whiplike ripostes that surely numbed the princess's shoulders.

Errol turned away, forced himself from the circus to walk the perimeter of their camp. For a few brief moments the sun shone below a break in the cloudbank, casting inky shadows in the orange-tinted light just before it set. Two hundred paces out from camp, he climbed the hill Conger had selected as his vantage point. Rale's decision to guard every approach to their camp would have seemed extreme a few weeks ago. Now Errol wondered if such measures had any chance to protect them.

Conger nodded his greeting as he scratched an armpit. "Evening, milord."

Errol shrugged off the greeting. "Errol, please. I've never even seen my holding, Conger, and I like the sound of my own name just fine."

The ex-priest nodded. "It fits you, if you don't mind my sayin' so."

"How do you mean?"

Conger's brows showed his surprise. "You mean you don't know what your name means? I figured you chose it because of everything that happened to you."

The man's store of minutiae never failed to amaze him. "No. I've been told it's the name I was born with."

Conger smiled. "Well then, maybe that's Deas's handiwork. *Errol* means *wanderer* in the ancient language of Illustra."

He took that in. His adopted father, Warrel Dymon, had told

him his mother had chosen the name as she faded, dying from the blood loss of a difficult birth. Errol shook his head. Was it prophecy or just Deas's idea of a joke? Maybe it was both.

"If you don't mind my asking, Errol, how come you're not with the princess?"

The clack of practice swords came softer out so far from camp, but he could still hear them. Not the laughter, though. The distance and trees muted that. "There's nothing in her lesson I want to see." He kicked a stick farther down the grassy hillside, then lowered himself to the turf and leaned against the rough bole of a glass-leaf oak. "She's got to be the most stubborn woman I've ever met. What can she learn in a few days?"

Conger nodded. "Aye, there's steel in that one. There'd have to be for her to defy the Weirs as she did."

"Why would anyone besides Lord Weir care?"

Conger laughed, then held up a hand in apology. "I keep forgetting you don't really know the kingdom, milord."

His envious sigh surprised Errol.

"I wish I could be a simple priest again," Conger said. "I'd find a village so far from Erinon that no one knew its name, and I'd stay there until the passage of time made me ignorant."

The naked yearning in Conger's voice pulled at Errol, and his eyes stung. "What happened, Conger? Why did you stop being a priest?"

The man in front of him, familiar and yet unknown, gave a soft laugh. "That's a short question with a long answer."

"Still," Errol said, "I would hear it if you're willing."

The ex-priest shrugged. "As you wish, but it's not a surprising tale. I grew up the third son of a very minor noble in western Avenia. The title went to my oldest brother, Alin. Father managed to arrange a favorable marriage for my second brother, Nicu." Conger spread his hands palms up. "With the title safeguarded by his first and second heir, it was up to me to find my own calling, not that I minded overly much. I didn't want the responsibility of the title, and poor Nicu married some chattering magpie of a girl.

"After some consideration I narrowed my options to three choices. I could enter the priesthood, offer my sword to the king or some other noble, or become a merchant. Father didn't have the money to set me up as a merchant, and my head for numbers isn't the best anyway."

Errol nodded. "So you entered the priesthood."

Conger raised one eyebrow. "No. I enjoyed the sword, and the idea of forsaking wealth and women didn't appeal to me. I became one of the countless swords for a very powerful duke." Conger's gaze became significant.

"Weir?"

"The very same. Father gave me a letter of introduction good enough to place me as a lieutenant. In time I might have become one of the duke's captains."

"What happened?"

"There was a fight, not much more than a skirmish, really, with a band of brigands in the Silviu Forest. We surrounded them, called on them to surrender, but they wouldn't. Can't say as I blame them. It was the blade or the noose after all. We beat them, but they carved us up pretty good." Conger stopped, lost in his memory.

"Then what?" Errol prodded.

"We took our dead and wounded to the nearest village, hardly more than a collection of huts on the edge of the forest, really." He shook his head. "I'm not sure how they managed to rate a priest, but it was a good thing for us they did. Pater Gavril came and tended us.

"As healers go, he was only fair, but I tell you, boy, the peace of Deas flowed from his hands. I saw men in horrific pain become calm and smile at his words. Dying men crossed to the other side with peace and surety. I thought I'd give up anything to be able to show the love of Deas like that. So I left my sword and became a priest.

"Then I met Mina." Conger hung his head. When he lifted it again a moment later, he avoided Errol's gaze, watching instead the empty road that wound down the hill. "Oh, Errol, do you know what it means to find the one? Such powerlessness is the boon and bane of Deas. Five years after I took my vows, I did what is not lawful for a priest to do—I took a wife."

"You left the priesthood?"

Conger shook his head. "No. The church might have forgiven me for that. We kept our marriage secret, instead. I employed Mina as my housekeeper." The ex-priest squeezed his eyes shut. For a moment Errol hoped he would stop, leave his tale unfinished.

"Of course we were found out. We were far too young and giddy in our love. The rest of the story goes quickly. The church stripped me of my robes, almost excommunicated me. A year later, Mina died of a wasting disease that no healer or doctor could cure. Everyone said it was Deas's judgment."

"What do you say?" Errol asked. For reasons he couldn't identify, Conger's answer would help determine his own response to the church and its compulsion. In the ex-priest he had at last found someone whose pain at the hands of the church approached his own.

"I say bad things happen. Sometimes it's because of the choices we make, and sometimes it's because of the choices other people make . . . and sometimes it just happens."

"Maybe that's all there is," Errol said. "Maybe there is no Deas directing our way."

Conger shook his head in denial. "I've often wondered that myself. It can seem that way, because we have the power to choose, but then I remember that priest on the edge of the Silviu Forest. There was more than just him at work."

Silence fell on the two of them. Unwilling to diminish Conger's pain by speaking of any other matter, Errol didn't speak. He waited.

At last, Conger sighed again, his eyes still lost in wishes and denied chances. "The Weir family is the most powerful in the kingdom, lad. Your princess has chosen to mortally offend them by spurning Lord Weir's suit and running away."

"But she's the niece of the king," Errol protested. "Isn't the king more powerful than the Weir family?"

Conger nodded. "That's what most common people think, and in Erinon that's probably true, but off the island the Weir family holds more power than you can imagine. Their wealth is nearly limitless, and that wealth is crucial in the event of war, boy. Swords have to be paid for. When the Morgols or the Merakhi come, it's the nobles that will be doing the paying—and since Weir will be paying more than anyone else, that gives him a hold on the king."

"And Weir's price is Adora." Lead filled Errol's stomach.

"The game goes deeper than that, boy. The Weir family boasts not only the most powerful duke . . ."

"But the most powerful benefice as well," Errol said.

Conger nodded. "The Weir family means to take the throne, lad. They deny it, of course, but the meanest peasant in Erinon or western provinces knows it to be true."

"But L—" Errol clamped his teeth against mentioning Liam's name. "The next king is supposed to be chosen by lot."

Conger's smile mocked his innocence. "Which benefice sent you out, boy?"

Errol shrugged. It wasn't news. Everyone knew. "You know as well as I—it was Benefice Weir. He wants Adora for his nephew."

Conger's smile grew. "Is that all he wants?"

The beginning of horror began to gnaw his gut, and his head spun.

"That's right, boy," Conger said. "Without an omne to verify the lots, Weir can buy or threaten every man in the conclave. Anyone who stands in his way will end up dead."

Errol turned to stare back at the camp. "The watchman who volunteered . . ." He couldn't finish.

"Right again. Every one of them will lay down his life for you to keep Weir from buying the throne after Rodran dies."

"But what about the barrier?"

Conger spat, punctuated the action with a few savory words. "The Weirs don't believe in anything but their own power, boy."

A distant clack brought his attention back to Adora. She knew all this. How could she not? "What can I do to help her?"

Conger laughed. "That's the spirit, boy, but the answer is right in front of you."

"Huh?"

"I've never seen anyone improve as quickly with a weapon as you, lad." Conger offered a diffident lift of his shoulders. "How did you do it?"

Errol laughed at the memory. "I spent every spare moment getting stronger or working the staff."

Conger nodded. "Aye, that's how it's done."

So. Errol braced his hands against a gnarled tree root and pushed himself to his feet. "Thanks, Conger." He grabbed his staff and headed back toward the camp.

The noise led him back, but the silence between sword blows grew. By the time he stepped between two of the flat-bottomed wagons, they'd stopped altogether. When he caught sight of Adora, he understood why.

Sweat stained the sleeveless cotton blouse that clung to her as she knelt in utter exhaustion. Her blond hair hung in a stringy tangle as she panted, face toward the ground. Adora's shoulders were a wreck. Welts and bruises covered every square inch of the princess's arms from shoulder to elbow. A trickle of blood flowed from a cut on the left one.

Rokha stood over her, sword in the ready position, waiting. "Do you think your enemies will stop because you're tired or hurt? That is precisely the moment they will strike hardest. Come, Princess. Summon some of that royal courage."

Adora staggered to her feet, her face slack with exhaustion. Her sword arm trembled, and she swayed as if drunk. Then she toppled to the ground, the sword slipping from her blistered hand. Rale came forward to gather the princess in his arms and take her away.

Adora's helplessness woke something within Errol, something that threatened to put him on his knees keening in grief or raging to kill Rokha. With a physical wrench, he shoved the emotion aside. He would end this. Rokha faced him at the sound of his footsteps, then retreated a step before she straightened to meet him.

"Is this what you call training?" Errol kept his voice low. If he started screaming, he might not find the will to stop. "It'll be days before she can lift a sword."

Rokha's eyes widened at the threat in his voice. "If you step in, boy, she'll hardly thank you for it."

"How can I not step in?" he asked. "You're practically killing her."

"Do you want her?" Rokha asked.

Errol clamped his teeth together around a curse. "What does that have to do with her learning the sword?"

"Everything, boy." Rokha came close enough to kiss him, pitched her voice so that only he could hear. "Do you want her?" she pressed.

"Yes."

"And she wants you, boy. She's run from every safety and security she's ever known to follow you into Merakh." Her mouth twitched in grim amusement. "We'll probably all die there."

Rokha's dodge confused him. She spoke of the princess in respectful, even warm tones mere moments after beating her to exhaustion.

He shook his head, trying to understand. "What does that have to do with anything?"

She lifted her hand to pat his cheek, but stopped just short. "You didn't learn very much about women in Erinon, Errol. You're a hero. Your name is on every tongue on the west coast. You're omne to the conclave of readers, you've had your story entered into the book of records, and the king elevated you to the nobility."

He shrugged away Rokha's list. "I didn't have any choice in the matter. I was just trying to stay alive."

She smiled, and for a moment he thought of Anomar, Rale's wife.

"You have to let her do this, Errol," Rokha said. "Adora was born to the nobility. Everything she has was given to her. She needs to prove herself worthy of you, to be able to marry you as your equal, not your inferior."

Inferior? Errol shambled away from Rokha in search of the princess, half afraid he'd find her conscious and wanting to talk. Just when he thought women couldn't get any more complicated, they said or did something so incomprehensible that he had to start all over again.

He found her by the lead wagon, the one Ru used to maintain his fiction as caravan master. Rale held a jar of salve that smelled of lemongrass and mint. Adora stared straight ahead, her eyes dulled by exhaustion.

"Is she all right?" Errol asked.

At his question, Adora stirred, blinked twice, and then faced him. "Don't try to stop me."

Rale caught his eye and gave a slight shake of the head.

Errol had no idea what his mentor tried to communicate, but Rokha's advice still resonated inside him. "I have no intention of trying to stop you, Princess, but if this is how you intend to abuse yourself, it will take you forever to learn the sword." His voice sounded harsh in the stillness surrounding Ru's wagon, almost a bark. He'd never used that tone with Adora before.

Her eyes widened at his response, and tears gathered at the corners.

Errol stifled the impulse to gather her in his arms. Instead, he held out his hands to Rale, who surrendered the jar of salve and left.

He didn't trust himself to speak yet. Instead he took a generous glop of salve and proceeded to rub it into the ruin of her right shoulder.

Adora winced and bit her lower lip but refused to give voice to the pain. Good. Maybe she'd be brave enough or stubborn enough to do what needed doing.

Errol tried to ignore the feel of Adora's skin. He willed himself to concentrate on the muscles beneath. The princess wasn't thin, but neither did she possess the broad-shouldered athleticism Rokha owned after years with the sword.

But the princess was built well. She was nearly as tall as Errol, and though he would never describe her as thick, neither was she as fine-boned as many of the ladies at court.

He moved to the left shoulder, his hands working to relieve a knot in her muscles. After he'd kneaded most of the tension away, he worked on her forearms, spending extra time on her sword arm. She'd taken fewer blows there, and the softness of her skin sliding beneath his fingers distracted him. By the time he'd massaged his way down to her hands, his ears were burning.

He capped the jar and stepped back. "How's that, Princess?"

"Adora," she corrected.

He nodded. "Adora."

The tears were gone from her eyes. She lifted each arm in turn. "Better. I think I might be able to fight again tomorrow."

Errol frowned at her ignorance. "No you won't. This bout was not like Rokha's earlier lessons—she was testing you. When you wake up in the morning you'll feel as if every wagon in this caravan ran over you. The day after that it will be worse."

Her green eyes narrowed to slits. "If I can't fight, then how am I supposed to learn the sword?"

Only brutal honesty would work. "You weren't fighting, Adora. You were taking a beating. Fighting is when you land a blow every now and then."

She bit her lip, but her voice was steady. "So what should I do?"

Better. "Don't abuse your body. It's your weapon as much as a sword. Care for it."

Her chin came up at the tone in his voice. "I want to prove myself."

He forced himself to laugh, even as he hated himself for it. "Getting beaten doesn't prove much." Errol shrugged. "Beating your opponent, on the other hand . . ."

Adora's eyes blazed, but she leaned toward him as if he had something she wanted. "How long before I can beat Rokha?"

Errol shook his head. "Probably never. She's worked at the sword for years, with her father, the best swordsman in the kingdom, training her. If beating her is your goal, put it aside and choose something more sensible. I can't show you how to handle a blade, but I can show you how to get strong. Then you'll be able to take what Rokha teaches and use it properly."

"I hate her."

Errol nearly asked why but decided against it. "Then use that, Princess . . . Adora. We'll be in Merakh all too soon, and I . . ." His voice caught.

"You . . . what?"

He swallowed. His voice rasped into the narrow space between them. "I would like for you to live to see home again."

Adora closed the space between them so quickly he hadn't realized she'd moved until he felt her lips pressed against his. He tasted the salt of her sweat. The way his head spun, it might have been the strongest mead. He tried to pull away, but her hands came behind his head, and her kiss became less aggressive, softer and more lingering. His awareness of everything but her lips against his vanished.

When she released him at last, the cultured face she displayed at court had returned, smooth and controlled except for a flush in her cheeks. "I would like for both of us to see home again, Earl Stone. Please see me in the morning so you may begin my instruction."

22

RIPPLES

ERROL TRIED TO IGNORE the pain evident on Adora's face. The challenge lay in ignoring his memory of Cruk's attempt to teach him the sword months before. Afterward he'd woken so sore that movement of any kind qualified as torture. Adora's beating exceeded his. The welts on her shoulders had faded somewhat overnight, but her skin was so mottled by bruises that her arms resembled molting snakes.

Even so, as Adora rode she hoisted a pair of bags filled with rocks, alternating lifts with each hand and then lifting them both in unison. The extremity of her exertions left channels on her face where tears washed away the dust from the road. Errol adjusted his view of the princess. Before, he had looked upon her as a work of priceless porcelain, of surpassing value, but fragile. The radiance of her eyes and the golden splendor of her hair had awakened protective instincts in him that had surprised him.

Now it seemed those instincts were hardly required. The glory of the princess's beauty—from her smooth, flawless skin to the lithe grace of her movements—still stunned him, but there was

222

more tempered steel to Adora than fired clay. She lifted the bags again, intent.

"Good, Princess," he said. "The motion will help work the soreness from your arms and strengthen the muscles for the sword."

"When can I spar again?" Adora asked with a grunt of exertion.

Errol laughed. "Whenever you want." Adora's face lit with anticipation. "But if you want to be able to get anything out of the lesson, wait until most of the soreness is gone."

Her delicate eyebrows lowered, casting the sea green of her eyes into stormy shadow. "Very well. I hardly think I need your supervision to heft bags of rocks, Earl Stone."

The tone of dismissal was unmistakable.

Errol tried to bow as he rode. He grappled with the saddle to recover his balance. "Your Highness," he said. Then he moved forward to ride with Rale.

Captain Elar Indomiel—who Errol would always think of as Rale the farmer—leaned forward as he rode, his eyes searching and intent. The captain's face, usually open and friendly, now looked harsh enough for him to be Cruk's brother.

His gaze snapped to Errol. "I don't like it, boy."

"What?" Errol asked.

Rale looked on the verge of giving him a tongue lashing, but he growled his impatience instead. "You need to think, boy. One well-placed arrow in my chest and, honorary captain or not, you'll be heading this church-forsaken mission into Merakh. In what direction are we headed?"

"South."

Rale gave an exaggerated nod. "And how long have we been headed mostly south?"

Errol shrugged. "Since we started."

"And if you were Valon or one of his circle, what would you think?"

"That we were coming for him in Merakh, but he knows that already," Errol pointed out. "He's known that since the attack at Steadham."

The captain inclined his head. "Good, but not good enough.

How many ports are there on our side of the strait? After that, how many ports are there on the Merakhi side?"

He shook his head. "I don't know."

"It's your job to know, boy."

"And when would I find time to do that?" Errol shot back. "I've been getting to know the men in the caravan, trying to keep Rokha from brutally beating Adora—who in turn, can't make up her mind whether to keep me or kiss me—and now you expect me to know things I have no way of knowing. By the three, I wish I were back in the ale barrel in Callowford."

Instead of getting angry, Rale laughed. The sound bounded among the trees in the cool air of the Talian hills, clean and fresh. When he finished, he clapped Errol on the back. "It's simple, boy. I'm one of the people you're supposed to get to know."

Errol hung his head in embarrassment. "They said you were the second-best tactician in the kingdom. I forgot."

"A woman can addle your brains sure enough, Errol, but you're second-in-command. You can't afford to get distracted. It's past time for you to begin your education."

"How long did it take you to become one of the best military leaders in the kingdom?"

"Decades, but I can teach you the rudiments along the way."

Errol settled in for a long conversation, and he wasn't disappointed. By the time the sun burned its way from bright yellow to orange to red, Rale had guided him through a mind-boggling array of military subjects that included pikemen, archers, light cavalry, heavy cavalry, sieges, supply lines, and more.

"How do you keep up with it all?" Errol asked in awe. "Your head should be as big as a castle holding all that."

Rale chuckled. "Years of study reinforced by experience in the field. I could have done without that last part. I hate war."

"But you're good at it."

The captain's lips tightened around his answer. "When I was a sergeant, I studied tactics because I wanted to live. The worst thing in battle is to have some popinjay of a noble giving orders while his head is filled with tales of glory. I disobeyed a lot of those. After they promoted me, I kept studying because I wanted my men to live. The higher I went, the more I studied. I've always enjoyed learning about war. It's using the knowledge I despise. Men bleeding to death calling for their wives or mothers never make it into the tales."

"Does it have to come to war?" Errol asked.

"Except, possibly, for a few of the nobles, the kingdom doesn't want it," Rale said, "but everything we've learned tells us that the Merakhi and Morgols do. War's not like dancing, Errol. It only takes one to start."

Ru called to them from his position on the lead wagon. The caravan master and Rale exchanged a long glance. Ru's head tilted and his lip curled ever so slightly. Rale stared through Naaman Ru as if the man were made of water.

"What do you want?" Rale asked.

"Darcy tells me there's a village a league ahead, watchman." Ru managed to imbue the title with scorn. "We need to resupply. Caravans have to do that every now and then, you know. We need to make camp there."

Rale's eyes flattened to slits. "How big is the village?"

"What does it matter?" Ru asked. "We need supplies."

"No. We'll camp here." Rale shrugged.

Ru's face flushed at the dismissal. "We won't make it to the coast unless we resupply. It's either at the next village or some other place."

"How big is the village?" Rale repeated.

Ru muttered genealogical imprecations under his breath and called for Darcy. The Gascon came forward, his smile fading as he caught the tension between the two men. "How may I serve you, Master Ru, Captain?"

"How big is the next village?" Rale asked.

"Minaccia?" Darcy asked. "It's more than a village, less than a town. It has three or four inns, I think." He kissed the fingertips of one hand. "Ah, but the women, Captain, they are a wonder."

Rale turned to the caravan master. "We'll camp short of the village by five hundred paces. You can take the supply wagon on in and get what we need." The captain gave Ru a long look. "I'll be sending a pair of guards with you, just to help you out, Master Ru."

The implication of distrust resonated in Rale's words and even more so in his choice of guards. Merodach and Orth were the two most skilled swordsmen in the camp after Ru himself. The master snorted his disdain and turned away.

Darcy followed Rale and Errol, his face lit from within. "I'd be happy to go with the good caravan master," he said.

Errol covered his smile with a fake cough. Darcy's sudden eagerness wasn't difficult to understand.

Rale didn't share Errol's amusement. "I expect you to remember your place and your duty, Darcy. I have no intention of letting you within fifty paces of the women of any village. You will stay here. Merodach and Orth will go."

"You expect trouble?" Errol asked. The choice to send the two best swords in the watch troubled him.

"I always expect trouble. The worst part is I'm usually right. The closer we get to the coast, the more Valon can concentrate his forces against us. There's a lot less ground to cover."

"Should I cast for danger in the village?" Errol asked.

Rale shook his head. "Not yet. Save your blanks for when we're closer to the coast. I think we're safe enough for now. If there's trouble, Ru, Merodach, and Orth should be able to handle it."

The caravan guards quickly set up camp—circling wagons, picketing horses, and preparing dinner without rush or confusion. Mindful of Rale's admonition, Errol studied their movements, taking note of who did which task and how.

After dinner, Adora approached Rokha across the cleared space inside the circle of wagons, her practice sword in hand.

Ru's daughter lifted one eyebrow in surprise. "So soon, Princess? You don't want another day or two to heal?"

"Will my enemies give me time to heal?" Adora asked.

Rokha nodded. "Well said." She rose to her feet and strode with a confident swagger to the closest wagon to retrieve one of the practice swords Ru carried for sparring matches. As she moved toward Adora, the princess held up a hand and turned to address Errol where he sat next to Rale.

"Earl Stone, would you be kind enough to excuse us? I'm sure the training exercises of a novice are hardly enough to hold your interest." She looked at him, her green eyes dark in the gray twilight and her face composed, expecting obedience. Behind the unblinking stare, Errol caught something more, a silent pleading in the tightness of her eyes that begged him not to stay, to avoid witnessing her humiliation.

Despite the hollow pain at her words, Errol rose with his staff in hand and sketched a bow. The king's chamberlain, Oliver Turing, had despaired of teaching him a proper bow, but Errol offered the princess the best he could.

"Your Highness, I remain your faithful servant." He would have added more, wanted to add more, but when he straightened, his eyes caught hers. And for a brief instant the veil he kept in place in her presence slipped, and he let his heart into his eyes. For a moment, he let everything he felt for Adora shine forth in his gaze even as he cursed himself as a fool for doing so.

Her eyes widened and her lower lip trembled. "Please." She cleared her throat, but her voice barely rose above a whisper. "Please go."

Errol turned with the feel of a dozen sets of eyes watching him. He passed through the ring of wagons as the first knock of wood against wood signaled the beginning of Adora's lesson.

He faced south toward the village. A hill rose above him, and he set his feet in that direction. At the top he could just discern the outline of the buildings, limned in the fading gray light of dusk. One of the guards, Nassep, a burly man with the pale skin and heavy beard typical of men from Dannick, stood watch on this quarter.

Nassep had proven useful in a fight—the Dann's sheer size and reckless style unnerved his opponents—but Errol didn't care for him much. He had a dour turn of speech that managed to find the worst in everything and everybody. The younger members of the watch had nicknamed him Daisy, but no one ever called Nassep that within his hearing.

"Good evening, Nassep," Errol said.

The watchman interrupted his survey long enough to toss a nod and grunt in Errol's direction. "I don't see what's good about it."

Errol clenched his jaws around his first impulse. "Have Ru and the guards made it to Minaccia yet?"

Nassep grew still, as if trying to find some potential catastrophe in Errol's question. Finally he shrugged. "About half an hour ago."

The village lay quiet in the distance. "It seems quiet enough."

The burly watchman to his left jumped on the innocuous statement. "With our fortune it probably won't stay that way. We'll be lucky to avoid pitched battle before dawn."

Errol sighed, fingered the polished wood of his staff. Nassep's company had lost its charm, and the sound of wooden swords behind told him the camp would still be off limits. Would the villagers of Minaccia welcome him? Errol longed for the company of regular people—he hadn't met any since leaving Callowford. A small voice in the back of his head cautioned him against taking an unnecessary risk. He told the voice to be quiet and set off down the hill.

The sounds and smells of the village urged him forward as he neared the outskirts. A woman's alto, sultry and intimate, sang words to a song that just evaded comprehension, but the good-natured laughter that accompanied it brought a smile to his lips and quickened his feet.

He walked through the broad open doors to the smell of roasting mutton and beer. The common room boasted two large fireplaces, cold and unlit in the late autumn warmth of Talia. An array of lanterns hung from the ceiling provided cheerful lighting, and in between the two hearths a small raised dais served as a stage for the evening's entertainment.

He edged his way through people clustered around tables like overripe grapes. At the bar he caught the innkeeper's attention and jangled his purse. The Talian, heavy and with the dark coloring and olive-tinted skin of his province, bustled over. "What can I get for you, good sir?"

Errol smiled, enjoying the company of folks with small cares. "Whatever you've got cooking in the kitchen and some water."

A frown creased the innkeeper's face and his mustache drooped. "We serve the best ale in northern Talia, good sir. It would be a shame for you to pass it by."

Errol nodded his agreement. "I'm sure it's excellent. Why don't you bring me water, and I'll pay you as if it were ale?"

The innkeeper brightened at the prospect. Before he could leave, Errol swept his arm in an arc to take in the crowd. "Is it always so busy?"

The Talian's face turned toward the singer. "It has been ever since she came here. I don't usually care for the Gitan—too many of the wandering people are thieves—but this one's different. I'll be seeing to your food now, good sir."

Errol listened to the song, a familiar tune sung in every province about two lovers from rival families who manage to overcome every obstacle in their quest for each other. He roared his approval and sang along with the refrain like every other patron in the inn, but deep inside, where he could almost ignore its existence, a little voice said, *If only . . .*

Evening wore on, and the locals started to drift away by ones and twos toward their beds in order to rise with the sun. A pair of merchant masters in opposing colors of blue and red haggled over the price of wine at a far table. By the windows a young man whined and wheedled a girl with jet-black hair and large brown eyes. He couldn't make out his words, but the young man's tone of voice and pleading features proclaimed his intent.

Errol's gaze swept across the room, acknowledging those few who noticed him. A man in the corner—tall, with hands and wrists that protruded from his sleeves—started as Errol made eye contact. With a smile the man rose and approached from across the inn, walking the planks as if he were a hundred feet tall. He leaned against the bar and gave Errol a smile that set his teeth on edge. It reminded him too much of Weir.

"She's not bad for a Gitan," the man said.

Errol took a sip of his water. How could he rid himself of this man? "She's not bad for anyone."

The man laughed as if he thought Errol's comment uproarious, but the notes of strain in his voice made it sound forced. "Such a belief in equality. You don't look like you're from Gascony, though."

What? Errol decided not to comment. It would only encourage the man to stay. He turned his attention back to the singer.

The man refused to leave. He made no further attempts at conversation, but he stayed by Errol as if the two were old friends sharing a night out together. The inn continued to empty. At last, the singer bowed to enthusiastic but sparse applause and stepped down from the dais.

To Errol's surprise she came straight toward him, her black hair and fair skin glowing in the soft lamplight. Her eyes, blue with a violet tinge, danced with laughter.

She stepped around Errol and draped an arm around the man, reaching up to run a slender forefinger down his jawline in a way that made Errol wonder if he should leave. She gave Errol a speculative look. "So, Rader, who's your companion?"

The man laughed as if the woman had made a joke. "I hardly know him, Sahra, but he took suitable offense to a slight against your people."

Sahra tapped his lips with her finger. "You're a pig, Rader. Why do I put up with you?"

He smiled a hungry wolflike grin. "Because I'm the best at what I do."

"Humph," she said. Sahra stepped around Errol and linked an arm through his. "Men often flatter me even as they revile my people. Why don't we go someplace where we can talk?" Her eyes glowed, catching flickers from the torches.

"I can't. I probably shouldn't have stayed this long." Errol moved to step away, but her arm tightened, and the man stepped closer, hemming him in. A long, thin dagger appeared in the man's hand, its point against Errol's ribs.

The woman cooed in his ear. "You really shouldn't turn me

down, Errol Stone. Rader dislikes it." The man's smile grew, and the point of the dagger wormed its way through his tunic to his skin.

Fool! The man's behavior should have warned him. Stupidity and bad luck had combined to dump him right in Valon's lap. "I have friends nearby," Errol said, trying to sound more confident than he felt. "If you start running now, you might actually get away."

The woman's eyes danced, and she purred. "Ooh, how very brave, but if you want to live past the next minute, you'll come with us." Rader's dagger pressed against his skin to punctuate her point.

"Where are we going?"

"Just out back."

"Why?"

She caressed his cheek in a gesture identical to the one she'd given Rader earlier. "I told you, dear boy—so we can talk."

Rader herded Errol with his knife out through the kitchen and into the stable yard behind the inn. Any hopes of escape were dashed when Rader and Sahra kept him so close no one could see the dagger pressed against his side. When they entered the yard, Errol noted it was deserted . . . of course.

The woman turned to face him, businesslike, the smile and flirtations gone. "My master wants to make you an offer, Errol Stone. Whether or not you live depends on whether or not you accept it."

Errol stared. "Valon has been trying to kill me for months. Why should I believe he would be willing to let me live?"

Sahra laughed. "I never mentioned Valon, dear boy, though I'm sure the scarecrow wants you dead. You're a threat to him and his circle."

The singer's eyes danced as she teased him with his ignorance. In the dim light of the stable yard they alternated between focusing on him and staring through him. Something about her seemed . . . off.

"How did you find me? Valon hasn't been able to attack us for weeks."

She laughed again, amused, but a thread of hysteria wove a note of discord in the sound, as if Sahra stood on the edge of anguish. "Gold loosens tongues, and Rader doesn't mind killing horses. We tracked you to the Arryth, but I didn't find you, dear boy. You found us quite by accident." Glee stretched her smile. Her eyes flickered. "I will be highly exalted by my master."

She flicked a finger at Rader. The dagger twisted. "It's time to choose, boy."

Errol licked his lips. He needed time. Someone must have noted his absence by now. "And what will your master give me?"

Sahra caressed his cheek, her hand unnaturally warm. "The mountains of far southern Merakh run yellow with gold, boy. An omne could name his price. My master would set you above Valon. Anything you desire would be yours." Her voice became low, cunning. "And you'd be free from the church."

The thought tempted him. "No more compulsions?"

She shook her head, her eyes practically vibrating now. "No."

"What about Adora?" Errol asked. He looked away, as if embarrassed by his own question. The yard and walls remained empty. By the three, where were they?

Sahra shrugged as if his question were of no importance. "You will be able to own any woman you wish, boy. If the women of Merakh are not enough for you, the princess is yours."

He tried to school his features to stillness, but his neck twitched in refutation and his mouth twisted. "And what makes you think Adora would ever love a traitor?"

The singer's eyes rolled and fluttered, mocking him. "Love? Why would you be satisfied only with her love when you could own her body and soul, boy? Don't you understand what I'm offering you? You could have power over others. Haven't you danced to others' tunes long enough? Women are fickle," Sahra purred. "Why depend on the princess's mercurial affections when you could simply own her instead?" Her voice dipped. "And if that is not enough for you, Errol Stone, there are ways of securing her devotion."

The back door of the inn banged open, and a hunched figure

bearing two large wooden buckets slouched into the yard. For an instant, Errol had hoped for rescue.

"No one's coming to save you, boy," the woman said. "Choose."

He did his best to ignore the eager look on Rader's face. "You said I could secure her devotion."

Her eyes lost their focus, appeared to wander in different directions. "All you have to do is open yourself to them, boy." Even as she said this, the woman's mouth narrowed to a rictus, and for a fleeting moment, horror that chilled Errol to his core shone in the depths of Sahra's eyes.

The servant with the buckets shuffled closer as he made for the stables. The tops of carrots peeked out over the edge of the buckets. He limped, dragging one foot behind the other.

Errol tried to recoil from the loathsome thing looking out through the woman's eyes, but the dagger halted him.

"Going somewhere, boy?" Rader asked.

The singer's face twisted into a look of gleeful hunger, her lips drawn tight against her teeth. "He's made his choice, kill him."

Rader nodded toward the hunchback with the buckets. "What about him?"

Sahra pulled a dagger that gleamed wetly. "Leave him to me."

23

MARKED

THE YARD DESCENDED INTO CHAOS. The flex of tendons in Rader's arm gave Errol his only warning. He threw himself back, away from the dagger, but pain exploded in his side, sharp and fiery. Errol rose, but instead of coming on, Rader smiled and backed away.

A wet chopping sound, like the hack of a knife into a watermelon, erupted. Errol turned to see Sahra, her smile gone, replaced by shock at the sword that had cut halfway through her side. The Gitan crumpled, her eyes focused on the man before her: Merodach.

The thrum of a bowstring, followed by the sound of a body hitting the dirt sounded behind Errol. He spun. Rader lay on the ground with half a yard of arrow sticking from his chest. His eyes had already emptied.

Errol pressed a hand to the cut in his side. Cold seeped from the wound, and the area around the cut throbbed. Gial Orth jumped from the roof of the tavern into the yard as Merodach reached him.

"Are you well?" the captain asked.

Errol nodded, then shook his head. The pain in his side moved from a throb to a tear, forcing him to speak through clenched teeth. "Get the man's dagger. I think it was poisoned."

Merodach snapped and pointed.

Orth scooped up Rader's dagger and sniffed. "It smells foul. There's a yellow tinge to it."

The pain in Errol's side continued to grow, and he growled to keep it at bay. He forced his eyes open. "The woman's dagger—did she mark you with it?"

Merodach shook his head.

A cry tore itself loose from Errol's lips, and he teetered. Merodach scooped him up as if he were a child and carried him back into the inn yelling for the innkeeper with each step.

The innkeeper came running down the stairs, lantern in hand, his mustache bristling. His face wavered through Errol's tears of pain.

"I don't like trouble in my inn," the innkeeper said. "You'll have to take him outside."

Merodach frowned in Orth's direction, and a sword appeared as if by magic at the innkeeper's throat. "You will get us a healer now," Merodach said, his voice all the more terrible for its quiet. "Lieutenant Orth will accompany you."

Orth's flame-red hair swam before Errol as if the lieutenant were on fire. "We need the caravan master's daughter as well. She might know this poison." He waved the yellow-tinted dagger for emphasis.

Merodach nodded, a movement Errol felt as searing agony in his side. "Ru is down the street loading supplies. Send him. I need a room with a bed, master innkeeper. I'll not risk moving him."

The innkeeper's drawling Talian wavered in the air. "Take mine, top of the stairs."

Merodach turned. Errol could hear the man's heartbeat, slow and steady, as though nothing of import had happened. The jolt of the captain's first step pulled a whimper from Errol. By the time they were halfway up the stairs his screams ripped through the inn. Consciousness faded before they reached the top.

He came to in agony as Merodach laid him on the bed. Screams tore his throat as pain ripped through him. Footsteps pounded in the hall. Errol felt the vibrations as knives of agony. Merodach's voice, harsh now, emptied the inn.

The sting of his sweat tore through him like the pulling of quills. Physical sensations magnified to the point of excruciating pain. The sensitivity grew worse with each second. He tried to hold himself still in a vain effort to minimize the torment, but the pressure against his back as he lay on the bed brought him to convulsions he couldn't stop. Before long he would die, thrashing and screaming.

He hoped it would be soon.

It wasn't. Errol spent an eternity trapped in searing pain. Crimson light filled his mind. Awareness of everything around him—the bed, the inn, even his screaming—disappeared into the unbearable heat of his growing pain.

Sometime after his ability to measure the passage of time had ceased, a new sensation intruded into his awareness. Cold. A chill deeper than of the Sprata's winter melt enveloped him. Shivers wracked him, turned his muscles into a quivering mass that vibrated against the convulsions of the poison. A semblance of awareness returned. Someone forced a stick between his teeth and liquid flowed down his ravaged throat.

The crimson light diminished, shrank from the size of the sun to a pinpoint, then winked out as he lost consciousness.

"Errol."

He passed without transition from black unconsciousness to pain. The rocking motion of a wagon sent spears of torture through him, but restraints kept him from thrashing to death. The effort of opening his eyes daunted him. He quit trying. There seemed to be enough muted light around him to indicate daytime. He couldn't be sure. Cold—thin and sharp like a dagger—covered him. Why was he so cold?

"Where?" The effort of that one word made him whimper. He tasted blood from the ruin of his throat.

"Oh, Errol."

Adora's voice. Broken. "We're headed toward a . . . a friend. The poison won't kill you as long as we can keep you still."

"Cold."

"We have you covered in ice we took from the inns. Rokha says we have to give your body a rest from the papaverine sap."

Papaverine . . . ? Where had they found that?

Adora's voice provided warmth to his hearing. "We've been covering you in ice to keep your convulsions at bay, but . . ."

A male voice broke in—Rale's. "But we have to let you warm up, Errol, or you'll freeze to death. We're trying to get you to a healer. Rokha thinks that if we can keep you alive long enough, the poison will pass from your system."

Chills shook him. Underneath the tremors he could sense the convulsions waiting. "How long?" He didn't like speaking. The red light in his mind flared and grew with the pain in his throat. His arms and legs twitched in warning.

"I'm not sure what you're asking, son. It's been three days since you were poisoned. We're making less than ten leagues a day. We headed west into the mountains so we would have enough ice to keep you alive."

Son. Rale hadn't meant it as Errol would have wished, but the word awoke an ache deep in his chest even as it warmed him. The cold surrounding him started to fade. Water flowed along the hair on his arms, his legs. A convulsion shook him, his back arching. The crimson light in his head exploded. Someone wedged the stick between his teeth again and a sticky-sweet liquid caressed his sore throat as he sank into oblivion.

Errol woke to darkness so black and unrelieved he thought ice had seeped into his chest, stilling his heart. The flare of red behind his eyes had receded to a pinpoint, leaving him lucid. He lay entombed in lightlessness, afraid to move lest the convulsions returned. His back ached as if someone had snuck up behind him and beaten him with punja sticks.

He was warm.

That last surprised him. He had come to associate any clarity of thought with a cold so deep it defied sun or fire. Was he dead? Months in Erinon had left him ignorant still of the simplest theology. What happened when a man died? He longed to speak, to have his loneliness relieved, but if he still lived and lay alone somewhere without help, the convulsions would kill him.

He didn't want to die. A thought occurred to him. If he still lived, the church's compulsion still lay on him. Errol turned his attention inward, seeking. Yes, there it lay, like a knot deep in his mind. He lived, warm and clear at the same time.

Why was he alone?

Or was he? He held his breath in an attempt to hear breathing other than his own, but the labored beating of his heart prevented him. With a deep breath, he tried again, with no better results. *Caution,* he told himself. He hadn't used any in the village, and a poisoned dagger to his side had been the price. As much as he wanted to know whether or not he lay alone, the answer wasn't critical.

And he was tired. His feeble efforts exhausted him. For the first time in an eternity of pain, he fell asleep without the use of drugs.

Errol opened his eyes an instant or days later. He didn't know which. A thread of sunshine shone through a thin gap in the curtains of his room. Adora sat in a chair at the foot of his bed. Dark circles of exhaustion rimmed her eyes, giving her a frantic look, as if she'd witnessed dire portents of the future. The light failed to catch the gold in her hair, and she slumped under burdens Errol couldn't see.

She blinked at him, her gaze going through him, and he shivered, remembering the eyes of the woman in the village. "Your Highness." His throat ached as though the entire conclave had used polishing cloth on it.

Adora's eyes came into focus, and she rose. Like a child, she tottered as she walked first to the door to lock it and then to the side of his bed. She knelt, her head with its glory of golden hair scant inches from his face. The patter of tears on the marble floor of his bedchamber came to him like the sound of rain on the rocks of the Sprata.

"Errol, will you forgive me? I should never have sent you away. You are the best and noblest man I have ever met."

He tried to clear his throat to speak. "Water?"

She rose, head still bowed, and filled a cup from a pitcher that sat on an ornately carved table across the room. She held the cup for him and he drank, tasting salt. His throat would take time to heal.

He closed his lips after a few gulps, ignoring what flowed down his cheeks. "You didn't send me to the village. That was my foolish idea."

"An idea you wouldn't have had except for my stupid pride," Adora said.

"Don't take burdens that don't belong to you, Your Highness. When I'm better I'll tell you just how many mistakes I made that night." Errol thought back. "It's a long list." He flexed the muscles in his legs, surprised at their obedience. "Can you help me up? I'd like to see Rale."

"I'll bring him to you," Adora said, moving toward the door.

He shook his head. "I want out of this room, even if it's to a chair just outside the door."

The princess smiled, her lips tight. "I'll get someone to assist you."

"You don't want to help me?"

The smile grew. "Earl Stone, in order to keep you cool, it was necessary to remove your clothes." She paused. "All of your clothes. You are quite naked beneath that sheet." The princess arched her eyebrows at him. "Do you still want my help?"

For a moment he considered teasing her in turn, but he considered the implications of his current state. Who had undressed him? He didn't want to know. "Uh, no thank you, Your Highness. Could you send someone else to assist me?" She turned to the door, and he remembered Rokha was the closest thing to a healer the caravan had. "Someone male, please," he called after her.

Conger came in a few minutes later. "Good to see you're still on this side of eternity, milord."

Errol shook his head. The room spun with the motion. "Call me Errol. How long since I was poisoned?"

"Seven days, mi—Errol." Conger helped him to a sitting position, then fetched a set of unfamiliar garments from a wardrobe in the corner and began to dress him as if he were a young child. "We had to cut your clothes off. It was the only way to get you into the ice without moving you too much."

Errol nodded. The motion came easier this time. "Where are we?"

Conger's eyes lit. "We are in Basquon, just over the border from Talia, but there is much more . . . Ooh, there's a story there, boy, but it's not mine to tell." He rubbed his hands with relish. "All in good time. First, the healer will want to see you. The princess has gone to fetch him."

As if the mention of him had the power to call him forth, the door opened and a young man, his head covered by a short, conical hat, moved to his bed. Dark-haired with a short beard, he looked hardly older than Errol.

He lifted Errol's shirt, removed the dressing on his side, and laid his hand on the wound, his fingers light and deft. With a nod, he replaced the bandage and the shirt. "You'll live." He said this as if he'd been uncertain of Errol's fate up to that point.

Errol smiled. "I'm glad to hear it. I had my doubts over the past seven days."

Conger snorted, but the healer only nodded, either missing the jest or ignoring it. "Styrich poisoning," he said. "You're lucky to be alive."

Caution, Errol told himself. "What can I do or not do?"

The healer waved a hand. "The poison has washed out of your system. You can do anything you have the strength to do. You haven't eaten anything for a week, so you'll be weak for a few days. Other than that, you're fine."

Errol tried to clear the scratch out of his throat again, but when he spoke, it still sounded deep and raspy. "When will my voice heal?"

The doctor's head tilted to one side. "It may not. They tell me you screamed the entire way here. A gargle of hot salt water may help the worst of it."

He didn't like the sounds coming from his mouth. The rasp sounded harsh, angry, like Cruk. With a push that made his arms tremble, he shoved himself off the bed. His knees buckled as his feet hit the floor, but his legs calmed to a minor quiver after a moment. His stomach emitted a low rumble that lasted for a dozen heartbeats. "Conger, can you find me something to eat?"

The ex-priest nodded and followed the doctor out of the room. Errol traveled toward the door, one hand on the wall as a support. He stepped into a broad, marbled hallway decorated with white statues. An archway in the distance opened to a large fountain topped by an ornate carving of rearing horses. Water cascaded over the figures with sounds Errol associated with the Sprata.

Outside of Rodran's palace, he'd never seen such opulence. He made for a bench across the hall with engraved horses on the supports, their manes flowing in some imaginary wind. The lines of the wood beckoned to his fingers, and he traced carved muscles, the heavy finish smooth beneath his hands. An urge to cast came over him, but he had no question that required lots.

"Here you go, lad," Conger said. He proffered a bowl of soup, thick with vegetables and lightly seasoned. "Thought you might want to start with something mild, and the soup might help your voice."

"Where are we?"

Boots echoed down the hallway in the opposite direction from which Conger had come. "You're guests in my house, Earl Stone." The man who sketched a fluid bow to accompany his words could have been Naaman Ru's older brother. Gray streaked his hair, but the mustache still glistened ebony beneath eyes the color of darkest onyx.

Errol tried to stand to return the courtesy, but shock and fatigue kept him on the bench.

"Do not trouble yourself, my friend," the man said. "You are fortunate to be alive." His voice, smooth as his bow, made common words sound as if he were reciting poetry. "I am Count

Rula. Please allow me to be your host while you recuperate. I understand that you are an honorary captain of the watch, yes?"

Errol nodded, bemused.

"Excellent. Please let my staff know of anything you require."

The man's effusive speech and flawless manners left Errol flat-footed. "Count, why are we here?"

The count's dark brows lifted as if he didn't quite understand the question. "Why, so you may heal, Earl Stone."

Errol shook his head, frustrated at his inability to communicate. "No . . . I mean, yes, I understand. But how did we get here? We're in Talia, and I was told that we detoured into Basquon."

The count's cultured manner remained, but his friendly manner cooled despite the smile he still wore. "You needed cold, Earl Stone. My estate is surrounded by the ice of the Apalian Mountains." He shrugged. "Let us say that Deas's providence has brought you here, shall we? Good day." He bowed and moved past Errol and Conger, his long strides taking him out of earshot in seconds.

"Why are we here, Conger?" Errol asked. "It doesn't take a reader to know something strange is going on."

The former cleric scratched his stomach as he answered. "I believe you have the compulsion the archbenefice placed on Master Ru to thank for that."

"What?"

"After you got poisoned, Naaman Ru became strange, gave orders to take the caravan over the border to Basquon. He and Captain Elar nearly came to blows before the captain figured out what was going on. It turns out Ru knew there would be help here, though he sweated and fumed and cursed like a sailor in a storm the whole way."

Errol nodded in understanding. "If I died he'd be free of his compulsion."

Conger shook his head. "I'm not saying you're wrong, lad, but there's more to it than that. Once we came onto Count Rula's estate, Master Ru ordered his daughter into the wagon with himself and refused to come out. He's still hiding there, so far as I know."

"Why?"

"Count Rula is his uncle and wants him dead."

Errol took another bite of soup, savoring the flavor and feel of warm liquid against his raw throat but suddenly feeling exhausted. "I've felt that way myself—many a time—but we need Ru to guide us into Merakh. He can't do that if his uncle has his head decorating a wall." He took a deep breath and looked at Conger out of the corner of his eye. "Why does his uncle want him dead?"

Conger's eyes fired with curiosity. "No one who knows is saying. Rula says we're welcome to stay as long as we like, but when we leave, Ru won't be going with us."

Errol rubbed a sudden ache behind his eyes, and he could think of little save returning to bed. He set down the soup bowl and leaned back against the wall. Why did everything have to be so difficult? "Does he have the men to stop us?"

Conger nodded.

"Please help me back to my room. I need to sleep. And then we'd better counsel with Rale"—he sighed—"and Naaman Ru."

24

THE SHADOW LANDS

MARTIN AND HIS FELLOW TRAVELERS halted in the pass, the scene spread before them like a storyteller's depiction. The mountains of the Sprata reared their crowns to the sky, cold and uncaring across an expansive sea of grass. The river, broad and sluggish a hundred leagues south of Callowford, created a border between the mountains and the plain.

"By the three," Luis said, his voiced muted. "It's more a land for giants than men."

Nothing to do with mankind stirred on that plain. In the distance a herd of wild horses ran, the thunder of their hooves silenced by the intervening space. They might as well have been phantoms.

"No men are there for a reason," Cruk said. After the cast, the captain had stifled his protests and led them south without complaint, but his voice carried a sharper edge. "That's where we're headed."

Martin followed his point to a spur of lower mountains, their peaks blunted by time and weather. The river turned to flow through a gap in the range. "How long will it take us to get there?" Martin asked.

"A day," Cruk answered, "perhaps two."

They descended the pass, and Martin's sense of self shrank as the press of the forest receded. Their mounts seemed comfortable in that open expanse. The wind moved over the grass like a wave, and Martin imagined he rode not on a horse but a ship.

They stopped past midday to eat and let the horses graze. Cruk scanned the horizon, his face hard. Lines of tension carved his face and forehead. "We'll want to make camp near one of the trees. We may have to alter our route a little bit."

"Why?" Karele asked. One hand made a circling motion. "There's nothing here save us and a few wild horses."

The muscles in Cruk's jaw jumped. Martin could almost hear the captain grinding his teeth. "You may be right, solis, but I'm not going to bet our lives on it. If it comes to a fight, I'll want to use that tree to protect my back." His shoulders bunched. "And if it comes to that, we may need to climb our way to safety."

Cruk seemed more cautious than usual. "What worries you?" Martin asked.

The captain pointed at the horses. "Meat usually means meat eaters."

As the sun set, they camped under a stunted oak tree, its leaves blunted by a yellowish cast when they should have been a glossy green. Scorch marks flared up the trunk as if someone had tried to topple it with fire. Despite the bare ground beneath the tree, Cruk dictated a cold camp. A gibbous moon provided enough light to distinguish shapes but failed to provide comfort.

"Sorry, Pater," Cruk said. He rubbed a few stalks of grass between his fingers. The grass gave dry whispering noises as it disintegrated. "One stray ember and the whole plain will go up." A rumble in the distance punctuated Cruk's warning. The captain pointed toward a dark cloud shaped like an anvil on the western horizon. "That may be our biggest threat. I'll take the watch."

Martin rolled his cloak into a pillow and tried not to think about the canopy of yellowed leaves above him that filtered the moonlight. Nothing could keep Rodran alive indefinitely. His last thought before sleep took him was a tired curse for Rodran's father, Rodrick, and the pride that had doomed the royal line.

Hands shook him. He woke to the smell of smoke.

"It's a grassfire. Time to ride," Cruk said.

Moonlight still filtered down through the leaves of the stricken tree. Perhaps an hour had passed, maybe two. Dawn still lay hours away.

"We can't run the horses in the dark," Karele said.

Cruk nodded. "We agree on that, anyway, and we won't until we have to. Let's move. That fire is leagues away. With luck we'll still be ahead of it when dawn breaks."

Behind them, made small by the distance, a wall of orange flared. Unseen tendrils of smoke reached through the darkness to sting Martin's eyes. If they failed to escape, the heat would boil the skin from their bones long before the flames engulfed them, burning them black as they raced to the river. With luck, the wind would shift and they would die from the smoke before the fire's heat took them.

After what seemed like hours of riding at a walk, Martin turned to see the wall of flame straining skyward for a hundred feet roaring in the distance—much closer now, close enough to hear. The blaze roared in hunger, the crackle of burning grass and scrub mixed with the rush of air.

Ahead the river glistened like a promise of rescue in the distance, too far for them to reach at their cautious pace. Yet Cruk held them to a walk. The horses strained at their bits, lathered and eyes rolling. Surely they had to make a run for it. Cruk kept to the same brisk walk, glancing back every few strides to gauge the distance between them and that swirling orange vortex.

Martin loosened the reins. His mount surged forward. The tendons in his arms protested as he sawed the bit to keep his horse from dashing away. "We can't stay at this pace much longer."

Cruk checked the progress of the wildfire behind them again before he gave a curt nod. "I know, Pater, but there are other dangers besides the fire."

Martin shook his head. Nothing stirred in that ocean of dry tinder except the fire and themselves. "What?"

Cruk pointed off to the right, toward the southern end of the plain. "That."

Martin squinted against the darkness, shielding his eyes against the light of the fire. Only shadows cast by the moon and flames were visible, but gradually the phantoms resolved into the shapes of horses streaming away from the threat. He shook his head. He saw nothing else—nothing to fear.

"Look at the grass behind the horses, Pater."

Martin peered into the darkness again. *There.* Behind the horses a wave of motion trailed the herd across the flat landscape. Something tracked them, something that hid below the waist-high grass. The stallion in front charged for the closest bend of the river, leading the predators to them.

The wave crept closer to the herd, the distance shrinking in agonizing slowness. Martin watched in horror as a colt, straggling behind, stumbled and disappeared. The deflection in the grass paused for a moment before resuming its track behind the herd.

Military training was as much a mystery to Martin as theology would be to most men, but even he could tell the herd and its predators would reach the river before them. What was Cruk thinking?

"We have to beat them to the river," he yelled ahead. "If they arrive before us, we'll never make it across." Fear wove strident threads into his voice.

Cruk shook his head. The man must be mad. Then the captain pointed toward the river, a bit to the north. Martin repeated his efforts to see in the dim light provided by the moon.

A child's prayer, desperate and fearful, sprang to his lips. An identical wave in the grass angled toward their path, making for the herd. Cruk's reckless strategy became apparent at a glance. The captain strove for just the right pace for their mounts, waiting for the predators to cross their path in pursuit of the herd. If they went too fast, the pack would catch their scent, fire or no, and they'd be torn to pieces; too slow and the fire would overtake them.

Cruk leaned toward him. "We have one chance, Pater. As soon as the pack ahead crosses and clears our path, we must ride for the river as fast as these sorry mounts can take us. Our only hope is that the approach of the second pack will slow the herd enough for us to get there first. When we reach the water, don't wait. Get to the other side. If we're separated, rejoin at the pass."

A hundred potential flaws in the plan battled for Martin's attention. "What if the current's too deep and strong for the horses to cross?" He didn't wait for an answer, as his thoughts swung to the opposite problem. "What if the water's not deep enough to keep those things away from us?"

Cruk spared enough time from his scan to grimace and spit. "Pater, you know what will happen as well as I do." He nodded toward Karele. "If you have concerns you might want to take them up with him." The captain bit his words, his voice clipped and tight. "I seem to recall this route was his idea."

The fire crept closer. Martin could feel heat now. The distances shrank and he could more clearly see dark shapes in the grass—forms that twisted and shifted in the moonlight as they ran, weaving shadows like dark tendrils of rope. In horror and guilt, he thanked Deas for each horse the first pack caught. Each time the mares panicked, the stallion brought them back under control, giving the second pack time to converge.

Thick smoke streamed past them as the fire roared and grew at their backs. A gust of wind brought a flash of heat like a premonition.

Cruk reined in, held up a hand, calling for a halt. "Any closer and they might smell us." Martin stopped, tried to ignore the feel of heat growing against his neck. In front of them, no more than fifty paces away, furred shapes streamed toward the herd. Over the roar and rush of flames he could hear the triumphant howls of the dark wolves. They bounded toward their prey, their eyes red with reflected fire.

Luis's eyes widened. The secondus leaned forward in his saddle, sweat streaming from the dome of his bare scalp down his face. He stared at the captain with single-minded intensity, never looking forward to the wolves or behind at the flames.

Karele sat his mount, his face pinched, but he looked at the river like a man seeing his salvation. Smoke settled into the lines of his face, painting his sharp features in soot. By the light of the fire, he looked like a ghoul. Doubt chewed Martin's insides. Why had they come this way?

The last of the pack cleared away, and Cruk's arm instantly snapped forward, waving them toward the nearest bend of the river. Martin required no additional urging. He dug his heels into his horse's flanks even as his hands slid forward with the reins. His mount sprang ahead, trailing behind Luis and Karele. The master of horses balanced in the stirrups, moving easily with his horse's gait, and he appeared to be talking to his mount. Martin surged past Cruk, who slowed, letting them pass before he closed in behind.

To Martin's right, the herd and packs angled in toward the river. The thunder of hooves rolled across the plain in defiant counterpoint to the howls of wolves and the roar of fire. The black water beckoned to him. He leaned forward to yell words of encouragement to his mount. The bay strove to keep pace with Karele and Luis, yet his horse, burdened with his greater bulk, slipped behind. Cruk came beside as they neared the water, one hand on the reins, the other holding his sword. Martin kept his eyes forward, willing and praying his horse toward escape.

Thirty paces from the water violence exploded around him.

The herd and the wolf packs surged around them. Howls merged with the screaming of horses, drowning Cruk's frantic commands. Karele and Luis had gained the safety of the river, their mounts splashing forward for half a dozen strides before they bobbed and started swimming.

Cruk swung his sword like a cleaver, chopping at wolf and horse alike, trying to clear a path. The horses milled in a panic, thrashing against each other. The herd's stallion went down under a half dozen wolves. Discipline among the rest of the horses vanished. Animals no longer made for the river but splintered into a dozen different directions. Cruk flailed at the press. Martin could do little more than hold on and try to follow. His sword bumped against his leg, but he'd yet to swing the weapon. Fear of losing control of his mount or, worse, going down in the melee, kept both his hands on the reins.

The shoulders of his mount dipped, and he cried out before the spray of water told him they'd made it to the river. A stream of horses swam away from the slaughter on the bank. After a few steps the bottom dropped away and his mount swam, its head tilted up to keep its nose clear.

Ahead, Cruk slipped from his saddle to float beside his laboring horse. Martin copied him, praying his horse had enough sense to follow. The water dragged at him, and he kicked, trying to aid the labored efforts of his mount. Behind him, fire reached the bloodbath on the shore. The howls no longer sounded triumphant. Water frothed as every animal left on solid ground threw itself into the water to escape the heat. The scent of scorched hair and burning meat blanketed him. He covered his nose with his cloak and kept kicking.

The far riverbank drifted by as the current carried him downstream. His horse's kicks grew weaker. Curse his fat priest's hide; they weren't going to make it. He yelled encouragement to the mare, to no avail. He smacked the mare's rump. For a few moments, the beast surged forward. Then it lapsed into weaker kicks than before. Cruk's animal must have been stronger or less burdened; the watchman was beyond reach.

Martin resolved to hold on to his horse for as long as the animal could make any progress toward the far shore. Dead animals—some horses and some wolves—drifted past him in the current, their coats covered with blood or burns.

Halted by the water and bereft of fuel, the wildfire began to die, pitching the river into darkness. Things bumped into Martin in the darkness—hairy things he shoved away in revulsion. His eyes readjusted to the lesser light of the moon. His horse bobbed below the surface, struggled upward, and then went under again.

Martin let go of the reins. Perhaps the animal would survive without his weight dragging it down. Regardless, it would no longer serve him. He surrendered his sword to the depths of the river, filled his lungs, and pulled through the water for the far shore.

Martin thrust himself against the current. Stroke and pull. Time after time, he thrust his arms forward, then brought them back to his side. His shoulders burned as if the conflagration on the prairie had settled there, punishing him for his poor judgment. Time slowed to a crawl, yet the moon dropped toward the western horizon behind him. Then the passage of time stopped altogether.

A shaft of sunlight stabbed his eyes. He held up a hand. Acrid smoke drifted across his vision painting the yellow-green canopy overhead with dirty brown smears. His shoulders trembled, and pain ripped through them when he levered himself to a sitting position.

On the far bank of the river, blackened scrub and ash spread as far as he could see. He wondered if the tough oak where they had camped had managed to survive. He hoped so. It seemed important for some reason.

His boots made squelching sounds as he turned a slow circle, searching for signs of Cruk, Luis, or Karele. A narrow plain separated him from the low peaks of the Sprata Mountains, which formed a wall between him and the shadow lands. Dead animals clogged both banks of the river.

There was no sign of his horse. He knelt to say his lauds, even though he'd missed dawn by two hours at least. What day was it? Sometime on the trip south from Callowford he'd lost track. Without knowing the day he didn't know which portion of the liturgy to recite. Did Deas care whether or not he recited the wrong portion? Did Deas care whether he used the liturgy at all?

He sank to his knees. A hundred petitions filled his mind. He framed them in accordance with the format of the daily office and began. "Hear, O Deas, the petition of our hearts that most earnestly . . ."

Martin stopped. For the first time in his life the familiar words failed to bring him the comfort of Deas. Instead a weight of separation fell on him as he used his words to hide his desperation and his fear.

His anger.

Martin stared at the ground, the practiced eloquence of his education and experience draining from him. He didn't know what to say, didn't know if he should say anything. He rose and turned north. Without a horse, it would take him hours to find the gap leading him into the shadow lands—his only hope of reuniting with his friends.

He moved away from the bank in an attempt to escape the mud next to the river that pulled at his boots. As he approached the mountains, the ground sloped upward. Ancient trees formed a thick canopy overhead. Boles two or three spans across supported limbs that were larger than the trunks of most trees. As he moved beneath the shade, the brush shrank until he walked on earth covered by nothing more than a carpet of leaves. Old scorch marks—testimony to the durability of those hoary titans—blackened the trunks.

Closer to the mountains, the suggestion of a path ran north and south. Curious, Martin scuffed at the detritus beneath his boots. Layers of dead and decomposing leaves peeled away, revealing a block of stone a foot or more across. A few paces away the skeleton of a forgotten road broke through the carpet of leaves.

Despite his circumstances, Martin found himself intrigued. The church's training covered the history of Illustra, and he prided himself on knowing that history as well as any professor at the university. Yet he knew of no civilization that had ever occupied this part of the continent. Where did the road go? What destinations had it connected, and what circumstances forced its builders and users to abandon it?

He continued north, the weight of his sodden clothes forgotten in his sudden burst of curiosity. The remnants of the road proved treacherous, forcing him to walk to the side. He detoured back into the forest, scanning the ground. When he found the object of his search, he hefted the oak branch and struck it against a tree. It felt solid enough. He leaned his weight on it. The wood flexed slightly but didn't break or crack. Heartened, he returned to the road.

After hours of walking his clothes were nearly dry, but the sensation reminded him that the river had claimed his waterskin as well as his sword. His stomach growled. Missing a few meals wouldn't hurt him, but he would need water. With a sigh he left the ancient road again and returned to the river.

Broad and deep, the Sprata flowed sluggishly. Martin sighed. Carcasses dotted both sides of the bank. If Cruk were there, the watchman could probably tell him how long an animal had to decompose before it ruined the supply. He looked closer. The animals hadn't even started to bloat yet, which meant the water was probably safe to drink.

The thought revolted him. Surely there would be some stream or brook he could find that fed into the river. He felt the end of his cloak, then lifted it to his mouth and pulled the moisture from it. It tasted like wool, but he detected nothing other than that. He pushed away from the bank and ascended back to the road.

The sun reached its zenith and began the long, arcing trek through the sky behind him to the west. The thrill of the unknown dissipated as his thirst increased and the gap through the mountains refused to show itself. Three hours before sunset he stopped.

The road ended.

A spur of the mountain range rose up before him, cutting across his path, blocking his way north.

For the next two hours he coursed along those hills, but they ran all the way to the river and ended in a sheer cliff fifty feet above the water. He had no doubt that he could survive the jump if the water was deep enough, but the current would be flowing against him. He would die of exhaustion before he regained the bank.

Not knowing what else to do, he returned to the ancient road. His mouth felt dry, but not enough to make him chance the river water. He seated himself on a broad stump. The road's existence mocked him.

He'd loved his history courses and fancied he knew the kingdom's annals as well as any man. Yet nowhere in the history of Illustra or in the time of the provinces before had cities in this part of the kingdom been mentioned. The implications disturbed him. And even more, the road didn't appear to go anywhere. It ran along the bluff that overlooked the river and then stopped at the mountain spur, blocking him from the pass to the east.

Why would anyone build a road that led nowhere?

He shook his head. They wouldn't.

He hefted his walking stick and retraced his steps to the end again. Trees on his left shielded the river from view. Enormous deadfalls blocked the way on his right. In front the mountains reared up, and behind the road stretched to the south. He stopped.

The deadfalls blocked his view. Cautious, he stepped across the jumbled blocks of weathered stone to the closest rotting bole. Climbing over it was out of the question. He backtracked around it, using his staff to force his way through the brush that had sprouted in the pools of sunlight. Deeper in the brush dwindled, and he made his way north. After a few paces he stopped, standing on the ruins of the road once more.

Of course. The road hadn't stopped. It had turned. The deadfalls kept him from seeing what should have been plain. The road now ran east. Perhaps, if he was lucky, the ruined street would offer a pass through the mountains. He snorted. If he was lucky, he wouldn't be thirsty, hungry, horseless, and alone. Besides, he didn't believe in luck. He believed in Deas's favor or its absence.

25

THE SWORD MASTER

TWO DAYS AFTER AWAKING in the villa of Count Rula, Errol walked with Conger toward the expansive back garden of the count's estate. The sound of practice swords drifted toward him as they crossed beneath one of the stone archways and onto the stone patio overlooking the garden. A red-banded hawk flew overhead, crying in defiance or frustration.

"No, Your Highness," Count Rula said. "You are too far forward. The secret to the sword is balance." Rula's hands adjusted Adora's stance, moving her shoulders back two fingers' width. "The weight of the sword must be compensated by the rear arm, placed on the hip or held so in back." He shifted her arm to match his instructions.

"Which is better?" Adora asked.

"Held back," Rula said. "But it is more fatiguing and requires greater endurance."

Clustered around the grassy area where Rula instructed, every watchman observed the count's directions with intense scrutiny. Errol knew little about swordplay, but he recognized the deft touch of a master swordsman, even so. Naaman Ru's prowess became easier to understand.

"Then I will train myself to hold it back," Adora said. She jerked upright as Errol came into her field of view. "Are you trying to kill yourself, Earl Stone?"

Errol smiled. "Not anymore, hopefully. Village inns are a lot more dangerous now that I'm sober. I might have to take up drinking again."

The princess smiled. "You're pert, my earl. You know what I mean."

He nodded. "Count Rula's healer has pronounced me fit enough to leave my sickbed."

The count eyed Errol with interest. "I'm told you're the premier staff man in the kingdom, Earl Stone. Your balance must be finely tuned for such a weapon. Have you ever given thought to learning the sword?"

Errol laughed so hard, spots swam in front of his eyes. "A captain of the watch tried to teach me. That's how I ended up with the staff. I'm probably the worst swordsman in the kingdom."

Rula sniffed. "Ridiculous. If you're that good with the staff, the sword should come naturally. You just need the right instructor." He came forward to rest his hand on Errol's shoulder. "Let me teach you."

Errol took a deep breath. He would never have a better opportunity to approach Rula about the caravan master. "May we discuss it as we walk, Count Rula? After more than a week on my back, I need to stretch my legs."

Rula nodded assent, but his eyes narrowed in speculation. "I am at your service, Earl Stone." He turned to those assembled. "Shall we meet together at the third hour tomorrow, my friends?"

The count moved at a leisurely pace toward his gardens. He pointed toward a myrtle tree, thick with vibrant pink blossoms. "That one is my favorite," he murmured. "The blossoms never fail to startle me."

Errol nodded his agreement. "It's beautiful. We have something like it in the Sprata, but it only blooms for a few weeks in the spring."

Rula gave him a knowing look. "You didn't really want to talk about lessons in the sword, Earl Stone. I love my garden, but perhaps we should address the concern that requires a private meeting."

Errol paused, searching the count's voice for any sign that he'd given offense. Basqus were given to be passionate people—quick to love, quicker to anger—but Rula's voice sounded open, courteous.

"Thank you, Count. I'm new to my title, so please forgive me if my manners are less than courtly."

"Earl Stone, that is as courtly and well-spoken an introduction as I've heard from a noble in some time. Most of us have forgotten our manners, I think. Please continue."

Errol bowed from the neck in a show of thanks. "I'll try to be brief. The details would take days." He sighed. "The Judica has placed me under compulsion to find a renegade reader and kill him."

The count's face darkened. "Monstrous. I thought the church had given up that disgusting practice."

Errol shrugged. "For the most part they have. I seem to be the exception. The worst part of their charge is that the reader in question has escaped to Merakh."

A kaleidoscope of emotions chased across the count's face—shock, rage, indignation, but also detachment, as if he knew what Errol would be asking. "Are your enemies so powerful, then?"

"They are. If I do not have a guide into Merakh, I have no hope of being able to satisfy the church's compulsion. I know of only one man with the knowledge of the Merakhi interior."

The count nodded. "My nephew."

"Yes," Errol said. He kept his voice as neutral as he could manage, neither asking nor demanding the count's favor.

Rula turned toward a stand of lilac. The heavy scent filled Errol with a longing to be back in Callowford.

"Do you know why I despise my nephew, Earl Stone?"

Errol shook his head. "I don't want to presume on your hospitality, Count."

Rula smiled. "You're plain-spoken, Earl Stone, but quite mannerly. Here, I will tell you the tale." He moved to a bench under a flowering tree Errol couldn't identify. "Naaman has a gift for the sword that comes once in a century. I've taught enough men to know. In my nephew Deas combined vision, quickness, and an aptitude for the blade that is startling." He spread his hands. "The sword is a tradition in our family. My brother and I were counted as the best swords in Basquon in our youth. In Naaman, our family's talent was distilled to its highest concentration.

"We trained him from the age of three, first in games children play with sticks, then with practice swords we cut to size for his stature, but by the time he turned ten he could best most men twice his age. By the time he turned fifteen, only my brother and I could match him." Count Rula shook his head, his lips pressed together in a sign of regret. "By the time he was eighteen, Naaman could beat my brother and me at the same time." Rula stopped.

"What happened?"

The count grew still, a stillness of suppressed rage. "Naaman's younger brother, Daman, fell in love with a girl, and she fell in love with him. Daman was a good lad, decent with the sword, but he would never have earned a spot in the watch, not even as a soldier, much less a lieutenant or captain."

"Naaman loved her too?" Errol asked.

Rula nodded. "I'm not sure Naaman knows how to love anything but the blade." He shrugged. "He thought he loved her— perhaps he did in the small, spare area the sword left in his heart. The end was so tragically predictable, it might have been laughable in a play." He lifted his gaze to the sky. "Naaman challenged his brother for the right to Fiora's hand. Idiots," Rula spat. "All they had to do was ask Fiora to decide."

Rula grew quiet before he spoke again, his voice as soft as the breeze that ruffled the pale blooms in front of them. "Daman died so quickly.

"My brother banished his son and heir. Naaman vanished

across the strait." Rula turned to look Errol in the eyes. "Your guide is an assassin. His heart is more quenched steel than flesh and blood."

"No," Errol said. "He loves. I have seen it."

Rula started. "You would defend him? The man took you captive and then tried to kill you."

"How do you know this, Count Rula?"

He lifted a hand. "I am a man with considerable resources. I have found myself wondering what has become of my nephew from time to time."

"I need him," Errol said.

Rula shook his head. "My brother and I vowed to give Daman justice if Naaman ever came within our grasp. The church's compulsion has inadvertently provided what twenty-five years and considerable wealth could not."

"Count," Errol said, "you may honor your vow to your brother, but my heart tells me he will not thank you for killing his son. Naaman Ru has a daughter he loves with all the passion the Basqus are known for. And he has a debt to pay to me. Will you let him honor it?"

Count Rula held Errol's gaze, as if considering a great request. "Perhaps . . . Earl Stone. We shall see what can be arranged."

The next morning long shadows from the dawn sun stretched before Errol as Count Rula pointed to a spot on the flagstones. "Stand, boy."

Errol obeyed without thought. Evidently his earldom ceased to exist the moment he became Rula's student. Errol didn't dare voice complaint. Despite the fact that his daughter would marry within the week, Rula was taking time from the preparations to exact his price for Ru's life—Errol would learn the sword. Naaman's freedom depended on honoring the count's request to train him, it seemed.

Without warning, Rula tossed Errol's staff. It floated across the space between them, and Errol's hands reached for it by reflex, his palms and fingers almost hungering for the feel of the smoothed wood grain against his flesh.

"Good," the count nodded. "Your balance is as good as any I've seen."

"As good as your nephew's?"

Rula nodded. "Yes, boy, it's as good, possibly better." He pulled the ash from Errol's grip and laid it aside. "Keep that balance in mind when you hold a sword, and the rest will flow from your experience."

The count pulled a practice sword from a rack, examined it, and put it back. He did this repeatedly, working his way through the whole rack before starting on another. To Errol's eye, each sword differed from its neighbor by negligible amounts. At last he stopped, brought the chosen weapon to Errol, and placed it in his hands.

"Stand like I showed you, boy."

Errol assumed the position—sword arm forward, relaxed, body turned to the side, and his free arm extended loosely behind him. He straightened in an attempt to correct a feeling of imbalance. Then he leaned forward once more. His free hand clutched at the air. Errol made a fist. Then he leaned back.

"What, by all that's sacred, are you doing?" Rula asked. "Be still."

Errol tried, but the emptiness in his free hand disturbed him, and he sought balance that continued to elude him.

Rula shook his head, no longer disgusted but perplexed. "It's that hand. Try holding the sword with your left hand instead of your right."

Errol complied, but no sooner had he assumed the stance when the small involuntary jerks in his posture resumed.

Rula frowned, his face thoughtful. "Perhaps I judged Captain Cruk too harshly."

A wave of relief washed over Errol. "Does that mean I'm not suited to the sword?"

The count shook his head. "No, far from it." He came to Errol's side and tapped him on the head with one finger. "Your sense

260

of balance is so developed that it's taken root in your mind. The emptiness of one hand while the other holds weight troubles you."

Despite himself, Errol felt a tug, curious. "Then I guess I should stick with the staff."

Rula smiled. "We're not done yet." He took the sword from Errol and replaced it in the rack. Then he moved down the line, the swords growing smaller until, with a satisfied smile, he selected two identical practice weapons from the rack and brought them to Errol.

"Here." Rula placed a weapon in each hand. "Now stand."

Errol stood; the sweat-stained leather of the hilts molded into his palms. He corrected once, lowering the forward tip an inch or so. *There.* The count regarded him, brows raised. "It seems your mind's demand for balance has been satisfied at last. Stay there."

Rula moved to the first rack, pulled one of the long, slender swords loose, and gave lazy waves through the air, testing it as he returned.

Without warning he lunged, the wooden blade whistling as it came at Errol's head with the swiftness of lightning. Errol parried with his lead arm, pivoted, and countered with what had been the rear weapon. His stroke missed the mark, leaving him open. Pain flared in his side like coals on his skin.

Rula stepped back, nodding in approval. "That was very good, boy."

Errol knelt on one knee, coughing. The count didn't train by half measures. Even Liam would have had a hard time matching the force of the stroke. "If it was so good, why am I the one with the bruised ribs?"

The count pursed his lips, the first sign of disapproval Errol had seen from him. "In any endeavor, boy, no matter how lofty or common, those who do it best are those who study it most. If you want to be a great master, you must first train yourself to be a great student."

The pain made it difficult to breathe. "What is the secret to being a great student?"

Rula's smile reminded Errol of Rale. "Excellent. The best

students are those who reflect on what has happened. They take every bout, every fight, and every move and break them down. They go over it and over it in their mind until they've gleaned all they can from it. Then they use what they have learned to improve."

Errol nodded, closed his eyes, and raised his weapons, replaying the attack in his mind. Rula had come at his head. He'd parried almost as he would have with a staff. Then he'd spun—the reaction automatic—and struck, or tried to.

His eyes popped open. "I missed. I tried to use a staff counter to strike below your knees, but my sword couldn't reach you, and I left myself open." Errol stared at the weapons in his hands. "I can't use these. The first time I do that in a real fight, I'm dead."

Count Rula waved his objection away. "Nonsense, you reacted automatically. We just have to train you out of the habit when you're holding swords."

The idea intrigued Errol. The swords' lighter weight and independence of motion would prove deadly in close quarters, situations where a staff proved cumbersome. Yes, he would be a good student. Errol sought Count Rula's face. "How good can I be, Count?"

Rula grew serious, almost somber. "Your speed and balance make you one of the deadliest men in the kingdom already, boy. If your blow had come for my side instead of my ankles, I'd be the one rubbing my ribs, not you."

The count hadn't given him the answer he needed. Errol dispensed with pretense and came to the issue. "You know I have no reason to trust your nephew."

Rula nodded. "You'd be a fool if you did."

"Will I be able to beat him?"

The count shook his head. "Not yet, boy, but given time, the issue would be in doubt. Past that, I can't tell you what would happen."

It wasn't the answer he'd wanted, but it was good enough.

26

RUIN WAY

FOR THREE DAYS Martin followed the ancient road. He found sufficient water in ponds and streams along the way, but he rarely found anything he dared consume. His progress slowed as the hunger grew, and as he crested another rise, he considered that his wandering was pointless and he would never rejoin his friends.

But as he descended into a sun-filled dale, an impression came to him from his environs, a sensation of order he couldn't quite define. He moved on, his ears straining for the sound of man or animal. He stumbled over the lip of a paving stone. When he righted himself, he saw it, and the hair on his arms stood out from sudden gooseflesh: The trees no longer lined the road in random design. The skeletons of huge oaks, their trunks black with age, ran before him, separated by the same distance from tree to tree.

He hurried forward, hardly remembering his hunger or fatigue in the thrill of discovery. The ancient remnants of the road rose before him, and when he topped a small rise, he gasped, the labor of his heart rushing through his ears.

Between two mountains, overgrown with brush, lay the ruins of a city, a city of which he'd never heard, a habitation that had surely passed from memory before the provinces had been conceived. The road he walked ran straight ahead into a broad, circular plaza from which other roads ran like spokes from a wagon wheel. He squinted, trying to accustom his eyes to man-made structures after so long in the plains and forest. He mounted the steps to what appeared to be a fountain, cracked and ruined in the center of the plaza.

Martin laughed under his breath. Some things seemed to be common to man no matter what the age. The steps must have been built for visual impact rather than function. He lifted each leg high to mount the oversized distance between them.

The sound of trickling water caught his ear, and he searched for it. Between cracked stones a clear stream flowed. Martin cupped his hands beneath the cool flow and took a cautious sip.

"Praise Deas."

A skittering sound behind him jolted his heart. He spun, brandishing his makeshift staff.

A small man dressed in tattered clothes with wisps of dark hair sticking out at odd angles ascended the steps with furtive jerks. He stared at Martin, then shook his head, mumbling to himself.

"I'm sorry, brother," Martin said. "You startled me." He gestured at the ruins. "This place . . ." He left it unfinished, kept his staff raised.

The man lifted his head to glance at him. "This one talks. Humph. Haven't had one talk in a while, eh?" He turned away, putting the mouth of a stained waterskin into the trickle.

Martin nudged him with his staff.

The man whirled, mouth and eyes wide with shock. He curled into a ball at the base of the fountain, water trickling unheeded over his head. He stared at Martin from underneath his arms. When Martin made no move, the little man unwound and crept toward him, his shoulders hunched as if expecting blows.

Half a pace away he extended his arm and poked Martin in his gut.

Martin grunted.

"Are you real this time?" His voice crackled with disuse. "This time?"

The man's breath whistled from his throat. "Never had one ask me a question before," he said to his hands. He poked Martin again.

Martin rubbed his belly. "Stop that. I'm as real as you are."

The man's head jerked back and forth, seeking shadows.

A sense of familiarity nagged at Martin. The little man's features and his quick, birdlike gestures reminded him of someone. "Who are you?"

The man straightened a little more. Then he laughed. "Real." Despite being a little taller than Luis, the impression of diminutive stature remained. "I . . ." He stopped, his brows furrowing in concentration. "N . . . Ni . . . Niel. Yes, my name is Niel Rohbe."

Martin stared at the little man in shock. "Teacher Rohbe?"

The man gaped. "Was that me?" He chewed a knuckle, his gaze vacant. "Yes. Yes, that sounds familiar." He squinted at Martin's face. "You have a horse? By the three, tell me you have a horse."

When Martin shook his head, Rohbe crumpled to the ground. Hysteria-tinged laughter bubbled from his lips.

"The teachers at the university said you'd disappeared, that you were dead."

Rohbe cocked his head to one said. "They're right, of course. No horse, no hope, and the spawn creeping closer. They're right, I'm right, but they'll never know it." He laughed a clear warbling sound.

Martin took him by the shoulder. The physical contact seemed to calm the man. "Do you remember me, Teacher Rohbe? Martin Arwitten."

The little man's eyes cleared a fraction. "Still getting into trouble, young Martin? Well, you're in the fountainhead of it now."

"How long have you been here?"

Rohbe shook his head. "I seem to have lost track of time. Yes. Time. I didn't expect to find ruins here. The rest of them must be long buried or covered by the seas. I've searched everywhere else."

Rohbe's chain of thought was too fractured for Martin to follow. He'd seen men like him before—hermits who'd gone into seclusion for years, who'd forgotten how to speak to others. It took a long time.

"There aren't supposed to be any ruins here, Teacher Rohbe," Martin said. He turned to take in the low hills that he could now see were concealed buildings. "You taught me that."

Rohbe gave a few quick nods, short jerks of admission. "Yes, and I was right. These ruins aren't ours, young Martin."

Waves of gooseflesh ran up and down his arms and legs like warnings. "Whose are they?"

Rohbe laughed. "I found them at last, young Martin. I found ruins of the"—his voice dipped—"malus. Do those fools in the Judica and the college still say the malus and the barrier are myths?"

Martin nodded, mute with shock.

Rohbe scurried down the jumble of broken steps. "Come, young Martin. I will show you something that would set the Judica and the college on end."

"How can you be sure?" Martin asked. He had never sided with the mythologists who refused to believe the malus once walked the earth, but the existence of such evidence seemed impossible.

Rohbe stopped. "Think, young Martin. Have you so soon forgotten that admonition I commanded you?" He pointed behind them. "Look at the steps."

Martin nodded. "They would have been elegant and grand once."

Rohbe snorted through his nose. "They were nothing of the sort. They were functional!"

He couldn't help but stare. "But that would mean . . ."

His former teacher nodded, his eyes alight. "Yes, yes. That's right. They were quite large. Eight to nine feet, I should say. Some may have topped ten. We're so small."

"Impossible."

A snap of fingers brought him up short, as if he were still a student under Rohbe's instruction. "Foolish word. I taught you to dispense with it. Come. Interpret the evidence." He pointed toward a ruin, hardly more than a pile of stone covered with vines a hundred paces away. "Are you hungry?" he asked.

Martin nodded.

"Come, my doubting student, I keep what food I can catch or grow in that building." He quickened his pace, and Martin hurried to follow.

As Martin approached the huge entrance, the feeling of strangeness swept over him again.

"It took me a year to clear away enough of the vines to find the entrance," Rohbe said. He stepped through an entrance five paces high.

Martin followed, his eyes trying to adjust to the gloom.

Rohbe paused to light a torch with flint. Then he moved around the room to light other torches that had been jammed into cracks in the mammoth walls. As the darkness fled, the indistinct shapes clarified. The hair on Martin's neck stood on end.

Rohbe cackled. "As you can see, there are plenty of seats, though I doubt any of them will serve our purpose."

Martin gaped, knew he must look foolish, but he couldn't find the words to express his amazement. Everything he thought he knew about the ancient history of his world had just been obliterated. "How old is this place?"

Rohbe nodded. "When does our history begin?"

Martin shrugged. "Two thousand years ago with the scattering."

The historian scratched his head. "Not possible to know. No. No. Twice as old, perhaps. Hard to date them. There are no reference points."

Martin couldn't help but look at the size of the chairs again. The malus had been . . . "Giants."

His teacher nodded. "Come, there's more. Bring a torch. Come."

Martin followed. The trip through the chasm could wait. His birdlike teacher had made the most important historical discovery ever. Rohbe led him to a small room off what looked to be a great hall. Whatever door had been there had long since rotted away.

His teacher crossed to the far wall. "Look. This room might have been a storeroom of some kind, but I can't be sure. It hardly matters. No, it doesn't. What's important is that the malus were possessed of artistic tastes, however twisted. Evidence."

"What do you mean?"

"Look, young Martin, at the walls. Look. They're covered in carvings."

Martin held up his torch to get a better view. The builders had overlaid the walls with a pale yellow stone he recognized from Erinon and his time in Callowford—opaque corundum; durastone. He raised his torch. The room was laid out in a hexagon, and every wall had been sheathed with the rock. Even without the carvings, the room would be worth a fortune. It took hundreds of man-hours to quarry enough of the stone for the conclave's most important casts.

The carvings. Martin held his torch back to look at them. He found himself confronted by faces of terrible beauty that, except for the dust, could have been carved yesterday. The corundum held the detail and gave the depictions a lifelike quality that disturbed him. In those eyes he saw nothing of mercy or compassion.

Male and female in strange, often revealing dress covered the walls, their beauty so perfect it seemed inhuman. Then he noticed the hands. Each hand had six fingers and each foot six toes.

"It took me months to clean out the chamber," Rohbe said with almost-normal speech. "Yes, months."

Martin ran his fingers on the bas-relief carvings, marveling at the skill that made the most adept reader's work seem crude by comparison. Scenes of war dominated. The artist depicted the brutality of war in such intimate, even sensuous, detail that Martin was taken aback. The malus had gloried in killing, taken pride and pleasure in it. Gaping wounds were given even more attention than the frightening faces of the beings that inflicted them.

He stopped. The victims in the scenes were small, much smaller than their killers. They wore crude garments of homespun.

Humans.

Martin tore his gaze from the scene, forcing himself to move on. What he searched for he wouldn't have been able to put into words. Perhaps it was some sign of a redeeming emotion in the countenance of that lost race. It never appeared. "What happened to them?"

His teacher gave a small squawk. "You know this, young Martin. Yes. What does your tradition tell you?"

Martin pulled his gaze from the carvings. "I know what our tradition says, but we lost Magis's book hundreds of years ago. Even the existence of the book is little more than a myth now. You taught me to question everything. Legend says Eleison killed the malus, but if that's so, where are their bones?"

Rohbe nodded. "Yes, yes. That would seem to be the question. But you must question everything. You must. Especially your assumptions."

Martin turned to face him. "What do you mean?"

The historian shook his head. "I've dug through these ruins for years. I have. I've never found a burial ground, a mausoleum, or a crypt. There's no evidence any of them died. Ever." His eyes were intent, his face lit with unuttered secrets.

Martin exhaled. "Of course they died. They probably burned their dead."

Rohbe nodded. "Possible, but I've seen no evidence of any kind of pyre. Not one." He took a deep breath. "The legends are true. Eleison bound the malus away from our world." He waved at the carvings. "I think *this* is what he's holding back."

Martin shook his head, adamant in denial. "No. That can't be. The malus are twisted, ugly things." His hand joined in his denunciation, thrusting the historian's theory from him. He gestured at the walls again. "These creatures are inhuman, but they could never be described as hideous."

Rohbe nodded, patient still. "Twisted by Magis's time, yes, but remember, Magis fought the possessed, not the malus themselves. It seems logical. Eleison disembodied the malus. Magis barred their spirits from the kingdom. And that barrier has been with us for centuries." His shoulders lifted. "Who knows what the malus look like now? Perhaps evil shows its true nature. It does."

Martin stared at the carvings. Dear Deas in heaven, what would happen when Rodran died? "Teacher Rohbe, the Judica is at war with itself. Half of them do not see the threat in Merakh, do not even believe in the barrier or that the malus ever existed. You have to come with me."

Rohbe shook his head, waved his hand to the south. "I'm sorry, Martin. There is no escape for us. No. I've been stranded here since my horse died. I've walked the length of this spit of land time and again. I have. No ships come to this coast, and the river is uncrossable. The barrier has some effect here, but it's weakening. The ruins are no longer safe at night. Things prowl the mountains." He shuddered and his voice diminished. "They do."

Rohbe's words went through Martin's midsection like a knife sliding through water. In the back of his head a desire grew to simply walk east, mountains or no, and a lassitude like a waking dream crept over him. He shook his head to clear his vision. This couldn't be the compulsion—Errol was nowhere near. Then he knew. He'd sworn to share Karele's amends.

He touched his teacher's shoulder. "I have to get to the shadow lands." In quick sentences he explained why.

Rohbe jerked his head from side to side. "You were always so full of passion, young Martin. So full. It is your gift and your curse." He scuttled toward the door. "We must leave now. We must."

A distant howl sounded, and Rohbe jerked, his face a mask of terror. "Quickly. The ruins aren't safe after dusk."

Martin followed Rohbe back through the oversized arch and toward the ruined fountain. Every line of his teacher's posture urged haste, but they stopped to fill the waterskins Rohbe had brought before moving into the forest.

"I have a nest in one of the trees," Rohbe said.

Martin looked at the giant oaks. "You live in a tree?"

Rohbe shrugged. "Yes. It is the only way to keep safe, the only way. The ferrals here can't climb. You'll understand."

They came to a tree whose trunk must have been three spans across. The first branch, a full span in diameter, shadowed them from ten feet above. At its foot, Rohbe pointed to the trunk.

"Look there."

Gashes so deep that sapwood showed cut the bole all the way around to a height of seven feet.

A howl sounded in the distance. Rohbe shook himself. "There's a rope ladder on the far side. My nest is a goodly ways up, it is, but it's big enough for both of us."

With his teacher's assistance, Martin managed to make it to the first branch, if barely. After that, the limbs grew closer together and provided access to the upper parts of the tree.

In his teacher's nest they ate a meager dinner of dried fish and apples. When dusk settled, an oppressive stillness lay across the ruins and the ancient forest. Though the forest seemed empty enough, Martin spoke in low tones, fearful of being heard. "I will attempt the river to the north tomorrow."

His teacher sighed. "No. I have tried, but the current is too strong." He gave Martin a sidelong glance. "You are too big to fight the current. Yes, too big. There is only one way that offers a chance of success, only one, but we will have to move quickly." A whine came from the back of his throat. "And trust luck."

His teacher curled himself into a ball and immediately fell asleep.

Hours later, Martin shifted away from the knot that poked him in the back. Fatigue, emotional and physical, pulled at him, but he fought the urge to sleep. He stared into the unrelieved darkness, but the absence of any visual reference point undermined him. He stirred once, jerked awake by the sensation of noise, but he heard nothing over the sound of his panicked heartbeat.

A scratch, as of someone clawing at the base of the tree, came to him, and he held his breath. With slow, soundless movements he unsheathed his dagger and waited. Minutes passed without the sound being repeated, and Martin relaxed. His back and shoulders settled once again into the contours of the tree.

Then a howl from the ruins sent tremors coursing through him. His hands shook as he gripped the knife and waited. Rohbe cried next to him, his sobs thin and childlike.

"Dawn will come," Martin whispered.

Rohbe nodded, shivering in the dark.

27

THE CUT

MORNING CAME gray and leaden under a blanket of clouds that withheld rain and blocked the light. Martin disbelieved his eyes, so gradual was the lessening of darkness. Tree trunks and branches resolved from the inky background with agonizing slowness. He peered into the gray light of dawn, searching for spawn. The same odd quiet still held the forest in its grip.

Rohbe sat up next to him, handed him a few strips of dried fish. "We must wait for full light before we set out. We must."

Martin nodded his agreement. He didn't need to be persuaded.

They clambered down an hour later. Scratch marks high on the trunk raised the hair on his neck. The owner of those claws could have ripped them apart without trouble. Praise Deas the thing couldn't climb. The blanket of dead leaves on the ground obscured whatever tracks might have been left. Only smudged impressions remained. With or without Rohbe, he must leave. He would not spend another night in a place of such horror.

With his oak-branch staff in one hand and his dagger in the other, he followed his teacher to the ruins. The mountains loomed behind them. Old and worn by time, they created a seemingly impenetrable barrier to passage.

His teacher stopped and pointed. "There is a chasm that runs east through the mountains. Yes, east. I've never reached the end. Don't know where it comes out or even *if* it comes out. We mustn't get trapped in it. The spawn would get us, they would."

"How far down it have you gone?"

Rohbe quivered at the memory. "Half a day's walk. Only half a day. Do you understand?"

Martin nodded. "We could be trapped, unable to get back to safety before dark."

Rohbe turned toward the ruins, his steps brisk. "We must pass through them to reach the chasm. Must. There are things we will need to take."

Sudden curiosity prickled Martin's skin. "What things?"

His teacher beckoned in answer.

Not for the first time Martin wished Cruk were with him. An overfed priest and an aging scholar were ill-suited to fighting spawn left behind millennia ago after the malus's attempt to corrupt the earth.

They entered the chamber of carvings and collected a pair of torches, then returned to the gray light and made for a large mound of scree. When they moved behind it, Martin's breath caught and he stopped. An array of six-sided columns that supported an enormous arch rose above him to a height of twenty spans. He looked left and right, his imagination filling in the parts of the building that time and debris had obscured.

Rohbe jostled his elbow. "Come, young Martin. More than anyone, I can appreciate your awe, but we cannot afford the time."

With a shake he followed his teacher into the darkness. They lit torches but gloom fought the light, refusing to recede from the illumination of his torch. Martin tucked two more brands under his arm and prayed they wouldn't stumble across the spawn's den.

A doorway sized for giants loomed before them. Niel moved ahead, confident despite the gloom. Martin lowered his torch to see the footprints of his teacher's previous passage. Beside them were the prints of pads twice the size of any dog's he'd ever seen. With a shake of his head, Martin drew a deep breath and followed Niel through and found himself in another large room much like the first. The firelight struggled to reach the ceiling, creating the impression of great height. They moved left, circling the room.

At the back of the hall they came to another door. They stepped through into a small room, and for the first time something in the ruins was truly different. The room wasn't empty.

Shadows moved across from him, and he gasped. His pulse roared in his ears.

But the shades that danced on the wall in his torchlight didn't come from any living thing. Rather, Martin found himself in an ancient armory. He moved to a stone rack thick with dust. Gray weapons with cruel edges lined the stand. A sword that dwarfed any he'd ever seen stood at the end. Curious, he wiped the dirt from the blade with the edge of his cloak and then started, surprised at the cut on his hand. The blade gleamed as if newly oiled and sharpened.

His teacher smiled. "The Judica and the council of nobles will find these interesting. They will."

Martin wiped his hand against his cloak. "That's impossible. No metal holds an edge for that long."

His teacher nodded. "I reacted similarly, I did. It is a good thing the malus in their physical form are interdicted from the earth. We should have no hope of defeating them. None."

The sword sliced through Martin's cloak with the least effort. He moved down the wall past large hooked axes and pikes four strides long. He searched for a weapon he could use for defense as well as proof.

A handful of rods, pointed like javelins and a little taller than he, lay grouped at the end. He hefted one of them and stumbled in surprise at the unexpected lack of burden. The rod could have been made of parchment for all the weight it carried. Martin gave it a tentative swing. The whoosh of displaced air sounded loud in the stillness of the armory. With a grunt he braced one foot against the middle and pulled, trying to bend it. The metal flexed slightly, but as soon as he relented, it returned to its original perfection.

No metalsmith in the kingdom could have produced an object of such perfection. Only readers had the gift and skill to do so, and they only made spheres. Martin left his wooden staff in place of the metal one. His teacher took one of the rods as well and led him to a door in the back of the room.

How far into the ruins had they already come? Surely they should be at the base of the hills by now.

Niel paused. This was no open doorway. A metal door the color of the rod in his hand barred passage. A latch three handspans long protruded from one end. His teacher waved him forward. "You are stronger than I."

Martin licked his dry lips, said a quick prayer, and pushed. The latch swung as if it had been greased the day before, but the door scraped through gravel. With an effort it opened to admit the gray light of an overcast sky. A noise—half sob and half sigh of relief—came from his throat. A path like a cut ran through mountains that rose up on either side toward the east.

A couple of steps along the path he turned to regard the door. On this side no latch or handle marred its blank, gray perfection. Once it closed, they would have no way back if the chasm proved to be a blind alley. If he closed the door and the passage to the east came to a dead end, they would die in this desolate land. Centuries would pass before anyone found their moldering bones. Yet if they left the door open to safeguard their return, the spawn could hunt them down. He held no illusions about their ability to outrun the beasts.

Loose rock littered the chasm that ran toward the shadow lands. Martin chewed his lower lip. Some of those rocks were too large to move, yet others weighed fifty pounds or less. He walked to the side of the chasm where scree and boulders piled against the rear of the ruins, searching for the right shape. He picked through the pile until he found a piece of stone two feet across and as thick as his hand.

Rohbe watched him, hunched over with beads of new sweat gathering on his forehead. "You understand that you are committing us to this one improbable chance, young Martin, yes?"

Grunting with effort Martin lifted the slab and carried it back to the door. He straightened. "We chance the chasm or the river, Teacher Rohbe. Soon or late, the spawn will be strong enough to hunt during the day."

His teacher nodded, licked his lips with a quick tongue. "Flawlessly logical." He sighed. "I'm not comforted. No, I'm not."

They piled rocks against the entrance, hefting stones beside the gray metal until they felt sure no man or animal could force it from the other side. With a last heave, Martin piled one more rock against the door, turned, and followed his teacher down the cut. As he picked his way he marveled at the skill of the fallen race that constructed such a passage. In its way, this road to the east impressed him more than all the ruins he'd left behind. How many years had it taken them to carve the vertical walls and craft the road that ran toward the rising sun without the slightest deviation? What knowledge had passed from the earth with them?

He checked himself. This race had slaughtered his. Perhaps their knowledge corrupted them, or perhaps they'd corrupted their knowledge. The barrier must be saved, whatever the cost. He prayed the herbwomen were wrong, hoped that no one had to die. Humans could not stand against these giants.

"Please, not Errol." The words passed Martin's lips before he realized his heart had spoken them. The shock of his request stopped him, his feet resting on a giant paving stone. For the first time he'd put Errol ahead of Liam. The realization stunned him as if he'd looked in a mirror and found his reflection strange and unfamiliar.

Someone had to die—Adele had said so. By the three, he hoped it wasn't true, but the truth of the herbwoman's words rang in his heart. What then? Did he want Liam to die? He started walking again. Of course not, but Errol had paid the price for the kingdom already. Why did one person have to suffer for everyone else?

They moved on. The sun passed its zenith. Rohbe stopped,

watching as the sun arced over the narrow walls of the canyon and was lost.

"We are committed now, yes," Rohbe said. "I hope they cannot gain the passage any other way. No."

Hours later, darkness fell. They kept going. Deprived of sunlight by the vertical walls and lacking soil, nothing grew in the chasm. Unrelieved stone, loose or fixed, surrounded them on all sides. They paused to light torches, then walked in the yellow pools of light. The deepening gloom pressed against the illumination, compressing it until their field of vision shrank to a pair of spans.

Martin fought his body's hunger for sleep. Until he came to the end of the road or emerged from the canyon into the shadow lands, he would keep moving. The shadows beyond his torch deepened. Then the torch died and the darkness became complete.

A boom sounded in the distance behind them. For a moment his heart leapt with hope as if a drum called to him. The sound came again and skittering chills ran down his arms and legs. There could be no mistaking the source: something had hit the door.

They broke into a run.

28

SPAWN

A SOUND—HALF SCREAM, the rest a howl—chased Martin and his teacher through the cut. He fell, not for the first time, and curled his arms to protect his head. Stunned, he lay on the unnaturally smooth ground littered with rocks from above. He waited, hoping. The boom sounded again, and his heart resumed its rhythm. A brief screech of metal against stone sounded, and Rohbe pulled at him, goading him to his feet.

The door was shifting.

A chorus of howls carried a ravenous note of hope. He followed Rohbe down the cut. Time and again he tripped, the stones casting him down to the floor. His legs ached with bruises as if he'd been beaten, and blood plastered his tunic to his right shoulder.

The booms continued to sound behind them, despite the distance. The channel funneled the sound toward them. Only his own labored breathing, whistling in and out of his lungs with notes of his desperation, kept him from hearing more.

The moon rose. Hints of silver light touched the rocks at the top of the chasm. He drove himself forward. If they lived long enough, there would be a window of time, an hour or perhaps two, in which the moon's light would enable them to see well enough to run without risk. He prayed their pile of rocks would hold through the night. Then he prayed that if they did not, the barricade would hold until they made it safely away.

He navigated his prayer as he negotiated the trail, moving from best to worst outcome. By the time he finished, all of his haggling had been reduced to a simple request to die well. Another screech came to his ears. It seemed his last prayer might be the one answered.

In some indefinable way, this calmed him. His vows had never promised him an easy life. They demanded he be ready to sacrifice himself. He banged his shin against another rock, stifled a curse. True, the sacrifice seemed to hint at a life of service, but no one guaranteed him that would be the case.

As he ran, Martin mourned the fall of Erinon, castigated himself for his weakness in failing to save Errol and, through him, the kingdom. He shook his head in the darkness. No. He could only do as much as his flesh could bear. The responsibility to save the kingdom did not fall to him. If Deas wanted it saved, then Deas would find a way to save it.

The moon's reflected light obscured the path ahead. He could no longer see the floor of the cut. Martin scrubbed his eyes with one hand and squinted, laboring to bring the path into focus.

He nearly ran into Rohbe. His teacher stood peering up at a pile of rock whose top was hidden in darkness. A rockslide filled the chasm.

Panic consumed Martin, eating away at his resolve. His teacher clambered up a few feet of rock, his breath whistling in panicked gasps. A cascade of loose stone flowed toward Martin, and his teacher slid back to his side.

Rohbe breathed a moan and scrambled upward again with the same result.

"It won't hold our weight. They're going to get us."

Martin slid the metal staff through the back of his belt and moved toward the wall. "I won't stand here and wait to die." He scrabbled upward, searching with his hands and feet for stones large enough to bear his weight without shifting. Ten feet up, he called to his teacher. "Try again by the chasm wall. The larger rocks will serve you better."

Howling screams chased him upward. Time after time the slide gave way, erasing much of his progress. Sweat poured from him, and his movements slowed. Against the far wall he could hear Rohbe's whimpering sobs.

"Climb, Teacher Rohbe. Climb. We are not beat yet."

And with a shuddering moan, Rohbe began to climb.

After what seemed like hours, Martin reached the crest. The moon still shone overhead, and across the top of the slide his teacher sat unmoving.

"Teacher," Martin called. "We made it. I think we should take our leave of this place."

Rohbe didn't answer, didn't even bother to acknowledge him. Then Martin saw the reason. The top of the rock pile, broad where Martin sat gasping, narrowed toward the other wall. His teacher sat on a large stone at the precipice.

The slightest move would pitch him down the way they had just come.

"Move toward me, Teacher. The pile broadens."

Rohbe stretched out his arm. A scree of rock trickled from beneath him. With a sob, he huddled into himself once more.

Cries of pending triumph and hunger called from the ruins.

Martin lay on his belly and slid toward his teacher. Two paces away, the rock crumbled beneath him, and he scrabbled backward.

Rohbe's eyes, widened in terror, reflected the moonlight.

Slowly, as if there weren't spawn behind yammering for their blood, Martin reached back and pulled the metal staff from his belt, extending it. Rohbe didn't grab on until Martin tapped him on the knee. When he did, Martin pulled him toward the far side of the slide—and their escape.

The slide gave way. The sound of rocks hitting the chasm floor echoed and reechoed around them as Martin fought to pull Rohbe to him. Rocks covered his teacher to the waist as they slid down, picking up speed. With a lunge Martin grabbed the man's robes and pulled him close, trying to lift him from the rockslide that threatened to swallow them both.

Rocks the size of his fists poured around them, and he flung his arms up over his head. At the bottom, he rolled to end up on the chasm floor once more. Moonlight streamed into the narrow gap overhead. To one side Rohbe groaned as he rose but seemed largely unhurt as he began to run. Martin longed to be away, but he'd lost the staff. Sense or intuition drove him, and he delved through the loose stone until he felt the smooth metal against his skin.

He lumbered after his teacher who raced away, twenty paces ahead. As he dodged the rocks and boulders littering the narrow canyon he listened for the telltale sound of ferrals.

Behind him, toward the ruins and the door, the howls turned triumphant. Sweat slicked his grip, and he tasted bile at the back of his throat. His heart hammered like a forge, and he labored to breathe. Ignoring the tightness in his chest, the fire in his lungs, he ran, praying the rockslide would keep them safe.

The howls grew closer, but soon, as the sky and the chasm grew completely black with the moon's descent, he heard howls of frustration. He picked his way forward, groping with the tip of his metal staff like a blind man finding his way in the street.

Moments later he blinked, stopped to rub his eyes and stare. Outlines. He could see outlines like faintest edges of gray against black. He surged ahead. Dawn was coming. The sky overhead appeared as a shade of charcoal against the ebony backdrop of the mountain. He prayed the sun would hurry.

A doglike yelp of pain sounded behind him accompanied by the sound of crashing rocks. Then snarls and more yelps. Martin exulted. They couldn't get past the slide.

Up ahead, no more than half a league distant, a hint of green beckoned to him. Renewed, he raced toward safety. Halfway there he caught up to his teacher. He sat huddled against the wall, his arms wrapped around his legs. Martin called to him.

"It doesn't end," Rohbe whimpered. "It's spelled, going forever and ever and ever."

He hauled Rohbe to his feet, half carrying him along. "Come, teacher, the shadow lands are just ahead. I can see them."

Seconds later the howls sounded again, louder, much louder. The spawn had cleared the slide.

Rohbe went limp at the sound, but the incarnation of Martin's fear calmed him. The tightness in his chest faded, and the fire in his lungs receded. He ran toward his hope, dragging Rohbe with him. The howls told him just how quickly he lost ground, but he didn't bother to look back. Doing so would only cost him time he couldn't spare. He bent his will toward his goal, concentrating on pulling from heart, bone, and sinew every ounce of speed his body could give.

He hoped for dawn with a desperation that passed beyond emotion to something physical. His feet flew, driven, yet the howls gained. The charcoal gray of the chasm lightened to the color of lead. He chanced a look behind.

A seething mass hurtled toward him. The pack was still too far away to make out individual entities, but they surged forward with frightening speed. Martin gripped his staff and ran even as a small part of his mind told him the truth he didn't want to acknowledge.

They weren't going to make it.

It would be close, less than a hundred paces, but they had his scent and his sight now. And dawn had been too slow. When he heard the sound of the pack's breathing and the pad of their feet, he turned, brandishing the staff.

By the three, they were huge.

Jet black with red eyes, they resembled a cross between a dog and a lion, except larger. Other than the eyes, which regarded him with unblinking intensity, the only part of the spawn that wasn't black was the teeth. They gleamed with a sickly greenish-white cast in the dim light. The lead ferral, bigger by far than any mastiff, raced forward, teeth bared and snarling.

Martin lowered the staff. The ends, pointed to needle sharpness, made it a lethal weapon.

"Come then, dogs! I adjure you by Deas in heaven, you may strike my flesh, but I deny you my soul."

An arrow sprouted in the lead animal's chest as if by magic. Martin stared at it transfixed.

"Run to us, you fool!" a voice called behind him. "The canis cannot abide light."

Martin turned, threw Rohbe's slack form across his left shoulder—the man was featherlight—and hobbled toward safety. A hail of arrows flew around him and over him to pincushion the spawn. But the beasts came on. Martin threw an awkward swing behind with the staff, smacking one of the beasts on the muzzle. The hound snarled. An arrow grazed Martin's right shoulder, leaving a streak of fire on his flesh.

The end of the chasm loomed before him. A dozen men stood on niches carved in the rock, pulling and releasing arrows as quickly as their hands could move. The first poor shot would kill him.

Weak sunlight opened in front of him beyond the shadow of the chasm. He fell forward into the light, landed badly, and rolled with Rohbe, struggling to breathe. Behind him the spawn, bristling with arrows, howled their frustration before turning back.

He sucked in air with a great whoop. Hands hauled him to his feet. Rohbe lay curled on the ground, his eyes unseeing.

"You run well for a fattened priest," the same voice said.

Martin waited for the spots to stop dancing in his vision. After a moment in which he savored each breath, he noticed he stood upon a grassy hillside that descended to a broad river. The sun faced him, cheerful and yellow.

"Did the dogs take your tongue, priest?" the man demanded.

Martin turned. He knew this man. Weeks after Martin's return to Erinon, Abbot Mann Lugner, an abbot of the Einland province under Martin's authority, had excommunicated this noble based on flimsy charges and had appropriated his land.

The man laughed at Martin's recognition. "So you remember me, eh, *Benefice*?"

Martin bowed. "Lord Waterson, I am in your debt."

One of the men approached Rohbe and spoke to him gently, encouraging him to sit up. The other men stood calmly waiting.

"I don't want you in my debt, priest. I want my life back, the life your corrupt little abbot stole from me."

No provision existed under church law that would allow Martin to undo Waterson's excommunication. Abbot Lugner's injustice would stand. He needed to change the topic.

"I had companions. We were separated on the west side of the Sprata. They would have come through the gap along the river. Can you take me to them?"

"Oh, you want something of me now, priest?" Waterson laughed. "I seem to remember a time when I wanted something from you, but you were unwilling." His face clouded. Then the cloud burst. "I was innocent!"

One of the other men, tall and dignified, stepped forward. "We've had no word of any newcomers to the land." He shrugged his shoulders. "But this is not surprising. We're not due to be relieved for another week. If your friends came through the gap, then they have been met and taken south."

"Enough, Lieutenant." Waterson made a cutting motion with one hand. "I'm sure you can find your own way, priest." He smiled without humor. "You can appreciate that our duty requires us to stay here."

The lieutenant turned to face Waterson. "This is unbecoming of you, Marcus. The canis are unlikely to attempt the passage again so soon."

"Then you take him," Waterson said. "I was told that in exile I would never have to look at a priest again. Now even that is taken from me."

The lieutenant nodded but gave no response or reproof to the ex-lord's words. "I will take you to the city, Pater."

"Thank you, Lieutenant." Martin gestured toward the huddled figure. "What about Rohbe? Can we take him with us?"

The lieutenant shook his head, but before he could speak, the man tending to Martin's former teacher stood. "His mind has been broken by his ordeal. We have a wagon back at our camp and will take him back to the city when we're relieved. So long as he is like this, he will be cared for."

Martin nodded his thanks and knelt next to Rohbe. "Thank you, dear teacher, for protecting me, instructing me. I pray Deas's blessing as you continue your journey."

Rohbe turned weak, rheumy eyes toward him and shuddered, "And . . . y-y-you."

With a heavy heart Martin picked up his metal rod and followed the lieutenant as he shouldered a heavy pack and led the way down the grassy slope toward the river, limping now that the danger had passed. In fact, he hurt in almost every place he could imagine. The man did not stop for his discomfort but led at a pace that allowed Martin to keep up. They followed a bend around the river that hid them from the rest of the party, and finally the lieutenant halted.

"Please forgive me for having you walk so far without relief, but I discerned no dire hurt upon you, and your presence causes Marcus pain." He pointed to a large rock. "Sit, and I will tend your hurts."

Martin complied with a groan.

"My name is Shal," the man said as he rummaged through his pack. "I noticed blood on your shoulder. My needlework isn't the prettiest, but I'm thorough, and it won't open up again once I'm done."

The shoulder still burned, and Martin's legs were a mass of aches and bruises. He laid his cloak on the ground beside him and doffed his shirt. If the sight of a half-naked priest seemed unusual to Shal, he gave no sign of it.

He poured a thick yellow liquid onto a square of cloth. It smelled of tar. "This will sting a bit."

When the cloth touched his flesh, Martin flinched and clamped his jaws around a scream. "You have a gift for deprecation."

Shal nodded with a smile. "Lana, my wife, tells me that is so." He tapped the wound with his finger. "Can you feel that?"

"No," Martin said.

His impromptu healer threaded a needle. Martin didn't care for the size of the instrument or the thickness of the thread, but under the circumstances there didn't seem to be much that could be done about it.

"Please forgive Marcus," Shal said as he worked. "He is still relatively new to his exile, and recognizing you stirred his resentments. Though dour, his skills have been useful in guarding the old passes."

"He's angry because he's innocent," Martin said. The admission cost him a pang that matched his external aches.

To his surprise, Shal laughed. "Many of the men and women here are innocent, but it doesn't matter. Guilty or innocent, exiles are welcome here. As the land of last resort, we have few problems with the lawless in Haven. There's nowhere else for them to go." He nodded toward Martin's breeches. "Let's have a look at your legs. When Martin revealed them, Shal gave a low whistle. "It's a wonder you can walk."

The exile pulled a jar that held a hint of the same tar smell as the liquid, though not as strong. When he poured a generous glop of the brown goop on his hand, Martin braced himself. Shal laughed.

"It shouldn't hurt so much, although it will feel very warm for a few moments." He continued to chuckle as he tended Martin's injuries. "We don't often see a priest in Haven. What were you banished for?"

Martin stared. "What?"

Shal raised his head, met Martin's stare with that same placid look. "If you don't want to talk about it, that's fine, but you'll find the healing process goes quicker if you get it out in the open."

"I'm not guilty of anything."

Shal nodded in an obvious attempt to humor him. "Most newcomers say that. Nobody will judge you here. You'll find sympathetic ears when you're ready."

Martin shook his head. "No. You don't understand. I wasn't exiled. I was led here by my guide to find a ship west to Basquon."

Shal's head snapped up, and his face closed, went flat and neutral. "You haven't been excommunicated by the church?"

The thought made Martin's stomach clench. "Of course not. I'm a benefice."

Shal stepped back and drew his sword, leveled it at Martin's chest. "I'll have your weapons, then, *Benefice*." The gravity of his tone matched his expression.

The sword precluded argument. Martin drew his dagger and handed it over along with the strange metal staff he'd brought from the ruins. "Am I under arrest?"

Shal nodded. "Exile is a death sentence for most of the castoffs the church banishes from Illustra. For the few that make it, our leaders, the council of solis, have declared Haven a sanctuary, a place of peace away from the judgment of the church. But, in truth, for all who enter, it is still exile. None may leave, ever. You are one of us now."

Martin swallowed and looked in the direction they had just come. "So will we return to your fellow guards?"

Shal rubbed a hand to his jaw, considered. "This will only cause Marcus more pain. I will take you to the city myself. I doubt I have much to fear from a fat benefice." His eyes were as hard as agates. "Your fate is for the council to decide, but if it's put to hands, I will urge imprisonment for as long as you live."

29

PASSAGE

MARTIN FOLLOWED SHAL along the banks of the Sprata. For an hour, perhaps more, the shadowlander followed behind him with his sword drawn as if Martin, bruised and battered as he was, presented some kind of threat.

With a laugh, Martin turned to confront the man's vigilance. "Tell me, Shal, does one priest present such a threat that you need to keep steel on me the entire way?"

Shal stared at him, then at his blade, before he sheathed it with a contemptuous thrust. "You should not be here."

Martin sighed. "I'm beginning to believe that, but the decision was not wholly mine."

A hint of doubt revealed itself in the lines of the lieutenant's face. "You told me you hadn't been exiled."

"And I told you the truth. There were four of us together on the western side of the mountains. Fire separated us, and I made my way into the shadow lands as you saw, but the choice to use this as our route to Basquon was made by one of the solis."

"You lie," Shal said.

"I'm a priest."

"Priests are not immune to deception. Offer some token of your words."

Martin shrugged, disinclined to attempt to open Shal's closed mind. "I'm a priest, as you say. What token would you accept?"

Shal walked beside him, still out of arm's length, hand on his sword's pommel, staring at the ground as he considered. "Only one in authority would attempt to bring outsiders here. What is this solis's name?"

Martin walked in silence. Shal's face assumed a self-satisfied expression.

"Please don't mistake my hesitation as refusal," Martin said. "I'm grateful for my life, but you've drawn steel on me, and I don't know you. I will not reveal the name of the guide who brought us here, but we traveled with the blessing of two women who held a position of authority or respect with the solis in Illustra."

Shal's eyes grew wide at Martin's words. "Names?"

"I knew them as Adele and Radere."

The lieutenant choked out his words. "*Knew* them?"

"They died not long after we left them."

"No." Shal shook his head in jerks from side to side. "You lie."

"I do not. They bought our passage through the theurgists of the Morgols with their lives."

Tears coursed down Shal's face. Martin's pastoral instincts overcame his caution, and he put a hand on the weeping man's shoulder. "I owe them my life and more." Then, because he wanted to offer Shal something more, he continued. "I have been chosen to present the knowledge of Aurae to my kinsmen in the church."

Shal's head snapped up. "You know nothing of Aurae."

Martin nodded. "Perhaps not, but I think I have shown enough for you to grant me civil passage to your city. My friends will be waiting."

After a pause, Shal gave a reluctant nod. He changed direction, heading straight toward the river. "Come. If your friends came to Haven through the gap, they've been met and taken to the city ahead of us. We keep boats docked at the river when the need for haste arises."

Martin stared. "And you were planning to take me on the slower, more arduous route?"

The look he received was filled with apology and a trace of defiance. "I wanted you to feel a bit of the punishment your church has meted out to so many. Not every excommunicate survives their journey to Haven."

"I have never sentenced any to such a journey," Martin said.

"Yet you are part of the church," Shal said in tones that said the matter was settled.

Martin let the conversation die after that. They walked another league to a broad bend in the river where half a dozen broad, shallow-bottomed boats waited, tied to the pier. A pair of guardsmen lounged, looking bored.

Shal moved in front of Martin and greeted the men with an open hand over his heart. "Greetings, brothers. I and my companion have need of a boat to hasten our return to the city."

The two men eyed Martin with a flash of curiosity that faded after the first moment. The older of the two men, a stocky man with sprinkles of gray in his dark hair, stepped forward. "Newcomers are expected to walk the length of their new home, Lieutenant Shal."

Shal nodded. "So they are, but this man is not an exile. He was sent here by the heads of the council of nine."

The other guard's eyes widened at this. "You know this?"

Martin's conscience impelled him forward. "That is what our solis guide told us, and I believed it to be true."

The shorter man's eyes narrowed.

"He knew their names," Shal said. "Adele and Radere told him to follow his guide, who led him here." He paused. "Our mothers are dead."

The two guards dipped their heads. "Death comes to us all," they intoned together. When they looked at Martin again, certainty showed in their countenance. "Your tale is beyond us to judge. Take the third boat from the end. It leaks less than the others."

Shal bowed, adjusted the pack on his shoulder, and moved out along the pier. Martin stepped into the boat, settled himself on one of the gunwales, and watched Shal pole them away from the bank.

"How long will it take us to reach the city?" Martin asked. Doubt and impatience gnawed at him. He did not know if his companions were safe.

"Four days, if my strength holds," Shal replied.

"What do you mean?"

"The current is with us. A journey that would take two weeks or more on foot can be accomplished in four days, but only if I take little sleep." The boat picked up speed, and Shal laid the pole in the bottom of the boat and sat at the rear with a hand on the rudder.

Martin watched the grassy banks slip by. Cottages dotted the hillsides a little farther up. They looked deserted.

"The spawn grow worse," Shal said in response to his question. "In the last couple of years their attempts to hunt on this side of the mountains have grown in frequency and intensity. The council has pulled people closer to the city until the attacks die down."

The windows of the cottage stared back at Martin like the eyes of the dead. He didn't want to tell Shal the attacks would only grow worse until a new king reigned in Erinon. He didn't want to admit to himself that a new king would reign only after either Errol or Liam died.

A few hours later, as the sun passed overhead and prepared to dip behind the hills, Shal broke the silence. "How long did you know the mothers?"

Martin sighed over the wasted opportunity. He hadn't really known them at all. "I lived near them for almost five years, though I didn't know their purpose until recently. I only knew them as herbwomen, healers for the villagers."

"A story would make the journey easier," Shal said.

Martin's desire for privacy warred with his compassion for the grieving lieutenant. With another sigh, he told how Adele saved him from poisoning, how Aurae told her what to use to counteract the moritweed.

Shal nodded. "Aye, they were both skilled."

The moon rose over the low-lying hills to the east as the sun's last rays winked out in the opposite direction. Martin shivered in the cool air. They drifted downstream, the landscape drifting by. They floated past a small town, the river sprinkled with piers and boats. Shal navigated through those still on the water.

"Do you have any other tales of the mothers?"

Martin exhaled. "Though I never persecuted them, I made it a habit to avoid herbwomen. Besides, I seldom strayed from my cabin in the hills, and they were busy tending to the hurts and pregnancies of the village. I've told you what I know to be true; anything else would be secondhand information."

"If you are willing, I would hear it," Shal said. The strident note no longer filled his voice when he spoke to Martin. Perhaps the knowledge that Martin knew Adele and Radere assuaged his anger. "The trip through the night will be long without a story to break the silence."

Martin nodded. A tug in his chest, like the prodding of a friend, told him what to say. "I will tell you a story in which Adele and Radere played a part, though it may seem small to you, but it explains why I'm here in your land. Will that suffice?"

Shal nodded in the purple hues of the fading light.

"Well then, let me tell you of Errol Stone."

Some hours later, long after the moon had risen and become a silver eye in a star-filled sky, Martin finished. Shal steered the boat without speaking, but his silence conveyed a troubled state of mind. The lieutenant's subdued movements carried hints of sorrow.

"This is true?" he asked Martin.

"Aye, it's true."

"Most men would have made some effort to cast themselves in a more favorable light than you did," Shal said.

Martin shrugged. "I made the vow I would tell him everything.

Such forthrightness may take some practice. I thought tonight might be a good place to start."

"Exile would have been kinder," Shal said. "We would have made him welcome here."

He nodded. "Agreed, but the kingdom has need of him."

Shal snorted softly in the dark. "So like a churchman to dismiss suffering by speaking of need."

Martin ached to protest the accusation, but he could not. He had told Errol more than once he was expendable. Yet he needed to answer the man's accusation. "Do you deny that Deas's hand is upon the boy?"

A moment passed before Shal answered. "No, not if your tale is true."

"Then do not speak to me of dismissal. Errol bears the need of the kingdom." Martin turned to face Shal in the darkness. "And of the shadow la . . . Haven, as well—or do you think the Morgols, the Merakhi, and the spawn will be content to leave you in peace?"

They did not speak again for a long time. The moon tracking through the southern part of the sky and the lulling rock of the boat pulled Martin into the depths of sleep, and when he woke, the sun was so far overhead he couldn't be sure it was still morning.

"Are you hungry?" Shal piloted the boat, his eyes bleary and smudged with fatigue.

His words drew an extended rumble from Martin's midsection. "Yes. I can't remember the last time I ate anything of substance."

Shal smirked without malice. "I thought the clergy made a discipline of fasting."

Martin nodded. "There, you have me." He patted his stomach. "Some regimens suit me more than others."

The lieutenant pointed ahead. "There remains three full days' travel, at least, but the town of Refuge lies just around that bend. I will put in long enough to procure food for the rest of the journey." He gave an apologetic smile. "It won't be anything fancy on a guard's pay."

A quarter of an hour later, Shal poled the boat to a pier with a soft thump. After he tied off, he held his hand palm out to Martin. "You should stay here. Refuge can be a rough place. They won't bother me, but if anyone suspects you're a priest, and even worse, a benefice, we could find ourselves in the middle of a riot."

"Do they hate the church so much here?" Martin asked.

Shal grimaced and lifted his shoulders. "Many of the people in Haven deserved their judgment, but there are just as many here whose only crime was being the victim of jealousy or ambition."

Martin nodded, aching to say it wasn't true, but he couldn't. His conscience forbade him.

He sat in the boat as Shal disappeared down an alley into the city. The existence of so many people in the shadow lands surprised him. The city rose on a hill overlooking the river, walled behind a bulwark of natural limestone. Its size hinted that it could boast twenty thousand people or more.

An idea bloomed in the depths of Martin's mind. Erinon needed allies. If the shadow lands could be persuaded to an alliance, any attack by the Morgols could be blunted. The men here wouldn't need to do more than make a show of military movement. The Morgols would have to divide their army to keep a hostile force from attacking them from behind.

Martin glanced at the sun. He'd missed his morning prayers. People milled around the docks, paying him little attention. He pulled the emblem of his faith from inside his tunic and knelt in the bottom of the boat, facing as close to east as he could approximate. As soon as his knees touched wood, the liturgy sprang to his lips.

Once he completed his daily office, he ran down the list he kept in his head of each intercession that needed to be made. It kept growing. So lost he became that he didn't note the sound of footsteps until they were upon him.

"Well now, what have we got here?"

Martin jerked at the nearness of the voice. Beside him, two men, rough and dirty, stood at the edge of the pier. They smelled sour, wearing the sweat of men drinking early or perhaps still drinking from the previous day.

He nodded toward the two. "Good morning."

"What's good about it, eh?" the first man asked.

"There's always something to be thankful for," Martin answered without thinking.

The hiss of daggers leaving sheaths raised Martin's hackles.

The first man gestured toward Martin with the point of his dagger. "Hulbert, I think this one's a priest." He caught Martin's eye. "I don't like priests."

"Nope, Orace, you don't," Hulbert said. "No reason for you to either, after that priest 'ad you excommunicated for messing with the mayor's twelve-year-old daughter. Nope, no reason you should like priests 'tall."

Martin looked left and right. The pier that had seemed so crowded only moments ago now appeared almost deserted. With an evil gap-toothed grin, Orace advanced toward the boat.

Before he could put foot in the boat, the blade of a sword appeared at his neck. "You know the rules," Shal said. "Any man who takes a life in Refuge forfeits his own."

Orace tried in vain to see the sword blade at the side of his neck without moving. Slowly, he replaced his dagger and lifted his hands. Hulbert copied the move. Shal stepped back but didn't sheathe his weapon. "I have your names. I think it would be best if I didn't see you anymore." At their blank looks, he ground his teeth. "Get out of my sight."

Orace gave Martin a flat stare. "If I ever get out of Refuge, I might just look you up, priest."

"What were you doing?" Shal asked after they departed.

"Morning prayers."

The lieutenant gave a deep sigh. "Can you do it without looking like a priest?"

Martin nodded. "Is there something about Refuge that you neglected to tell me?"

Shal gave a brief shake of his head. "You're an outsider. Whatever the council deems necessary to tell you about Haven, they will tell you. Until then, draw no attention to yourself."

Shal loaded a pack he'd dropped into the boat and followed

it. He cupped a handful of red berries and popped them into his mouth.

"Do you have any more?" Martin asked. The groaning of his stomach made him less courteous than usual.

The lieutenant laughed. "Yes, but I don't think you want any. These are chara berries. We use them to help fight off sleep—effective, but bitter." He pointed to the pack. There's cheese, bread, and water in the pack. It should last us the three days to the capital city."

After Martin ate, a process that took a considerable time, the boat's gentle movements lulled him back to sleep. One day, he hoped to sleep in a bed again.

30

BLOOD ROSE

LIGHTS FESTOONED the rolling hills of Count Rula's estate. In honor of his daughter's wedding, the count produced barrels of the finest wines his vineyards produced, and a steady stream of the area's nobles rolled onto the estate by carriage. Men in tight-fitting hose and doublets with boots polished to a high sheen accompanied radiant women in the traditional dress of the region. Each man wore his sword, the thin dueling type, strapped to his waist. Every woman wore a chain of coins around her neck, a white blouse surmounted by a heavily embroidered vest, and a skirt belted with another chain of gold coins. Though each woman's dress strongly resembled the rest, disparities remained that allowed Errol to perceive differences in wealth or status.

Rokha and her father emerged from their self-imposed exile to attend. Errol breathed a sigh of relief when he noticed Naaman Ru kept his distance from the count. Rale stepped beside him, resplendent in an all-black outfit Rula provided for the occasion. Each member of the watch in Errol's company was similarly attired.

Except for Errol. Rula's chamberlain had taken charge of Errol's appearance, showing an attention to detail that Oliver Turing would have admired. Errol strove to keep himself from fidgeting in the finery; he was Rula's guest, after all. As his host introduced him to each new arrival, he bowed politely. Men squinted at him, tomcats eyeing a rival, while women gave him speculative glances as they smiled and checked his hands.

A raven-haired beauty with large brown eyes and olive skin, the daughter of a minor noble, gave him a smoldering look that made his ears burn. Errol stammered his greeting, then found himself being pulled aside by Rale.

"How much do you know about Basquon weddings?" Rale asked.

Errol shook his head.

The captain winced. "Take care, lad. These people are as hot-tempered as they are hot-blooded. A wrong word and you'll find yourself dueling or betrothed."

Errol swallowed with difficulty. "Did I do anything bad just now?"

Rale laughed. "No, but be careful. Basquon weddings often flow red with more than just wine."

Errol gulped and kept his greetings perfunctory after that. His hands hung at his sides, empty, and for the first time in his life he wished he owned a sword. At least then he could rest one hand on the pommel as the other men did. Not for the first time, he reflected that the world would be a better place if more men used a staff. His two spans of ash would have been totally out of place at a wedding—even he realized that—but he missed it all the same.

"Honored guests," Rula said from atop a balcony overlooking the courtyard, "be welcome to the wedding of the flower of my life, my daughter, Elaia. Once you have refreshed yourself, we will begin our celebration in earnest."

Errol looked around trying to determine what he should do next, but Rale was nowhere to be found. He spotted Rokha surrounded by a cluster of women who all seemed intent on getting to know her. Of course. She would be a long-lost cousin to many of them.

With a deep breath, he squared his shoulders and headed her way. She turned as he neared, warned by the glances her companions sent his way. Rokha dropped a perfect curtsy, her skirt flaring. "Earl Stone, how may I serve you?" The rest of the ladies mimicked Ru's daughter. For a moment Errol felt sure they were making sport of him.

"Uh, I was hoping you might spare a moment to advise me." He stopped, unsure of how to address her. "Lady Ru."

Rokha's full lips pursed in amusement as she rose, taking his arm. "Certainly, Earl Stone. Shall we walk?" Without waiting for an answer, she led Errol away.

"I'm surprised you sought me out, Errol," Rokha said once they were beyond earshot of the other guests. "I'm sure your princess looks ravishing tonight. That golden hair of hers will make her stand out like a peacock among ravens."

Errol scratched his head. "I can't tell from one moment to the next what she's thinking. Ever since we left Erinon, it's like she's a different person."

Rokha nodded. "She's the same person, Errol, but she's in a completely different environment. I have to admit, I was surprised she wanted to learn the sword." She gave him a sidelong glance and a smirk. "I think you're going to have your hands full with her. Are you sure she's the one for you?"

"Can we talk about something else?"

Rokha's deep-throated laugh brought a touch of heat to his cheeks. She lifted a wine glass from a passing tray, took a deep pull. For a moment Errol wished he could join her, but his stomach roiled at the thought.

"If you didn't want to talk about the princess, why did you seek me out?" Rokha asked.

Errol swung his arm in an arc. "This. I don't know what to do. I thought you might be able to tell me."

She smiled. "Just enjoy yourself, Errol. It's a wedding, not a fight." She paused. "Although Basquon celebrations include those on occasion. We're a passionate people." She patted his arm. "Just watch what the other men do and do the same."

Errol nodded, but the constant attention he received as the highest-ranking noble present and his unwanted fame made him very ill at ease. He wanted nothing more than to find a secluded place and work with his staff or the twin swords.

A plump woman—the count's cousin, he thought—approached and linked her arm through his. He groped for her name. *Lady Pelela.* "Come, Earl Stone. The bride is about to dance the desposorios."

Helpless, Errol accompanied the woman to a large tent where Rula's daughter and several striking young women about his age formed a line on a wooden floor that had been installed for the occasion. Errol joined the throng at the edge as a drummer began a slow, rhythmic beat. An instant later a stringed instrument joined in, its high, clear notes enforcing and accentuating the strike of the drum.

The women on the floor linked their hands in a weave pattern, swaying side to side with the music. Rula's daughter, similarly dressed but adorned with a crown of white roses, stood in the center. Then, as the pace of the music increased, the line of girls advanced in a challenging swagger, their eyes flashing.

A girl close to the end locked gazes with Errol as she came forward. He felt his face redden. As the line came to the end of the platform, the girls stomped in unison and retreated back to the far end, where they resumed their rhythmic sway.

A line of men stepped forward onto the platform, their hands joined as the girls had, and began stepping toward the line of women. The heels of their boots tapped a counterpoint to the music as they approached the women, almost stalking them. Step. Step. Step-step-step.

The women danced forward, their feet pounding the floor, and the men retreated. Once again the girls stomped and returned to their starting place, except for the girls on the end, who took the hands of the men opposite and departed the floor. The process repeated, the crowd clapping in time to the music.

"Have you ever seen the desposorios, Lord Stone?" Lady Pelela asked.

Errol shook his head. "It's beautiful."

The countess laughed. "Oh, that was only the prelude. Now you will see why the women of Basquon are counted the most beautiful in the world."

All of the girls danced their way off the stage accompanied by men, until only the prospective bride remained. Four young men, nobles who appeared to range in age from twenty to forty, stood at the corners of the floor. Each held a rose of a different color. Elaia, raven-haired and dark-eyed, moved forward from the center of the floor, her feet pounding a staccato challenge in time to the music.

"She dances well," the count's cousin said. "But in my day I was accounted the best in Basquon."

The idea that this plump, simpering woman on his arm could have made men's faces heat the way Rula's daughter did startled him. "Truly?"

Her eyes flashed beneath lowered brows. "Believe it, Earl Stone. I could have turned your knees to water." She turned back to the dance. "Elaia will dance with each man, taking his rose at the end. Then she will present all four to the man of her choice. If he accepts them, the priest will bless them and they will be married."

Errol looked at the four men on the floor. Each looked upon Rula's daughter with single-minded intensity. "Who will she choose?" Errol asked.

Lady Pelela sighed. "Back in my mother's day, or even in mine, you wouldn't know until the end, but too many duels spoiled the tradition. We've become much like the northern provinces." She shrugged her ample shoulders. "The dance is mostly for show. Elaia is betrothed to Count Maren." She pointed. "That's him in the red shirt."

Errol had to admit Elaia's choice looked impressive. Maren stood a good four inches taller than the other men, and his face filled with adoration when he looked upon Rula's daughter. Errol wondered if he looked like that when Adora was near.

The count's daughter danced with each man, her steps fluid and her skirt accenting her flirtation. One by one she collected each of the roses. Spinning in time to the music, she curtsied low at Maren's feet, holding the roses in offering.

Maren knelt on both knees to accept them.

"That was unexpected," the count's cousin said.

"What?"

A tinge of pink decorated the woman's cheeks, and she wiped away a tear. "A bridegroom usually kneels on one knee to show that he will honor his wife and his duty equally. Maren's gesture says he will place his wife above all." She sniffled. "Forgive me. I'm a sentimental old woman."

"Oh," Errol said. He didn't quite keep the note of disappointment from his voice. From the lady's reaction, he'd expected something more.

"We are a passionate people, Earl Stone. Once done, such a gesture cannot be undone. For the rest of his life, Maren will be judged by how he lives his vow."

A priest, robed in gleaming white, came forward to perform the rite of marriage. A few sentences later, it was done.

Errol turned to leave, but Lady Pelela restrained him. "Oh, you can't leave yet, Earl Stone. The maidens will expect you to dance the eskaintza."

Something in her manner warned him. Perhaps it was the hint of a smile he feared was at his expense or the way her eyes fluttered, but his first instinct was to get as far away as possible.

"I don't know how to dance, my lady. I'm afraid I would dishonor the count's hospitality by my clumsiness."

"Nonsense, my lord. The count would only be dishonored if you refused. Just do what seems right to you." She clenched his arm and guided him toward the floor. Errol floundered, helpless to escape. He either allowed himself to be herded or risked making a scene by fending off the count's cousin in front of Rula's guests.

Lady Pelela deposited him on the dance floor and returned to her place on the perimeter. At the far end of the floor a group of young women jabbered excitedly. They each rushed to a table next to the musicians to grab a pink rose and then formed a line.

As the music played they came forward. The laughter of the crowd, raucous and focused on him, reminded him too much of his days as the drunken buffoon. He looked about, panicked, searching for an escape. The first woman came forward, lithe, athletic.

Rokha.

With a saucy glance she spun around him, brushing his shoulders with hers, holding the rose out for him to accept. Without thinking, he reached for it. She spun, keeping the bloom beyond his grasp, and then leaned in.

"Whatever you do, don't take the rose," she said through her smile.

He rubbed his nose. "Why not?"

"It's a betrothal dance, you idiot. You're an unmarried earl at a wedding filled with mothers who are trying to set up an advantageous marriage for their daughters."

He stared.

Rokha brushed his cheek with the petal of the rose. He cringed as if it were the sharpest steel. "You're the biggest prize here, Earl Stone."

He clenched his hands into fists at his sides, afraid to move or even breathe.

Rokha put on a show of being chagrined and twirled away. Moans of disappointment and cheers came to him on the edge of his consciousness. The next dancer came forward—a slender, willowy girl whose direct glance and pout made Errol sweat. He wanted nothing more than to run away. He caught Rula's eye on the edge of the floor, clapping and cheering him on.

The girl swayed and bent like a sapling in a gale, her long hair flying. Fingers caressed his cheek, his brow, his neck. The crowd roared its approval. Sweat ran from Errol's palms. At last she moved on, only to be replaced by another.

Errol retreated into his mind. One by one, he recalled every attack on him since he left Callowford. He reveled in the fear and the pain, seeing through the dancer of the moment to each stroke, blow, and injury. By increments, his breathing slowed and his pulse returned to normal. The noise of the crowd faded and the blood left his face.

Then the last dancer stepped forward, her feet light, barely touching the floor as she glided toward him. His protective shell crumbled when her eyes flashed with challenge, with passion. He swallowed, his throat tight.

She swept toward him, the rose in her hand less an ornament than a partner in her dance. Her blond hair, thick and lustrous, caught the light, amplified it and reflected it. His breathing stopped.

Adora.

His hands unclenched as she brought the rose forward to caress his lips with the petals. The music swelled to a crescendo, and the crowd, as if sensing his state, hushed, waiting. Unshed tears filled Adora's eyes as she spun and then came face-to-face with him, extending the rose for his acceptance.

Or his denial.

Errol went to both knees, reached for the bloom.

Adora pulled it away, out of his reach.

The crowd gasped.

A hole, black and bottomless, opened in his chest where his heart had been.

Adora held the rose over her head for everyone to see and then closed her hands over the long stem, over the thorns. She held them there, squeezing tighter and tighter until Errol could see trickles of blood between her fingers. Adora lowered her arms, cupped the blossom in her hands, and let the blood from her palms run over the pink petals. Absolute silence fell across the courtyard as she knelt and presented the stained flower to him.

Powerless to refuse, Errol took it. Driven by instinct and drowning in the startling green of her eyes, he squeezed the bloody thorns into the center of his palms. Then he covered her blood with his own. Thundering applause cascaded over him in peal after peal, but nothing except Adora filled his vision.

31

Dextra and Sinistra

Not a cloud marred the blue of the sky overhead when the next morning Errol rode out from Count Rula's estate accompanied by his own caravan and a score of Rula's men. The count insisted on sending the escort with Errol as far as the boundary of his territory, and no amount of arguing could dissuade him. The parting looks from Rula and his cousin Lady Pelela had been embarrassing. If his caravan didn't leave this land and its people with their infectious passions, there was no telling what trouble he might get himself into.

Adora rode close beside him. Errol shifted in his saddle. Despite the amount of time he'd spent riding, he couldn't seem to find a comfortable place to put his hands. As they rode, the princess's expression moved from shock to adoration to smoldering and back again. Several times she seemed on the verge of speaking, her mouth open to draw breath, but each time she simply wet her lips and continued her mute regard.

A hawk cried, fierce and defiant, overhead. Errol shielded his eyes against the yellow glare. Red bands marked the wings and a suspicion sprouted in Errol's chest. He turned to Adora to beg her leave to talk to Rale, but the passion in her gaze seared him.

The air seemed too thick. He fought for breath. "Would you pardon me, Princess? I need to speak to Captain Elar for a moment."

She regarded him beneath lowered lashes. "Certainly, my Earl Stone." The stress she placed on the word *my* combined with the heat of her glance made it even more difficult to breathe. He nodded and kicked Midnight forward to the front of the caravan.

Rale—the kingdom's second-best tactician—rode at the vanguard, his eyes sweeping the landscape ahead for threats. He acknowledged Errol's presence with a nod, his manner stiff, almost formal. Errol sensed an undercurrent of disapproval in the captain's manner.

Not knowing how to broach the subject, he pointed overhead, but the hawk no longer floated above them. "It's gone."

Rale caught his gesture. "You mean the hawk?"

Errol nodded. "It has red bands on the wings. I've seen it or one just like it since Gascony. How common are they?"

The former watchman nodded. "Hawks as a rule are fairly prevalent, but the large ones, like the red-banded one you've noticed, are rare. It's surprising to see one so often."

"Are we being followed?"

The captain grimaced. "It's likely."

Rale gave no indication of speaking further. "That's it? Shouldn't we send scouts back to see who it is?"

His mentor gave him an inscrutable look. "I have. I noticed the hawk a couple of days before you were poisoned. The scouts couldn't find anything. Whoever is following us is too far back, which means they're too far away to attack us." He pointed at the blue-liveried men Rula sent. "And I have no doubt the count's reinforcements will discourage them all the more."

"What will we do when we get to the coast?" Errol asked.

Rale shrugged away the question. "We'll take a ship and hope that the Merakhi are fooled by our disguise."

"Won't our pursuers follow us across the strait?"

"No. I've sent word ahead. The garrison at Monett is one of the largest in the kingdom. Nobody will be allowed to port after we do. As long as our friend with the hawk is content to follow at a distance, there's not much we can do to stop him, but once we reach the coast, we'll be beyond his reach."

Rale's certainty comforted him.

In desperation, Errol blurted the question that burned inside him. "What did I do wrong?"

Rale sighed and shook his head. "Errol, you have a way of taking a game and raising the gamble to insane heights. The Basqus are going to be talking about your dance with the princess for generations." He grunted. "Don't you ever ask for advice before you do something?"

Errol dropped his gaze. "Lady Pelela dragged me out to the floor. She said the count would be offended if I didn't dance. Rokha told me not to take any of the flowers offered to me."

"By the three, man, why didn't you listen to her?" Exasperation laced Rale's voice.

"When Adora came and offered the rose to me, I couldn't think of anything I wanted more. Before I could take it, she pulled it away." His shoulders hunched at the memory. "I thought she was saying she didn't want me anymore. She's been strange since we left Erinon. Then she squeezed the stem until her hands bled."

"Don't remind me," Rale said.

"I didn't know what else to do. Her blood was on every petal, and she was kneeling to me—the only princess in the entire kingdom was kneeling before me as if I really were an earl and not some peasant who used to sleep on tavern floors. What was I supposed to do?"

Rale squeezed his face with his hands. "You were supposed to show some sense even if the princess didn't. What do you think will happen back at Erinon when the king and Duke Weir hear of this?"

"I don't care," Errol said. "You're the one who told me to fill that hole in my chest. Well, I love Adora, and she loves me."

His mentor rolled his eyes. "I didn't tell you to fall in love with the princess, boy. She's royal. Adora doesn't get to choose who she marries."

"Why not?"

"Because she belongs to the kingdom!" Rale's chest expanded as he took a deep breath. "Rodran needs her, boy. When Adora swore to die before marrying anyone but you and you returned the oath, you put the kingdom at risk. In terms of power and money, Weir is practically king. We can't win this war or any war without his men."

"He's a murderous pig," Errol spat.

Rale nodded. "Yes, and he's a necessary ally."

Errol rode in silence, cursing the kingdom's need in his mind. He played through half a dozen schemes for running away with Adora to start a new life somewhere else, but he discarded each one. He could abandon his title and become a guard or a farmer with little trouble. His newfound fame would fade, and his ordinary face would allow him to resume a life of anonymity.

But Adora could never vanish. Even if she were not one of the great beauties of the kingdom, the princess represented power and access. They would never let her leave. Duke Weir would insist on the princess as the price for his support, both in money and men, for the upcoming war.

Errol traced the punctures and scratches on one palm with his fingers. He hadn't changed his mind. He would die before he married any other, but could the princess afford to keep her vow? Could the kingdom afford it? The question carried the answer.

"She'll have to renounce her gesture," Errol said.

Rale nodded. "Probably."

Errol sought his gaze. "But that doesn't mean I have to renounce mine."

Rale's eyes were sympathetic above his broad nose. "No, lad, you don't."

A cry overhead that echoed the longing and loneliness in

Errol's heart announced the hawk's return. His next course of action seemed obvious—convince the princess to reconsider the wild extravagance of her actions for the sake of the kingdom. He snorted. All very well for him to say. He didn't have to marry that useless peacock. Errol regretted not smacking him with his staff when he had the chance.

"How am I supposed to convince her?"

The captain opened his mouth, closed it, and then sighed. "I don't think you can, lad. She's not likely to see the sense of the political stakes."

"Maybe I could find a way to drive her away?" Errol asked.

Rale shook his head. "It's courageous of you to think of it, my lad, but it won't work. The princess is smarter than you are and would see right through a tactic like that. You'd only end up binding her to you more tightly."

"You're remarkably little help," Errol said. "I thought you were supposed to be one of the finest tacticians in the kingdom."

His mentor shook his head. "That's warfare, boy, which is simplicity itself compared to affairs of the heart." He grunted. "Besides, women don't fight fair. They never have."

Errol started in surprise. "That's kind of harsh."

Rale laughed at him. "You think so? Take another look at your palms and tell me who pulled the strings and called the tune during that dance."

They camped that first night in the Basquon countryside less than a fortnight's ride from Monett, where they would hire a ship to transport them and their phony caravan across the Forbidden Strait. Errol followed Rale as he moved among the guards. Gial Orth, his violent red hair braided behind him, joined them as they set the guard.

"Double the guard and the scouts," Rale instructed the watchman. "Keep it that way until we board ship."

"Do you expect trouble, Captain?"

"It's my job to expect trouble. Someone's been following us, Orth. If they weren't planning something, they wouldn't keep on. The closer we get to the coast, the more desperate they'll become."

Orth smiled and fingered his dagger. "I could slip out of camp tonight and discourage them, Captain."

Jared Achio, the head of Count Rula's detachment, approached, officious and deferential as always in Errol's presence. "Your pardon, Earl Stone," Achio said with his customary bow.

Rula's man held his tongue until being acknowledged. Errol nodded, trying to ignore Rale's amused look. "Yes, Lord Achio, how may I help you?"

Achio repeated his bow, though not quite as low. "My count's orders were clear—to accompany you to the edge of his estate and then return. I expect we will reach the border tomorrow, midday. The neighboring lords would take offense at Count Rula's armed men entering their territory without permission."

This last piqued Errol's interest. "Are they that threatened by a score of soldiers?"

Count Rula's man cleared his throat. "Ahem, well, you may have heard that Basqus are a touchy people. Skirmishes between nobles are not uncommon, and our long history encompasses quite a number of grudges. We've all been allies or enemies at some time in our past."

"Count Rula seems to be quite mild-mannered," Rale said.

Achio knuckled his thin mustache and darted furtive looks from side to side as if afraid of being overheard. "I can assure you it was not always so. My master had a reputation for impulsiveness in his youth."

"Thank you, Lord Achio," Errol said. "Please convey my thanks to Count Rula."

Achio inclined his head. "On the contrary, Earl Stone, it is Count Rula who wishes to thank you."

"Me?" He shook his head, bewildered. "I don't understand."

Achio laughed and snapped his fingers twice. "My count wishes to express his gratitude by presenting you with gifts."

Two of Rula's men came forward, each holding a long wooden case. The first man opened the lid of the simple wooden box he held and leaned forward to reveal its contents—a pair of practice swords, light but well made.

"The swords are fashioned from banbu wood, incredibly light but very strong." Achio wore a sheepish grin. "The count's reputation as a master of arms will be greatly enhanced when word spreads that one of the heroes of the kingdom received instruction at his hands."

Errol smiled as he considered the count's arduous instruction in the days leading up to his daughter's wedding. He took a sword in each hand and hefted them. How had Rula had them made so quickly? "Their balance is perfect. Please tell the count I will practice with them at every opportunity." With a twinge of regret, Errol replaced them in the case. A sudden desire to work the forms swelled in his chest.

"Nothing would please my master more," Achio said. He waved to the second man, who stepped forward and opened his burnished wood case. "Count Rula earnestly hopes you never need these, but should you require them, he says they will serve you well."

The second man opened the case. Light glinted off of twin steel blades inside. A pair of rapiers lay before him, their workmanship apparent despite their lack of ornamentation. Errol took one in each hand. They responded to the slightest pressure of his fingers, so finely were they balanced. "It's as if they anticipate my thoughts."

Achio bowed as if Errol had paid him a personal compliment. "My lord will be pleased you find them so."

"You made these," Errol said.

Achio bent low from the waist. "My master sees fit to employ me as his arms smith. I try to justify his faith in me as much as possible."

Errol lifted the twin swords as the arms smith watched with paternal pride. "Have you named them?"

Achio laughed and reached out. He lifted Errol's right arm.

"I call this one Dextra." He lifted the other. "And this one, Sinistra."

Rale whistled. "Boy, do you know how much those swords are worth? Any noble would pay you a ransom for them. Lord Achio isn't a smith; he's an artist."

Achio smiled at the compliment. "Any artisan wants his work to be appreciated, Captain Elar. I don't accept a commission unless I believe the skill of the recipient matches my own." His eyes sought Errol's as he said this.

"You flatter me, Lord Achio," Errol said. "I'm new to the sword."

"I do not indulge in flattery, Earl Stone."

Errol nodded. "Please accept my thanks and convey them to Count Rula as well. His gift surpasses me. It is fit for a prince."

Lord Achio's laugh took him by surprise. "But, Earl Stone, you accepted the princess's gesture of undying love and matched it with your own extravagance. What do you think you will be?"

Errol gaped. "What?"

"Oh yes, Earl Stone. Soon Basquon's people will speak of little else. Such a thing has never been seen before. Already men and women are making plans to match your gesture. The 'Blood Rose' they are calling it. You and the princess would have made fine Basqus."

Achio clicked his heels and left.

Rale shook his head. "Well, boy, I've got to admit it. You don't do anything by half measures. We'll be lucky to land in Merakh before the tale reaches Duke Weir's eyes and ears."

Rula's men left midafternoon the next day, and the caravan, reduced to its previous size once more, seemed small and vulnerable. He itched to complete their journey to the coast and fidgeted as if his saddle no longer fit. Though it pressed the integrity of the wagons, Rale ordered a quicker pace. Errol worked his worry over their pursuers like a toothless man working a piece of dried beef. Each time he heard the cry of a hawk, he jerked as if struck.

A hand reached over and caressed his. "You're uneasy today, *maitale*."

Adora's eyes held him, trying to communicate something just between the two of them, but Errol couldn't discern it. "Ma . . . what?"

She laughed, gave his hand a squeeze. "Maitale. It's an old word from Basquon. It means 'heart of my heart' or something to that effect."

The glint in her eye told him there was more to it than that. He pushed the thought aside. She would have to recant her gesture, but he didn't want her to do it yet. For a while he wanted to pretend they could outrun her duty, her destiny. "We're being followed."

Alarm widened her eyes. "By whom?"

"That's the problem. They're staying too far back for us to find out, but I've seen the same hawk over us every day since we entered Talia." His heels itched to push Midnight into a gallop. "I wish we were at the coast already. As much as I hate ships, I'd gladly board one to be away from whatever's behind us."

Adora leaned over and covered his mouth with hers. Errol gasped, pulling her breath into his lungs. Heat spilled from her lips, spread across his face until he ached with it.

"You seemed surprised, maitale," Adora said. "Do you think I offered my gesture lightly? I know you will find a way to keep us safe." She laughed. "But in the meantime, I think I need to petition Rokha for a few more lessons." With a twitch of her reins, the princess headed for the back of the caravan, where Ru's daughter rode next to Merodach.

"That didn't look like you were trying to persuade the princess to do her duty," Rale drawled. "You could light a fire with your face, you know."

"She called me *maitale*."

Rale slumped as if defeated. "Don't be alone with her, boy. Not if you want to keep your head attached to your shoulders." No trace of mirth showed on Rale's face or sounded in his voice.

"She said it meant 'heart of my heart.'"

Rale nodded. "And so it does. A less literal translation is 'lover.' The princess seems to think your mutual gestures signify something close to marriage. If you entertain any thoughts in the direction of consummating those gestures, you won't have to worry about Duke Weir; the king will have you killed himself."

Desperate to change the subject, Errol pointed ahead. "How long before we reach the coast?"

Rale grunted. "At this pace and with longer days of travel, a little more than a week. If a wagon fails, we'll leave it behind. Tonight will be the last camp in the open. The villages start getting more frequent from here on out." He turned toward the rear of the caravan and bellowed. "Orth."

The red-haired guard bounded forward, a smile on his lips. "Yes, Captain?"

The watchman's smile deepened the frown on Rale's face. "I'm taking you up on your offer to trail back and see if you can discover who's following us."

Orth's eyes caught the light and his smile turned wolfish. "Thank you, sir."

Rale raised a hand. "I don't want bodies, Orth; I want information. Don't bloody your sword unless you have to."

The watchman's face fell, and he donned a look of injured dignity. "Why, Captain, would I fight unnecessarily?"

Rale just stared at the lieutenant. "I need knowledge, not casualties. Understood?"

Orth saluted, all trace of banter and jesting gone. "Yes, Captain."

"Good. Get going."

Errol watched him leave. "Will he be safe?"

Rale shrugged. "As long as he doesn't give himself away. But there are no guarantees. He's the second best among the watchmen with us, after Merodach."

"Why didn't you send Merodach?" Errol asked.

His mentor nodded. "That's a fair question. You don't put your best weapon in jeopardy unless you've got no other choice, lad. Whether it's with a bow or a sword, he's the equal of ten men. We can't afford to lose him. Orth is expendable, and he knows it."

Errol laughed, but there was little humor in it. "I guess I'm like Gial Orth. The kingdom doesn't need to keep me safe, so they sent me out after Valon."

Rale's eyes conveyed his disapproval. "You should know better than that, boy. You were given this quest because someone is trying to defang Illustra before the war starts."

They set up camp against an elevated outcrop of rock that afforded an unobstructed view in all directions. Errol avoided contact with the rest of the caravan. His extravagance at Count Rula's in front of hundreds of strangers left him with an acute need for privacy. He hid in the shadows, using skills from his days as a drunk he hadn't realized he still possessed.

He noted Conger still engaged in prayers at vespers before pouring himself into another tome on church history. Errol edged farther into the shadow of one of the wagons. Across the camp Adora approached Rokha as Ru's daughter spoke with Merodach. The blond watchman's face verged on the edge of emotion, and Rokha smiled as she traced her fingers along the back of the captain's hand.

At Adora's arrival, both gave a bow of respect. That wouldn't have happened before. A moment later, Rokha nodded and left, returning with a pair of practice swords. The women squared off. The effectiveness of Rula's instruction showed in Adora's movements. She glided across the ground, and though she couldn't yet breach Rokha's defenses, neither did she take as many hits as she had in past sessions.

After a half hour they broke, sweat streaming down their faces. The feeling of being watched made Errol's neck itch. He shifted and found Merodach staring at him through the shadows. He remembered his promise to Count Rula. On impulse, he stepped out into the soft light and headed for the tall, blond captain of the watch.

Errol bowed. "Captain Merodach, would you help me keep a promise to a friend?"

Merodach nodded without committing himself. "If I can. What is this promise?"

"I told Count Rula I would practice with the swords each day.

I have neglected that promise since leaving his villa, but now that I have his gifts, I hope to start immediately."

The watchman stepped closer. "Do you think that is wise, Captain Stone?" His voice was pitched so that it hardly carried past Errol. "I have avoided sparring in the camp to keep Naaman Ru from observing."

Errol blinked. "Do you think you'll have to fight him, then?"

Merodach answered with the slightest shrug of his shoulders. "I don't know, but I would prefer not to give him opportunity to search me for weaknesses."

Errol's surprise deepened. "Everything I have heard about you says you don't have any."

Merodach didn't smile at the compliment. "Such flattery only reveals the ignorance of the flatterer. I have striven to diminish them, but every fighter has flaws."

The watchman's modesty stoked Errol's curiosity. How good was he? "If I have Captain Elar keep Ru occupied, would that free you of your concern?" At Merodach's nod, he left in search of his mentor and his practice swords.

Errol's heart raced as he stood across the space from the best fighter in the watch. He stood with one sword in front and one to the rear, as Rula had taught him, holding his balance in his mind as well as his hands. His fights with Skorik and his bouts with Liam had been with a staff, movements quicker than thought. Would he be able to think fast enough to keep the tall captain at bay?

Merodach circled without attacking. Errol shifted his feet, keeping his balance centered through the middle of his chest and down through his legs. The captain gave a nod and reversed direction. Errol followed. Merodach feinted and lunged, the blunted end of his weapon leaping like a viper toward Errol's midsection. Errol parried with his lead sword at the last moment and spun, driving his rear sword with a flick of his wrist toward Merodach's unprotected waist.

Shock numbed his arm as Merodach parried. Impossible. No one could move that fast.

The stray thought, the slight break in concentration, cost him.

Merodach's sword found his side, and the feel of hot coals spread from the contact. Errol stepped back, his hand raised.

"You must never let your concentration waver," Merodach said. "Against a lesser opponent it leaves you open to the unexpected. Facing a more skilled foe, it creates an opening."

The man was a sorcerer. "How did you know?"

"Your eyes showed your surprise when I parried. The merest fraction of a second, the slightest hesitation, can be the difference between living and dying."

Errol nodded. "Again?"

Merodach smiled; the expression all the more surprising for its rarity.

They sparred for another hour. Half a dozen times, Errol's staff instincts betrayed him, and welts bloomed on his skin. Yet as the bout progressed, those mistakes came less frequently, and he began to find a rhythm to the swords and a freedom that opened new possibilities for attack.

He parried, twisted and struck. His sword whacked against Merodach's side. The captain stepped back without grimacing, but sweat beaded more heavily on his forehead. "That was well struck."

Errol smiled and bowed. "I would like to spar again, if you're willing."

The captain's nod might have been the highest compliment he'd ever received as a fighter. "I am. I haven't been touched since Captain Cruk bested me ten years ago."

"Cruk beat you?"

Merodach nodded. "A decade ago he was the best in the watch. Time has slowed him, though, and I would beat him at sparring. Steel might be another matter. A man as tough as Cruk doesn't go down easily."

If possible, Merodach became even more serious, and his gaze bored into Errol. "There are times when you must accept your enemy's strike in order to kill him. The trick is to make sure you permit an injury that is less than a mortal wound."

The captain spoke with the air of a man sharing a prophecy.

The following afternoon, after an uneventful day's travel, they stopped to camp just outside of a small village. Errol breathed a sigh of relief at the absence of the red-banded hawk overhead. As he and Merodach prepared to spar, Orth rode back into camp. The watchman dismounted from his horse, took one step, and collapsed.

32

BLOOD CLUES

ERROL RUSHED TO ORTH'S SIDE, started to lift his head.

"Don't move him," Merodach ordered. "You may worsen his bleeding."

Errol lifted his hands and found them stained with blood. Orth was covered in it. Half a dozen rents in his clothing testified to the extremity of the watchman's struggle. Rokha arrived with her kit, with Rale half a second behind.

Errol's mentor took one look at Gial Orth and gave a brief shake of his head, his face closed to any emotion. Only the necessity of the moment showed on Rale's face.

"Will he live?" he asked Rokha.

The truth written in Orth's blood and wounds waged war on Rokha's face with her desire to tend the watchman's injuries. Blood and wounds won. She gave a shake of his head. Orth moaned, his head rolling to one side.

"I can make him more comfortable."

"Do you have any fein powder?" Rale asked.

Her eyes widened in shock followed an instant later by indignation. "He needs belladon. Fein powder will just kill him more quickly." She pressed a folded cloth onto a thrust wound in his chest.

Rale grabbed her shoulder, forcing her to face him. "He's dying. If you want to avenge him, give him the powder to wake him, but avenge him or not, I need to know what he knows."

She looked on the verge of refusing, then swore and pulled a stoppered vial from her bag. "It's not fein powder, but it will accomplish the same thing. I need water."

Someone thrust a skin into her hands, and she poured a stream into a shallow bowl and mixed a pinch of green herbs into it. Rokha raised the bowl to Orth's lips, coaxing him to drink. Most of it spilled from his mouth, but the watchman mustered a weak swallow. A moment later his eyes fluttered open.

Rale came forward, bent over his subordinate, his face sympathetic. "We have you, Gial. Who did this?"

Orth's bloodless lips parted in the barest of smiles, and he drew a shuddering breath.

Then his eyes glazed.

Rale growled a curse. "I need to know who follows us."

"You may yet, watchman." A cold voice behind Errol spoke. The group clustered around Orth turned. Naaman Ru stood a few paces away, his face composed, serene. Uncaring.

Rale's face clouded. "Speak."

Ru shrugged as if the matter were of no import. "His wounds may tell us much. Orth was an accomplished swordsman, at least in the estimation of the watch. To someone who knows how to read these things, the watchman's wounds will tell the story of his struggle."

Rale stood. "Bring him. We'll need light."

They laid the body of Gial Orth on the floor of Ru's wagon. Lamps turned the cabin into day. Besides Ru and Rokha, Errol, Rale, and Merodach crowded into the small space, sitting or standing shoulder to shoulder in the confines.

The caravan master pointed at the dead watchman's legs. "There's blood, but there are no wounds. He wasn't on horseback."

"How can you be so sure?" Errol asked.

Ru shrugged. "Horses move during a fight, boy, sometimes unexpectedly. If so, at least one blow would have found Orth's legs or his horse." He cast an insolent look at Rale. "While you were trying to get information out of a dead man, I checked his mount. The animal is winded but unhurt."

Merodach's face, cold and merciless as winter, caught Ru's attention. "I think it would be better if you spoke in terms of respect for one of the watch who died on our behalf."

For an instant, doubt cracked Ru's impenetrable facade and something akin to fear showed through, but the caravan master snorted his derision a split second later. "And what will you do, Captain, place me under another compulsion? I was not aware the watch held that power."

"No," Merodach said without changing the bitter cold of his expression, "we do not. The watch limits itself to weapons."

Ru turned back to Orth's body. "Remove his shirt, daughter. Let us see what his wounds will tell us."

Her hands sought the buttons and laces that held the shirt in place, her movements gentle, solemn, as if preparing a loved one for burial. Out of the corner of his eye Errol saw Merodach nod in approval.

With the shirt removed, Errol could see the indignities that had taken his friend's life. Most of the wounds were concentrated around the left side of the chest and up toward the throat. Rokha wet a cloth to wipe away the congealed blood from Orth's wounds.

"Not yet, daughter." Ru bent to point at the wounds. "Whoever bested him preferred to attack on the high line toward the head and chest. Orth's opponent was likely taller than he was."

Errol tried not to look at Orth. His skin, growing pale and bluish, sickened him. Yet Ru's comments aroused a curiosity within him. "How do you know he only faced one man?"

"A fair question, boy." He pointed. "Look at his abdomen—no wounds. What does that tell you?"

"What?" Errol asked.

Ru snorted his contempt toward Rale and Merodach. "Don't you teach those puppies anything in the watch?"

Rale frowned but turned his attention to Errol. "Soldiers are taught to attack on different lines if two men are facing one opponent, one on the high line and one on the low. If Gial had faced two men, he would have taken wounds to the midsection. He didn't."

"So Gial fought someone tall and someone better," Errol said. "How does that help us?"

"Wait, boy. I'm not done. Daughter, wash away his blood now."

Rokha complied, her movements tender, almost as if tending a brother. She edged back after she finished until she brushed shoulders with Merodach.

"No Merakhi did this," Ru said. "Orth was killed by a kingdom man."

Rale and Merodach nodded, but Errol needed an explanation. Despite Ru's demeaning tongue, he asked for it.

"Merakhi use a different style of sword than we do, boy. It's curved and only has one edge. In a fight, the Merakhi come at you with a flurry of slashes. The wounds they leave are long, deep cuts. And they never thrust. They're not trained that way."

Errol nodded with the rest of the group, but something in Ru's manner roused his suspicions. The caravan master had presented his explanation as if he'd known what he would find. Orth had been one of the best swords in the watch. How many men in the kingdom could have beaten him so thoroughly? He looked around. Two of those men stood in this cramped room with him, and another was traveling with Martin and Luis.

But he knew of one, one who had trained with the best blade in the world, one who had a grudge worth exploiting.

"Skorik."

Ru nodded. "It's possible, but there are other swordsmen in the kingdom equal to the watch, despite what is claimed."

"And we make it our business to know them," Merodach said. "This Skorik would have a reason to want to betray Earl Stone to the Merakhi, yes?"

"Yes," Rokha said, "but perhaps not for the reason you think." She wet her lips. "He saw Errol as a rival. Skorik was in love with me—or as close to it as he could come. At one time I thought I might have returned the favor, but his jealousies became too unreasonable, and I spurned him." She shrugged her shoulders. "He didn't take it well."

"Why didn't you tell me, daughter?" Ru asked.

"Because I didn't want you to kill him."

"We would have been better off if I had. Now we have this dog following us."

"A dog you trained, Naaman Ru," Rale said. "I would suggest you give some thought to choosing your students in the future. You've given the enemy a weapon to use against us."

Ru scowled but said nothing.

Merodach, closest to the door, put his hand on the latch. "The need for information remains. I will go in Gial Orth's place."

Rale raised a hand. "No. You will not."

Merodach raised a pale eyebrow. "Not? I am a captain of the watch."

"Nevertheless, when you joined us you became subject to the mission. As leader of that mission, appointed by Archbenefice Canon, I order you not to go." Rale turned to regard Orth's body. "Besides, Orth gave us the information we need. We are being pursued by kingdom men." He pointed at Ru. "At daybreak, we will abandon the wagons and ride hard for the coast. By the time Skorik and his companions realize our plan they will be too far behind to catch us.

"Captain Merodach, would you help Errol and me bury Lieutenant Orth's body? I think we'll require the services of Conger. I'm sure he knows the rites."

On a nearby hillside they took turns with the shovels, attacking the rocky soil of Basquon until, by tradition, the hole matched Orth's height. After they interred the lieutenant into the bosom of the cold, damp earth, they piled stones to mark his final resting place.

"Won't his family want to know where he's been buried?" Errol asked.

Rale shook his head. "The watch have no family save each other. When word reaches Captain Reynald of Gial's death, the sergeants will duel to see who will take his place. Then the corporals will do the same for the empty sergeant's slot and so on. Then we will accept a new recruit. The members of the watch serve as brothers, fathers, and uncles to each other. They have no other family."

"But you do."

His mentor nodded. "I was removed from the watch by the archbenefice. My reinstatement is temporary. If we survive, I will return to my wife and daughter."

Conger bowed his head to recite the panikhida. "Deas, we commend into your mercy all your servants which are departed away from us with the sign of faith and now rest in the sleep of peace: grant unto them, we beg you, your mercy and everlasting peace."

The ex-priest shrugged as if in apology. "It's not the high canticle. My tongue gets all twisted up around all those *thee*s and *thou*s."

Rale rested his hand on Conger's back. "I think Gial would have appreciated it just the way you said it. The lieutenant had a familiar sense of humor."

Errol visited his pack, then moved into the shadows, a pair of blanks and his knife in hand. The thought of Skorik stalking them raised the hackles on his neck. If the man managed to betray them to the Merakhi or Duke Weir, Errol held little doubt as to his own fate. A long, weary sigh escaped him, and he let his shoulders fall. How could one village drunk accumulate so many enemies in such a short time?

He sat away from the others where they'd gathered by the fire to share stories of the dead watchman. Errol bowed his head and cleared his mind. The question framed the answer. A simple cast such as this one hardly required all of his concentration, but despite the accolades of the conclave, he was still a novice. With single-minded intensity he pictured Skorik following them and focused on the word that would embed itself into the grain of his lot to be read by him alone. That word was *Yes.*

The knife slid over the grain as easily as water flowed over the rocks of the Sprata, molding and shaping. The pungent odor of pine shavings filled him, and his mind sharpened further. His hands moved of their own accord. After the space of a few minutes, he looked down to see a rough sphere in his lap. He marveled again at his gift, that he should be able to create this thing.

He reached for the next blank, repeated the process with Skorik and the opposite answer held in his mind until he completed the carving. In the dim glow of the firelight he could just make out the word *No* against the yellowish grain of the wood. He reached into his pack for the rubbing paper. He probably didn't need it; the lots could be cast now if he required haste, but he found the ritual of lot-making comforting. Gial Orth was dead, his life drained away along with his blood and his body entombed under six feet of earth and a few hundred pounds of rock.

But where was he? Was a man nothing more than the sum of the parts of his body? That didn't seem right. Errol had met old soldiers, veterans of the Steppes War and subsequent skirmishes, who had lost an arm or leg to injury or infection. They struggled with certain tasks, but their personalities, the essence of themselves, seemed undiminished. Did a man simply wink out like an extinguished candle when he died, or did he go somewhere? He rolled each blank through the rubbing cloth, chasing slight imperfections as his mind ran in circles around the watchman's death.

"What's your cast?"

Errol looked up to see Rale standing over him. His mentor crouched so that they were on eye level with each other. He nodded at the blanks in Errol's lap.

"I wanted to confirm whether or not Skorik is the one following us."

This earned a raised eyebrow. "Will it make any difference?" The question held a slight note of challenge.

He rolled his shoulders. "Probably not. An enemy is an enemy, but I needed space to think about Gial Orth, and casting just felt . . . right."

"Every watchman knows his duty, Errol," Rale said. "We fight for the kingdom, and if necessary . . ."

"We die for it," Errol finished. "But I'm so very tired of people dying for me."

Rale shrugged. "It might help to look at it a different way. They're not dying for you; they're dying for the kingdom. You might be called on to do so as well."

Errol looked at the lots in his lap. "I don't want to."

Rale laughed, and Errol jerked his head up to see if Rale mocked his cowardice, but he could only find sympathetic agreement on Rale's face. "Me neither."

He pointed to Errol's lap. "Let's see what the lots have to say. It never hurts to know your enemy."

A few minutes later Errol pulled the same lot from his makeshift bag for the twelfth time. "I guess I wasted a couple of lots."

"Perhaps not," Rale said. "What kind of man is Skorik?"

"I saw him cut through half a dozen bandits in less than two minutes. He's fearless and not shy about spilling blood."

"And he hates you."

Errol shook his head. "I don't think so, or at least not exactly. He loves Rokha and thinks I'm in the way." He laughed. "If he knew who Rokha favored, he might be less inclined to follow us."

Rale's brows framed his question.

"Merodach," Errol said. "Rokha spends her free time sharing his company."

The captain grunted. "Merodach has always attracted women, but he hardly knows they exist."

"I think you might be surprised. When Rokha is near him, he borders on the verge of having a personality." He shrugged. "I'm glad he's better than Skorik."

"You know this?"

"I beat Skorik at his best. Our fight was a sparring bout only in name; Skorik wanted to kill me and I knew I had to beat him senseless to escape. Both of us threw everything we had at each other. I've gotten better since then. Merodach beat me just to make a point in a lesson. I can believe what the others say about him."

Rale stirred himself before turning away, his manner that of the captain in charge once more. "Be ready to leave at first light."

Errol looked at the wagons they'd hauled south as their disguise. How much money would they be leaving by the roadside? "What will we do when we get to the coast?"

Rale shrugged as if the answer were obvious. "We'll buy new wagons and a cargo to go with them, something the Merakhi prize."

With a frown, he searched his pockets. He had perhaps a couple of gold crowns and a little more silver, certainly not enough to outfit a caravan. "With what?"

Rale laughed and patted his breast. "The pockets of the church are deep beyond imagining, Errol. Before we left Erinon, the archbenefice gave me a letter of declaration." A mischievous grin split his face. "The benefice of Basquon will find his treasury somewhat lightened when he returns from the Judica."

Errol stopped. The Judica. He hadn't thought of them in weeks. What had they decided about Illustra's future king?

33

COUNCIL OF SOLIS

MARTIN WOKE to Shal's hand pulling at his shoulder. "Greet the city of Phos, priest."

Three days after leaving Refuge, their boat slowed between two barges and bumped softly against a massive wharf. The dawn sun crept up over the plain that stretched away to the east, and on the near bank of the river stretched the city. Martin gaped. It wasn't possible. The shadow lands couldn't possibly hold a city so big. Why, over a hundred thousand people might live inside the walls alone. His mind reeled at the implications. The shadow lands probably held as many people as any of the largest provinces of the kingdom.

"Where did they all come from?"

"I believe this is one question I can answer," Shal said, "since you would come to the answer yourself, eventually. How long has the church been excommunicating its people?"

Martin shrugged. "Centuries."

Shal nodded. "And does anyone ever return?"

When Martin shook his head, still held in dumb fascination, he continued. "Few born in Haven leave."

Martin stammered. His brain refused to accept the reality of the sprawl before him. "But no one knows you're here. We could trade. We could treat and set up mutually defensible borders."

"With a country of excommunicates? What would Mother Church say to that?" Shal smiled as he stepped out of the boat. "Come. If your friends are here and they are as important as you claim, they'll be in the citadel."

Martin's head swiveled as he tried to catch every sight, smell, and nuance of the city as if he were the rawest peasant in from the country. Everywhere he looked he saw signs of a prosperous, thriving culture. And it was hidden from the kingdom as if it didn't exist.

"How have you managed to keep this a secret?"

"I think that's a question for the council, but I can tell you that we are still ten leagues from the coast. The city is not visible from the Forbidden Strait." He pointed ahead to a building whose size rivaled that of the great cathedral in Erinon, but where Erinon's cathedral was laid out with perpendicular wings, this building appeared to be circular. A great dome sheathed in white stone capped the center of the building, rising a hundred feet or more into the air.

Martin could see five entrances to the grand building, each an enormous arch that led to the interior. He surmised at least seven additional entrances filled the outer wall as it curved out of sight. The enormous construction embodied a symmetry of surprising elegance.

At the nearest entrance a pair of men, unarmed and clothed in simple gray robes, stood duty—answering questions and directing the foot traffic to the proper destination.

Shal pointed toward them. "Those are the dirigio. The citadel houses most of the government of Haven, and the dirigio help sort out who goes where."

"Why are they not armed?" Martin asked.

Shal's gaze, somber, caught his. "Haven is committed to nonviolence. Despite the animosity you've seen from some of our people, most of the populace was exiled here justly. Men who have paid such a high price for their violence come to accept the necessity of living in peace with others."

"Surely there are still some among you who would use violence to accomplish their ends," Martin said. "And you guard your borders with weapons." The idea of even a remotely peaceful society arising from the kingdom's penal colony sent tremors of disquiet through his midsection. "No society can be totally peaceful."

Shal nodded. "You're right, but if the question is important to you, it should be posed to the members of the council, who can answer it better." He stepped forward and spoke to the dirigio in murmuring tones. Martin tried to hear the conversation without giving the appearance of doing just that, but the words were lost amidst the noise of the crowd.

The men at the gate bowed toward him. The one on the left, who had the pale hair and ruddy complexion of a Soede, turned and called into the citadel's shadowed interior. A page, a boy of ten or perhaps eleven, appeared, barefoot and panting. "Imprimus, take these men to the council."

"Follow me please, sirs," the boy chirped. He set off at a pace on his spindly legs just shy of a jog. Imprimus led them along a corridor that followed along the outermost wall until they reached a hallway to the left and turned, heading for the center of the citadel without deviation. The citadel's interior appeared to be laid out in a series of concentric rings joined by hallways like the spokes of a wagon wheel. At any juncture where closed doors and attendant men in gray blocked their path, Imprimus's name gained them access. The boy, his bare feet dirty and his hair matted with sweat, seemed unaffected by this treatment. Within minutes they reached a large circular chamber with thick wooden doors.

"The council deliberates here," Shal said.

Imprimus swung the knocker on the door. A gray-clad servant poked his head out. At seeing the boy, he swung the door open to admit Shal and Martin.

"Your page seems to carry some authority," Martin observed.

The boy and Shal shared laughter. "I'm only one of the pages assigned to the council today. I drew the first lot, which makes me Imprimus. The most important visitors are given to me. The rest stand in line at the other entrances, waiting for an opening once more urgent matters are taken care of. When the sentry saw my face, he knew *you* were important, not me."

Martin nodded, impressed by the efficiency of the arrangement.

The interior of the council chamber mimicked the citadel's exterior—a large circular room with a series of doors evenly placed around the perimeter. Martin, Shal, and Imprimus stood at the door directly in front of the men and women in the council. The council members raised their heads from their examination of three figures in front of the dais, and Martin endured their silent scrutiny.

Besides their obvious positions of authority, there was nothing remarkable about the council, other than their variety. It seemed every province of the kingdom had found representation here. A thin Soede man sat next to a plump Gascon woman. A Basqu, her telltale dark hair and eyes shining in the bright lamplight sat next to a couple of Talians, a man with a waxed mustache and a woman, her face intense and angry. They in turn sat beside a Dann and then a Bellian and an Avenian. In all, nine people examined him from their council chairs.

Then the three figures turned.

Martin surged forward, his feet carrying him almost without his knowledge to embrace Luis and Cruk as they rushed to meet him.

"You made it," Luis said. His voice choked over what he would have said next.

Cruk gave a sober nod, and for once his smile actually raised both sides of his mouth. "We feared for you. Karele said you lived, said Aurae told him you'd make it into the shadow lands by another route. I didn't believe him."

Luis smiled. "Our captain is somewhat miserly with his description. He refused to move one step east until I cast to see if you were alive. Three times a day, I cast to see if you'd made it across the mountains."

Karele, the third person in front of the dais, turned from them to face the council. "Did I not tell you he would live?" He drew himself up. "The priest has done what no one has ever done—he has come to Haven through the cursed city. Now will you accept my authority? Now do you accept that upon their deaths Aurae chose me to head the circle of nine?"

Tension Martin just then discerned crackled between the council and the figure of Karele standing below them on the dais. The rigid postures of the men and women spoke of a battle of wills, their bodies thrust forward in their seats as if to ward against threats.

"Authority?" the Talian woman said. "You bring no written word from the mothers verifying this authority, *and* you bring outsiders to the city. Everything we have striven to build and keep safe from Illustra is in jeopardy because of you." She rose from her seat to speak to her fellow members of the council. "Why should we accept the authority of a man we do not know—based solely on his say-so?"

Luis left Martin's side to stand by Karele. "Perhaps I can help. You know that I am a reader. Before leaving Erinon I was secondus, the second-highest reader in the conclave. I am willing to cast any question you choose to ask."

Far from being mollified, Luis's offer enraged Karele's accuser. "You dare? Here in the highest chamber of Haven, you dare to espouse casting lots?" She stood, pointed a finger at him. "Do we need to hear any more? Throw them in prison."

The other council members kept their seats, waiting, it seemed, for Karele to speak, to offer some refutation of the charge. The man who'd proclaimed himself head of the solis eyed the members of the nine, his face calm.

A council member with the bushy brown eyebrows and swarthy skin of a Lugarian turned to face the Talian woman. "Sit down, Marya. You've fulfilled your duty." Turning to face Karele, he cleared his throat. "Marya takes her duty as accuser seriously. You have brought trouble to Haven, solis."

Karele nodded at this. "It was necessary. In fact, it was

commanded. Adele and Radere told the solis decades ago that our exile would come to an end."

"Not exactly the end we wanted," Marya said. "What will the kingdom do once they discover our true nature? We cannot hope that they will leave us alone."

Martin stepped forward to stand by Karele. "The kingdom is the least of your worries, madam councilor. Once Rodran dies, war will sweep over the earth. You cannot hope to be spared."

"You are wrong, priest," Marya said. "The Merakhi and the Morgols know as little of us as the kingdom does. The routes to war are far to the north and west of our little corner here."

Martin swallowed. "And if the accursed ones awake at Rodran's death . . . ? Their city lies on your border. Do you think they will fail to notice you?"

The Lugarian held up a hand. "Enough. Such questions will have to wait. It is the immediate purpose of this council to determine the head of the solis."

"You mean to entertain this man's assertion, Garet?" Marya asked. The Lugarian, along with several council members, including the Soede, nodded at this.

"I do," Garet answered. "Karele, do you mean to call Aurae to witness your claim?"

Karele bowed to the council. "You know I can only call, not summon. Whether Aurae comes is up to Deas."

The Basqu woman smiled. "If Aurae does not come, we can always have the reader cast."

Marya bristled. "You would trust him? A churchman?"

"Your opinions are colored by your personal experiences. Most churchmen are good men who follow as best they know," the Basqu said. She pointed a finger toward Luis. "See him, Marya. He is nearly solis himself."

She scoffed but turned to peer at Luis as if she were reading a text whose words were too small to make out. After a moment, she sat back, her eyes wide. "Strange tidings."

The Basqu nodded. "Indeed."

Garet rose to address the attendants. "Seal the chamber. Let no one enter until we are done." Two dozen gray-clad men with serious faces departed, sealing the doors behind them as they went.

Garet faced Karele. "Call and let us see if Deas's favor names you head of the solis."

Karele stepped a little apart and bowed his head. For long moments that Martin tracked by the anxious beating of his heart, nothing happened. The nine members of the council sat with the patience of stones, as if prepared to wait as long as necessary. Even the air, disturbed before by the movements of the chamber's occupants, grew still, settling like a blanket over Martin as he held his breath. His heart hammered against his ribs, shaking him where he stood.

Aurae's appearance would destroy the last vestige of doubt left to him. If the spirit of Deas appeared within the chamber, all of Martin's teaching, the sum total of doctrine and theology he'd learned and espoused his entire life, would be torn to tatters.

And he would be required to present the truth to the Judica.

The college of benefices would already have censured him by now for leaving in the midst of deliberations. They would hardly welcome news that challenged their most cherished beliefs and traditions. Aurae's appearance would cost Martin dearly.

Yet Martin watched Karele with an anticipatory hunger that frightened him, even while it washed him from head to toe. With everything that was in him he wanted Aurae to appear, thirsted for it like a man in a desert. Tears of longing welled in his eyes.

But nothing happened.

Karele knelt now, both knees on the ochre stone floor of the chamber, his head bowed, hands raised in an attitude of beseeching. The council members leaned forward, their faces moving from anticipation to vague embarrassment as time slipped by and Aurae did not appear. Martin's chest heaved, acquiescing to his body's demand for air. His breath stirred the air, and his heart thrummed in expectation before the chamber stilled again.

Garet shifted his weight in preparation to rise from his seat.

No. They had to wait. Everything Karele had done and said had borne witness. A plea that captured all the longing of his call to be a priest, of his deepest desire to know Deas, came as a wordless cry from his lips, and he sank to his knees to mimic Karele's supplicant posture.

34

BREATH OF WIND

A WHISPER OF AIR brushed his cheek, flowed past him and grew, ruffling Cruk's hair. It circled the chamber, growing in intensity to ripple Luis's clothes and flow from one council member to the next. It wheeled around the wall, lifting motes of dust to wink and sparkle in the lamplight before spinning and concentrating on Karele. It coalesced upon the healer. Tendrils emerged from the vortex and he rose to his feet. Then it encompassed him, enveloped him in swirling currents.

Beginning with Garet and the Basqu, the council rose to their feet and bowed. "Karele is head of the solis."

Martin sank back on his haunches, smiled through tears that blurred his vision and turned the room into a waterfall of color. He blinked in an effort to see. The wind increased, lifting the hair from his forehead. With the coarse weave of his cloak he scrubbed his eyes. He needed to see.

Breath left him. The vortex of wind surrounded him now. Tendrils of substance appeared in the wind like tentative suggestions of fog or mist, yet they moved of their own volition, first following the circular wind, now up and down and against it. He reached out, tentative, to touch a tendril that somehow faced him, stationary within the tiny maelstrom.

Warmth and chills ran over his skin, lifting the hair on his arms. Then, without warning, the wind ceased and the chamber returned to stillness, as if it had never been.

Martin wiped his eyes, found Karele and the rest of the council staring at him in shock, as if he'd become strange in their sight.

The Basqu man cleared his throat. "I'm sorry, Marya. I think you were saying something about not trusting churchmen."

She sniffed at his jibe, but the look she turned on Martin held surprise and a fading hint of reverence. "My objections are unimportant. For whatever reason, Aurae has chosen the priest as well." She shook her head, the motion of her black hair echoing the departed wind. "I dislike such tidings."

Garet nodded. "As do I. However, it may be that we stand on the edge of our gloaming. Representatives from the church and the kingdom know we are here, and if the kingdom's theology proves true, the barrier will fall with Rodran's death." He looked down the curved table at the rest of the council members. "We must choose our path."

The Soede snorted. "Choose? What is there to choose? We must align with the kingdom—else the light of the world will be buried beneath a tide of ghostwalkers and theurgists."

"I think the issue is deeper than that," the Talian woman said. "No one questions whether we will fight on the side of light or of dark." She leaned back and tapped a long, tapered fingernail on the table. The click against the stone sounded loud in the silence. "The real question is, will we submit to kingdom authority or marshal and command our own troops?"

The Soede's brows rose. Garet gave a thoughtful nod. Martin stepped forward, trying to smooth his features to hide unexpected nervousness. If the shadow lands fought how and where they chose, the kingdom would never be able to coordinate a successful defense. "If I may speak?"

Garet nodded. "Speak, solis."

It took Martin a moment to realize that the leader of the

council addressed him. He cleared his throat. "The kingdom possesses fine generals. There are currently five captains within the watch who have mastered the art of war. If we were to offer them a coordinated army under one command, we would have a much better chance of winning."

The Soede sniffed. "I fought in the Steppes War, priest. I saw how the conscripts drew duty in the vanguard. Tell me what assurances you can provide that the army of Haven will be treated better than draftees."

Every member of the council leaned forward, awaiting his answer. This, then, was their biggest concern: how to protect their people. His throat clenched. He squared his shoulders and cleared his throat. All of his years in the priesthood and the Judica had prepared him for this. "You have the best assurance of all, my lords and ladies. If you do not receive fair and equitable treatment, your forces can quit the field. You are a sovereign country."

"I doubt the church will see us that way," Marya said. "To them we are nothing more than a seldom-remembered penal colony. Once they learn of our numbers, they will see us as a cheap source of manpower and goods." She pointed. "Mark my words, solis, news of our prosperity will awaken a hue and cry among the nobles and the church to assert control over Haven."

Garet and the rest of the council nodded, waiting in expectation for Martin's reply. He licked lips gone suddenly dry. This was not some debate over obscure theology. The freedom and autonomy of the shadow lands—or Haven—was at stake. His stentorian cadences were of little use here. Only the truth would suffice. He caught himself. *The truth?*

A whisper in his mind, like the sighing of trees, urged him to speak to the point. "Friends," he said, "what you say is true. The kingdom is as it ever has been—a collection of men, good and bad, compassionate and ambitious. There will be men who will see the unexpected bounty of Haven as nothing more than ripe fruit for the plucking. There are powerful men who crave yet more power. The Weir family continues as the strongest hand in the nobility after the king, and they have influence in the venerated halls of the cathedral as well.

"But there are also good men, men who will see what you have accomplished here as a miracle and a treasure, men like Archbenefice Canon and Primus Enoch Sten." His voice caught. "I know these men. They would treasure and strive to protect your people as their own."

Garet nodded, his eyes moist. "As would you, Solis Martin. Yet kingdom politics may turn with the swiftness of the tide. What can be done to safeguard our people?"

Martin took a deep breath. If the powers of the kingdom objected to what he was about to suggest, he might well end up in the shadow lands himself. *Ha. If* they objected? By Deas in heaven, he should save himself the time and begin looking for a place to live here and now.

"My friends, I think there is a way, though my superiors will dislike the fact that I have suggested it to you." He paused, out of respect, to make eye contact with each of them. "I will ask the king to declare a writ of recognition for Haven. His declaration will make you a sovereign nation."

Raucous laughter burst from the Basqu. "Dislike? You have turned mountains into anthills, Solis Martin. The kingdom's numerous exiles have brought us extensive tales of the kingdom over the years. We are not ignorant of the power Duke Weir exercises. The man may just kill you outright." He turned to Marya. "What say you now?"

"I say that if the church had more such men, she would be a light to illuminate the world."

The mercurial councilwoman looked upon Martin with fierce admiration and something he hadn't seen from a woman in over twenty years. It made him uncomfortable, and he felt his ears grow warm.

Garet clapped, calling the attention of the council. "I propose that we send Solis Karele and Solis Martin on their way with all the speed and aid they require. In addition, I propose that the writ of recognition be delivered by the king. If the kingdom grants recognition to Haven, then we shall fight under their banner. How say you?"

Martin lifted his hands in protest. "Rodran would never survive the journey."

Garet nodded. "Then he must send his niece. Agreed?"

Martin scanned the council. "I will communicate your terms."

One by one, each member of the council laid their right hand upon the stone table. Garet nodded. "It is decided. Solis Martin, our blessings and prayers go with you." The members of the council filed out of their seats and moved out in front of the arc of their table. As each member passed Karele they laid their hands upon his head and kissed him. Then they repeated the gesture with Martin.

Marya's warm hands cupped his face, but instead of kissing each cheek, she pressed her lips against his. "If you ever tire of the priesthood, Solis Martin, I think you would make a fine husband."

Laughter, not unkind, filled the chamber at Marya's words. Even Cruk joined in, and after a moment, during which tension spilled from him like water through a sieve, Martin's gales rebounded from the wall.

The next day they stepped from a flat-bottomed riverboat onto the dock in order to transfer to a ship that would take them to Basquon. Unlike the ports in Erinon or Port City, the docks at the southern tip of Haven did not boast much seafaring capability. In fact, only one small pier jutted out into the hidden harbor that provided access to the strait. Two ships, one on each side, waited with furled sails.

As their party drew closer to the vessels, Martin's stomach roiled at the thought of daring the straits in the craft before him. Both ships appeared seaworthy enough, except that, to all appearances, neither had been to sea in years. A handful of men with fishing lines hung about the docks, regarding the three-masted cogs as fixtures in the landscape rather than means of transportation.

Cruk strode forward shaking his head, muttering under his breath. With tentative steps he crossed the gangplank, feeling each as if he expected the wood to break beneath him and dump him in the gray waters of the harbor. He stepped onto the ship with visible relief.

The deck of the ship was dry. Cruk fingered one of the ropes and snorted. "I wonder how many years it's been since they put to sea."

Luis made a slow turn. "Where is everybody?"

Cruk shook his head. "On permanent leave, most likely. If anyone's on board this dried-up tub, he'll be in the captain's quarters." He moved toward the hatch and broad stairs that led down to the next deck. When they reached the captain's quarters, Martin was surprised to find the door's wood polished and gleaming, casting the rest of the dusty interior in stark contrast.

"At least we know somebody's onboard this hulk," Cruk said.

"Go easy, friend," Karele said. "You forget that Haven is first and foremost banishment for those who have been excommunicated. Those who have been sent here are under a death penalty if they return to the kingdom."

"Why did they build ships, then, if they couldn't use them?" Luis asked.

Karele shrugged. "Many who are exiled find it difficult to adjust to a different life. It is likely a few shipwrights and sailors gathered to re-create the life they could no longer have."

This simple assessment conveyed to Martin the despair of excommunication more than anything else. "I think it's a beautiful ship." He stepped forward to rap on the door. Muffled voices, a man's and a woman's, came from the interior, the thick oak not quite masking the surprise in their tones. A moment later, the door cracked open to reveal a squat, middle-aged man holding a short sword with rust on it.

His eyes bugged at the sight of Cruk.

"What might you fellows be wantin' of old Amos Tek?"

Cruk's brows rose at the name, but Karele stepped in front of the watchman. "I am Solis Karele. Are you the captain of this ship?"

The man blinked in incomprehension. "Captain? Hmm, I guess I be the captain. It be more of a floating home than a ship." His eyes narrowed. "And why would you be wantin' to know that?"

Karele drew a sealed letter from within his cloak. "I have orders from the council for you, Captain. You're to take us to Basquon."

The captain's fingers trembled as he reached for the letter. Lightly, he stroked the wax seal before breaking it. He bit his lips as he read the instructions within, then turned toward the interior of his cabin. "Brandy, I'm going to sea. The council says I can go to sea."

A woman dressed in sailor's clothes came into view, snatched the paper. She read it twice, her lips moving in time as her eyes scanned the few lines within the missive. "Aye, it's true." She turned dewy eyes upon Karele. "You've made Amos very happy." She rested a hand on the captain's arm. "Do you think you still remember how to sail?"

He drew himself up. "I be captain every night in my dreams, woman. Of course I remember." He swatted her on the rump. "Go gather those layabouts and tell them we sail with the tide." A cackle of mirth bubbled up from somewhere inside him. "Captain Tek be on the seas again."

35

NETS

ERROL MOVED DOWN the gangplank of the ship, his legs swaying and buckling in time to the swells of the strait. Much of his dawn breakfast of ham and cheese was no doubt still attracting gulls somewhere out in that accursed expanse of water. Even zingiber powder hadn't helped. Of course the crossing had been less than smooth. For the fourth time in eight days their ship had been met at the halfway point in the strait by Merakhi longships ready to attack and board.

Every time they'd turned tail and fled back to Basquon, relying on their greater speed to reach the safety of kingdom ships that patrolled Illustra's side of the strait. Four different trips in four different ships led to the same conclusion: The Merakhi knew who they were and knew when they were coming.

He grumbled around the taste of bile in his mouth. With every failed attempt, the church's compulsion grew within him—frantic thoughts of swimming across the water filled his mind. His temper frayed and his friends and companions avoided him. They did not possess the power to lessen the church's compulsion. Even Adora, after being rebuffed twice, found reasons to be elsewhere. Only Rale sought him out, standing next to him on the dark gray planks of the pier as Errol looked out across the waves toward the south.

"We will find a way," Rale said.

He shook his head. "If they can turn us back at night, there's no way for us to slip through their blockade. We're beaten."

"We're not beaten 'til we're dead, lad."

Rale's words, meant to cheer him, focused Errol's thoughts on the subject of his concern. "What happens to a person if he is prohibited from fulfilling a compulsion?"

Rale grimaced and shrugged. "I don't know. There may not be anyone who does know. Archbenefice Gayle issued a decree limiting the use of compulsion three hundred years ago. No doubt some members of the church have used it in secret since then, but that's the kind of information that doesn't make it out to the village goodwife, if you take my meaning."

Errol gazed at the water—longing to cross the strait filled him like a hunger he couldn't feed. "I think I'll just lose myself and walk right into the sea and die."

Rale growled. "We'll find a way, boy. If need be, I'll set a watch on you or have you tied to the mast to keep you from drowning yourself."

Errol shuddered as he envisioned himself raving and tied to the main, his mind in tatters, unable to fulfill the church's penance. "Don't keep me alive if my mind breaks. I don't want to live like that."

"You're not going to go insane, boy. We'll find a way."

"How?"

Rale's posture sagged as his mouth worked to find an answer. Errol watched, grateful, but his friend's efforts only heightened the morbid fascination he felt for his unavoidable demise. What would it be like to go insane? Would the thinking part of his mind just shrink until nothing remained, like snow melting in the sun? Or would he simply snap, one moment himself and the next moment broken like a branch during a flood? He couldn't decide which he preferred.

"Errol!" A voice hailed him from out in the bay. "Errol!"

He squinted, labored to focus on the source of the call. Out in the harbor, running with the wind, came a small three-master, its captain calling the order to furl sails, his voice filled with salt and laughter.

"That's not possible," he heard himself say. The compulsion must have been altering his mind already. There was no other way to explain the hallucination, but Rale's laughter contradicted him.

The ship glided into the slip two piers over, where dockhands tied it off with thick hawsers. Errol followed Rale over to the craft, numb with surprise and shock. A moment later he found himself smothered by cloak and arms as Pater Martin wrapped him in a bear hug.

"It's good to see you alive, boy," Martin said. "I was afraid we'd be too late."

Errol shook his head, trying to clear the clutter of the previous night's failure and the compulsion from his awareness. "What are you doing here?"

Martin smiled, but his eyes looked pinched, closed. "We're going with you to Merakh, boy."

Errol shook his head. "Nobody's going to Merakh. We can't get across the strait. The Merakhi know our every step."

A small man with dark eyes and sharp features stepped forward, squeezing through the space between Cruk and Luis to stand before him. "I might be able to do something about that, Earl Stone."

The set of his eyes—calm and assured—exuded simple confidence. Errol looked to Martin, who gave a slight nod.

"You know this?" Rale asked Martin. "He can get us through Valon's net of readers?"

"I have seen it," Martin said. "This is Solis Karele. If anyone can get us through to Merakh, it is him."

Rale eyed the ship Martin and the rest had just left and rubbed his chin in thought. "It's obviously not a kingdom ship. Is there any chance your captain is available for hire?"

Cruk barked a laugh. "Just assure him you won't send him back to the shadow lands, Elar, and he'll probably do it for free."

Rale started, shook his head in shock. "Cruk? Is that you? You still look awful."

Cruk grunted. "I'm no wiser about the company I keep. It's not very restful."

Rale cut his eyes to Errol. "I know what you mean."

Cruk nodded. "I see you do."

"What's your captain's name? He might do it for free, but I'll feel a lot more comfortable if he knows I've bought him."

Cruk's mouth pulled to one side. "Amos Tek."

Rale's eyes widened. "The pirate? I thought he was dead."

Cruk laughed. It sounded like a saw rasping through a board. "No, it was worse. He got himself exiled to the shadow lands."

Rale looked as if he'd begun a long list of questions. Errol stepped forward to catch his attention. "How soon can we leave? I'm slipping."

"What?" Cruk asked.

Luis nudged him. "The compulsion is taking him."

Cruk spat. "Foul thing to do to a man. Better to kill him outright," he said. Then he looked at Luis and away again, his color rising.

Luis didn't appear to take offense. "Despite the evidence to the contrary, I have to say I agree."

He glanced at Martin with an indecipherable look. Errol restrained a sigh. More secrets. A wave of fatigue washed over him, sapping his strength. "I'd give anything to be back on your farm shoveling manure and working the staff," he said to Rale.

"I know what you mean, lad." He turned to Cruk. "We'll have to transfer our goods to the hold of Tek's ship. But that should take less than three hours. Can we leave then?"

Cruk shouted up at the captain. "Tek, you cursed pirate, can you be ready to sail in three hours?"

"Reformed pirate," Tek shouted back. "Yes, I be ready to sail now. The waves call to me, they do."

"Excellent," Rale said. He wheeled, giving orders.

Errol stood rooted to his spot on the pier, searching within himself to determine if the compulsion had lessened at the news. He couldn't tell. The pull seemed as strong as ever, as if the church had tied the end of a string to his chest and given the other end to the entire nation of Merakh and ordered the country to pull him across the strait. The thought sent his consciousness slipping, and he took an involuntary step toward the water.

"Errol." A hand on his shoulder stopped him, pulled him around. Awareness returned. He blinked. Rokha stood before him, shoulder to shoulder with Merodach. The fingers of their hands fluttered as if they'd just then separated. He nodded, requiring the physical motion to chase the last of the compulsion's somnolence away.

Rokha peered left and right before speaking. "He's hiding something, Errol."

"Who?"

"The priest."

A snort vibrated in the back of his throat. "Martin. He's always hiding something. The man has more secrets than Weir has gold."

"Did you know he's under a compulsion?" Rokha asked. She went on as he gaped. "That's my ability, remember?"

His guts couldn't seem to figure out where they were supposed to be. "Shouldn't you be telling Rale this? He's the man in charge, not me." He didn't wait for an answer. His curiosity rushed out of him. "Can you tell who put it on him?"

Her dark brows met over the ridge of her nose. "No. That's beyond me, but it's strange. It doesn't look like the compulsions I've seen before. It's strong, very strong."

He tried to keep the frustration out of his voice and failed. "What does that mean? Aren't they all?"

She shrugged. His irritation had no effect on her. "Yes, but I think this one has something to do with you. From the moment he saw you he's looked like a man in pain." She shrugged as if her revelations weren't making his insides dance. "I thought you'd want to know."

He didn't want to think about it. Rokha was wrong. He didn't want to know. A nod came as close to thanks as he could muster. Then he spun on his heel to help port their goods to Tek's ship. There seemed little point in worrying over things beyond his control—and Martin, with his multitude of secrets, had always been one of those.

Two hours later, they cast off the mooring lines and unfurled enough sail to drift into the harbor. Errol stood in the prow, hoping to lessen the pull in his chest by the scant advantage his position offered. Why was the wind so still?

"Once we clear the harbor, you should go belowdecks," Rale said. The erstwhile farmer had a way of appearing out of thin air. "Valon knows what you look like. He may be confident in his circle's ability to find you, but if he's smart, he'll have men using their eyes as well."

It only made sense, but he loathed the thought of being unable to see their progress. With a nod, because words seemed burdensome, he made his way aft to the stairs that led down to the sleeping quarters and the hold. He found Luis, Martin, and Karele in the galley seated around a long trestle table nailed to the floor. They smiled at his approach, but Martin's eyes flinched as if at a sudden discomfort.

Even so, the priest waved to a seat. "It's good to see you, boy. I think we have some catching up to do."

Errol nodded his reply but left the indicated spot on the bench empty. The abstraction from the compulsion and the flare of pain in Martin's eyes made him too uncomfortable to sit. "I need to find Cruk." He didn't really, but in the absence of Rale, who remained topside, he craved Cruk's plain speech.

Martin nodded, his eyes strained and relieved at the same time.

Errol moved aft, seeking not so much company as a way to escape his own thoughts. Each time someone desired speech he begged off and continued his search for Cruk, hoping all the while that he wouldn't find him.

He wandered topside, then ascended to the elevated deck at the rear of the ship. Tek's first mate manned the rudder. To one side, his face toward the sea, Luis stood alone. A yearning for the reader's peaceful company came over Errol, and he moved to stand beside him at the rail.

"Hello, Errol." Luis's eyes still held their accustomed serenity, but the calm assurance had been replaced by something closer to doubt. His gaze refused to settle anywhere for long.

Perhaps some of the reader's diffidence communicated itself to Errol. He didn't know how to respond. "It will take us a few hours to make it to Merakhi waters. The four times we tried we were met by longships."

Luis faced him. "They turned you back?"

Errol chuckled softly. "No. They tried to chase us down and board us. We used four different ships, and they spotted every one. No other kingdom ships were threatened. Only us."

Luis nodded. "Valon has readers aboard those ships. Even without a circle, it would be a simple matter to cast for your presence."

Errol watched the water. He couldn't think of anything else to say. This had never been his strength, ferreting out information. Plain speech suited him better. "Rokha says Martin is under a compulsion."

"She's right," Luis said.

Errol fought to hide his surprise. No slippery speech. No half answers. Just open acknowledgment. "Does it have anything to do with me?"

Luis sighed as if trying to rid himself of a burden. "It seems everything has something to do with you, Errol."

He smiled at the reply. Except for the mournful tone, this was closer to the reader's usual manner of speech. Luis put a hand on his shoulder as if trying to comfort him.

"I'm sorry, Errol. I would have stopped him if I could have. Martin is passionate. His sense of justice could no longer tolerate your circumstances. He placed a compulsion upon himself." Luis shrugged. His shoulders twitched during the motion.

Emptiness opened in the pit of Errol's stomach, spreading outward with the dawning comprehension of Luis's words. Why was he sorry?

"What . . ." He couldn't seem to push enough air through his voice. "What does he have to do?" He might as well have been an eddy in the wind.

Sorrow and tears filled Luis's eyes, but he held Errol in an unwavering glance. "He has to tell you the truth—all of it."

Of all his desires, visible or locked away in his heart, knowing the truths Martin had kept hidden ranked as the third most important. Only Adora's hand and the identity of his parents ranked higher. Yet now he feared the resolution of Martin's compulsion. Luis had not flinched at compelling Errol to the conclave, had barely blinked at telling him he was expendable, yet now the secondus stood with tears in his eyes.

Enough. Whatever secrets Martin might bring into the light, Errol didn't want to know. "Tell him to remove the compulsion. I have enough burdens."

Luis's face tightened. "I'm sorry, Errol. He can't. In this Martin is now as powerless as you are. The compulsion can only be removed if Martin fulfills its demand." He shifted to gaze out across the sea. "He acted in haste, before he learned the full truth. Every moment he tarries is painful for him, but he loathes adding to the weight you carry."

Luis gave a rueful laugh. "Martin thought to give you what you wanted, not realizing what might happen. There's a lesson there." He sighed. "I think he means to defy the compulsion for as long as he can. He's strong, Errol, so who knows how long that may be?"

"We're headed into Merakh," Errol said. For months, even years, all he'd wanted was the truth, but now the truth had turned out to be as ugly and misshapen as everything else in his life. *Why?* "It's supposed to be my death sentence." Bitterness laced his voice. "Perhaps Martin will be able to keep his secrets after all."

He wanted no more of this conversation with Luis. It was obvious the reader would not divulge the secrets Martin carried, and his empathy for the priest rankled in a way difficult to define.

He couldn't decide which he wanted more: to let Martin suffer with the pain of his own stupidity and compulsion, or to force the priest to tell him the truth and know that he'd placed another wound in his soul. A part of him savored the fact that someone else suffered as much as he.

Then, with a suddenness that surprised him, he ached for Adora's company. The princess loved him. She would know what to do. He thrust himself away from the railing and Luis's sympathy and went in search of her.

As he stalked through the ship, some intuition seated deep within his chest told him Adora would be able to see a solution he could not, that the wisdom she'd garnered by her years in the palace would be equal to the task.

When he found her with Rokha in the small cabin Tek had set aside for the women on board, Adora stood to greet him with a polite nod, but the tension at the corner of her eyes said plainly she had not forgotten his behavior. He rushed across the room to enfold her in his arms and kiss her.

It was the first time he'd ever kissed a woman. True, women had kissed him, but until this moment he'd never initiated that sign of affection. He half expected Adora to push him away, but after a muffled exclamation of surprise, the princess melted into his embrace and her hands rose to lock in his hair. The kiss lasted longer than he'd intended. When their lips parted, the ship seemed to be rocking with the waves more than usual—and from across the room, Rokha grinned at him.

"I'm sorry," he said.

Adora broke from his embrace and took a step back, the picture of cool serenity once more, with the exception of a flush in her cheeks. "You make apologies where none are needed, Errol. No man alive carries a burden such as yours."

"Actually, someone does." He couldn't stop a sardonic chuckle from escaping his lips.

"What do you mean?"

Errol recited his conversation with Luis, watched as Adora's eyes grew wider until the whites showed around the emerald green of her irises.

"Unheard of," she said. "I never suspected a priest could lay a compulsion on himself."

"What should I do?"

She wheeled away from him to pace the confines of her cabin. "My heart tells me you should go to Martin and demand he tell you the truth, but I mistrust myself in this." She pivoted on one foot and came toward him again, head bent in concentration. Rokha was uncharacteristically silent as she feigned interest in something outside the porthole she stood near.

Adora stopped to look at him, her eyes locked with his. "I think you have three choices available to you, Errol."

He sighed. What he really wanted at that moment was for Adora to tell him what to do, but she would not. No one would, not even Rale. Though the watch captain commanded the mission, Errol's circumstances placed him beyond Rale's authority. "What are they?"

She held up a finger. "First, you can have Martin tell you what he knows at a time of your choosing."

"Isn't that up to him?" Errol asked.

Adora shook her head even as she gave him a fond smile. "You know, one of the reasons I love you is that such things as I'm about to suggest never occur to you. If you want to force the information from Martin, simply stay in his presence until the pain of his compulsion forces him to speak."

His eyes widened at the cold calculation of that suggestion and what it said of the intrigues that had surrounded Adora during her upbringing. He kept any trace of accusation from his face and voice. "I don't think I'd like that. It seems cruel, but I thank you for making me aware of the option. I hope I don't have to use it."

She nodded. The set of her shoulders relaxed. "Second, you can wait until he chooses or the compulsion forces him to tell you. I would advise against this. It puts you at the mercy of circumstance." She touched the scar in his side. "You don't seem to have much luck with circumstance."

His hand probed the flesh around the wound. Scar tissue covered the area, and he seemed to have suffered no permanent physical damage from Sahra and Rader's attack, but memories of screaming convulsions plagued his dreams. He couldn't jest about it yet. "No. I don't. What's the last option?"

Adora's shoulders, beautiful with new strength from her sword work, rose and descended. "Avoid him. Don't give him a chance to confess. Confine him to the ship once we reach Merakh and order him back to the kingdom."

For a moment, he latched on to that idea, until the somber look in Adora's eyes opened his own. "But that would be worse than forcing him to tell me, wouldn't it? Sooner or later the compulsion would take him, and if I'm not there . . ." Errol left the statement unfinished. He didn't know how to finish it.

To her credit, she didn't try to talk him into the obvious option, the one he hated and feared. She simply waited. He turned an idea over in his mind. Could he persuade Martin to satisfy the compulsion without telling Errol directly?

He stepped closer to Adora, taking her hands in his. They fluttered, birdlike, before gripping his own. "I would request something of you, Your Highness."

Her eyes narrowed at the use of her title, but her mouth pulled a little to one side in a smile. "Speak, Earl Stone. Fear not to reveal your mind to us, as all the world knows you bear the utmost regard of the crown."

Her voice dipped as she finished, and he felt his mouth go dry. "Would you approach Martin on my behalf? Have him tell you these truths that pain him so much. Then advise me on how to proceed."

She stared at him. "You would trust me with this? Not knowing what he might reveal?"

He held up his scarred palm. "Better you than any other."

Tears splashed against the wood of the cabin floor as she curtsied to him.

36

BROKEN

SHE DID NOT COME BACK to him for the rest of the day. Or the next. The princess dropped from sight as surely as if she'd been swept overboard. One time Errol saw her, but she scurried away, her face stricken, before he could approach.

Thus engaged, the ship passed through the Merakhi blockade almost without his notice. Karele stood on the deck as Tek guided the ship between a pair of sleek longboats.

As the ships to their stern vanished over the horizon, Errol questioned the small man.

"It's not me but the power of Aurae," Karele explained. "The power of the lot is written in the fabric of our world. Think of it like water running its course along a stream. The spirit of Deas, Aurae, has the ability to alter that course."

The idea didn't make sense to him. Either something worked or it didn't. "But how?"

Karele smiled. "Do you have any blanks with you?" At his nod, the little man continued. "Why don't you go get them and I'll show you?"

Errol went to the quarters he shared with the rest of the men

355

on board and pulled a pair of pine blanks, some rubbing cloth, and his carving knife from his pack. He hurried back to Karele, grateful for the opportunity to do something that would take his mind off Adora's protracted absence.

"Cast for something easy," Karele said.

Errol nodded. A yes or no question would be simplest. It would require little concentration to form the answers into the two blanks. "Is Martin a priest?" he said out loud in order to help him frame the question. Fifteen minutes later the lots lay carved and sanded in his palm, but only he could see the words reflected there.

Karele gave him an encouraging nod. "Now cast as many times as you need to reassure yourself they work as intended."

Errol dropped them into the large pocket of his cloak and drew one at random, then repeated the process. Twelve draws later, he gestured toward Karele. "Ten out of twelve says he's a priest."

Karele leaned forward with a smug expression. "How many times picking the opposite lot would it take to convince you that Aurae's power supersedes that of the lot?"

He shrugged. "Ten?"

Karele laughed. "Then let's make it twenty."

Errol snorted through his nose. "Impossible. Not with wood. I couldn't cast the surest question and pull a draw twenty times in a row."

"You're not Aurae." Karele pointed north, to the empty horizon. "If you do not believe me, then believe our passage. No one is following us."

Errol jumbled the lots together and thrust his hand in. "No." He put the lot back in, and for the next nineteen times—while Karele relaxed beside him on the weathered planks of the deck—he drew the same lot. His feel for the cast ceased to exist, as if he no longer held the power to read. "You can do this anytime you choose?" he asked.

Karele nodded. "So long as Aurae guides me."

This troubled Errol. A small knot of distrust formed in his

stomach. "What if Aurae decides not to guide you or suddenly chooses not to shield us from Valon's readers?"

Karele shrugged as if the question held no import. "Then we would be killed or captured."

"That's small comfort. Why should I trust it?"

This received a shake of the head. "Don't you know Aurae is the spirit of Deas, Errol?"

Errol shrugged. "No, not really. Some of what I know of Deas comes from the tales Conger has told me, or Martin's liturgy, but mostly it comes from Antil." Errol watched Karele's face stiffen into a mask at the mention of Callowford's priest.

"Antil doesn't speak for Deas, Errol."

He shrugged. "He says he does, just like you do. What's the difference?"

Karele pointed south to the still-out-of-sight shoreline of Merakh that awaited two days hence. "With the help of Aurae, I can get you to Merakh."

Errol permitted himself a grudging nod. "Granted, but the way you hedge your speech and refuse to make guarantees reminds me too much of the churchmen I've known."

"Do you mean Martin?" Karele asked.

"Among others. When you speak, I hear unspoken secrets running through your words." Errol gestured at the ship, the sky, the water. "Churchmen and their secrets are the reason I'm in this mess. I didn't do anything to deserve it. I've been driven with a goad every step of the way—first to Erinon, now to Merakh."

As he spoke, he realized he wanted Martin's confession, after all. What could a few words do to him that Antil's whipping rod had not? "After I start getting the truth out of people, the whole truth, you might find me more willing to listen to your version of Deas."

If Karele took affront at his words, he showed no sign of it. His face softened before he spoke. "I hope you still feel that way once you get your secrets." He moved away, his stride adapting to the pitch and roll of the ship as if adjusting to the gait of a horse.

Errol, left alone with the consequences of their conversation, faced forward and closed his eyes to concentrate and enjoy the easing pressure in his mind where the compulsion lay. It hadn't vanished completely. It wouldn't leave unless and until Valon lay dead. He permitted himself a bitter snort. For all their talk of peace, the church had turned him into a glorified assassin.

Hours later, a touch on his arm, light and tentative, broke his reverie. Adora stood behind him, her eyes pinched with worry, and something else. For a moment, he quailed and questioned his resolve, but he threw his shoulders back and gulped deep breaths of salty air. Martin, the whole church, owed him. He would never be able to extract a price for pain, but he could force them to tell him the truth. Gulls cried in the distance, harbingers of their destination, heralds of his appointment with death. By the three, they owed him.

Adora bit her lip, and her eyes darted as if she sought escape from his presence. "Let him keep his secrets, Errol. You don't have to do this."

His peripheral vision shifted back and forth in time to the shake of his head. "There is nothing words can do to me that has not already been done and more by Warrel and Antil. They are only words."

She turned from him. "You mean to pursue this?"

Her uncharacteristic fear almost persuaded him, but the desire to collect a portion of the debt the church owed him proved too strong. "I do. Where is Martin? I want to get this done before we land in Merakh. He is a man of many secrets; his confession may take a while."

Adora shook her head. "Not so long as you would think. There is, in fact, very little that he hasn't told you." She faced him, knotted her hands in the loose folds of his shirt. "I have prepared for this. Martin, Luis, Cruk, Karele, and Rale wait below in the captain's quarters."

Like an ill-weighted staff, this announcement threw him off balance. "I understand the need for Martin's presence, but why the rest? I don't want them there. If that priest wants them to know, I can't stop him, but he can do it when I'm not around."

She refused to look at him. Her gaze locked on his shirt, stayed there. "I did not ask your permission in this, though I knew you would see it this way, but you said you trusted me, so I prepared as well I could a means for you to hear Martin."

A means? What was she talking about? Adora lifted her head then, and the naked fear behind her eyes persuaded him in spite of his ignorance. "As you will. Are they ready?" When she nodded, he took her by the hand and led her to the stairs that led below toward the captain's quarters.

She moved in front of him at the door, raised a trembling fist to knock. The first rap barely sounded, the second more so. Cruk answered, looked to Adora, who nodded, and then to Errol. The look on the watchman's craggy face conveyed approval mixed with resignation.

"Can't say I blame you, boy." His voice held none of its usual accusation.

Errol moved past him into Tek's snug quarters. Luis and Karele sat on a bed built into the wall. Martin and Rale occupied a bench at a table in the middle of the room. All rose as he entered. Martin's face distorted, moved from peace to pain.

"Is it bad?" Errol asked. Perhaps the priest's experience fighting the compulsion could help him if they could not kill Valon. Maybe there was a way to live with it.

Martin ignored the question. "Don't compound my foolishness, Errol. Let this be. I will live or die with the consequences." A spasm twisted his face.

Pity wrenched through Errol. No compulsion had ever wracked him like this. What had driven Martin to this extremity? "And leave you like this? Would you do that to me? Speak, Pater."

Again he was ignored. Martin reached for Rale. "Before I fulfill my vow, Rale has a request to make of you."

Errol's mentor stepped forward.

"You came to me an orphan, son." He chuckled. His smile almost reached his eyes. "Actually, you came to me a drowned rat, more dead than alive." Rale's voice cracked. "But there's more steel in you, boy, than the entire watch has in their armory. Any man would be proud to call you his son. If you're willing, I'd like to be that man."

"What?" He turned to Martin, who managed to look hopeful despite his pain, then to Adora, who stood with pleading in her eyes. Then it hit him. Martin knew. Somehow, he'd uncovered Errol's parentage. A bolt of anger flashed through him. Only his respect for Rale kept him from lashing out.

"Thank you, Rale." His voice sounded overly formal, but he couldn't soften it without letting the anger loose. "I think I need to hear the good priest before I decide, though any man would be honored to be your son. My presence is causing Pater Martin pain. I think it best if we lift his compulsion as soon as possible." He considered Martin's pain-filled eyes. "Compulsion is evil."

Martin winced at the rebuke, even as he nodded in acquiescence or surrender. "I think Karele should begin."

This surprised him. What possible part could the solis have to play in Martin's confession?

Karele came forward. "You should know, Errol, that my presence here is my penance for my earlier failure. Aurae charged me with escorting you to Erinon while I was yet on the steppes. I tarried." He exhaled.

Errol almost laughed. "Is that all?"

"No. Had I been with you, the malus in Morin's dungeon would never have recognized your importance, or Liam's. You would have been safe." He sighed. "I was supposed to be your guide. Because of my failure, you almost died."

Now he understood. For an instant, the depth of Karele's failure yawned before him, but Rale's presence mollified him. "Why did you delay?"

"I was loath to leave my master, Ablajin."

Errol pressed. "Why?"

Karele's lips pressed into a line before he answered. "He is like a father to me."

His reticence stabbed Errol's middle. "Do you not have one?"

A shake of the head. "No. I am also an orphan."

Errol shrugged. "I would have done the same. I'm surprised you're here at all. I would have stayed."

Karele panted as if he'd run miles in the intervening moments. "Don't you see, boy? I was supposed to be to you what Ablajin was to me."

Errol lifted his hand, let it drop. "I think I see pretty well. You wanted to be with your father."

He turned to Martin. "Is there anyone else who needs to speak before you?"

The priest shook his head. The rest of the occupants of the cabin retreated to the walls, granting them a measure of privacy, though they could doubtless hear every whisper that might pass between them.

"Much of what I tried to keep from you, Errol, you've surmised and so becomes moot." As Martin spoke, the tightness around his eyes and the furrows that split his brow eased, until he looked almost normal. "It is true that I was certain Liam had been chosen by Deas to be king, and I still think he may be, but when Luis finally cast the lots he spent five years crafting, your name came up as often as his."

Errol inhaled to pose a question but stopped. Martin's geas would leave him no room for omission. He waited.

"In our blind trust for the reader's craft, we failed to seek out answers to what made you and Liam so important. So the archbenefice granted that Luis, Cruk, and I could return to your village.

"On our way we were met and aided by Karele." His shoulders shifted beneath his tunic. "That tale itself deserves to be told, but it has nothing to do with the vow I took."

Errol leaned forward. "What does?"

Martin exhaled into the silence, loud, pained. Despite the pressure the compulsion placed upon him he seemed more than reluctant to speak. The muscles at his jaws clenched. Around the room everyone leaned forward, waiting for that moment when Martin would succumb and break the silence.

"You and Liam are of an age, Errol," Martin said, "brothers

by circumstance though not by birth. Before they died, Adele and Radere told me the circumstances of Liam's birth. The timing of his conception and yours was no coincidence. You were both sired when Rodran's brother, Prince Jaclin, came through on his way to the gap. Callowford had to billet the prince and his men." He waved a hand. "Soldiers . . . well . . ."

Errol wanted to laugh. This is what they feared to tell him? "So I'm the son of a soldier and some . . . some tavern wench?"

Martin shook his head. "No. Not you. Liam. But you, Errol, were a mystery to us," Martin said. His eyes tightened with a different kind of pain. "And a surprise to the herbwomen." He stopped, his teeth clenched.

"Who is my father?" Errol asked. "If he was not some soldier, who?"

Tears gathered at the corner of Martin's eyes. "I found him by accident. Please understand, I'd already vowed to tell you everything."

"Who?"

Rale spoke. "Remember, Errol, every man decides what kind of man he will be. You have chosen well, no matter who your father might be."

"And I will never give my heart to another," Adora added.

He stepped toward Martin, hoping to force the truth from him by proximity if nothing else. "Who?"

Martin Arwitten licked his lips. "There was a man with Prince Jaclin, a . . . a servant in his command. Every large contingent has one to . . . to perform the rights of the church, to say the prayers over the dead."

A horror began to grow in Errol's mind.

"This man was found in the act with a young girl in Callowford. Jaclin gave him a choice—marry the girl or remain in Callowford as its priest."

The blackness in his mind grew, threw tendrils into his heart.

"He chose the priesthood. Months later the girl died giving birth to a son. The infant boy was given to a stonemason named Warrel and his wife." Martin swallowed.

"Please," Errol whispered. "Please tell me there was a different priest. Please."

Martin shook his head, the tears spilling down his cheeks.

"Antil is my father." Errol spoke it, his voice wooden. Something in him bent like a sapling in a gale, threatened to break.

Martin squinted and bit his lip. "Please, Errol, please leave."

It seemed he looked on Martin from a great distance as if through a long tunnel. What he saw would have stunned him had he been capable of anything more than numbness. "What more do you have, Martin?"

Martin locked his jaws around his secret.

Adora came forward. "What? There's more?"

Nothing could touch him now. His torturer had been his own father. What could compare to that? Errol took his arm. "Let me have it all, Martin."

Invisible hands pried Martin's jaws apart. "Somebody has to die."

Errol shook his head.

Martin vomited the words into the confines of the cabin. "The kingdom can only be saved by blood. You and Liam must fight on behalf of Illustra. One of you must die."

The bent thing in him broke with a soft snap in the depths of his mind. No physical death could touch him now.

He was dead inside already.

37

MERAKH

THE SHIP COASTED into the dock, hitting the pier with a soft *thunk* that testified to the longevity of Captain Tek's skill. Sun-browned men in loose white clothing shouted orders in the deep-throated language of the Merakhi, sending cold prickles that defied the heat up and down Martin's skin. He stood on deck, watching, standing as close to Errol as he dared without drawing the boy's attention. Horses passed before them with tentative, clopping steps down the gangplank to the thick wooden timbers that framed the pier.

Errol stood alone. He held a space about him that none dared violate, not even the princess. Her brief attempt at conversation had been met with some reply that had sent her to the hold red-eyed and biting her lip. After the horses, the ship's passengers began to disembark. Rale moved next to Errol and rested a hand on the boy's shoulder, which Errol didn't appear to acknowledge, then said something with his head bent close that Martin couldn't hear. The two of them moved to follow the mounts.

Martin noted the city's multi-arched, white-stone buildings that reflected the too-bright sunshine. Plants bloomed everywhere, serviced by irrigation pipes that ran to the river in the distance. Up a gradual incline decorated with a riot of colorful flowers, a building festooned with countless spires reached to the sky. In one—impossible to tell which—a bell tolled. The dockworkers huddled together for a brief discussion, then faced approximately northwest and bowed in time to the bell, which tolled eleven times.

"A strange custom," Martin mused.

Naaman Ru, standing close, shrugged. "The people of the river worship many gods, one for each day of the year. Each day they will rotate where they stand and bow once for each hour of daylight." The caravan master sighed, his eyes wistful. "Do you know why they're called the people of the river?"

Martin nodded, but Ru either didn't notice or ignored him in his desire to tell his story.

"The Altaru River winds back and forth, east and west, for thousands of leagues, beginning in the mountains that separate Merakh from Ongol, hundreds of leagues to the south. The river cascades from the mountains in a torrent, gradually slowing as it approaches the coast, where it splits over and over again. All along the river's incredible length, the Merakhi irrigate their fields from its massive flow." He gestured to the irrigation channels in the distance. "Maybe one Merakhi out of ten lives more than a league from the river. It is their life."

Martin surveyed the strange people milling around him. Away from the docks, men and women worked together at the market—the women dark-haired, their eyes and lips heavily painted in blues and greens. Yes, a very strange people.

Luis spied him and broke off from the main group to come stand at his side. "Merodach has found a stall in the city market that sells Merakhi clothing." His voice sounded almost normal, but the effort made it too bright, like the sunshine on this side of the strait. "Rale says it would be best if we wore clothing to blend in."

Martin nodded to show he'd heard. "I've been watching Errol for hours, Luis. He's dead inside."

"Perhaps not," Luis said. "The shock of the truth may wear off in time."

The words were meant to comfort, but they only drove the barbs of Martin's guilt deeper into his heart. "*Perhaps, may.* The boy believes he must die."

"And he may be right," Luis said.

Startled, Martin faced him. "Harsh, my friend. Has your heart become like one of your casting stones?"

Luis's brown eyes tightened at the accusation. "Is it harsh to desire the survival of the kingdom? From Soeden to Basquon, there are millions who will fall to the Merakhi and the Morgols if Errol fails. He and Liam must fight this evil. Someone must die if the kingdom is to survive."

"What makes you think it will be Errol who dies?"

Luis pointed to the object of their conversation. "Look at him. Even if he survives this trip and the coming war, do you think he would ever consent to be king? Can you see him working with Duke Weir or the Judica, the body that tried to kill him? He's nearly used up, like a fire running out of fuel."

"You should be more consistent. Didn't you argue with me when I insisted Liam would be king?"

"Things change." Luis shrugged. "You should never have made the vow."

Martin sighed, his anger turning back on himself.

Luis's hand came to rest on his shoulder. "If he lives to save the kingdom, he will be revered as the kingdom's greatest hero, even more than Magis. The kingdom and its people will live."

Martin nodded. "But what of Errol?" He pointed to the figure standing wooden and lifeless some little distance away. "What of him?" He noted the sudden lack of warmth as Luis lifted the hand meant to comfort from his shoulder and moved away.

Rale moved among the company and crew, speaking in low tones to issue orders. He spoke to Errol, who only acknowledged him by moving to follow as they headed deeper into the city.

"I'm sending most of our company back to Erinon with Tek," Rale said.

A sense of vulnerability threaded its way into him. "Won't we need the watchmen?"

"A thousand of them wouldn't be enough to force our way to Valon, and too many of them look like watchmen no matter what clothes they wear."

"Who's going on?"

"Errol, myself, you, Luis, Karele, Merodach, Naaman Ru, Rokha—" he paused, looking angry—"and Adora."

"You're letting the princess come?"

"She outranks me, Pater. I'm not *letting* her do anything. She threatened to follow us on her own."

"A kingdom woman in Merakh?"

Rale gave a curt nod. "I'm glad you appreciate the problem."

Knowing there was nothing they could do, Martin simply nodded and said, "I have information the archbenefice needs. Which of the watchmen should I give it to?"

"Give it to Conger."

"What?" Old prejudices bubbled up in him at the mention of the defrocked priest. "What if he reads it?"

Rale regarded him under heavy-lidded eyes. "Does it matter at this point, Pater? We left enemies behind us. The last person they'll suspect of carrying messages is Conger. I've paid Tek to drop everyone off in Erinon and then meet us back here."

Martin noted the captain didn't bother to expound on any of the hundred things that might go wrong. He was just as happy for Rale's silence.

An hour later Tek's ship unfurled the foresails and drifted away. Their company was reduced to nine, of which only five were accomplished with a sword. Martin, Luis, Karele, and Adora would be of little use if it came to a fight.

"We will not have to worry about bandits," Ru said. His mouth twisted to one side. "The akhen take pride in devising . . . creative ways for criminals to die. It discourages people from taking up the practice. Executions, though rare, are a very popular form of entertainment." He laughed at the look on Martin's face.

They rode out of the city, past whitewashed walls and laughing women with water jars on their heads, and took the road south following the river. A sense of absence nagged at Martin for a mile or more until he realized that he missed the sound of wagons. They didn't have any. Their cargo—medicines and herbs from the kingdom—didn't warrant the use of the clanking, horse-drawn contraptions. Instead a train of mules—bored, disinterested-looking creatures—carried the cargo. Their group seemed pitifully small as they followed the verdant path cut by the river along with the other caravans. Rale and Naaman Ru dropped back to speak with Luis, who rode a piebald just in front of Martin.

"Your services are needed, Secondus," Rale said.

Luis nodded and pulled a knife and a bag of blanks out of a pack behind him. "What's the question?"

Rale looked toward Naaman Ru, who spoke. "This road follows the Altaru River, which winds east and west repeatedly through the entire length of Merakh. A hundred leagues south from here lies the city of Guerir, where the ilhotep rules." He turned from his survey of the road to Luis. "The ilhotep pretends to be the power, but it is the six hoteps that advise him who hold sway. They are rumored to be ghostwalkers. If your Sarin Valon is here, I think he is in that city, which makes this little more than a march to our death."

"Do they allow traders in that city?" Rale asked.

Ru nodded. "Traders who are willing to make the trek are handsomely rewarded, but the slightest offense against Merakhi custom turns you from a trader to a slave. And they are easily offended."

Luis nodded. "It is a simple cast to see if that is where Valon is, a yes or no question."

Ru darted glances everywhere. "Keep your movements small. Readers are forbidden in Merakh. If an akha sees you, we'll envy the fate of bandits."

Luis worked as he rode, his hands hidden in his bag.

"Can you do that on horseback?" Martin asked.

Luis shrugged. "It's clumsy, but for a question this simple, I hardly need the quiet of the conclave."

Martin edge his horse closer, dropped his voice. "Why did we not just ask Karele? Aurae could tell us with more certainty than lots."

Luis continued to focus on the work beneath his hands. "The solis is wary of revealing his ability to Naaman Ru. Lots will take longer but will provide the same answer."

Some moments later, Luis grunted, sounding unsurprised. "It is as Ru suggested. Valon is in Guerir."

"Won't he see us coming?"

"Karele says he will not." Luis nudged his horse forward toward Rale and Naaman Ru. Martin followed.

With reluctance, they left the lush green of the river and set off south across the sand.

"There's a village halfway between loops of the river," Ru said. "A place called Shagdal. There was a man who ran an inn there who helped me and Rokha escape. We can camp there."

"Thank you," Martin said.

Ru spat, jerked his head in Errol's direction. "Don't thank me, priest. I'm under compulsion to help that whelp, and I'd like to live to see my way out of Merakh again."

Two hours before sunset they rode through the hard-packed dirt of the village. A man in a white conical cap standing next to the well in the center of town surveyed their arrival with narrowed eyes.

Ru steered them well clear of the man toward the inn. He drifted back, whispering instructions. "The fellow in the hat is an akha, a servant of the hoteps in their high council. Keep your eyes down. Direct eye contact is a challenge. Gather at the back of the inn. I will bring up the rear. Say nothing until I arrive."

When they rounded a corner a voice rose to greet them. The

owner, a tall, broad man with heavy jowls and sun-browned skin, yelled what must have been a welcome in his native language. Seeing Rokha, he approached, a smile broadening under dark curls fading to gray.

Ru stepped into his path, speaking quickly in the same language. The man's face showed surprise and recognition. He clapped Ru's extended hand, pointing to the rest of the party. Ru shook his head. The man nodded in resignation and greeted them, bowing as he touched his forehead with both hands. "Your caravan master says you need lodging. I am Sahion. Welcome to my lokanda, my inn. Please come in. I will have my sons care for your animals."

He barked a command over his shoulder through the rear entrance of the inn. A stampede of boys and young men—all younger versions of Sahion—came pouring out to take reins from each member of the party.

"Are all these yours?" Martin asked. There must have been close to a dozen boys in the penned area behind the inn, laughing and kicking up dust as they worked.

Sahion rested his hands on his belly and gave a proud laugh. "Yes. My wife has blessed me with many children, all boys. Every man should have a passion—mine is sons."

His good-natured laugh drew a smile from Martin and everyone else—except Errol, who merely waited. They stepped forward into an open-air dining area filled with small tables and old men who drank dark, strong-smelling drinks and played a game that looked similar to chess. Looks directed toward the group ranged from curious to hostile.

"Perhaps you would like a little privacy," Sahion said, his face troubled. "Come. I have a room where you will be away from those who object to Illustra's people."

They passed by a series of pointed arches covered with intricate wooden lattice screens and into the inn. Broad windows filled the interior with light, and the smell of unfamiliar spices emanated from the kitchen.

Sahion beckoned to a young man standing by the door to

the kitchen. "Amun, check the roof." They followed him into a private room, and Sahion gestured to the lattice roof overhead. "My son will guard to make sure nothing that is said is heard by the wrong ears. Be seated, my guests. I will bring date wine."

He departed to return a moment later with a stoneware pitcher and a tray of cups filled with a dark brown beverage. Martin took a sip, coughed. Sahion laughed, his eyes narrowing to slits with his mirth.

"Careful, my friend," his voice rumbled. "Kingdom men find our date wine to be heady stuff."

Ru tossed back the contents of his cup and smiled at the goblet before he refilled it. "I'd forgotten how much I'd missed it."

Despite his assurances, Sahion leaned forward and his voice dipped so that any eavesdropper on the roof would have to strain to hear. "What trade brings a shade and a spirit back to the sand between waters, my friend? I thought you were dead."

Ru didn't blink. "Medicines. Profitable and easily transported."

Sahion dipped his head once. "Well spoken. What I do not know, I cannot reveal. But be careful, old friend. The ranks of the akhen swell to keep the populace in line, and any male above the age of fourteen is conscripted into the army."

Martin looked around the table. Rale and Merodach sipped from their cups as if they held only a passing interest in their innkeeper's news. Errol stared through the walls to the south, his eyes dead. Everyone else showed signs of the fear Martin felt.

"We saw no signs of war preparations on our way here," he said.

"Yes, and you would not," Sahion said. "They are hidden out in the sand. The desert teems with the sons of the river waving their swords and screaming whatever the akhen tell them to scream. The chieftains are powerless against them." He leaned back, shaking his head in confusion. "The tribal leaders, our sultans, were always able to keep the akhen in check before, balancing the power of the religious leaders. Things are different now."

Sahion leaned farther in to Ru, his voice a whisper. "A year ago the armies to the south broke northern Ongol's resistance. Gold and slaves with skin like midnight flood the streets of Guerir, and the akhen are drunk with power. If a chieftain objects to the orders coming from the council, he finds himself short of a head before sunset. Only an outrageous bribe allowed me to keep my sons here with me to run the inn."

He leaned again, until his nose almost touched Ru's. "Go home, my friend. When your king dies, Merakh will erupt with warriors. The people of the river do not like the cold. Find a place far to the north of your kingdom where you can hide."

Ru leaned back and laughed, but there was no mirth in the sound. "You have no idea how much I would like to follow your advice. Perhaps I shall."

Martin spoke, hoping he wouldn't unknowingly give offense. "Your words surprise me, my host. I had not thought to find such opinions in the river kingdom of Merakh."

Sahion chuckled. "You thought we spent all our time waving our shirra and screaming, eh? Well, I screamed much in my youth, but I find myself desiring peace for myself and my sons as I grow older."

Sahion leaned back and surveyed the company one by one. His gaze moved over Karele as if the solis's seat were empty. Martin felt himself weighed and dismissed before Sahion's attention rested on Rale and Merodach, but he still spoke to Ru. "You travel with dangerous companions, my friend, but I seem to remember you as one such."

His eyes snapped to Rokha and Adora. "Would it not be wise to leave your daughter and the kingdom woman here until you return?"

As one, Rokha and Adora crossed their arms, looking defiant. Sahion noted the look and laughed. "Sons are a blessing to the mind," he murmured.

"And daughters a challenge to the heart," Ru finished. They laughed together.

Ru refilled his and Sahion's cup. "Now, what can you tell us of Guerir?"

In the fading light of the afternoon, a hawk cried, but Martin paid little heed. He hung on every word of their host.

38

TAKEN

ERROL STOOD IN THE INNER ROOM, leaning against the wall, feeling the gritty texture of whitewashed sandstone through his shirt. He heard the conversation between Sahion and Naaman Ru in the same vein as one of Quinn's lectures on the casting properties of different woods. His sense of abstraction had grown since Martin's revelation. The image of Antil's face, clenched into a rictus of blind hate, hovered in Errol's vision over everything he saw—the sand, the buildings, his friends.

Adora, clothed in the garb of a Merakhi merchant but clearly still a woman, almost held the power to break through the walls his mind had erected. Almost. The squeeze of her hand on his and her whispers of encouragement touched the surface of his emotions, but failed to break through his shell.

Then the hawk cried.

His eyes met Rale's across the table. Ru pulled his sword, held it against Sahion's throat.

"I'm sorry, my friend," Sahion said. "Kill me if you must, but they arrived before you. At least this way my sons will live."

Errol broke for the door the same instant as Rale, who shouted commands to flee. He paused for a heartbeat to grab Adora's hand, then joined the press that streamed out the back toward the stable. The sounds of men, a lot of men, and horses came from the front of the inn. Their only chance would be to outride them.

They poured out the back door and stopped—those behind crashing against the ones in front. Errol pushed Adora back toward the inn and shouldered his way out into the light. Ringed around the entrance were a hundred white-robed horsemen, curved swords drawn and pointing toward their group.

There would be no escape.

A rider at the center of the arc with a pair of blue stars stitched into the shoulder of his shirt moved forward on his dappled horse, his dark, dark eyes hard. "I am Kayeed Rayn. You will all accompany me to Guerir. If you attempt to escape, you will be killed. Place your weapons on the ground before you."

A clatter of arms—swords, staffs, and daggers piled high.

Ru stepped forward, bowing and touching his forehead as Sahion had. "Surely there is some mistake, good kayeed. We are merchants carrying rare medicines and herbs. Please, check our packs—you will find I speak the truth."

The kayeed smiled. "I have no doubt you carry those items of which you speak. The most cunning spies are always the best prepared. But checking your packs will not be necessary—though they may accompany you on your trip south, if you wish. There is one in your caravan my masters have been seeking."

Ru's eyes betrayed his nervousness, and he pressed his lips into a line. "Good kayeed, I have no idea whom you might mean. We are just traders, as I said."

The captain's eyes glittered, and he considered Ru and the rest with the hint of a smile on his lips. "Perhaps I was mistaken," he said. His tone contradicted his words. "Like all officers, I rely on external sources of information." He snapped his fingers twice, and the horses behind him parted to reveal a lone rider, wearing kingdom dress.

Lord Weir. He prodded his horse forward and scanned the

crowd until he found Errol. A triumphant smile split his face. "Well, peasant, I see you've gotten yourself into a bit of trouble." He leaned back in his saddle and took an exaggerated look at the mob of Merakhi soldiers. "Somehow I don't think you're going to be able to fight your way out of this one." He pursed his lips. "Pity, really. Now the king will have to find some other little urchin to play with."

The numbness in Errol never wavered. His eyes saw Lord Weir, but even this betrayal couldn't rouse him to response. He merely stared at the excuse for a man before him and waited.

Weir looked away. "I will take my price and go," he said to the kayeed.

"You may go," the captain said. "But my orders are to bring *all* suspected spies before the holy council at Guerir. We leave in the morning."

Weir's face reddened. "My father will hear of this disrespect, Rayn. But I will travel with you to Guerir—to take my price from there." He dismounted and threw his reins to the soldier next to him. "Make sure my horse is well cared for." He turned to Errol. "You don't mind if I make use of your room, do you, peasant? After all, you won't need it."

He strode over to stand in front of Adora, his face growing hard. "It was most ill-mannered for you to run off, my lady. Once we are back in the kingdom and married, I will ensure you know the proper way to behave."

Adora's eyes blazed. "We will never be married. And I will see you cut in pieces for this."

Weir smiled and turned away.

The ranks of the Merakhi parted to let him through, but the eyes of the kayeed and his soldiers went flat and hard as they watched him leave. Men gathered Errol and the rest into a knot and roped them together. A dinner of flavorless flatbread and water followed. A ring of guards remained around them where they sat in the middle of Sahion's stable yard.

Errol noted these things peripherally. Deep inside, a twinge of regret nagged him. At least Adora would be safe back in the kingdom if she returned with Weir. Perhaps Liam would manage to see her married to a more worthy man after he became king—perhaps even himself. It was out of Errol's hands now. They would kill him in Guerir. After the sun went down, he slept, dreamless and sound.

A boot in his side woke him the next morning. Moments later he sat his horse, his hands tied to the pommel, as they thundered south. The pack animals had been left at the inn. By Rale's estimate they covered perhaps twenty leagues that day, twenty leagues in which the air grew sultry as they approached the next loop of the river. Unrelieved stretches of scrub, sand, and rock gave way once more to crops, gardens, and exotic flora. They camped near a bridge that stretched across the river. Once the captives were fed, soldiers tied their wrists and staked them to the ground.

Weir sauntered through the camp, flicking his sword in casual disdain at the fronds that grew too close. "Hello, peasant."

Errol didn't bother to meet Weir's gaze, but Rale muttered something that earned him a kick in the ribs from the noble. "Watch your tongue, Captain," he said, "or I might have to relieve you of it."

Rale laughed. "You must be singularly stupid, Weir. Even if they let you take the princess back to the kingdom, she'll denounce you at the first opportunity."

Weir laughed. "The princess will be too overcome by her ordeal with the traitorous peasant to speak publicly for quite some time. By the time I let her see the light of day, no one will have any reason to believe a word she says. Women are so very fragile, you know."

An expulsion of air sounded through Rale's nose. "I was wrong, Weir. You're not stupid, you're insane. What do you think will happen when Rodran dies and the barrier falls? The whole kingdom will be at war."

Lord Weir threw back his head and laughed. "The barrier? You actually believe in that myth? The only thing that will happen when Rodran dies will be the elevation of my father to his rightful place on the throne."

"Elevation?" Rale said. "The next king will be chosen by lot, Weir. Even you must have sense enough to know that. Or do you think Deas favors your father over all others?"

Weir squatted between Rale and Errol, his grin growing malicious. "Of course they'll draw lots, Captain, but those lots will choose my father, and without an omne to gainsay them, no one will have cause to question the results." He rose and moved closer to Errol, until he towered directly over him. His sword twitched. "But I didn't come here to converse, not when the peasant can offer me a few hours amusement." The sword flicked, just missing Errol's face.

His detachment didn't lift, but he thought it would be nice to be free and cave Weir's skull in with his staff. He savored the image and smiled.

"You find this amusing, peasant?" Weir snarled, and his grip on the sword tightened. "Let's see how entertaining you find this." His arm drew back.

Before Weir could follow through on his threat, a hand clamped his wrist from behind. "We do not deliver injured slaves to the council," Kayeed Rayn said. "These captives are the property of the ilhotep. To damage his property is to invite his wrath."

Rale laughed. Almost Errol joined in, but his indifference to his fate and that of Weir wouldn't lift enough to allow it.

As soon as full dark came upon the camp, he slept.

The next day and the day after were the same—a fast ride and then a stop before sunset on a different bank of the river that looked the same as before. They were fed and staked.

On the fourth day out from the village of Shagdal, Kayeed Rayn set a slower pace, his manner almost casual. One of the guards, a talkative middle-aged fellow with a thick red scar on one cheek and a pointed beard shot with gray pointed ahead.

"Now, infidel, you will see a sight of which you would tell your children's children if you were fated to have any. Behold"—he swung his arm wide—"the countless spires of Guerir."

Errol interrupted his disinterested contemplation of the horse in front of him to follow the guard's gesture. Off in the distance, shimmering through the warm Merakhi air, rose a city the likes of which he'd never imagined. Behind a towering white wall rose a city of hundreds of needlelike spires clustered around one predominant building with a spire sheathed in gold that rose higher than all the rest. Sunlight blazed from the city and reflected off the broad river running before it.

Errol shielded his eyes from the glare.

Their road joined with others, and traffic began to slow. Painted women and men in dirty white robes jeered at them in the Merakhi tongue, making cutting gestures across their throats. Their guards boxed them in, and the kayeed sent riders ahead to clear the way.

They passed through enormous iron-bound gates of wood, swung wide to accommodate the traffic. The clamor from the market rose to a deafening crescendo with screams and epithets for the guards as Captain Rayn forced his way toward the inner part of the city. Strange-looking animals with long, curved necks and slit noses rested by a well.

One of the animals spat as they rode by, striking the talkative guard on the chest. "Filthy creatures. You are lucky you do not have to ride such as those, infidel. They are a trial to the spirit."

The farther away from the market they rode, the more the noise faded. The hooves of their mounts no longer crunched on sandy gravel but clopped instead on broad white sandstone. Always they ascended toward the golden spire. They passed a huge amphitheater on their left, and noise washed over them like a tidal wave.

Errol tried to see into an arena revealed between the massive pillars.

"You may see the *stadi* soon enough, my friend," the guard said. Then he gave a raucous laugh.

Half an hour after entering the city they arrived at the inner wall, behind which rose the central spire and a score of other buildings. Guards in white with red sashes and bared swords patrolled the entrance. At a salute from Kayeed Rayn, they opened the iron gates and stepped aside to let them pass.

Inside, they were relieved of their horses and escorted toward the central building. Weir walked next to the kayeed with darting looks behind at the gate that now blocked their retreat. Servants or slaves—Errol couldn't tell which—moved through the alleys, intent on the myriad tasks it took to keep the capital city functioning.

At last they stopped. A dozen white-robed guards stood watch at iron-grated doors. A man in rich blue robes stepped forward, and as one, Kayeed Rayn and the guards surrounding him dropped to one knee.

Hands forced Errol down into the same position.

"Get your hands off me," Weir yelled. "I am a lord."

Errol jerked his head up to see a pair of guards in the act of forcing Weir to obeisance. Their hands, heavy on his shoulders, pressed down, and he struggled to shake them off. The man in blue held up a solitary finger. The guards stilled.

"Please forgive our soldiers' rough handling," the man said. His voice flowed like honey, but his dark eyes, lids painted red, glittered with malice.

Either Weir did not notice or chose to ignore the man's intent. "I do not bow until I know whom I address."

The man in blue smiled. Despite his numbness, it chilled Errol to see it. "The world has need of such boldness. I am Ilakhen Osiri, servant of the council."

Weir drew himself up. "I do not bow to servants."

The guards hissed. "Foolish man," one of them muttered.

Osiri's cold smile never wavered. "A messenger tells me you have delivered a valuable captive into our hands. Who might this be, and how might we verify his identity?"

Weir pointed at Errol. "That is the one you seek, Errol Stone, omne of the conclave. As for verification, you have no need of it. I have just told you who he is."

The guard next to Errol shook his head and mumbled something under his breath that sounded like a prayer.

"Bring them all," the ilakhen snapped. He moved deeper into the building without waiting to see if they obeyed. The guards rose and escorted Weir and the rest inside. Errol noted with grim satisfaction that a quartet of guards now surrounded Weir. They did not walk so closely as those who kept the prisoners, but they left no doubt that Weir must obey.

Slaves and servants in the halls prostrated themselves as the ilakhen passed. Errol raised his assessment of Osiri. The man might serve the council, but there remained no doubt he wielded the power of life and death. Most of the slaves and servants who bowed themselves out of their way wore looks of profound respect—some wore terror.

Light from grates in the ceiling overhead threw scrollwork shadows across the intricate patterns in the tiled floor as they moved inward. Fewer guards and more servants patrolled the halls. A dozen guards in white with gold sashes across their chests stood before a dark, ornately carved door. At a signal from the ilakhen, they bowed and opened them both. The guards drew swords and put them to the necks of their prisoners. Even Adora and Rokha had bare steel against their skin.

Errol stepped into a world such as he had never seen—or imagined.

Opulence on a staggering scale filled the huge hall. A pool twenty paces on a side filled the center of the room. At the far end, on a raised dais of stone, bare-chested guards, their skin as dark as midnight, protected men and women who reclined on long couches covered with colorful pillows. Next to each, an elaborate water pipe bubbled, and wisps of aromatic smoke drifted, swirling on eddies in the room. To one side below the dais, courtiers lounged, their clothes a riot of color and styles. A babble of voices floated from that direction, excited and mocking.

Their escort halted at the door, and the prisoners were turned over to black-skinned guards wielding huge curved swords. Weir came with them, moving as if he owned the palace. Perhaps he didn't notice the hulking servant holding a bared sword behind him. Guards marched them around the pool to face the men on the dais.

A man with a dark, bored face in the center couch lay surrounded by four men and two women in gold silks who watched the prisoners with the avid concentration of vipers about to strike.

Ilakhen Osiri stopped short of the steps that led up to the dais and bowed. "Exalted ilhotep, your servants have brought you a gift."

The bored-looking man raised his head and surveyed the men before him without interest until Weir's presence caught his attention. "A kingdom man."

Weir possessed enough sense to bow to Merakh's ruler. "Lord Weir—at your service, most exalted ilhotep." His head nearly scraped the floor.

The men and women reclining near the ilhotep regarded Weir like snakes watching a rat. Wrong emanated from them in waves, and Errol stifled a chill as he recalled the malus in Morin's dungeon and the Gitan, Sahra, who almost managed to kill him in Minaccia.

The ilhotep clapped his hands like a child. "A well-mannered kingdom man at that. What have you brought us, kingdom man?"

Irritation flashed across Weir's face at the omission of his title, but he bowed again and pointed to Errol with a savage grin. "One you seek, most exalted one—the peasant Errol Stone, omne of the conclave."

The six surrounding the ilhotep jerked in surprise, their mask of indulgent self-control slipping.

"Impossible," one of them, a young man with hot eyes and a hooked nose, yelled. "The circle has said nothing of this."

The ilhotep laughed, obviously enjoying his council's dismay. "Perhaps your security is not as impenetrable as you believe, Belaaz."

Weir bowed again. "I assure you, most exalted ilhotep, the man is indeed Errol Stone."

"Have the prisoner speak," Belaaz said. "What is your name, slave?"

The guard behind exerted the slightest pressure on the sword at his neck. Errol hesitated. The guard shifted his sword and clubbed him across the head. "Speak, cur. What is your name?"

Errol's vision swam, but he said nothing. Out of the corner of his eye he saw the ilakhen gesture to a servant and say, "If I may suggest a course of action, Exalted One?"

The ilhotep, no longer lying down but sitting and leaning forward in anticipation, waved his assent.

"In this very room we have the means to procure the slave's name," Osiri said. "A pipe with ahrat sumac will loosen his tongue."

"Make it so, Ilakhen," the ilhotep said. "Let us see now, honorable Belaaz, whether Valon's circle is as powerful as you believe."

A servant brought a lit pipe that smelled of sulfur and strange spices forward. Errol clenched his teeth, but the guard's hand on his jaw forced his mouth open, and the tube snaked down his throat, making him gag and cough. Reflexively, he inhaled. The room spun as the drug took effect.

"Who are you?" the ilakhen asked.

Errol tried to remember why he was supposed to hide his name, but the thought wouldn't come. The room seemed very beautiful, and the ilakhen's smile comforted him.

"Who are you, friend?" Osiri asked.

There, the ilakhen called him friend. It must be safe to speak. "Errol Stone."

39

SLAVE

THE ILHOTEP LAUGHED, his joy apparent at the consternation among the six who yelled and jerked like puppets under the control of a drunken puppeteer.

Belaaz recovered first. He snapped his fingers at a black-skinned servant and pointed at the exit.

"Bring Sarin Valon to us."

The servant left at a run. Belaaz bowed, slightly, to the ilhotep. "I do not know how his art was thwarted, Exalted One, but the stars shine on your kingdom. Without its omne, Illustra will move hesitantly, leaving itself vulnerable to attack."

Errol blinked at the mention of *omne*. The word seemed important somehow, but he couldn't quite place why. The room felt very warm, and the cool tile under his feet invited him to lie on it.

The ilhotep indulged in a lazy smile. "I should like to add those northern lands to my rule. Tell me, Belaaz, with the omne captive, why should I not order the attack now?"

Belaaz laughed, his face swimming in and out of Errol's focus. He looked like a man trying to deflect the question, and his eyes stared off in different directions. "O Ilhotep, the stars are not yet aligned. Soon, however, the way will be open and all barriers will be removed from your glorious conquest."

The ilhotep pursed his lips above his neatly trimmed beard. "I hate waiting. My family has waited half a millennium for its revenge."

Belaaz blinked and gave the ilhotep an oily smile. "Then what is a few days more, O light of the stars?"

The ilhotep settled back, puffing on the tube to his pipe. Bluish smoke wreathed a splotchy crown around his head. The room waited for Valon to appear. Errol bent his legs to lower himself to the floor, but the guard jerked him upright. When he looked up, he found himself looking at Karele. The little man's lips moved without ceasing. A corner of Errol's brain tried to tell him there was something important about Karele, something having to do with Valon and the people here in Merakh, but the thought slipped from his grasp, like a perch in the waters of the Sprata.

The guard holding him up shifted, and Errol forced his eyes to focus on a tall, slender man with a neatly trimmed beard sauntering in the room. From feet to head, he emanated meticulously groomed confidence that made Weir appear rough and uncouth by comparison. Decked in loose yellow silk, he glided across the room, his steps light and graceful. Only the man's eyes contrasted with the fastidious care he exercised with the rest of his appearance.

They burned in their sockets with undisguised hatred.

Through the drug-induced fog that lay across his mind like a sodden blanket, Errol knew this to be Sarin Valon, the man who'd tried countless times to kill him. More, he knew Valon to be hopelessly insane.

Belaaz looked on the former secondus with savagery. "Come, Valon. This northern lord"—he pointed to Lord Weir—"claims this"—he pointed to Errol—"is the omne Earl Stone."

He glared at Valon. "Since one of your circle has seen him face-to-face, perhaps you can confirm this."

Valon shrugged as if the command was of no import, then closed the distance, gliding toward Errol. His eyes flared, and breath hissed from him like that of a trapped animal. "How did you get here? The ships did not let you pass."

Errol didn't answer. He knew the answer, or rather, he knew he should know the answer, but he couldn't seem to bring it forth from his mind.

"So his reader's art has failed him." The ilhotep bringing. "Perhaps you should find yourself a more reliable traitor, Belaaz."

Valon wheeled toward the ilhotep, brought his rage under control with a visible effort. "I know not which of my circle has been suborned, O light of the stars, but I shall find him and flay the skin from his bones. The music of his screams will fill your palace for years."

The ilhotep chuckled, his eyes languid. "And what shall I do with these prisoners?"

"Kill them." Valon made a dismissive gesture with one hand. "If they have discovered a means to subvert my circle, they are dangerous."

"Yes," Belaaz said. "We could make an example of them. I'm sure your council could devise an amusing end for them, Exalted One."

The ilhotep frowned, his face petulant. "I don't want to just kill them. They don't look dangerous to me. They look scared."

For the briefest instant, hatred raged in the glance Belaaz gave the ilhotep before the advisor managed to smother it. "As you wish, light of the stars. What do you desire?"

The ilhotep rubbed his hands like a miser over his hoard. He pointed at Rale, Naaman Ru, Merodach, and Cruk in quick succession. "Those four have the look of fighting men. Let them test their skill in the arena. I will place them in my stable. You have been winning too much from me of late, Belaaz. Perhaps these northerners will set the balance right." He paused. "Give the other men to my slave master. Perhaps they have some skill that will make them useful."

His eyes moved at last to Adora and Rokha, who still knelt, heads down. "Kingdom women. I don't usually care for the large, ungainly females. And they are dressed like men!"

Tittering laughter came from the courtiers. The ilhotep reclined on his divan. "Bring them to me."

Errol struggled against his drug-laced lethargy to protest, but no words would come.

Guards escorted Rokha and Adora to the ilhotep with firm hands. Both of the women kept their heads down, refusing to meet the ilhotep's inspection.

"Let me see their faces," the ilhotep ordered.

As hands forced their heads up, Rokha's dark mane and Adora's golden hair tumbled loose. The two women directed their defiance at the ilhotep. His eyes sparked with interest. "What have we now? Kingdom women, but hardly ungainly. One is as dark as the night, while the other wears the light of the morning." He laughed. "And both with spirit. But they smell of horses and dust.

"Guard, take them to my chief eunuch. Tell him to have them bathed and dressed in silk and satin. If they please me, I will keep them for myself. If not, I will give them to my ilakhen. Would you like that, Osiri?"

Weir stepped forward. "The golden-haired one belongs to me."

The ilhotep frowned at the intrusion. "Why is this one not a prisoner?"

The ilakhen bowed. "This is the one who delivered the kingdom spies into our hand, Exalted One."

Lord Weir sneered. "And the price for my aid is the girl. She belongs to me."

The ilhotep's casual manner evaporated like water on a sun-scorched rock. "By way of thanks, I will overlook the fact you make demands in my palace." He waved a hand. "Take my forgiveness and go. The females remain."

Weir goggled. "You would dismiss me and deny me what is mine? Do you know who I am and who my father is?"

The ilhotep's face darkened. Without taking his eyes from Weir, he crooked a finger at his ilakhen. Osiri mounted the dais and stooped to whisper in the ilhotep's ear. After a moment the ilakhen straightened and stepped away.

The ilhotep stood. "My ilakhen tells me you are the son of a powerful ally in Illustra. But you are not in your kingdom, worm. You stand in my throne room beneath the greatest of the three hundred and sixty spires. I rule here. However, I offer you my forgiveness a second time. Take our blessing with you and go . . . now."

Weir's face reddened. "You stupid barbarian. Nobody—"

The lord's next words never made it from his mouth. The ilhotep lifted his arm, and in a single motion the guard next to Weir drew his sword and cut Weir's head from his shoulders. Blood fountained, splattering thickly on the tile floor, as the body collapsed at the guard's feet, arms and legs twitching.

The ilakhen closed his eyes and sighed. "Your ally the duke will be displeased at the dispatch of his son, Exalted One."

The ilhotep looked bored and petulant once more. "He dared offer an insult to me in my palace."

"Agreed," the ilakhen said, "but the duke is a powerful man within the kingdom. He has agreed to withhold his support from the kingdom's war effort in exchange for the crown. News of his son's death, deserved as it is, may change his heart."

Belaaz laughed. "Then he shall not hear of it that way. The duke's son was killed by the omne, Errol Stone. The ilhotep, wise beyond measure, imprisoned the omne and all his companions and sentenced them to a life of slavery in recompense."

The ilhotep waved a hand. "Make it so." He looked to Adora and Rokha. "And take those kingdom women to my eunuch."

As they passed, Rokha stared straight ahead, showing no fear, but Adora stopped and looked to Errol, her eyes wide. Errol struggled to say something, do something, but all he could manage was a feeble "Ad . . . ora."

Prodded by the guard behind her, she bowed her head and stumbled forward.

As the women left the throne room, the ilakhen asked, "And what of Errol Stone?"

The ruler of Merakh no longer attended Osiri. He sucked on his pipe, and his lids grew heavy as he lay indolent on his couch. "Let us see how well the omne fights in the arena. Perhaps he will provide some amusement before he dies."

Belaaz looked at Errol with hunger raging in his eyes. The ilhotep's councilor unfolded as he rose from his couch. Tall, nearly as tall as the dark-skinned guards, he approached Errol where the guard held him upright. "Such a waste, O light of the world. Would it not be better to offer the omne a place among us and so serve you?"

The ilhotep's eyes drooped ever farther. "Do I have need of other servants, Belaaz?"

The councilor's face filled Errol's vision. Belaaz's eyes dilated, his lids drawing back to show the whites all around as he came within arm's length. "Surrender to us, omne. Is it not better to live as one of us than to die in the arena, even as Weir died here?"

Underneath the drug's influence, Errol's mind screamed in revulsion. Behind the raw appetite of the councilor's gaze lay a stark, raving terror no amount of compulsion or possession could completely disguise. Somewhere beneath the malus's dominion, the person that had been Belaaz still lived, screaming in silent horror and trying to break free.

Despite the heavy calm induced by the drug, Errol edged back, repulsed. "I think I prefer the arena."

Belaaz's snarl, joined by Valon's, ripped the air. Relief flooded through Errol so that he almost fell. Only the guard's strength kept him on his feet. The black-skinned guard murmured something in a tongue Errol did not recognize, but the tone, deep as the ocean, sounded like approval.

"If you will not surrender, then you will die, Errol Stone—like your friends, like your women, like your kingdom."

The palace guards, their skin dark as night, marched Errol and the rest of his company single file out of the ilhotep's throne room. In the broad expanse of the palace hallway, Cruk walked with his guard behind Errol and snorted. "You might have pretended to join them, boy, and then worked out a plan to escape."

Errol almost laughed. "There's no escape for me. Not that it matters. I don't know who Belaaz and Valon used to be, but the things speaking through them aren't men. I'd rather die in the Merakhi arena than live imprisoned in my own mind."

Beside him, his guard gave a curt nod of approval, his shaved head reflecting the light darkly. "Well spoken, northlander. Perhaps you will die well."

In the air outside of the palace, Errol's head cleared of the drug, but the Judica's compulsion nagged at him, growing with each step away from Valon. They passed beneath the needlelike shadows of the spires as they trudged back to the arena. The guards led them through one of the arches, and they emerged into an enormous bowl lined with rows of stone blocks for seating. No noise greeted them. The stadium lay empty. Only a few servants in ragged clothing circulated, their movements slow and dispirited as they cleaned.

They descended the steps and entered the chambers beneath the stands. The air cooled as they turned down another flight of stairs and moved into a set of large rooms. The guards split and herded Luis, Martin, and Karele away from the rest of them.

Errol, along with the remainder of his company, doubled back and followed the guards down a long hallway to a cavernous room beneath the amphitheater of the arena. Men of every possible description trained under the watchful eyes of palace guards. Sweating Merakhi grunted their way through various exercises. Armed guards stood everywhere. No prisoner came within five paces of them. Among the slaves were men who could have been twin to the black-skinned guard watching over him.

Errol pointed at them. "Why are your countrymen here if you serve the ilhotep?"

"You are curious for a slave, infidel."

Errol shrugged. "I'm dead, anyway. Why not ask?"

The huge guard nodded. "Again, well-spoken. This hall houses the ilhotep's jabari, his stable of arena fighters." He pointed to the dark-skinned men who stood in a group, staring back with hatred in their eyes. "Those are the captives of my country's army—Ongolese who refused surrender and have been taken prisoner."

"And what of you?"

The guard's broad face grew distant. "I was born into the ilhotep's service along with the rest of the Ongolese guards you see. Our forefathers were captives from previous battles throughout history. We are his most trusted bodyguards precisely because we are not his countrymen."

His brows drew together beneath the naked dome of his head. "I owe the ilhotep my life. The protection of his well-being from any threat is my sole concern."

The guard's voice hinted, but did not reveal.

"Any threat?"

The barest nod was the only reply.

Through a pointed archway at one end of the room, men ate from piles of food stacked before them. On the opposite side, through a similar doorway, men slept on comfortable-looking bunks.

The guard must have sensed his surprise. "Those who fight in the arena are well cared for, infidel. The ilhotep desires to provide suitable entertainment for his people."

Errol's head cleared enough for him to be curious. "Who will we be fighting?"

The guard shrugged; a mountain shifting. "You will battle the jabari of the ilhotep's councilors. Their stables are much as this—enemies of the river kingdom, criminals, or those who have displeased the ilhotep or council members."

Errol met the guard's gaze, surprised to see the man's eyes were an olive green instead of brown. He sensed a question lay somewhere within their depths but had no idea what the guard might want of him.

The guard smiled, showing white teeth against the deep charcoal of his skin. "Rest now, infidel. They will send you to the arena tomorrow."

"What's your name?" Errol asked.

"You may call me Hadari, infidel, for as long as you may live." Almost, he smiled.

"And how long will you be my guard?"

Now the smile came. "Who can say?"

Errol drew away from the hulking guards who lined the walls

and drifted over to a block ledge along the wall where Rale, Cruk, Merodach, and Naaman Ru had gathered. Several paces separated them from the other slaves in the hall; they wouldn't be heard.

Ru looked about with disgust. "This is what comes of getting involved with the church, boy. You're a thousand miles from home, doomed to die so that you can give these howling barbarians a few moments' pleasure."

The caravan master's caustic, demeaning tone grated on him. "And what makes you think I'll die, Naaman Ru?"

Ru shook his head as he laughed. "You're still too easy to provoke, boy. Learn to control your emotions if you want to survive. You spurned the ilhotep's chief councilor. Do you think he'll let you live? If you beat one man, they'll send two, then three. You're good, boy, good enough to beat my best student, but how many men can you defeat at once?"

Errol shrugged, lifting his hands. "It doesn't matter whether I die here or back in the kingdom."

Ru's eyes widened. He turned to Rale. "What have you people done to him?"

Rale closed his eyes, sighed. "Earl Stone received some distressing news before we landed in Merakh. He's still wrestling with it."

"Well, wrestle faster, boy. I've got no intention of dying here. We need a way to escape."

Errol turned his back. "When you figure one out, let me know." He moved to the sleeping room. The aftereffects of the drug and the turmoil of the throne room had left him fatigued, and Ru's need tired him all the more. They all expected him to save them. What did it matter if he died in the process? Enough was enough. If Deas or the Judica required his death to save the kingdom, they would surely have it, but Errol Stone would no longer be a willing participant.

The other slaves in the sleeping room noted his presence, but he ignored them. He sought out an empty bunk as far from the noise as possible, covered his eyes with his arm, and slept.

In his dry, dusty dreams Adora appeared again and again, her face marked by the freckles she'd garnered in the southern sun. Her dream image issued the same command over and over— "Live."

He woke to Hadari's hand on his shoulder.

"But I'm so tired," Errol said to the fading traces of his dream.

His guard laughed. "You have yet to fight, infidel. How can you be tired?"

Errol shook his head to clear the sleep and dream from it. "Am I to fight already?"

"Already?" Hadari laughed. "You have slept for a day." He signaled another guard standing next to him, and the man moved forward with a plate of food. "You show courage, infidel. I would not have you defeated by hunger."

Errol took that plate and ate without question. The meat tasted unusual.

"Goat," Hadari said in response to Errol's questioning look. "The rest is rice and dates."

Errol wedged the mouthful aside with his tongue to ask a question. "How long before I fight?"

"A few minutes," Hadari said. "Perhaps a bit longer."

He set the food aside. A heavy meal would slow him down. Perhaps he would be able to eat afterward. If he lived.

"You are wise, infidel. Many of the men who come here think only of their belly and pay the price for their lack of discipline."

The guard's compliments might have warmed him once. Now they were just words. "Everyone must die sometime, especially me, but today I will try to live."

Hadari considered him, his smile in place, his eyes intent with unspoken plans, but the guard let slip nothing that might give Errol insight to his thoughts. "Come, infidel. Let us see how you fare before your Deas."

"I have no Deas, Hadari."

Sorrow showed on Hadari's face, etched in the lines of his charcoal-colored skin. With a gesture he invited Errol to precede him, and they moved out of the slave quarters toward the entrance of the arena. The temperature rose as they ascended the bowels of stone, and the smell of people, a lot of people, drifted to him.

Then he heard the noise of a multitude, like the distant roar of the sea. They turned into a hallway with the light of the sun showing at the far end, and the sound and smell redoubled.

Errol's hand strayed to his hip out of reflex before he realized he had no weapon. "Do I fight with my bare hands, Hadari?"

The guard laughed. "By no means, infidel. You may arm yourself in any way you desire, save the bow. Your weapons are waiting for you up ahead."

When they entered the light, the noise swelled into a crescendo and broke upon his hearing like a physical thing. He squinted against the glare across a circle of hard-packed earth a hundred paces across. Across that expanse stood a shirtless man armed with a sword, his muscles oiled and rippling in the sun. He waved to the crowd, pointing in Errol's direction and laughing. The crowd above him joined in the taunting, but since most of those taunts were in a language unfamiliar to him, he paid it no mind.

Weapons were racked to the side. He searched for his staff, found it propped like an afterthought at one end. His hands caressed the smoothed wood, then caught sight of the polished wooden case Count Rula had given him. Errol rubbed his side as he turned to Hadari. "How good is he?"

The guard shrugged his massive shoulders. "He has fought before. There can be only one survivor in the arena, infidel. For you to win, he must die."

Errol nodded. "I thought as much." He didn't fully understand the reckless impulse that led him to open the polished case and extract the two swords Rula had given him. Deep inside, he knew his choice was foolishness, but the rebellious indifference that had covered him since Martin's revelation still held him.

He stepped away with Dextra and Sinistra in his hands, reminding himself not to strike for the legs.

His opponent waited for him at the center of the arena, turning circles, arms raised for the crowd. Errol approached, and the man, tall and dark-skinned, sneered at him. "Northern cur, do you think two swords will help you against me? I will give your flesh to the crows."

Errol checked his footing. The dusty ground would demand balance. The Merakhi's threats meant nothing to him. "When do we start?"

The man snarled, pointing his sword. "When the trumpet sounds, I will spill your blood into the sand."

A voice, loud and brazen, shouted from one end of the stand, speaking in Merakhi to the enthusiastic roars of the crowd. He went on for some few minutes, his speech punctuated by boos, laughter, and hissing. With a final flourish, he fell silent.

The horn sounded.

40

A STAFF OF METAL

THE MAN LAUGHED as he charged, his sword falling in a fierce overhand chop. Errol slipped the blow off his front sword and riposted, spinning. His combatant leapt back, but not before Errol's strike furrowed a deep cut in the man's chest. Blood welled in the cut.

"Cur! I will leave you in pieces for the birds." The Merakhi charged again, his sword coming from the side this time.

The man had to be the worst opponent Errol had ever faced. He wouldn't have been worthy to be Ru's fifteenth. Even Weir would have carved him up with little trouble. Errol grimaced as he parried. It somehow seemed unfair to kill the man . . . but only one could leave the arena—so he thrust with the same sword, his body gliding forward into a lunge that slipped his sword through the Merakhi's ribs and into his heart.

The man fell backward off the sword, dead before he hit the ground. Noise intruded its way back into Errol's awareness, the crowd hissing and booing again. He looked around, but no sign of what to do next seemed to be forthcoming. Was he supposed to wait?

The brazen-throated man remained in his perch in the stands above the arena.

At the entrance where he'd selected his weapons, a trio of guards waited. Hadari beckoned to him, then held up a hand palm out that stopped Errol while he was still twenty paces away. The other two guards held bows with arrows trained on his heart.

"Leave your weapons where you stand, infidel." Hadari smiled. "They will be cleaned and cared for until your next fight."

Errol dropped the swords. Dust clung to the wetness on the blades. He followed Hadari out of the light into the comparative darkness of the tunnel back toward the slave quarters.

"They did not tell me you were a warrior," Hadari said.

"It's not by my choice."

Hadari's eyes sparkled with interest. "Do you have a tale, northlander?"

Errol shook his head. "There is a tale, but there is no point to my story."

"The people of the verdant say all tales hold import."

They turned the corner, and the sounds and smells of the arena diminished. A question nagged at Errol, growing with each step until it forced its way into the air. "Who did I just kill?"

"Does it matter, infidel? Someone must die."

Errol laughed at Hadari's choice of words, his detachment threatening to break. The sound echoed against the block stone walls, bitter, harsh. "So I've heard, but it matters to me."

"He was a murderer, northlander, whose name is not important."

They entered the slave quarters where Ru, Cruk, Rale, and Merodach waited, pacing or sitting as their dispositions dictated.

Rale put a hand on his shoulder. "It's good to see you alive, lad. You've barely left and you're back. Did you not fight?"

Errol exhaled, weary with the conversation already. "It wasn't much of a fight. If that is the best of what this kingdom offers, it's no wonder they need the malus to fight their battles." He snorted in disgust at the memory. "Some people shouldn't pick up a sword."

Surprise showed in the jerk of their postures, but he couldn't place the cause. A discomfited silence filled the space around them, and a sudden desire to be elsewhere, to be away from them, overtook Errol. He stepped from beneath Rale's hand and moved back. "I need to eat. And sleep."

He woke in the middle of the night to the catarrhal sounds of soft and not-so-soft snoring around him. Torchlight cast creeping shadows along the walls. At the entrance the guards stood vigil, their skin blending with the night so that they appeared to be shadows in linen and armor. The occasional glint of fire reflected from steel moved across his vision. How long had he slept? Errol sat up, a longing for the woods around the Sprata stabbing through him.

A vision of the falls in spring, heavy and chill with winter melt, coursed through him. But his memories of Callowford led step by inexorable step back to Antil. His father. Errol looked at his hands. He'd killed a man today. And hardly cared. Was that Antil's legacy to him? Perhaps the time would come when he would seek others' pain, revel in it.

He thrust that thought away, chose to think on Adora, but he found no comfort there either. The princess slept in the ilhotep's slave quarters, taken to please him. Errol's imagination conjured images that disturbed him. The tenor of his heartbeat increased until it pounded against his ribs.

Pushing himself away from his thoughts and his bunk, he walked toward the entrance. The guards, unfamiliar to him, paid him no mind until he came within five paces. Then they snapped weapons to the ready, and Errol found himself staring down several feet of naked steel.

"Where's Hadari?"

The guards exchanged an inscrutable look. "What do you wish of the kayeed?"

Kayeed? Was Hadari the leader of the palace guards? Errol lifted a hand. He wasn't really sure how to answer the question. "I wanted to talk to someone who doesn't know me."

One of the guards slipped away, and another took his place. Errol almost laughed. Where could he possibly run? He probably couldn't find his way out of the maze of the arena. A few moments later, the guard returned with Hadari at his side.

The big man looked sleepy, but his tone was warm as he greeted Errol. "Do you always arise so early, infidel?"

Errol gestured at the blank, featureless walls. "There are only slits and it's dark; I have no way of knowing the time."

"Two hours before sunrise," Hadari said. "Come, I will check the other guards. If you still feel the need to converse, infidel, we can do it as we walk."

The threat of swords held by those walking mountains rooted him where he stood. "Is it permitted?"

The two guards flanking Hadari laughed until he looked their way. Errol recognized the reaction of soldiers to a superior's displeasure.

"It is permitted. I will have a guard trail us. If you seek to attack me, infidel, he will kill you where you stand."

Errol shrugged. "Death comes to everyone, some sooner than others, but I'm in no hurry to meet it."

Hadari smiled. "Have I not said you are wise? Come." He turned and made his way out of the slave quarters. Errol hastened to catch up. He fell in step next to his warden, but now that the opportunity to speak lay open, words failed him. They walked in silence past a guard station within the arena. A motion along with a curt command in a lilting tongue brought a man with a bow and quiver from within that room to trail them.

"You are quiet, infidel. Why is that?"

He looked at the intricate patterns along the walls, the dominant form of decoration here in Merakh. The patterns repeated themselves on a smaller and smaller scale until they were lost to sight. "Your fellow guards called you *kayeed*?"

Hadari smiled. "Ah. You are observant."

Errol cocked his head to one side. "I know the look of men confronted by their superior. No more."

"It is given to me to know much about you, infidel. There seems to be much you know, perhaps too much."

How Errol wished it weren't so.

"The other guards call me kayeed because I am their captain, the head of the ilhotep's personal guard."

"Then why does the ilhotep not have his personal guard with him?"

Hadari stopped, turned sideways to face Errol, and held a hand up, palm out, to the guard behind them. The guard following stopped. Hadari guided Errol farther along the hallway before speaking. "That is a dangerous question, infidel. You should find another."

Errol pulled at his jaw muscles, the bristle of whiskers raked against the palm of his hand. "Why do you call me infidel? None of the other men from Illustra have been called that."

Hadari's black eyebrows crept up the dark charcoal of his skin toward his bald head, and his eyes widened in surprise. "Are you not? I have said much is known about you. Your refusal to acknowledge your Deas looms large in the ilhotep's councils. It is one of the reasons the chief councilor desires you."

The accusation grated. His unbelief belonged to him. After everything he'd been through, he shouldn't have to justify it to anyone, much less the Merakhi ruler who was trying to destroy his kingdom. He set his jaw.

They passed another guard room. Hadari stopped to speak to the men within for a few moments before moving on. The halls changed, and Errol sensed they had passed beyond the confines of the arena. A tug within his chest pulled him left. He could have pointed without error to Sarin Valon's chambers. How long would it be before the church's compulsion took over his mind? "Where are we?"

"Under the gallery of victories, the ilhotep's storeroom. There is something within I wish to show you."

"Why?" Errol asked.

Hadari laughed. "An interesting question, infidel, but not the right one. Come, you will see."

They climbed a narrow stone stairway that wound upward in darkness, Hadari in the lead, until they emerged into a domed-entrance antechamber. Torches burned in sconces beside an entryway, but no guards kept watch. Hadari led him to a door and produced a key from within the linen folds of his uniform.

The door swung open. Hadari grabbed a torch and entered. "Follow."

Errol stepped behind him, but the other guard remained outside.

With each step into the chamber, Hadari's former ease diminished until the guard's manner radiated intense anticipation. Stacks of artifacts surrounded them. Gold, silver, and precious stones reflected torchlight in a dozen different hues. Errol goggled at the fortune, but Hadari moved with purpose past rows of treasure to the far corner of the room. When he stopped, he lifted the torch high above his head to illumine a massive black marble obelisk, and his manner became deferential, reverent.

On the obelisk sat an ancient book, tattered and yellowed with age. Smudges of handprints on the glassy marble surface around the book testified to recent visitations.

Somewhere within Errol, a memory stirred but refused to surface. Hadari reached forward and opened the book as gently as hands nearly twice the size of Errol's would allow. His expression as he faced Errol became closed, his eyes narrowed and probing.

"Do you know what this is, infidel?"

Errol shook his head. "How could I know something I've never seen before? It's a book. I've seen lots of books."

His answer appeared to frustrate his companion. Hadari huffed, and his hands wandered in aimless gestures, as if he no longer knew what to do with them. "It's from your kingdom," he said at last. "It is very old."

Errol's natural curiosity had been so dulled by the revelation of his ultimate fate he could not muster an interest in the Ongolese guard's convoluted guessing game. "If there is something you want me to know, tell me."

Sorrow wreathed Hadari's face. "I cannot give you the knowledge that way."

A sigh building in Errol's chest came out in a soft hiss. "You speak in such riddles. Are you sure you are not a priest? You sound like Martin."

Hadari laughed and stepped back from the book. "Would you like to read it?"

Errol leaned forward, preparing to take that first irrevocable step to discovering Hadari's secret. He stopped. There was no point. Someone had to die, and it didn't take a scholar to see that the kingdom needed Liam more than it needed a former drunkard like himself. No, let Hadari keep the knowledge of his book. Errol's destiny lay in the arena.

"No. I am done with books and secrets. Whatever you want from me is beyond my ability to give."

For the barest instant, the guard's large face, dark and blunt, showed a longing almost beyond human capacity to express. Hadari wheeled, his shoulders taut, and closed the book. "Perhaps another time, then, infidel." His tone carried a note of finality, and the way he said *infidel* no longer spoke of teasing but of wrenching loss.

Errol followed him from the ilhotep's treasure room. The other guard fell in line behind them, and they followed a twisting route that Errol could never have duplicated back to the slave quarters underneath the arena. Neither Errol nor Hadari made any further attempts at conversation.

Back in the sleeping room, Errol sat on his bunk amidst the sound of men dozing around him. His subconscious found a spot in the upper part of the wall through which an unobstructed arrow would find Valon's heart. Books and questions faded from his awareness.

When the morning meal and light through the slits announced sunrise, the guards came for Naaman Ru and Merodach. Both men returned within an hour, dusty but hardly out of breath.

Merodach, his silver blond hair glinting in the light, returned to his whispered consultations with Rale, his blue-eyed gaze darting often to Errol.

Ru, meanwhile, walked about the quarters snorting and voicing his disgust. "We're wasting time. The ilhotep's councilors will tire of our easy victories and begin sending us against their best."

"How would you propose we escape?" Rale asked. "I'm open to suggestions."

Errol returned to his bunk. There would be no escape, and until whatever end awaited him arrived, there was little to do except eat, sleep, and fight. He was ready to accept his fate, but when he thought of Adora . . . He tried not to think of the princess.

He slept often and spent his waking hours following Valon's movements as surely as if the man walked before him.

Cruk and Rale visited the arena and returned as quickly as Ru and Merodach. Hadari came for Errol the next day at noon to lead him to his next battle. "The crowd does not like you or your friends, infidel."

"Why is that?" Errol asked.

"They are here for a show, and you disappoint them with your quick kills."

"Then they should send us better opponents."

Hadari laughed as if Errol had made a great jest. "Well spoken. The men you have defeated were counted fierce among the bandits and criminals they lead. It is a great honor to have three captains of the watch fighting in the arena, but who is this other man, Naaman Ru?"

Errol did not trust Hadari's companionship despite their visit to the treasure room. "He is a caravan master who is good with a sword."

"You weave a rug with missing threads." Hadari smiled. "There are some who have noticed Ru is . . . comfortable here, as if he has seen Merakh before."

Errol let the unasked question slip by. "I'll wager he would rather be in the kingdom right now."

"Perhaps we will talk on this again, infidel."

Errol couldn't tell if the man's words were an invitation or a threat. But thoughts of Hadari and his secrets faded as he entered the glare of the arena to choose his weapon. Swords or staff? He moved along the rack toward his sword case and stopped, his attention arrested by a smooth, gray rod.

"What is this?"

Hadari approached. "It is a metal staff. Your priest, the one you call Martin, had it with him."

Errol lifted it from the rack, amazed at its light weight. Despite the sweat on his hands, the metal gripped well. It did not slide from his grasp. He stole a glance across the circular stretch of ground. His opponent stood impassive under the noise of the crowd, waiting.

Foolishness, he told himself. Only an idiot would take an untried weapon into battle. Doing so practically begged for death.

He grabbed the staff and returned to Hadari.

"You would face a sword with a glorified stick, infidel? I thought you wise. I see my estimation was in error."

Something about the feel of the metal staff, lighter than ash and stronger than oak, made him want to laugh. "You may be surprised, Hadari, what may be done with a stick."

The guard nodded, and Errol left him to approach the center of the ring.

The jeers of the crowd faded as his opponent came forward. "I see you, northlander," the man said. A thick black beard covered his face and waggled when he spoke. "You insult me with your choice of weapon. Do you not realize I have killed over a hundred men, both northlanders and countrymen alike? Pig."

Errol stepped forward, the staff moving slow circles in preparation.

Moments later Errol replaced the staff in the rack with a pang of regret, the crowd silent behind him. Hadari inclined his head in acknowledgment, less than a bow, more than a nod. "You surprised many today, northlander. There has never been a warrior in the ring who has chosen to fight with a stick."

"Staff," Errol corrected.

"Hardly the weapon for a warrior of renown, but now it is easier to believe the tales," Hadari said.

"I never wanted renown or to be a warrior." His voice thickened as his detachment cracked and a wash of emotion that threatened to become a tidal wave came through. "Maybe I should have. But getting other things I wanted hasn't helped much."

A glint appeared in Hadari's visage, of cunning or something else Errol couldn't tell, but the big guard escorted him back to the slave quarters with the abstraction of a man making plans. When he stopped at the door and motioned Errol inside, he gave a cryptic smile. "It would be good for you to rest now, infidel. Unforeseen circumstances come to us all."

It was barely an hour after noon. Sleep seemed a ridiculous notion, yet conversation with the rest of the company did not interest him. He lay down on the bunk. His gaze traced invisible paths along the upper part of the wall, following Valon's movements. Errol's mind wandered through the days of the past year, seeking an escape from the pull of the Judica's compulsion.

The message. If he had refused to take the message, Luis would never have discovered his talent. There would have been no compulsion to force him to Erinon. He would have remained in Callowford with Cilla.

With Antil.

He rolled, tangling himself in the thin blanket that covered his pallet, found himself staring at the stone slabs that formed the floor. His answer must lay further back. The face of his adoptive father, Warrel, loomed before him again, pale and closed with pain.

The fracture in Errol's detachment widened, threatened to burst, allowing emotions he'd locked away to drown him. When had he ever been in control of his own life? He pressed the heels of his hands against his eyes, trying to shut away the useless memories. What would have been different if he had never crawled into the ale barrel?

No. It was no use. The seekers for the church would have

tested him at fourteen and taken him to Erinon. He would have been spared Antil's abuse and his own intemperance, but in all likelihood he would be dead now. The conclave would have uncovered his talent as an omne. Valon would not have left him alive. A knot of rage built in the back of his throat. The grip of destiny had its foot as firmly planted on his future as it did his past. There had never been any escape for him.

The struggle to keep his emotions in check exhausted him. He slept.

A hand on his shoulder brought him to wakefulness. The sighs of men dreaming of freedom surrounded him. Hadari's silhouette hovered over his bunk. Errol rose and followed the guard as before, but this time Hadari seemed uninterested in conversation.

At the entrance to the slave quarters, guards removed Errol's clothes and outfitted him in the white linen of a Merakhi soldier. A guard bent and belted a curved sword, a shirra, at his waist. Curious, Errol tested the edge with his thumb. It was dull, so dull it could only be used as a club.

Hadari stepped in front of him and wrapped Errol's face with the linen cloth attached to the shoulders of the uniform. "With your sun-browned skin and dark hair you could almost pass for a Merakhi." He leaned close. "Keep your hands empty. To draw that weapon is to die. Do you understand?"

Errol nodded.

"Good. Do not speak. Your voice would give you away."

With two guards in front of them and another two behind, Hadari led them through the tunnels that connected the buildings of the ilhotep's city until they arrived once again at the treasure hall of Merakh's ruler.

This time all five guards accompanied Errol into the room. Without preamble, he was escorted to the back corner where the book lay. When they turned the corner, Errol stopped short. In front of him, surrounded by another five guards, all of them as big and dark as Hadari, stood the ilhotep.

The guards with Errol knelt. Oversized hands moved to pull him down before the ilhotep's raised hand stopped them. On impulse, Errol completed the gesture on his own, his right knee cold against the polished marble floor. When he rose, Errol looked upon a man who wore the ilhotep's features and rich clothes, but whose posture and personality bore no resemblance to the indolent pouting man he'd seen in the palace.

41

MAGIS'S FOLLY

ARE THE ENTRANCES SEALED?" the ilhotep asked.

Hadari bowed. "Yes, my ilhotep. None may enter without your knowledge or permission."

Merakh's ruler turned his eyes to Errol. Away from the indulgence of his throne room, the ilhotep seemed more like a panther than a kitten. Black, shoulder-length hair accentuated the intensity of his face. His eyes, dark to match his hair, had lost their heavy-lidded somnolence, burning instead as they scrutinized Errol from eyes to soles, noting every detail. Yet the smile that appeared in the midst of his neat beard seemed welcoming enough.

"Doubtless, Earl Stone, you wonder why I would have you brought here in the middle of the night."

Errol nodded. "Ilhotep, I'm surprised that you would address me by a title few of my own countrymen use. To most of them I'm a boy, or a peasant."

The ilhotep's eyes blazed. "Yes, so my informants have told me. Yet you have accomplished great things, and the hope of Illustra rests on your shoulders."

"No," Errol said. "I do not think so, or they wouldn't have sent me on this fool's quest."

Laughter greeted his statement, showing the ilhotep's white, even teeth. "Do not confuse those who vie for power with those who work for good. Men like your Duke Weir would rather perish as king than live as duke. Unfortunately, he is powerful enough to obtain his desire."

"Pardon me, Ilhotep, but why are you telling me all this? If you know as much about me as Hadari says, you know I must kill Sarin Valon or go insane. Merakh will be at war with the kingdom when Rodran dies, at any rate."

The ilhotep stepped closer. Errol kept his hands in plain view, away from his sword, surprised to discover the ruler was his own size. The intensity of his face and manner had made him seem larger. "What would you think if I said I do not desire war?"

Hunger flared in Errol, then died almost as quickly. "I have seen too many men die, Ilhotep—some of them by my own hand—to wish for anything but peace, but I must kill Sarin Valon or lose myself."

The ilhotep brushed aside his objection. "Valon will die. He is insane and serves Belaaz rather than me. The spirits—the ones we call the roukh—have eaten his mind. The intelligence you see looking out from his eyes does not belong to a man. After you left the throne room he went mad with fear. He knows why you are here." The ilhotep paused to laugh. "And now that he knows he cannot see you coming, he is petrified along with the rest of the council. Beware, Earl Stone, they will not be content with waiting. Every moment you draw breath is one in which a sword stroke may deprive the roukh of their host."

The ilhotep ran his fingers along the edge of the book, then nodded to himself. "The matter is simple. In four days we will celebrate the feast of the god Belaaz."

Errol started.

The ilhotep's lips parted in a sardonic grin. "No, northlander, it is not a coincidence. My chief councilor has taken the name of the roukh that possesses him. His feast will be our opportunity." His face grimaced in disgust. "The roukh drive their hosts relentlessly on such occasions as they indulge their . . . appetites. Eventually, even they must rest. On that day you will be provided with a map and allowed to escape. If you wish to avoid war, as I do, kill Valon and the council."

The enormity of the ilhotep's request daunted him. "Ilhotep, even if they are unconscious, they will be guarded. Any alarm will put the council and Valon beyond reach."

Instead of answering, the ilhotep turned from him. He stilled and for a moment appeared to doubt himself. "The council thinks me safely under their influence, but I do not want war." His right hand came to rest on the book Hadari had shown Errol before. "I have come to see things differently. Errol Stone, you are Illustra's—and Merakh's—only hope for averting conflict."

Errol pulled his gaze from the ilhotep's with an effort. Almost he confessed that it was Karele who protected the Illustrans, that alone, Errol might be visible to Valon and his circle. But the presence of so many guards silenced him. He trusted Hadari, wanted to trust the ilhotep, but the rest of the Ongolese guards were unknown to him.

He bowed. "I will consider your plan, Ilhotep."

The leader of Merakh didn't bother to hide his disappointment, but instead of trying to persuade Errol further, he turned his full attention to the book. He knelt to press his head against the cover, and his lips moved, though Errol could hear no sound. The ilhotep ruler rose. "Do you know what this is, Earl Stone?"

"Hadari showed it to me," Errol said. "It's a book."

The ilhotep laughed, joyful and light. "Yes, he showed it to me as well. Though a good number can speak it, not many in Merakh can read the language of your kingdom. But my father, who was ilhotep before me, gave me the finest education in the world, and I require men of intelligence to guard me." He turned to Hadari. "Because he discovered and showed me this book, he has become more than a servant; he has become my greatest friend."

Hadari smiled and bowed, bending at the waist until his head faced the floor.

The ilhotep's fingers traced the book with reverence. "In the kingdom, the loss of this book is known as Magis's folly."

Remembrance flooded through Errol. "It can't be."

The ilhotep smiled, pulled his mouth to one side in a smirk. "When the roukhs were all destroyed? Yes, but there were men with that army as well. They fled with the book and brought it back here. Anything the kingdom thought precious enough to guard, they thought worthy enough to take. When they discovered the book held no incantation or secrets of power, they put it here to gather dust. But the power of the book is far beyond mere chants, Earl Stone. Can you read?"

"Yes."

"Then I would have you read the book," the ilhotep said. "Time is short, but we have some few days yet. Hadari will bring you here each night."

The enormity of what the ilhotep proposed began to sink in. "If your council discovers your plan, they will kill you."

The ilhotep smiled. "Yes, Earl Stone. My life hangs by the thinnest of threads, but in you I have found a weapon that may defeat the council and their roukhs and prevent war."

The simple admission caught Errol off guard. "I am your slave, Ilhotep. Why not just order me to do it? You could have me killed if I refuse to cooperate."

The ilhotep's face softened. It retained its fire, but something gentle came into the set of his features. "Since I have read the book, I find that I no longer desire needless deaths."

He left surrounded by eight of the ten guards. After he left, Errol shook his head. "He is very different than what I expected."

"He is very different than what he was, infidel," Hadari said.

"But not as wise as he should be." Errol bit his lip. "Ten men are too many for the secret he's trying to keep."

"You know not of what you speak, infidel. The nine are my brothers, sworn to his protection. None would betray him."

"For all our sakes, I hope you are right."

Hadari pointed toward the book. "We have a few hours before dawn."

Errol stepped to the table and opened the cover.

He fought in the arena again the next day. His opponent, dressed in rough, ill-fitting rags, blustered and yelled, inciting the crowd. Someone threw a melon that landed a few feet from him as Errol stood, waiting for the introductions to end. One of Hadari's brothers jumped the barrier that separated the stone seats of the coliseum from the arena proper. No one threw anything else.

The brazen-throated sound of the horn signaled their bout, and Errol's attention snapped into focus. The man facing him, broad-shouldered and narrow-waisted, moved across the hard-packed sand with surprising grace. Errol circled, trying to make sense of the conflicting impressions.

The man's clothes and manner marked him as just another bandit or criminal sent to meet his eventual end in the arena. But his movements and the neatly trimmed beard and hair said something else. Errol backed away, ignoring the jeers of the crowd. His opponent took a casual swing with his shirra, and his ragged sleeves inched up his arms. *There.* Errol recognized the tattoo on his forearm. He had seen the same three indigo circles marking some of the soldiers of the spire.

He was fighting a palace guard.

"Why did they dress you like a bandit?"

Surprise showed in the man's eyes. "You have good eyes, north-lander." He bowed in respect, his hand scraping the ground.

A cloud of sand covered Errol, blinding him.

He backpedaled, blinking. His vision rippled, his opponent and the arena undulated like a mirage. He caught the first blow by luck. Riposted with the staff and caught the man with a grazing blow to the head.

The Merakhi guard wobbled. Errol retreated, scrubbing his eyes. The Merakhi attacked again, his sword catching the light. Wet. The blade gleamed with a yellowish cast.

His opponent needed only mark him and Errol would die.

Panic coursed through him, shattering his detachment. He pushed the light metal staff he had once again chosen for this bout, spinning it ever faster until the ends disappeared in the sound of a thousand angry hornets. He moved on the guard, striking his sword hand with a crunch of broken knuckles. The sword fell to the ground, and the guard clutched for a dagger Errol saw strapped at his side.

Before he could draw, Errol struck. Driving faster than ever before, he beat the Merakhi on the head, hitting him over and over again, striking even as he fell.

Sightless eyes gazed at the sun. His opponent's guards came forward at a run to reclaim the weapons. Errol stooped, pulled the dagger from the dead man's waist, and scooped up the sword before running back to Hadari.

Ten paces away, drawn bows stopped him.

Hadari cut his gaze left and right. "Drop the weapons, infidel. The fight is over. Your opponent has paid for bringing a hidden weapon to the arena."

Errol let them hit the ground. "They're poisoned, Hadari. The sword and the dagger have styrich on them." He stepped well away from the weapons as the men caught up to him from behind.

Hadari acknowledged them with a brief nod. "The infidel says the weapons are poisoned, Jaba."

A tall man with narrow eyes spat. "You would believe a pale barbarian?"

Hadari approached, coming close enough to dwarf his counterpart. He made a show of looking at the poison on the sword and then smiled. "Of course not."

Back in the tunnel he pulled Errol aside. "You must decide quickly, northlander. Belaaz grows impatient for your death."

Rale's brows furrowed when Errol related the events in the arena, as well as the details of his conversation with the ilhotep. Cruk made extensive use of his vocabulary. Ru echoed him, and even Merodach's stoic impassivity cracked enough to show concern.

"I don't have any choice, do I?" Errol asked. "I have to try and kill them."

Naaman Ru growled in disgust. "Of course you don't have any choice, boy. You never had any choice."

Rale nodded. "He's right."

Errol slumped onto the stone bench that ran the length of the room. "But it's still three days until the feast of Belaaz. How am I supposed to stay alive?"

No one answered.

Hadari came to him again that night to take him to the book. Errol donned the white uniform of a palace guard once more and walked side by side with Hadari back to the treasure room.

Errol broke the silence as they entered the ilhotep's hall. "I will try to do as the ilhotep has requested, though it is unlikely I will succeed. Valon may not be able to see me through his cast, but the simplest guard will spot me with his eyes."

Hadari's eyes narrowed as he squeezed Errol's shoulder. "It is a special occasion. I will make sure the council is watched by the ilhotep's most trusted guards."

Fatigue clouded Errol's thoughts. When he realized what Hadari proposed, a thrill of hope, like a splash of ice water, coursed through him. If there were no guards to raise an outcry, success was possible, perhaps even likely.

Hours later, Errol rubbed the sleep from his eyes, forced himself to focus on the page in front of him. The enormity of the task daunted him. "I'll never be able to read it all in three nights."

A smile played around the edges of Hadari's face, showing a glimpse of white teeth. "You do not have to read the whole book now, Errol. You just need to read the *right* part. The ilhotep and I found that a certain part of the book spoke most strongly to us."

Errol pointed to the pages in front of him. "Show me that part."

His guard's face fell. "They were not the same. It has been different for all of us."

"All of you?"

Hadari's eyes twinkled. "My brothers and I."

"Then what do I do?"

The dark-skinned mountain shrugged. "Keep reading."

Errol turned the page.

Two hours before dawn, unable any longer to make sense of the words on the page, he returned to his prison and collapsed into his bunk. He fell into dream-filled sleep where he fought a score of enemies wielding poisoned swords and throwing choking clouds of dust at him. He couldn't breathe.

He woke. Spots danced in his vision, and his lungs burned. He struggled to tear the cloth from his face, but his arms were pinned to his side. His vision narrowed to a pinpoint of light that danced behind his eyelids.

Impact knocked him to the floor and he sucked air. He rolled to his hands and knees, his head pounding. Someone kicked him in the side, and he curled around the blow. Instinctively, he grabbed his head.

A moment later, hands pulled him upright. "Sit up, boy. He's dead." Ru.

Errol rubbed his neck. "Thank you," he croaked.

"Thank your church friends. This compulsion forces me awake whenever you sleep."

The slave room seethed like an ant colony in a storm. Guards shouted as they charged into the sleeping quarters brandishing swords. Slaves, bleary-eyed and frightened, backed away from the tangle Errol, Ru, and the dead man made on the floor. Harsh torchlight threw frantic shadows against the walls.

The guard closest to Ru kept the point of his shirra at his midsection until Hadari marched in and ordered him to withdraw.

"What happened, northlander?" he asked Errol.

Errol pointed to the dead man. "He tried to choke me in my sleep. Ru saved me."

Hadari nodded. With minimal conversation, he ordered the prisoners segregated and posted guards to watch over the men as they slept. Errol sat in the torchlight on the bunk above Naaman Ru's.

If not for the caravan master's compulsion, he would be dead now. Belaaz had attempted to kill him again. He hoped to Deas it was only because Valon couldn't see him coming.

Two days later Errol sat on his bunk and stared at the window slit as the night purpled, then lightened to rose. The feast of Belaaz would begin at sundown. Sometime after dark, Hadari would come to him and dress him in the white linen of a palace guard.

Then he would kill the council and Sarin Valon. In one more day he would be free.

He thrust his dread and doubt away with a mental push, pondering instead what he had read just hours before. Over half the book remained unread, but the words he *had* read seem etched in his mind. Hadari had said he would know the passage meant for him, but indecision clung to him. Much of the book felt like truths he had never heard, but had he read the passage meant for him? He thought it was possible but wasn't sure.

The first night he'd read—as Hadari, torch in hand, stood watch over him—how Deas, Eleison, and Aurae had molded the world, and how the malus, who walked the earth in bodily form, corrupted it. Betrayed by the fallen ones who promised knowledge and power, men became chattel.

The second night he'd read how Deas sent his son, Eleison, through the gate of time and space to rescue his creation. For the first time since Martin's disclosure, the beating of Errol's heart seemed less than a burden to be borne. Hadari had pulled him away from the book at first light. Dawn threatened to expose them.

As the sun began its descent the previous night, Errol had waited in the slave quarters under guard, yearning to return, watching the light outside their narrow window, hungering for darkness. It came finally. And he'd read a passage that confounded him.

He sat on his bunk now, the same question echoing in the astonishment of his mind. Who would believe him? The words of the book came to him again and again in refutation of a liturgy he'd heard his entire life. He grieved the knowledge that had been lost and the conflict that had arisen because of it. Would Martin believe him?

Aurae was knowable.

42

COUP

HADARI CAME FOR HIM a few hours after noon.
"Come, Errol. They want you to fight again."

Disappointment, thin and sharp like the blade of a knife, stabbed him. "Do I have to?"

His guard nodded. "Once more. I have told the ilhotep of your decision. We will have you and your friends away from the city after tonight. The one you call Karele has impressed the stable master with his knowledge. He has been given authority to exercise the horses. Have I not said that Deas weaves events to his desire? The ilhotep has ensured you will not be threatened. Your opponent is vicious, but lacks the skill of a warrior."

"I will use the staff," Errol said, "and try to avoid a killing blow."

Hadari nodded as if he expected nothing less. "The guards will kill him if you do not."

Errol nodded acquiescence to this truth. "But at least it will not be me."

He stepped out of the gloom of the tunnel into the arid sunshine of the arena. Behind him he heard Hadari gasp. The big man closed the space to stand behind him while Errol chose his weapon.

"Something is wrong," Hadari said.

Errol followed his gaze into the arena. "Three of them?"

Hadari shook his head. "Those men are not bandits. They are janiss, warrior elites and captains of the guard."

Errol trusted the Ongolese now with his life, and more. "Can I win?"

"Not with the staff, brother. You will have to use the blades."

Hadari proffered the case that held Dextra and Sinistra. Errol sighed. Would he ever be able to stop killing? "I am tired of taking lives, Hadari." He appeared not to hear.

"Hadari."

The guard started, and the eyes he turned to Errol were wide, intense.

"What does this mean?" Errol asked.

"Three have never fought against one in the arena—two, maybe, but never three. The council has overruled the ilhotep. They want to make sure you die," Hadari said. "I must return to my master. I will send one of my brothers to take you back to your quarters, if you live."

He turned to give Errol a last warning. "The six would not overrule the ilhotep in such a way if they did not suspect. Strike quickly."

The twin swords felt alien in his hands after fighting with the staff. He walked toward the center of the arena, circling to his left to keep the sun from his eyes and working through the forms Count Rula taught him. His opponents moved with the purposeful strides of experienced soldiers. They did not bother to wave to the crowd or make taunts. Their grim faces held the implacable resolve of men bent on a swift kill.

Errol concentrated, reaching for his former detachment, but his nightly sessions reading the book had made that impossible.

The men spread on catlike feet to surround him. Death sought him here, but a thought struck him and he smiled. If he lived, he might get to read the book again. His heart swelled at the thought, and in the midst of the arena, he laughed.

The man upon the raised stone platform signaled, and the trumpet sounded.

They rushed him, coming at him from three different sides. Errol charged the closest, parried the stroke and slipped by, slashing with the rear sword to make space. He wheeled. For an instant he faced the man alone while the other two moved out from behind him. Errol struck with both blades. The top line was parried but the lower line found the man's thigh. He grunted in pain and stumbled back.

The other two slowed at the sight, paused to coordinate their attack, then struck. Steel whistled as their blades sliced the air, one high, the other low. Errol rolled as he parried the low strike, riposting. His sword found the back of the man's legs. He went down screaming. The other man swung an overhand strike at him, and Errol squirmed, flailing as he tried to open enough distance to rise, but the man stayed on him.

Desperate, he let go of his right sword and flung sand. The man threw up an arm to block, and in that instant Errol regained his weapon and his feet. The crunch of a boot behind him sounded and he threw himself to the side. Steel parted his shirt, whispered across his back. He wheeled, backing away.

Two of his attackers still stood, the first man with his thigh still bleeding, and one unmarked janiss. The third man was down, his hamstring severed. Dextra and Sinistra once again in hand, Errol circled, keeping the wounded man between him and the last whole adversary.

Errol lunged, took the parry on the fore sword, moved close to hold the janiss in a bind, and took him in the throat with Sinistra. He backed away as the body collapsed into the dirt. The last man, eyes so wide they looked lidless, screamed and charged. Errol parried the blow and lunged, his steel grating on bone as the man's momentum forced the blade through his ribs and into his spine.

He fell, his dead eyes staring at the sun. Errol pried his sword from the man's body and returned to the gate. The crowd, near to overflowing, was silent. A royal guard, a brother of Hadari's, waited for him.

"Leave your weapons and follow me," the guard said.

He set a pace that set Errol running. White-robed soldiers and hulking palace guards roamed everywhere, moving quickly, scanning the halls with staccato jerks of their heads.

"What's going on?" Errol asked.

"No questions."

The slave quarters were in turmoil, like a school of fish thrashing in the shallows. Unfamiliar noises sounded outside the walls. Shadows danced through the narrow window slits in counterpoint to guttural shouts. The guards stood, wary. Messengers came and left at a run.

Night fell, and the royal guards were called away, replaced by a pair of white-robed janiss with bows.

Errol gathered with Rale, Merodach, Ru, and Cruk. "What do we do?" he asked.

Ru turned away from the guards. "Be quiet. Be still," he whispered. "There's fighting in the palace."

"What does it mean?"

Ru scowled at his question but answered it anyway. "It means someone is trying to kill someone else, boy. Now, be quiet so I can hear."

Another runner came, and two more guards joined the first pair.

"That's not good," Ru whispered. "There's only one reason I can think of to arm guards with bows in the slave quarters."

Rale nodded. "I suspected as much. The ilhotep?"

Ru shrugged. "Him or the council. Merakhi politics are ruthless and bloody."

"Spread out, but be casual about it," Rale said. "If they start shooting, charge the guards after the first flight."

Errol's heart threatened to force its way into his throat. He tried to look nonchalant as he walked away from the group. If the guards fired, he would have bare seconds to close the distance before they fired again. If he was more than ten paces away, he wouldn't make it in time, but being any closer meant he'd be the primary target. He scanned the room, looking in vain for something he could throw.

Sometime after midnight, a runner came, breathless, his eyes frantic, to speak to the guard in charge—a tall, gangly janiss with a hooked nose. The man's eyes went flat at the news. He barked an order as he fit an arrow to his bow.

Ru's voice cracked like a whip. "Dive, boy!"

Bowstrings twanged as the janiss fired. Errol threw himself behind the nearest bunk. Arrows hissed, striking sparks from the floor and sending splinters from the wooden bunk. Sounds of struggle filled the hall. Errol rolled to his feet to see Merodach give a violent twist to the last remaining guard's head. The sound of snapping bones reverberated off the stone. The four guards lay dead. The other slaves in the room flooded out and away.

"Fools," Ru said. "They'll be dead in minutes."

"How do we keep from joining them?" Rale asked. He and Merodach held bows.

Hadari stepped into the room. Rents in his clothing and armor testified to a struggle. Rale and Merodach trained their bows on him, but he ignored the threat to address Errol. "Come with me, brother. We must get you out of the palace. The ilhotep is dead. Belaaz rules now." Tear tracks lined his cheeks and his eyes were red.

"What of Martin and Luis?" Cruk asked.

"My brother has them near the stables with the one that knows horses," Hadari said.

"What about Adora?" Errol asked.

"I'm not leaving without my daughter," Ru said.

Hadari shook his head. "No harm will come to the ilhotep's harem. I will send one of my brothers for them."

Errol shook his head. "No. I will go to her."

"I'm not leaving without Rokha," Ru said.

Rale stood from a bunk. "We stay together—to the women first."

The charcoal skin of Hadari's face wrinkled into a scowl. "Foolish kingdom men. You seek the lion's maw when you should be running away."

Ru nudged one of the dead guards with his foot. "We could wear these. There's no blood on them."

Hadari looked heavenward and sighed. "Quickly, then, and we'll need weapons."

They scrambled into the uniforms and made for the armory. The sounds of fighting outside intensified, and the screams of dying men echoed and reechoed around them. Errol grabbed Dextra and Sinistra and was belting the sheaths that fastened them to his waist when he noticed the metal rod. He grabbed it, his hands automatically seeking the balance point toward the center, as if it were his wooden staff.

"Leave it, boy," Ru said. "Merakhi don't use the staff."

"I will carry it," Hadari said. Grabbing the rod, he broke into a quick trot, leading them away from the skirmishes, always working his way toward the palace. They came upon a squad of white-robed guards who saw Hadari and attacked. Errol slashed at his opponent's head with his swords. By the time it was over, his comrades' white uniforms bore stains and streaks of red.

Pain, like a tug in his mind, pulled Errol's attention to the west. He put out a hand to steady himself. Valon was moving.

"Everyone?" Rale asked.

Cruk had a cut on his leg, but besides that, the blood on their uniforms belonged to the guards.

"You all fight well," Hadari said. "Were you Ongolese, I would have placed you in the royal guard." He moved up a narrow hallway. "Come." He moved toward the ilhotep's throne room. Away from Valon.

Errol grabbed Hadari's sleeve. "Valon's moving. I have to take him now. Save her, please." At the man's nod, he set off.

An instant later an echo of boots behind startled him, and he swung the sword in his right hand. The shock of steel and Naaman Ru's face registered at the same time.

Ru gave him a wicked smile. "You're almost fast enough, boy. But not quite. Now hurry and find this reader you have to kill so I can get my daughter."

Errol didn't bother to thank him. Ru didn't want his gratitude.

As he ran the corridors, Errol tried not to think about getting trapped in a blind hallway. They avoided the skirmishes when they could. If Ongolese were not involved, it was impossible to determine who fought for whom. When forced to, they fought. Naaman Ru moved through opposition like a phantom, and the touch of his shadow brought death. Most men never saw the strike that killed them.

They ran on, following the tug in Errol's head. As they raced up an inclined hallway, a stench of animal musk and corruption filled the air. He swallowed against the gorge rising in his throat and covered his nose with his sleeve.

When they turned a corner into a broad hallway, Valon stood before him, surrounded by a mass of ferrals. The renegade stood relaxed in expectation, the hint of a smile showing above his neatly trimmed beard. He looked down his nose at Ru, dismissed him before returning to Errol.

The ferrals scented the air, their muzzles showing jagged teeth, their eyes burning. They gnashed at Valon's upraised hand, straining to attack. The spawn seethed, a boiling mass of barely restrained violence.

"Come, Errol Stone," Valon said. The glare of his eyes belied the honey smoothness of his speech. "You cannot win. Even if you kill this body, I will simply find another. There is no lack of people willing to accept us for a chance at immortality." Valon smiled and his eyes vibrated. "Join us. As omne within my circle, you will be second only to me."

Errol shook his head. Revulsion and loathing turned his stomach.

"If you're concerned about the compulsion those churchmen laid on you, you have no need. We supersede that authority." Valon beckoned as if to an old friend. "Come. This conflict is pointless. Rodran's breaths are numbered. At his death I and my brothers will become invincible. Even now we have power you cannot withstand."

Errol spat. "I've seen your kind die before. You're not invincible." He smiled as a passage of the book sprang to his lips. "'In that moment, Eleison bound the malus so that they could never return in physical form. The evil ones were imprisoned beyond the great circle of the earth.'"

Valon threw back his head and howled like a dog, and the ferrals attacked in a seething wave. Errol and Ru parted, met the swirling rush. The mass of bodies pushed them back, and they fought at first simply to avoid being swamped by sheer numbers.

Valon and Ru vanished from his awareness, hidden by blood and fangs and fur. Again and again, he was forced to give ground. Dextra and Sinistra jumped almost by their own accord, and in a small part of his mind not occupied with staying alive, he exulted in their use. Rula's swordsmith had crafted weapons that anticipated his commands, and the touch of their edge was death.

Months of using a heavy staff had given him unexpected endurance with the swords. By increments, the press of ferrals thinned, until Errol fought and finished one alone. A moment later Ru dispatched the last of the spawn with a contemptuous thrust. A long, low mound of dead filled the hallway. At the other end, Valon stood, his smile amused. He toyed with a long rapier, flicking the tip at the dead ferrals at his feet.

"It's really too bad, you know," Valon said. His face was wreathed in mock sympathy. "You could have joined us, but it's too late now." He smiled. "Death has come to you at last, Errol Stone."

He picked his way through the mass of the dead without looking down, his steps sure and confident.

Errol took a deep breath, forcing himself to relax. "This isn't your fight, Ru. Go save Rokha." He took a step back, away from the treacherous footing of the ferrals' blood.

One step sounded behind him, then another. "I can't, boy. The compulsion won't allow it."

Valon stepped forward, his eyes vibrating.

Pain blossomed in Errol's front hand before his mind registered Valon's stroke. Ru lunged, his body and arm stretched, thrusting for Valon's throat, but the renegade countered. The hall thundered with the crash of steel as Errol and Ru attacked. It was impossible for Valon to counter them both.

But he did. The rapier flicked in and out of Errol's perception as every slash and thrust he and Ru attempted was countered.

Valon's swordsmanship lacked skill, his stance unbalanced, but the rapier danced and forked in the air like lightning. Errol shuddered to think of the inhuman strength required to push that length of steel to such extremes.

He and Ru were forced back. Valon's grin stretched as he sensed their fatigue. A cut blossomed on Errol's forearm, his parry a fraction too slow. Ru took a shallow slice across the ribs.

They couldn't win.

With the strength of the malus driving him, Valon would wear them down. Another cut opened higher up on Errol's arm, deeper this time. Beside him Ru growled a curse. With a yell, Errol put his all into an attack, striving to open a line Ru could use.

It failed. Valon twisted and coiled like a viper, beating the attack with a series of strokes that nearly pulled the swords from Errol's grip. Ru threw himself back to keep from losing his head.

Valon laughed. "Now, Errol Stone, you will die."

With a savage beat, he swung to knock Ru's sword from its line. It never landed.

Naaman Ru lifted his arm, allowed the stroke to take him in the side, and wrapped his hand around Valon's rapier, holding it.

Valon's eyes widened. Unable to follow with a slash against Errol, he pulled the rapier toward himself, out of Ru's grasp.

But the move gave Errol the opening he needed. Lunging as he swung, he cut for Valon's throat. The tip of Dextra passed through the soft tissue as if it didn't exist. Blood oozed from the cut. Valon clamped his hand to the wound, tried to speak, his mouth working.

He fell to his knees instead. The madness cleared from his eyes as they stilled, replaced by a knowing horror.

The compulsion in Errol's mind vanished. He dropped, kneeling in blood at Ru's side, his hands trying to staunch a wound that went halfway through the caravan master's torso.

"Don't bother, boy," Ru said. "It's too deep." His brown eyes glared for a moment before softening. "This is what comes . . . from getting involved with the church."

Errol nodded. "I know. The compulsion made you do it."

Ru gave a weak shake of his head, pushed his sword toward Errol as his gaze grew distant. "No . . . I chose . . . Tell Rokha." He pulled a shuddering breath. "Tell my father . . . and Rula . . . I . . . chose."

43

FLIGHT

ERROL ATTEMPTED to backtrack away from the bodies. In moments he'd lost his way. Sounds of fighting drifted down the massive hallways. The ilhotep's palace held as many twists and turns as the entire imperial compound in Illustra, and he had no compulsion to guide him.

He didn't even know where Adora and Rokha were being kept, and without a knife or blanks, he had no way to cast for their position. Every hallway seemed familiar, but the absence of bodies in many of them told him he hadn't been there before.

He rounded a corner to see a royal guard, one of Hadari's brothers, and a handful of white-clad janiss fighting a greater number of soldiers. Even so, the contest looked even. The Ongolese counted as three or even four of the janiss. Errol moved to the flank and began mowing down soldiers. Three men were down before they turned to counter. That gave the rest the advantage they needed.

The soldiers broke and ran. Errol grabbed the Ongolese by the arm. "I need to find Hadari."

With a nod, the guard moved in the opposite direction from the council's forces. "I am Bamba. Follow."

Leaner than his brother, Bamba set a pace that left Errol straining. They came to the ilhotep's slave quarters as Adora and Rokha stepped through the wreckage of the doors with Hadari behind. At the sight of Errol, Adora gave a cry of greeting and hugged him, her fingers digging into his arms.

Another Ongolese, showing the blood and sweat of fighting, joined them. "It is done," he said to Hadari. "The false one is dead."

"Who betrayed the ilhotep?" Errol asked. He prayed his instinct was wrong, but the tightness of sudden pain at the corner of Hadari's eyes told him otherwise.

"Fairhan, the youngest of us."

Errol nodded.

Hadari squeezed his shoulder. "Have I not said you are wise? Those of us that live, if any, will mourn for him. We must leave. They will block us from the horses if they can."

Rokha's eyes sought Errol's. He shook his head, trying to think of some way to lessen the blow. He stepped forward and placed Naaman's sword in her hand. She pivoted, ran after Hadari, weeping as she went. Errol wanted to offer her some word of comfort, but he was the reason behind Ru's death. She would not welcome his solace. Ahead, Adora ran, her golden hair reflecting the torchlight. A catch in his throat made it difficult to breathe.

They moved down a long passage of rough stone. The smell of horses came to him. A pair of royal guards, sweating and bloody from a dozen minor cuts or more stood at the entrance.

"Where are the rest?" Hadari asked.

The two shook their heads. "Adar led four of us and some of the janiss loyal to the ilhotep against the council forces to keep them from taking the stables. They cannot win. Time is short."

The taller one, who looked even bigger than Hadari, pointed into the stable. "The northern slaves wait with the horses. The short one has left three for us. The rest of the mounts are sleeping and will not awake for some time."

Hadari caught Errol in a bear hug, his head held against the big guard's sternum. "Go now, little one. Merakh is lost. You must carry word back to your kingdom, to Illustra—war will certainly come."

"Come with us," Errol pleaded, "you and your brothers. There is nothing left for you here."

Hadari smiled, glanced in the direction of the ilhotep's palace and treasure room. "There you are wrong. Go now. If you ride swiftly you will beat pursuit back to the strait."

They thundered through the streets of the city, Merodach clearing the way of guards with unerring shots from his bow. The soldiers at the gate, confused by the sight of several of them wearing the white of the guard, did not recognize them for northerners until too late, and they had no means to pursue.

A league from the city, they left the lush vegetation that bordered the river and entered the barren sand that filled Merakh between the loops of the Altaru. Rale held out his arm, palm down, and they slowed the horses to a trot. The moon tracked overhead, washing the brush and rocks in the sandy landscape with silver hues. Soon after slowing, Karele called for a halt.

"Why are we stopping?" Cruk asked.

"I want to check the horses. Even such power as theirs must be tended. The Morgols would prize them above their finest." The solis moved from mount to mount, his hand sliding down the foreleg and checking the occasional hoof. "Keep a tight rein on your mounts. They'll want this." He untied a bag from behind his saddle and began broadcasting bits of something that glinted in the darkness.

"What's that?" Rale asked.

Karele smiled. "The ilhotep prized my knowledge of horses. When I requested extra apples they never questioned me. Those slices I just laid across the road are laced with cardamom. The horses will pick up their scent from a mile away."

Errol's horse jerked on its reins, trying to get at the fruit Karele had so generously distributed along the road.

"So?"

"They've also been soaked in sleepwell. Any horse that eats it won't be able to manage more than a walk for at least a day."

Cruk laughed. "You're starting to come in handy, solis. You really are a master of horses."

Karele gave a mocking little bow. "Thank you. I thought it would be better than poison. I don't like killing."

In the distance the sounds of pursuit drifted across the sands.

Merodach pulled his horse around to face the others. "Go. I will stay here and make sure the horses don't gallop past their refreshment." He unlimbered his bow.

"I'll stay with you," Rokha said.

The moonlight glinted off Merodach's white hair and his stricken expression. "No. You cannot. They'll almost certainly have bows."

Her mouth set. "I've already lost one man I loved tonight. I will not lose the other." She glared at him. "And curse you, you stone head, for making me say it first."

The cold reserve of Merodach's face melted. A smile blazed forth in the moonlight that turned the stoic captain into a boy. He urged his mount next to Rokha's and caught her in an impassioned kiss that lasted long enough to embarrass the rest of the company.

"There," she said with a voice both rough and breathless, "that's how you're supposed to treat the woman you love." She loosened the bow attached to her saddle. Merodach nodded.

They left the pair there and set a ground-eating trot that ate up the miles. Five hours later they stopped as the sun cleared the horizon. Errol's legs and midsection ached from the ride. He stopped at moments to stretch as he cooled his horse.

The sight of Martin breathing his mount filled him with an obscure guilt, as if he'd deceived his friend. In halting words, he told Martin of his encounter with the ilhotep and of the existence of the book.

Loss and pain wreathed Martin's face. He spun south to face Guerir. Even from such a distance, smoke from the city was visible. "We have to . . ." He swallowed. "Oh, Deas, it's lost. We've lost it again."

Errol looked at the ground, abashed by the priest's anguish. "I'm sorry. I didn't think to retrieve it."

Martin put one hand on the back of Errol's head. "You were fighting for your life, lad. You've given the kingdom the chance to fight another day. It's not your job to do it all."

Errol nodded, but in his heart he wondered. They walked their horses over to Karele. The master of horses moved down the line of mounts, checking the legs and hooves of each. He pried a stone out of the frog of one, then ran his hand up and down the leg before giving a satisfied nod.

"They need water," he said to Rale. "We'll have to give them a longer rest at the next loop of the river."

Rale nodded, not looking pleased.

"We need some way to slip through the towns without attracting attention," Cruk said.

"It's going to be a little hard to go unnoticed with most of us wearing blood," Rale said.

"What if we pose as merchants?" Martin asked.

Rale shook his head. "Ru's not here to bluff us through."

A touch on Errol's arm diverted his attention from the discussion. Adora stood behind him wearing the ilhotep's silks and an expression that conveyed hope and doubt at the same time.

"Are you well, Errol?" she asked.

The sun glinted off her gold hair. The sprinkling of freckles around the delicate perfection of her nose only made her more beautiful. With everything in him, he wanted nothing more than to sweep her into an embrace as fierce as Merodach's with Rokha, but he schooled himself to stillness. Still, he allowed his smile to communicate everything he would not grant his body.

"I am well, Your Highness." He bowed, took her arm, and stepped a few feet away. "Will you forgive my absence?"

Surprise lifted her blond eyebrows. "What absence would that be, Earl Stone?"

His smile deepened. "The one I so rudely took after Martin shared his truths with me. I am back now, and I won't leave that way again." Before she could ask for clarification, he pressed on. "Are you well? When the ilhotep claimed you for his own, I thought . . ."

She cut off his question with a chop of her hand, but red tinged her cheeks. "We do not need to speak of that. The ilhotep did not take me." Her blush deepened. "But Merakhi men and women are much more . . . familiar with each other."

"Errol." Rale waved him over.

Not knowing exactly what she referred to but relieved, Errol bowed to Adora and rejoined the rest of the company.

"You and I will pose as the merchants," Rale said. "The rest will be our servants."

A tingle of fear raced up his neck and into his scalp. "Us? Why us?"

"Because we look more like Merakhi than anyone else. We have dark hair and, with the sun's help, the complexion to go with it."

Errol shook his head in denial. "If they get close enough to look me in the eyes, they'll know I'm not one of them."

Rale nodded. "I know. I'll lead. Just keep your head down."

They mounted and set an easy trot to the next loop of the river. By the time they got there, Merodach and Rokha were coming up from behind. The pair shared triumphant smiles as they rejoined the group. Merodach cast frequent looks toward Rokha, wonder and desire written on his normally impassive features.

"We'll have to dress Adora and Rokha in whatever clothing the rest of us can spare," Rale said. "They draw too much attention dressed as they are."

Rokha sat her horse, her head high, her bearing almost regal. Her silks fluttered in the breeze. Adora matched her beauty, blazing like the sun. The two women looked like rare flowers against the washed-out color of the road.

Which gave Errol an idea. "They can be the merchandise."

"Are you trying to get us noticed, boy?" Cruk asked.

Errol shook his head. "That's just it." He pointed. "Look at them. Do you think any man will notice us with them dressed like that, looking that way?"

Adora's face showed her surprise, but Rokha tossed her head

and laughed. Rale rubbed at his jaw muscles. "They are distracting, aren't they."

"Better than that," Martin said. "The ilhotep has presented them as a gift to the royalty of the kingdom." He gave Errol a lift of his eyebrows. "You are part of the royalty of the kingdom, are you not, Earl Stone?"

They formed up the company with Adora and Rokha in the middle, surrounded like precious cargo, and rode north. The women donned veils, but the sheer cloth only accentuated their beauty. Men and villagers gaped.

Three days later, they arrived at Shagdal, Sahion's village. But as they stopped on a low rise overlooking his inn, there was no sign of their betrayer or anyone else. Dust blew through the streets unimpeded by man or horse. Rale sat his mount at the head, staring at the scene before him, his brows furrowed over his broad nose, and scratched at his short beard.

"It looks empty," Errol said.

Rale pointed. "Perhaps. A carrier bird could have beaten us here, or perhaps Belaaz has managed to appropriate Valon's circle. If the village is empty, there's no threat. If it's not, then trying to skirt it will only bring investigation." He sighed. "The horses can't take this heat for more than a day without water."

They rode into Shagdal, each with one hand on the reins and the other on their weapons. Merodach guided his mount with his knees just behind Rale and Errol, both hands free to hold a bow. Cruk brought up the rear, his blunt face more grim than usual behind the red of his beard and mustache. Adora and Rokha held swords low and out of sight, flanked by Luis, Martin, and Karele.

Furtive figures appeared, then disappeared as quickly. Elsewise, nothing stirred.

Rale pointed to the well in the center of the village. "Merodach, take everyone and check the water. Make sure it's safe. Come with me, Errol." He turned his horse toward the inn.

"Why are we going there?"

Rale's face hardened, like stone. "Never let an enemy think

you are soft, Errol. Mercy is a fine thing, but if it costs you men, you can't afford it."

Errol dismounted and tied the reins of his horse to one of the posts that supported Sahion's porch. Rale had his sword out. They entered the large, open-air room next to the kitchen. Sahion sat at a table as if asleep, one hand clenching a dagger, the other pressed against a dark stain in his side.

Rale put the tip of his sword against the innkeeper's throat.

Sahion's eyes fluttered open at the touch. He laughed. "Ru would not have paused. Ha. Ruthless enough to rule the sand, that one."

Rale increased the pressure on his sword. "You may find me less merciful than Naaman Ru. What happened here?"

Sahion laughed even as his face contorted in pain. Instead of answering, he pointed. Across the room the village's akha lay dead, cut from shoulder to sternum. A headless messenger bird lay like a pile of discarded feathers on the floor next to him. Flies buzzed over the carcasses. "They took my sons. Even the youngest. Liars."

He pointed across the room at the dead man. "That stupid pig came to gloat, bragging—with messenger bird in hand—about how he'd been the one to arrange the conscription of my sons and about how my friends would never make it to the coast alive. I killed the bird first and finished him—" he spat—"with his own dagger. Akhen aren't supposed to carry weapons. You can't trust anyone anymore."

"Where is everyone?" Errol asked.

Sahion waved a hand. "Gone—or preparing to leave. Killing an akha is mal-un. Everyone in the village dies."

Rale sheathed his sword. "Let's go. If we hurry, we might be able to make the strait before the news of the ilhotep's death does."

Sahion touched his forehead, then his lips at the news.

They pushed the horses as fast as they dared. Karele checked them every four hours. The fast trot gradually beat Errol's legs into jelly. Even the horse master began to look uncomfortable.

But they crested the rise overlooking the port of Oranis early the next morning.

The city teemed with Merakhi guards. Errol nudged Rale's shoulder and pointed by turns to four ships tied up at the dock. "Those look familiar."

Rale nodded, his face creased with disappointment. "I'd hoped I was wrong. Those are the ships that turned us back. Now they're in port with us."

"What does that mean?" Martin asked.

"There's no way to know for sure," Rale said. "Once Valon learned Errol was in Guerir, there was no point in trying to keep him out." He turned to Luis. "What happened to Valon's circle when he died?"

The reader raised his hands, palms up. "It is impossible to say with certainty. His death may have broken their minds. Perhaps one of his subordinates assumed power. Possibly, Belaaz took over somehow."

"What's the worst possible outcome?" Rale asked.

Luis stared at the ships in the port. "Belaaz. If he was able to take control of the circle, then every reader down there knows what we look like. Karele will be able to shield us from their lots, but they still have their eyes."

"This just keeps getting better," Cruk said. "Even if we get past the readers and their guards, we have no ship to take us home. Anybody care to take bets on how long it will take our pursuit to catch up to us?"

Rale looked back to Luis. "We need information. Where is Tek?"

Luis shook his head. "I'm sorry. I don't have any blanks, and there's no wood here in the desert for me to use."

"What can you tell us, Karele?" Rale asked. "Martin says your power exceeds that of a reader."

Karele shook his head. "It's not my power. It's whether Aurae, the spirit of Deas, chooses to communicate or act."

"And?" Rale prompted.

Karele shook his head.

A breath of wind ruffled Errol's hair in the moment, whispered in his ear. An incomprehensible thrill of hope, like a drink of cold water in the desert, coursed through him, and he wanted to laugh at the joy of it.

Martin and Karele lifted their heads and spoke at the same instant. "Tek will be here just before sunset."

"Are you sure, Pater?" Cruk asked.

Karele nodded, laughing. "Aurae has spoken."

Martin added his confirmation to Karele's.

Cruk grimaced but swallowed his doubt. "If you say so, but how are we going to get on board?"

"Fire," Merodach said. He lifted his bow. "We'll have to get close enough for me to put arrows into the ships." He pursed his lips. "I wish I had a longbow. It's got twice the range of this."

Two hours past midnight, fire still raged on two of the Merakhi ships, and the other two were useless wrecks. Errol still marveled at Merodach's skill with a bow. His ability to plant burning arrows in the furled sails of the Merakhi longships amazed them all. Now the flames were bare pinpoints of light astern as Tek sailed away from the port of Oranis.

The sea was almost lake smooth, and Errol felt only the slightest twinge of queasiness. Karele stood next to him with Martin and Luis on the other side. The three men listened raptly as Errol told them everything he could remember of the book three times over, and still they asked for more.

"If only we could have brought it back with us," Martin said. "The Judica would have to believe."

Karele shrugged. "Perhaps, but some would no doubt question its authenticity or interpretation."

Errol gazed off the raised deck in the stern of Tek's ship, holding the decision he'd made in Guerir close in his heart. He would not chance interference, not even from these men who received unexpected knowledge from Aurae.

Without warning, a stab of pain in his chest like the thrust of a dirk left him clutching the rail for support. He groped with one hand against his unbroken flesh. Luis reeled like a drunkard, holding his head. Beside him, Karele and Martin dropped to the deck, gasping in shared pain. The priest, his face ashen, lifted a trembling hand to point northwest, toward Erinon.

"My Deas," Martin breathed. "Rodran has died."

Errol didn't need Karele's tortured nod to know it was true.

ACKNOWLEDGMENTS

This second book of THE STAFF AND THE SWORD series contained its own challenges, and I would like to thank my agent, Steve Laube, for going to bat for me and being the voice of experience and wisdom; my critique partners, Austin Deel and Tori Smith, for giving me the feedback I needed and for putting up with me when caffeine made me long-winded; the students at Martin Luther King Magnet High School and Croft Middle School in Nashville, for being interesting enough to be characters themselves; and as always, you the reader, for giving me the opportunity to tell you my tale.

After graduating from Georgia Tech, **Patrick W. Carr** worked at a nuclear plant, did design work for the air force, worked for a printing company, and was an engineering consultant. Patrick's day gig for the last six years has been teaching high school math in Nashville, Tennessee. Patrick is a member of ACFW and MTCW and makes his home in Nashville with his incredible wife, Mary; their four awesome sons, Patrick, Connor, Daniel, and Ethan; and their dog, Mel.

If you enjoyed *The Hero's Lot*, you may also like...

Made in the USA
Middletown, DE
11 August 2018